Cordelia & Mel and the

WITCHES OF ICE

Book One: Gloom

by W. F Gadd

Third Edition

Completely Revised & Edited April MMXXIII

"A pile alane stod ageyn al fere,
Wacched bi magike lest sum neah,
Caste it doun to asch and fyre,
Graunt ne witche alane soche dire."

Anon.

TheMerryspel Cottage

iii

Thanks to My Nieces Amy and Holly, for their Inspiration, laughter and Sunshine.

Cordelia & Mer and the
WITCHES OF ICE

Book One: Gloom
by William F. Gadd

Copyright ©William F. Gadd *MMXXIII*

Editor: Emily-Oscar Siggs.

Cover Design & incidental illustrations by William F. Gadd,
with additional artwork throughout by Maxine Gadd & W.F. Gadd.
Both Maxine Gadd and W.F. Gadd have asserted their rights under
the Berne Copyright Convention.

Copyright ©William F. Gadd *MMXXIII*
Copyright ©Maxine Gadd *MMXV*

ISBN: 978-1-9836-9977-1
ISBN-10: 1983699772

10 12 15 14 13 11 9

Third Edition
This work first published in electronic form June 2011
Printed and bound in the U.S.A.

Typeface: Hoefler Text Regular & italic
Digital Image Creation: (Maxine & William Gadd):
Adobe Photoshop CS
Typesetting & Page Layout: Adobe In-Design CS

Contents

Preface

The seed of an idea for this story grew in the summer of 2008, after a visit to The Faerieworlds Convention in beautiful Eugene, Oregon, U.S.A.

The event opened my eyes. It celebrates the mystery of faeriedom, and involves mums, dads, kids, –everyone!

Each fashion themselves into a world of wonderful make-believe. The music, dancing, craft and art, was so unique, so back to the Earth, so necessary in our troubled world.

Faerieworlds was a buzz of excitement, and, along with all the American friends made, the adventure set my imagination racing.

Upon returning home to Australia, everything that I'd seen and vividly experienced still remained in my thoughts.

Three months later, I kept thinking of my magical journey and decided to write about two harmless, fun-seeking and daring little white witches: Cordelia & her older sister Mer. It was naturally entitled '*Little Witches*'

After a while, I further developed these daring characters; and they emerged as the main protagonists of my story '*Out-Witching Witchdom*', which in turn became '*Cordelia & Mer and the Witches of Ice*', also published as '*The Horrible Witches of Ice*'.

I trust you enjoy the read.   *William F. Gadd, May 2023*

About the Editor:

Emily-Oscar Siggs is a writer and editor in Boorloo (Perth). They studied Creative Writing and Publishing at Curtin University and completed Honours last year. He has had work published by Aussie Speculative Fiction (Cancer and Leo Anthology), the Centre for Stories, and Peter Cowan Writer's Centre, and works as a freelance editor.

Emily possesses some witchy pagan knowledge that assisted the development of this manuscript. Here, she provides a counter-curse to the medieval-style typological gremlins that inhabit this book:

> *Bothersome book, tricky type,*
> *Commas keep me up at night,*
> *Gremlins curse kerning with ghostly power,*
> *I wrangle them at witching hour.*

Illustrations & Plates

Plates

Illustrations

Glossary of Character Names

Name	Meaning	Pronunciation
Cordelia	Heart	cor–dee–lia
Chantress	Stone	chan–tress
Cragertha	Craggy – hard	crag–earth–ah
Delia	Of the moon	dee–liah
Eloisa	Warrior	el–oh–iss–ah
Estoriah	Frozen soul	est–story–ah
Gawain	White hawk	gah–wain
Hepsibah	Delight	hep–see–bah
Jemimah	Dove	jeh–mime–ah
Kaldre	Goddess	kell–drah
Kosovskaia	Woman of the valley	kosovs–kay–ah
Maxim	Great	mac–simm
Meag	Pearl	meeg
Melchior	Wise King	mel–key–or
Mer	Of the ocean	Merr
Meryl	Sparkling sea	mare–rill
Myrtle	Aromatic evergreen	merr–tall
Nevara	Snows	neh–varr–ah
Olivia	Olive	oh–liv–ee–ah
Persimmon	Fruit of the Heavens	per–simm–on
Persis	Woman of Persia	perr–siss
Pfirsich	Peach	furr–sic
Pitheringae	Particular and dithery	pither–in–gay
Rioghnach	Queenly	ree–owe–nah
Sarabeth	Princess	sarah–beth
Ulla	Exalted ruler	oo–lah
Vago*	Mysteriously vague	varr–goe
Wistar	Steward of food supply	wiss–star
Wyn	Friend – white	win
Xylia (Vago)*	Woodland; wood-dweller	Zye–lee–ah
Zylphoriah	Darkest feeling	zill–four–riah

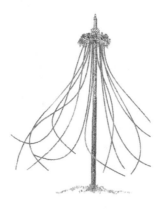

Prologue

Once, once the
Holly tree dead

Twice, twice the
Briar claw sharp

Thrice, thrice the
Nightshade blood

First, first the
Awakening eye

Last, last the
Changeling froze

Death, death the
Friend inside.

Many hundred years ago, eight good, trusting and dearest friends invoked a most terrible spell.

They all lived together as a coven of witches in a stone dwelling deep in a forest, far away from prying eyes and minds. It was only there that they could practice the mysteries of witchcraft, safely hidden from a wisely mistrusting world.

Once in a while though these eight witches would venture out to nearby villages to sell herbs and welcome advice. Yet, those innocent dealings soon turned darker, offering not only cures for the ailing, but curses for their enemies too, which is what the coven always intended.

With powerful spell after spell, potion after potion, they became well known across the cold, miserable land.

Most of their magic worked, but there were certain times when it didn't; and those times were shocking to say the least. Some who had requested a particular charm or a sip from a vile bubbling brew, would, without warning, endure unimaginable pain as their faces, arms, legs and torso blistered, shrivelled and buckled unto a twisted mess.

Their victims' screams were horrendous, leaving the witches no other option but to flee from their crimes.

Eventually, the coven's reign of misfortune became known everywhere; and instead of being welcomed, they were hunted down.

Upon brooms charmed and obedient, they frequently had to swoop and swerve back to their hidden retreat: miles upon twisted miles away from their baying bloodthirsty pursuers.

In only a few weeks, every village it seemed had built fire-stacks, drenched in pig fat with a stake at the heart waiting to burn each of them alive. The stacks were stuffed and ready with driest kindling covered with cowhide to fend off the rain.

In no time there wasn't a village, market or fair they'd dare show their presence. So, they took to disguising themselves. This worked for some while, yet their magic became even more deadly and foul. Consequently, honest folk were forced to shun anyone not known to them. This caused much distress and unfair punishment to many a traveler, tinker, or wise-woman.

'Sheep brained fools, the lot of them!' scalded one of the eight witches during a particularly cold wet day of endless confinement.

'It surely rains in my heart as well,' she moaned, peering out of their one tiny window, and onto the dark soggy forest.

'Heart's blood!' screamed another, *How this selfishly steals our freedom!*'

'We must implore something from hell,' spoke a witch named Lavender, though very far from smelling as sweet.

'Yes, my dears,' she continued, 'let us set a table of blood and skulls and lizard tongue potion so that we may curse unto curse 'til the moon doth rise!'

The room filled with cackles and laughter as the eight went about their task.

Their chants began. The table moved and shook, candles came ablaze, thunder roared without. Then, something black and ghostly appeared above them. It circled the room.

'What have we this day unleashed?' worriedly asked Delphine.

The black swirling mist took form and made itself an arm with a hand, old and nails like claws. From these it offered a glowing rolled parchment and Lavender stood fearfully to snatch the scroll. The blackness disappeared and the eight gathered around to read the ancient words scratched into its ethereal skin.

They placed the open scroll before them on the table between man-skulls, worm piles and blood bowls; as well as wreaths of fresh cut nightshade, henbane, willow and putrid garlic. In one voice they chanted and chanted the strange words upon the glowing parchment.

Hours passed by and through weariness, their voices croaked and ceased. The candles finally spluttered and forsook their light. The moon, she had now risen high.

'It works not!' snapped Lavender, holding and waving her hands, seeing that she possessed no additional powers of hand or mind.

'I neither,' agreed another, placing an empty jug over her head to try see through it. She tripped and fell instead, breaking the jug, and nearly her head.

'I have it; we need a girl!' reasoned Primrose.

'One who is young of years, yessss!' cried the witch Hawthorne. 'But, many would be better!' added Lavender.

'Yessss, my lovelies,' sighed the witch Everlost, 'let us then visit on the morrow, where such do gather, and we'll take and wither their souls under a Yew tree, so that we should bring them hither to this place and better strengthen our hex.'

So on the following morning, the eight flew by broom to the village Oak-Over-Rye, and lurked by the village Maypole, where young folk do usually mischief and frolic.

The witches' evil eyes and minds were soon rewarded and they gathered unto themselves by spell and charm all the young ones that suited their need. In a trance, the girls followed the vile witches home.

Back at their loathsome cottage their eight victims, one for each of them, had their souls wrested from them, leaving them to be at the mercy of the floating entity the witches had invoked to complete their spell.

Whereupon the dark swirling mist returned, gathering these innocent souls and using them to transform the eight vile creatures into something far, far worse.

As the deathly magic performed by the dark swirling spirit took hold, the witches bodies became frozen, each cracking and snapping until they were half their former size; and as dried as a lightening-struck carcass. The new forms of these eight foul witches then floated out of the cottage and up above the scurrying clouds.

They had become dormant, and would remain so until their chrysalis-like forms had been fully transformed. Unknown to them before they had commenced this wicked spell, their transformation would be slow and awful.

It would take many a year, many a decade, and many a century in fact, before complete. But, such endurance would thus grant each with extraordinary magical powers, well beyond those possessed by earthly witches and wizards.

Thus, the centuries duly passed, and only a few years ago, floating high above the dark clouds, their chrysalis skins finally split and ruptured to spew the eight transformed creatures; awake and death-hungry, upon an unfamiliar world of witches, warlocks and wizards.

The eight so renamed themselves as: Zylphoriah, Nithenamie, Kirku, Pheobeth, Estoriah, Myrithian, Zyliesiah and Horrolin.

Frozen they still were, yet animated; frozen to their very cores, though well able to see, move, and practice the most darkest forms of magic.

Now they had become reformed, they wanted what they felt was rightfully theirs. Enduring such a dire change of body and soul would have to be paid for, and the only ones qualified to repay them were those who practiced magic here on Earth, either innocent or powerful.

It had been two years since the frozen witches began their reign. In that time, they were fully industrious with their evil labour. They had built themselves palaces of ice to dwell in that floated well above the clouds we see.

Aside from this, they laboured incessantly upon the willpowers of several great witches and wizards to convert them to a new kind of witchcraft, but understandably, not one of them would choose to follow. So their powers of persuasion took on a more deadly earnest.

The terror and death left in this frozen wake was increasing day-by-day, hour by painful hour. And only one wizard refused to bow: Melchior Fizz.

He simply called all of them: ***The Witches of Ice***.

Chapter 1: Peculiar.

Summer had begun peculiar, and by the end of it, things weren't much better. Take what happened down the road at a certain little shop in the old village of Lower Wyshing.

Mrs. Huggitt's *Last-Chance Shoppe of Magical Curiosities* is a grand but somewhat tumbledown store. And, if you ever cared to visit, you'd certainly agree. Not grand in the sense of stunning architecture, clever lighting or the flow of majestic music proudly announcing how wonderful the place is. No, certainly not that kind of grand, but something much grander –it is a shop of wonderful and mysterious magic.

To the casual visitor, it is dusty, poorly lit, cluttered; and viewed from the road, clearly and precariously leaning over to one side. Yet, it is exactly this ramshackled appearance that attracts the eyes and minds of many a witch and wizard in the land.

Magical people fly to, or mysteriously appear in her store, just to gawp or possibly buy anything from the most breathtaking collection of magical items in the world. Mrs. Huggitt is understandably proud of her grand little shop that leans to one side, and which doesn't appear grand at all to most of the ordinary folk who wander past, or even enter.

But on one particular day, just after she'd finished an afternoon tea with her good friend and best customer, Mrs. Valerie Pitheringae, the shop seemed to suddenly lose its grandness. And, to make matters worse, Hilda Huggitt was immediately overcome with a strong feeling of anxiety.

She'd not felt this way before, and to her, even the

wonderful pile of magical odds and sods, reaching well up to her marvellously cobwebbed ceiling, seemed especially dark and foreboding on that fateful afternoon.

Hilda was determined, though, not to let her feelings be known to Valerie, and, in a trembling sort of voice, responded to Valerie who was now holding up an item of great interest to her.

'Ah, yes' said Hilda straining to be positive 'that one is only £5.20, it's on special; does the price suit you, dear?'

But, before Valerie had even agreed the cost, Hilda snatched it from her and began nervously wrapping the strange object.

Valerie noticed her fidgety attempt and remarked 'Everything all right, Hilda dear? You seem upset' Hilda made no reply, continuing with her clumsy attempt at covering the object with fancy paper; and copious lengths of coloured ribbon, tied in an array of misshapen bows.

The magical item she had shakily wrapped was none other than an original Charmers' Chest, and yes, it still had its small golden key, essential for it to turn on the charm.

No matter the foulest mood that the owner of this fine piece of magic machinery would be in, one twist of its filigree-rich key, and they would turn into one of the most charming persons you'd ever want to meet.

This inspired piece of mystical invention would certainly help Valerie, who wasn't known for her diplomacy, especially in the genteel circles she mixed in. In fact, the chest was an absolute snip at the price. But this brilliant Charmers' Chest with its amazingly low price; and how it would make Valerie actually appear charming, wasn't important at all to Hilda for the moment.

Suddenly, she snapped.

'Valerie!' she gasped 'I must talk to you!'

'But I thought you were!' answered Valerie.

'No, *really* talk to you.' replied Hilda.

Her friend frowned at this, staring at Hilda with concern,

'Go on.' said Valerie as calmly as she could, what's on your mind?

Hilda leaned over the counter, and in a secretive undertone, she asked, 'Did you feel something just then, like the whole place becoming instantly depressing, as if there was no point to anything?'

She asked with a voice as grave as the expression upon her face.

'And, have you wondered why just lately we've had difficulty unlocking any of those odd *Witch-Whispers* we chatted about —I mean not one of us could fathom them out!'

Valerie well knew that the importance of a 'Witch-Whisper'; the mysterious way of whispering a jumbled-up secret magical message which becomes immediately recogniseable by the person they were destined for. They are whispered along witch-by-witch and warlock-by-warlock, until reaching the right person.

Yet, even though the witch-whispers correctly arrived at their nearby coven, not one of them could be translated, even by the correct recipient: That was very peculiar.

Hilda continued speaking very lowly convinced someone unseen was overhearing every word.

'I'm certain there's something very sinister going on' she strained.

Valerie looked dumbstruck, but she wasn't; and nodded

thoughtfully in agreement. 'Well, now that you come to mention it, I suppose I have.'

Her acknowledgement was met with a swift ghostly rush of cold air and distantly sighing voice. The disturbing sound sent a shiver down both their spines. It emanated from a tall dusty ebony-framed wishing mirror behind her.

The huge mirror, resting on the floor against a locked wardrobe, and with a faded sale-price ticket of just £67, shook a little as if disturbed by a tremor.

Both of them moved back, suspiciously looking around from side to side. The presence they felt was a lot stronger now, so both kept their voices low.

The hardly lit store, cluttered as usual with witchy curiosities, was empty of people, except for these two of course.

Hilda darted forward once again, eyes squinting and whispering;

The Wishing Mirror

'Olivia couldn't unlock any of her witch-whispers either. You know Olivia, dear! Olivia Jute, the lady we go weaving with Thursdays! Come on, you must know her!' she said accusingly, almost as if Valerie didn't know whom they went *spell weaving* with on Thursdays, which naturally, she did.

Valerie looked stunned by Hilda's outburst.

'Oh sorry, forgive me for that rare bit of anger dear' she offered 'I think I'm being badly affected by this

4

disturbance in the ether.'

But Valerie, a tall overly particular type with fastidiously tidy clothing and sharp mind, who was also quite an experienced witch by all accounts, wasn't really listening.

Instead, she now peered clear through Hilda's pallid grey eyes, right through her brain and out the other side onto the tall wishing mirror behind. It was reflecting, through the leadlight dimple-glass bay window of Hilda's shop, a sky unexpectedly thunderous and dark.

Vacantly, Valerie forgot her purchase, turned and walked, though to her it felt more like she'd floated, toward the shop door. She opened it, tripping the little customer bell which was occupied by a ghost named Cuthbert, and drifted out almost in a daze.

Hilda Huggitt looked on in surprise but wrote a docket for the woman's peculiar purchase anyway, quite sure of her return.

'I've added a few special charms with it too' she called as if providing Valerie with a temptation beyond refusal.

Outside, and standing gormlessly in the street, and lucky not to be run over by any passing cars, Valerie Pitheringae stared up at this now foreboding sky.

It was yet another indication, as Hilda Huggitt had reminded her, that things had been getting rather nasty lately in the world of witchcraft. Not only for these two, but most witches in fact, including her good friends the Merryspells.

Yes, something was definitely and seriously wrong. Spells were reversing, charms no longer charming, and innocent incantations leaving people in a terrible condition.

All across the country there were broken keepsakes,

broken promises, broken bones and even broken spirits.

Yet, whilst Valerie in her long brown coat, garish silk scarf and pointless wobbly hat peered into this thunderous scene, a puff of light blue mist drifted in below the dark clouds above. Nothing particularly unusual about that in itself; until, that is, it took on the shape of her late Great Aunt Agatha, who'd passed away only days ago.

The apparition of her Great Aunt appeared angry, waving a cloud-like walking stick at her. Valerie stared up at her ghostly Great Aunt, almost in disbelief. Bravely, she spoke to her, not from fear you understand, but dread of getting an *ear-bashing* argument from this late and previously very intolerant relative; and that's putting it nicely.

'What's that Agatha? I can't hear you, your voice is still on the other side. You're very much in spirit dear...I'm happy, err, sad to say.' Valerie bit her lip over this slip of the tongue.

Mrs. Pitheringae's head was cranked so far back, her wobbly hat slid off, only to be saved from flying away into the stormy wind by her late Great Aunt still wielding that cloudy walking stick in a war-waging manner. With puckered lips Agatha blew the rescued hat back down to her.

'Thank you Aggy!' yelled Valerie, knowing full well how much her passed relative disliked being called by this nickname.

Surprised though amused by the visitation, Valerie could only suppose Aggy's angry appearance was because she'd placed far too few flowers on her grave during the recent funeral.

Mrs. Pitheringae muttered 'Flowers indeed! Serves the

old goat right for being such a mean cantankerous so and so.'

Ponderously, she watched the apparition of her Great Aunt gradually disappear from sight then walked back to Hilda Huggitt's little shop of mystical peculiarities.

If that wasn't enough, on the following night, past witching hour, young Cynthia Grosselearne, also a witch as well as a star pupil at a nearby college, distantly related to Mrs. Pitheringae, became convinced she'd spotted something moving about inside her tall bookcase in the corner of her bedroom.

The glass doors were open, which was odd as she usually kept them locked due to the disturbing contents of her many books on extreme magic.

Inside she could see a glow; and the more she looked, the more this glowing moved. It was as if the thing couldn't settle. She knew it wasn't her cat familiar playing in the bookcase though, because *Duddles* was outside the house, sitting on the window ledge, clawing and hissing at whatever weird materialisation had just taken place inside her room.

'Odd that' she breathed fearfully whilst staring at the bookcase from her bed. Cynthia dared not move; and anxiously gripped her drawn up eiderdown firmly between clenched teeth.

A few days later, something else peculiar happened. Henry Leaflove –apprentice warlock to old Florian Phumbleppot, a very experienced wizard indeed– as well as being a part time daredevil, woke early one morning in a start. He'd just had a powerful dream that demanded immediate action, somewhere in a wood nearby.

He raced down the rickety back staircase of the rickety

but hugely popular establishment, *The Charming Crust Bakery*; and once outside, Henry recited the few special words he recalled from the dream to his newly made and spell-woven broom. Then, he jumped on and soared above the dawn dark deserted streets of his village *Whizz-on-the-Floss*.

He arrived at goodness knows where deep in a blur and deep in woodland. Henry was utterly confused by his inexplicable venture, and stood stupidly in his pyjamas. OK, so they were his favourite pyjamas, black with a pattern of silver broomsticks and funny warlock hats, but totally embarrassing for him all the same – even in the middle of nowhere.

The apprentice warlock blinked a few times and looked about. Then, he noticed it; a tall strange-looking building with a pointed roof that rose up along with the tall trees.

It was the Merryspell cottage. This was very odd, as he'd never been to the Merryspells before.

But he did remember vaguely meeting them in this dream. And another thing that stuck in his mind; he needed to tell them about being handed a book made of ice: All very peculiar.

Yet, he couldn't deliver his message; the place was absolutely deserted.

Through dirty and broken windows Henry cast his eyes around a dark neglected interior. He could barely perceive anything. Only some old threadbare furniture laced with grimy cobwebs, and what appeared to be dusty cauldrons hanging over a long dead fire in the hearth.

'What am I doing at a derelict old house in the middle of nowhere?' He questioned, 'There's something very freaky going on here!'

But the house wasn't derelict. No indeed not, not at all. You see the Merryspell Cottage had been enchanted to appear this way to deter unwelcome visitors. If the truth were known, the Merryspells had merely gone out for the day. Though, if he were more experienced at his craft, he'd have seen beyond this convincing enchantment.

Inside, the floors were actually polished, covered with a scattering of exotic rugs. The furniture was clean and well-loved, the hearth roaring with a welcoming fire.

The lad simply couldn't see it, and dispiritedly flew back to his dingy flat above The Charming Crust Bakery, still mystified as to the purpose of his visit.

That night, when the Merryspells returned home, Mrs. Merryspell's youngest daughter, Cordelia, sneaked down to her mother's library of deep magic to find a gut wrenchingly good book on spells. Though, in truth, she was about to acquire a great deal more. As she recited a charm to overcome her mother's unnecessarily punitive *spell-lock*; a magical lock to prevent nosy visitors just like her; Cordelia witnessed with astonishment a strange translucent book suddenly appear before her eyes.

Cautiously, she reached out and took hold of the glowing book. It was freezing cold, which made her hands tingle at the touch, yet she didn't let go.

Cordelia just couldn't resist opening this weird see-through oddity either; her curiosity knew no bounds. Turning each of the ice-like pages carefully, as though they might snap with the lightest touch, she began reading the fragile book then and there. Cordelia quickly learnt that white witchcraft, and all of witchdom in fact, was on the verge of becoming embroiled in a terrible and utterly magic-shattering event, something that would change magic forever.

The book went on to reveal that *The Witches of Ice;* ruthless beings hell-bent on complete control of witchcraft, will soon rule witchcraft entirely. Not a single spell or witch, white or dark, would survive unless they gave their undying allegiance to the Ice Witches. If any refused, only death awaited them for opposing their evil intent.

Melchior Fizz, a formidable and incredibly inquisitive wizard, wrote this tell-tell book, and entitled it *Out-Witching The Witches of Ice.* The book was a wealth of uncovered truths and warnings about this future event.

By use of deep magic the wizard had caused it to materialise in countless bookcases of witches and wizards across the land, including Mrs. Merryspell's, to alert everyone on the coming danger.

Someone's bound to read it, someone's bound to take notice –or so he thought.

So, carefully, Cordelia carried her newfound treasure up to her bedroom, hiding as best she could its intense green glow. The light was certainly bright enough to awaken anyone it may land upon.

As she read page after page, the more she read, the more she became intrigued; and the more she was inveigled by something very nasty. Worse still, the simple act of reading this alarming and somewhat treacherous book; put her, her sister, and all their friends' lives in peril as well.

Chapter Two

Chapter 2: Inconsequential Spells

Despite the winter sun doing everything in its power to warm things up, the Merryspell cottage remained bitterly cold.

In a certain room of this old and peculiar cottage, things were even more chilling; *Dark magic* was stirring.

Cordelia and her older sister Mer, who both happened to be young witches, were being severely punished. Their mother had grounded them indefinitely for something that wasn't really their fault.

So miserably, it has to be said, the two were sat in their study forced to read a particularly nasty book on how to be more obedient.

And, what they'd done to deserve this awful punishment had only helped the canker of evil that was already working against them. Their mother's unfair retribution was in fact, because of the girls', and particularly Cordelia's, outrageous misuse of magic.

Against wise caution from her sister, she had encouraged them both to attempt a very powerful protection spell.

It somehow reversed, causing severe damage to everything around their cottage. Worse still, its unpredicted explosion of fire and ice had resulted in the loss of several priceless family relics of witchcraft that simply disappeared into a cloud of ice-blue smoke, including, it must be admitted, a relic that would have gone a long way in saving them both from the predicted catastrophe.

Their mother was hopping mad. And Cordelia's explanation that the wizard Melchior Fizz had strongly advised using the spell against *"the coming danger of The Ice Witches"*, in his mysterious book *Out-Witching The Witches of Ice*; didn't help.

Mrs. Merryspell had scoffed at her plea, despite being shown the ice-like curiosity. Instead, she harshly confiscated the strange book, barking; *You've gone too far this time, and your nonsense stops right here!*

So, for punishment on this freezing winter's day, the witches were each condemned to reading from a particularly heavy looking volume on discipline.

Even as they studied, the evil in the cottage was already taking hold of their destiny, eating away at their freedom *second-by-second, charm-by-charm.*

After several hours of tiresome reading, their yawns occasionally broke the peace of utter quietness. This yawning though soon evaporated into thin air returning the room to excruciating silence and hard study.

Except for yawns, the creaking of their chairs, and the sporadic turn of a page or so, neither made hardly a noise. They wouldn't dare.

The afternoon sun had lazily, incredibly lazily, moved the shadow of cobweb curtains and other items across their study at an agonisingly slow speed. The two had watched this subdued drama happen without even a murmur, which was quite an achievement.

For Cordelia the approaching turmoil for witchcraft was simply a thread of thought, like so many other threads tangled throughout her mind.

Melchior's previously confiscated book *Out-Witching The Witches of Ice* was proving to be quite a headache to take in. So, in a way, this punishment, although undeserved in her mind, was a welcome break from reading such a direful work.

Mercifully, their stringent mother was out visiting Mrs. Pitheringae; and had left Meldrick, a strange ghoul, half-ghost half-real, to keep watch over them. But, inexplicably, and rather fortunately to Cordelia, he'd gone missing.

'Psst...Mer, can't we cast a small spell or something... cheer the place up a bit?' Cordelia's impatient whisper echoed around the room and across the long table, now deep in shadow. Her warm breath formed a tiny cloud of vapour, which she arranged into the shape of a puppy seeking attention.

'Nobody would ever find out!' she added.

'No!' snapped Mer sharply. 'I told you before, spells are strictly forbidden, so keep quiet or we'll be in even more trouble. And, stop using magic on your breath too.'

'But Meldrick has gone!' returned Cordelia more enthusiastically.

'I don't care' answered Mer 'he'll probably be back any second.'

With that, she returned to reading the book chosen by her mother.

The work they were forced to study was thoroughly recommended for all wayward witches; Prunella Primm's *The Young Witch's Guide to Becoming Sensible*.

It's a truly dreadful book. Even looking at it would be enough to scare any poor child witless. Thrusting out from its front cover is a realistic cast of Prunella's grim face, showing every disconcerting detail. Upon her accurately portrayed and outrageously protruding nose, loosely rests a pair of jewel incrusted gold-rimmed spectacles.

Prunella Primm's dreadful book.

And woe betides anyone, either daring or foolish, who

who tries removing them, perhaps, for example, to attempt selling the glasses for a small fortune at a nearby pawnshop. It's a trap, with a real shock in store for those that try.

This despicable work by Prunella is painful in the extreme. Simply a casual glance at the chapter titles would be daunting for anyone no matter how tough they pretend to be.

Chapter One: *Knuckling Down to Hard Work*

Chapter Two: *Obedience is Your Master*

Chapter Three: *Accepting Punishment Gladly (Smiling through the pain.)*

Chapter Four: *Talking Out of Turn (and what you can be turned into for doing so.)*

Chapter Five: *The Pleasure of Studying for Hours*

Chapter Six: *Tedious & Tidy (two of your best friends.)*

Chapter Seven: *Neat Straight & Correct (everything you need to know.)*

Chapter Eight: *Strict & Severe (two more of your best friends.)*

Chapter Nine: *Hard Work & Deprivation Never Killed Any Witch*

Chapter Ten: *Nonsense & Sense-ability (spotting the difference.)*

Another terrible thing, quite unbeknown to any unsuspecting reader of this horrid work, is that once they open the book and start reading, they are bound by magic to keep every one of its harsh rules and incredibly difficult and sometimes distressing exercises.

There's no escaping it either; one can only look forward to a lifetime of drudgery andobedience the moment one takes hold of its scaly, leathery cover.

That's unless one obviously happens to possess a

Brechen-Knott by the famous wizard Hieronymus Startle. This knotted piece of cord, mixed with a variety of dead insects and other disgusting items, along with a reading of various spells written by Hieronymus himself, is indeed a very powerful device.

Fortunately for Mer, her sister had made up two of these *Brechen-Knotts,* and had slipped the spare into Mer's satchel completely unnoticed. Not that Cordelia knew it had any power over Ms. Primm's awful book, but simply they were kind of handy to have for a variety of grave situations.

Thus, because of Cordelia's act of benevolence neither her nor Mer was bound by the book's magical hold; so, nothing horrible happened at all. This was just as well, for many hours ago Cordelia had decided instead to use Ms. Primm's book for flick animation, drawing her characters on the top right corner of each page.

Once finished she would delight in the scene of her excessively severe school headmistress, Miss Emily Starch-Stiffington, walking up and sitting upon the loo.

But something remarkable happened once she'd completed drawing the last picture. Her figure of Miss Starch-Stiffington sprang to life. Instantly aware of Cordelia's surprised face staring down at her, the miniature figure stood and pulled up her over-large black bloomers, scowling and wagging an accusing finger at her as she did so.

"Ol' Starchy" as everyone nicknames the draconian Miss Starch-Stiffington at school, then turned to flush the cistern, whereupon was duly sucked down into the basin, causing her and the remains of Cordelia's drawing to disappear into the page with her.

This had greatly amused and occupied Cordelia for a while. But, now that the angry headmistress and her enormous black bloomers were sucked into oblivion, boredom really set in.

'*I'M SO BORED!*' She exclaimed loudly at last, putting the emphasis on *bored,* thus noisily interrupting Mer's determination to finish this wretched book by an equally wretched writer of discipline.

'Our den is boring,' she complained 'our books are boring, and our brooms are boring. Even our stupid black cat is boring!' Radmila, their cat familiar, gave Cordelia a piercing glare from a mantelpiece where she'd sat happily observing the girls' detention.

'I'm bored too.' said Mer. 'Well there you are, why don't we do something?' pleaded Cordelia. 'Like, maybe just... one spell? Come on, I've got a really good book here for a small enchantment.'

Mer yawned, frowned, looked back at Prunella Primm's distastefully thick book, and looked away from it. As she stared into empty space, a gleam appeared in her eyes.

'Well, perhaps maybe...' she said vacantly.

'Oh great!' cried Cordelia.

'Yes, but use only the tiniest spell, nothing more. We're in so much trouble already because of your stupid *Out-Witching book* insisted Mer indignantly.

'Oh, I promise.' replied Cordelia, knowing full well she had no intention of keeping this promise.

Cordelia's cheeky look matched her bright obstinate red hair. Being twelve, and one year younger than her sister Mer, didn't seem to matter. Cordelia was very quick thinking and often figured out a plot way before her sister had even thought such a thing was needed. Mer, on the other hand, had raven-black hair, tended to be wiser and more thoughtful about her actions.

19

Mer and Cordelia Merryspell lived happily here, along with their rather strict mother, Hepsibah, their favourite grandmother, Daisy, and bossy eldest sister, Myrtle. All of them were witches, though Myrtle rather felt she was more worthy of being a wizard, but to this Mer would say, 'Nose down, sis, it would take you a hundred years to become that good at magic!'

The round stone cottage was in the deepest part of Broomsnest Wood, and lay some miles from the village of Lower Wyshing. Both the wood and cottage were far from anybody; which was just as well for all concerned. And those not so concerned.

'What spell shall I do first?' asked Cordelia whilst rubbing her hands together excitedly.

'First!' objected Mer, 'You're only doing one spell, that's all.'

'Of course, just the one –duh!'

With that, Cordelia picked up her favourite book on small spells; *Amethyst Tryte's Little to do About Anything.* It was a trifling volume on idiotic spells that even Cordelia's mother allowed her to keep.

'Here's one.' she said, hoping that it wouldn't upset her sister too much. '*The Golden Hat spell* it says here. Shall I read it?'

'Go on then if you must' replied Mer with an impatient sigh.

'OK, You take a small square of paper,' read Cordelia in an annoyingly loud voice 'fold it in half so you end up with a triangle shape, and fold the left and right corners of the triangle into the centre. Next, fold the points of these lower ends upward in line with the bottom edge to form a witch's hat. Lastly, say these words; *"Paper, paper, fizz and splat, Become now a golden hat!"*

Cordelia smiled looking a teensy bit abashed, and admitted 'Yeah, I know... that does sound a bit stupid and childish, but still, Mer, you never know with some spells these days, do you?'

Mer never answered as she was back reading her book, so Cordelia followed the spell exactly as written; looking hard at the little piece of paper neatly folded into a triangle shape, now lying flat on their study table.

She stared at it for some while but nothing happened. Then, gradually at first, each corner of the paper started to curl fizz and spark.

'Crumbs, it's working!' she cried in shock, and Mer looked up in surprise. But within seconds it had burst into flames and all that was left was a pile of ashes.

'Oh, that's really rotten.' she protested to Mer 'Hardly what you call a spell -shall I try another one?'

'No, I said one spell only.'

'Yes, I know' argued Cordelia 'but you can't exactly call that a spell, now can you?'

Mer was far too anxious to argue with her sister; especially feeling she'd have to finish reading Ms. Primm's book before their mother returned; and instinctively knowing for sure that Cordelia would probably end up getting her own way anyway.

'Go on get it over with.' sighed Mer as she rested her head between her hands. She wasn't looking inside Ms. Primm's book, but over it; momentarily dreaming about better things to do.

Cordelia looked around intently for something worthy of practicing upon. There wasn't a lot to choose from owing to a great deal of unfair confiscation precipitated by an overly zealous mother.

There was one thing though that did catch her eye; a dusty old wooden bucket lying on its side in the corner of the room, and obviously unworthy of Mrs. Merryspell's scouring intent to remove any objects of pleasure from the girls' lives altogether.

Instantly, Cordelia sprang to her feet and picked it up. Mer looked up to watch her carry it into the centre of the study.

I don't think she can do much harm with that old thing. Mer thought quietly to herself. But she was wrong. Radmila disagreed, and jumped from the mantelpiece to a hasty exit.

'Shall I begin?' asked Cordelia.

'Alright' said her sister, 'cast your stupid spell but be very, very careful.'

Cordelia raised an index finger and waved her arms in the air muttering strange words that were completely unnecessary.

Using a totally banned spell book, she read out a curious old spell, wisely hiding it from Mer. *More Mayhem*, by her favourite wizard Melchior Fizz.

Cordelia had read a lot of books by Melchior lately, though *Out-Witching The Witches of Ice* had been the cause of more than a sociably acceptable amount of sleepless nights.

Understandably, *More Mayhem*, although packed with powerful spells, was a great deal easier to digest, and on page sixty-two, she'd located the perfect charm:

> *"From the deepest fathoms,*
> *To the highest hills,*
> *I command of this vessel,*
> *All gifts and ills."*

Mer, looking up from her reading.

'Where did you get that spell?' she enquired.

'Oh, nowhere in particular,' fibbed Cordelia.

Mer walked over for a closer inspection. Cordelia discretely slipped Melchior's dangerous book back into her inside pocket.

Mer peered inside the bucket, then wisely stepped back. The room was filling with smoke, yet there was no fire. Miniature lightening darted erratically around the bucket's rim. Its fizzing was quite unnerving.

The two of them moved even further away. It was evident that the vessel had begun reacting to the spell by Melchior Fizz after all, and in a manner that even surprised Mer.

But, no sooner had it started, the drama ended with a large whomp and a cloud of thick black smoke.

'That just so totally failed,' scoffed Mer. '…Is that the best you can do?'

Cordelia looked embarrassed, but as the smoke cleared, she could see something sticking upright out of the bucket. 'Look Mer, brooms!'

Because they'd both had their brooms confiscated earlier in the week, for something else that wasn't really their fault, Cordelia thought that they would be quite a treat.

Mer though was still unconvinced. 'You can have the brooms; they don't look up to much. Besides, I think we've had enough spells for the present.'

'Yes, but look!' drooled Cordelia, holding up one of the brooms. It was tatty and had definitely seen better days. Mer viewed it with disdain.

'It's disgusting and ratty, actually!' she objected. 'I

wouldn't be seen dead with anything like that, but if you want it, take it. Anyway, your problem not mine, does it work?'

'I don't know,' answered her sister 'but I'll give it a try. Hey, look at the other one though, now that's more your sort of broom, Mer!'

Cordelia knelt down and grabbed the other broom, which looked quite exotic. It sparkled with gems and magic stones ingrained into the very broom itself.

Mer's eyes widened and the '*I want it*' part of her brain instantly sprang into action. Awkwardly, they began flying the two brooms. But it was far too difficult manoeuvering around the cramped study.

Cordelia's broom was getting harder to handle by the second and she crashed into the bookcase. The impact knocked it over sending rows and rows of very large heavily bound books, presumably all by Ms. Primm, scattering to the floor below.

'This is crazy!' she complained 'we're going to do ourselves serious damage if we go on like this. Why don't we take them outside for a small flight, we'll be back in no time, I promise?'

The promise part didn't wash with Mer, but she did accept they needed to put them through their paces if they intended keeping them, definitely as Mer now possessed a very strange if not attractive-looking broom.

'OK, let's go, but we'd better not be gone too long.'

The windows creaked open to Mer's command and they both shot off into the bleak woodland, completely putting out of mind the fallen bookshelf and scattered books. The two even forgot the likely return of Mrs. Merryspell's ghostlike entity Meldrick. He'd really create a fuss if he found them missing.

No matter, they'd been cooped up for most of the boring day, and it was more than a lot of people would bear, especially if they were witches, especially for that reason alone.

Cordelia led the way, flying well above the bare lain trees. The brooms were fantastic, gliding easily through air. Before they'd realised it, the two had flown well beyond Broomsnest wood, and into a place neither of them were familiar with.

'Hey!' called Mer 'I thought we were only trying these out; we'd better turn back Cordelia. If we're discovered missing, well, it would have to be a life sentence at least!'

Reluctantly, her sister agreed. They both pulled hard on the handles to turn their brooms. Nothing happened.

'Damn!' yelled Mer. 'For some reason mine's not working.'

'Same here!' Cordelia cried.

'What are we going to do?' asked Mer 'this is just soooo annoying!'

'Well, we'll just have to see where they take us I guess' answered Cordelia 'Unless I can find a spell or something' She fumbled through her pockets for a book of magic verse to overcome the broom's obstinacy.

She managed to find Maurice Pussot's *Un-Curse* book of common counter-charms. But it was of no use. Eventually however, the broomsticks, one ratty, the other sparkling in the late sunlight, did slow down. Understandably, Cordelia thought it was due to her frantic chanting. It wasn't. Mer, looking down in anticipation, spotted something of interest.

'Hang on,' she called, interrupting Cordelia's desperate readings, 'there's an old ruined mansion down there, maybe that's where the brooms are headed?'

The foreboding walls of a once grand and palatial building looked impressive and the witches flew around at the will of their odd-looking broomsticks. The glass windows, those that remained unbroken, were bare and uninviting.

The brooms jerked upward, flying over the roof and swooped into a courtyard below. They held on tightly and landed outside a large door, partially open. After dismounting, the two strode over.

'Do you think we should ask someone first if it's okay to walk in and look around?' questioned Mer.

'No, there's no-one about, the place is obviously deserted!' said Cordelia shrugging her shoulders. 'Trust me, I'm a witch –it'll be fine!' So, she pushed it and walked in. Perhaps this wasn't the wisest thing to do.

Inside was amazingly dark, and the whistling wind, speaking from thousands of different cracks and gaps in the walls and windows, announced a strange presence all of its own.

'Crumbs!' said Cordelia. 'It's bloody creepy in here, don't you think?'

Mer nodded, and cautiously made her way forward, keeping a wary eye out for any dark or hard-to-see entities which might have been lurking in the shadows.

Eventually, carefully tip-toeing over broken vases, chairs, sofas and all sorts of smashed objects; not to mention brushing past countless cobwebs, they came to a door. Beyond it, at the end of a long twisting corridor, they arrived at a white marble statue of a witch, pointing. At its base, it simply read *"This way"*.

'OK, lady, we'll go that way,' said Cordelia. 'Alright with you, Mer?'

'Well, I'm hardly going to stand here on my own, am I?'

So they followed the direction down another long corridor to where it terminated. There, a further corridor crossed it. At this little junction there was a second white marble statue, this time of an archer with a drawn bow. At its base was an inscription *"I be Artemist –most feared by mine enemies."* She was facing and aiming toward the right. So, ignoring the left turn, they proceeded to where the ghost white statue of Artemis pointed her rather sharp arrow, and took this narrow passage to its very convoluted end.

They'd walked quite a way, and were now at a door that was both tall, and old, crumbling and splintery. Before Cordelia could about-face and say *"I think we should go in,"* the white marble arrow they'd just seen shot past her left ear, imbedding itself in the thick rotten timber.

'I could have been killed!' she cried.

The statue of Artemis the archer had obviously loosed it.

'Oohh, that's an omen for certain!' mused Mer.

And, maybe it was. Nonetheless, with a creaking moan, the door unexpectedly opened from the arrow's force. A ghostly rush of cold air and a distant sighing voice accompanied it.

Mer appeared unsettled, her eyes wide and scared, face as white as chalk. Cordelia strained to look through the darkness as the ancient door slowly opened wider. She reached for her not-so-trusty torch. As her eyes adjusted to the light of it, she noticed a flight of stone stairs descending toward some kind of cellar; and she could swear another light was shining from down there within.

'There's something glowing down there!' she called. Quietly, they began creeping down the long stone stairway, grateful at least there were no creaking boards to give them away to whatever maybe waiting for them. It felt decidedly colder, and distinctly unnerving. As they neared the bottom, they could clearly see the opening into the hardly lit cellar.

Probably a dungeon thought Cordelia.

Hesitantly peering inside, they noticed an old oil lamp on the corner of a table and a stack of books next to a very large cauldron; which appeared to be boiling without any sort of flame under it. The room was dead quiet.

Out of the dark shot a voice cracking open the eerie stillness.

'WHO'S THERE!' it snapped.

'AHHHHH!' screamed Mer responding in fright.

Mer's scream shook Cordelia who nervously shouted back; 'No-one much, just two young witches... nothing to be scared about... I mean it's not that we'll change you into a bat or anything...even though we do possess tremendous magical powers!'

Cordelia's voice echoed throughout the dingy room.

'Come in!' said a friendly sounding voice at last 'Come in, I don't get many visitors these days, so you're more than welcome.' As they cautiously entered, they saw a tall woman skulking in the corner near an old cupboard. She was dressed in amazing clothes. Although nearly charcoal black in colour, each garment seemed to glow and sparkle.

'Obviously a *charmed dress*' said Mer out loud. Not hearing Mer properly, the woman replied 'And I'm charmed to meet you too!'

By her looks she was clearly a witch. 'My name is Penelope Plowright, and I may be ugly, but I am a *white witch*' she said, introducing herself whilst trying to hide

'Why ugly?' asked Cordelia.

'Well, that's what everyone thinks of me' replied Penelope.

'But, you're beautiful!' proclaimed Mer insistently.

'Oh, what, really? Surely not, I mean, I'm ugly! Do you really mean it though? Oh, gosh...yes I suppose it's true, I haven't any warts or anything like that!' she said feeling her face 'Perhaps in the right kind of light, I could be considered....'

At that, she burst into a kind of embarrassed manic laughter.

Penelope beckoned the witches in for a Romani tea, though sadly she had none. Although she had a teapot, but it was housing her frog familiar for the time being, and consequently of no use at all for refreshments, unless one had a peculiar desire for drinking the slimy water that stagnated in the bottom.

'Would you care for a biscuit?' she asked with a very sweet smile. She fumbled around the table, and eventually found a tall black tin. Opening it, she jerked her head backwards in shock saying 'Oh dear, I don't think so!' and started that laughter once more.

The woman promptly strode away from the table to a dark ebony cupboard, her dress shimmering in the poor light.

'Come over and take a look at this!' she said inviting them to the ominous cupboard in the corner of the room. Opening it very carefully, she remarked 'Don't be scared now!'

The two hadn't realised till that moment they had any reason to be scared. The cupboard, quite tall as it happened, was very spacious, and the dingy light from the oil lamp made it difficult to see inside.

'There's nothing in it!' complained Cordelia shining her rapidly dimming torch around.

'Ah, but there is you see, something very special, so I'm sure you won't want to miss it' replied Penelope.

Cordelia was no coward, but stepping into a strange cupboard at the behest of some loony witch seemed a bit risky to say the least. Mer appeared worried and whispered 'I'd be careful if I were you.'

Cordelia looked back at Penelope who smiled just as sweetly as when she offered them tea and biscuits. But bravely, nonetheless, she slowly extended her arm and left leg into the strange looking cupboard, whilst feeling about for that something special as promised. Her torch wasn't much help as the batteries had all but died; and she didn't have time now to find a suitable glowing spell.

'Don't be shy now,' encouraged Penelope whose wide-eyed expression, Mer noticed, had become one of anticipation, rather than delight.

It seemed as though the cupboard had no end as Cordelia moved her arm and body further and further inwards. Mer was holding the end of her sister's cloak, just in case. At last, Cordelia's fingertips touched the back of the cupboard.

'It's still empty!' she yelled.

'Well, just move your sweet little arm to the left' added Penelope 'that's right, you'll find a wonderful surprise right in the corner.'

Mer gripped her sister's clothing even tighter.

Cordelia let out a shriek.

'Wow!' she squealed 'It's a jewelled casket!'

'Let me see!' urged Mer as Cordelia brought the prize

out into the dingy light. The casket's jewels sparkled and glinted even in the dimness. Again came a rush of cold wind and that same ghostly sigh they'd heard before.

'This is unreal!' continued Cordelia trying to open it. They should have seen Penelope's face. It wasn't filled with jubilation, more like someone about to unwrap a diamond the size of an apple. There was certainly lust in her eyes, and more than a smidgen of evil contemplation. They never looked though; and if perhaps they had, they wouldn't have been caught up with what happened next.

Penelope snatched it from Cordelia's hands as her and her sister ogled at it. 'We'll put it on the table here' she said 'then you can both have a good look at what's inside.'

Their eyes were unashamedly glued to the casket as she walked it over and set it in the middle of the table, moving aside a pile of dusty old books and the spluttering oil lamp.

'It belongs to both of you now, I want you to take possession of it entirely' she said as if handing them an ancient family heirloom.

They took no notice of what she'd just said as their eyeballs and minds were still transfixed by the precious object.

'I'm going to open it for you' said Penelope with excitement 'and I want you to promise me that you won't *ever, ever* let it out of your sight.'

'Y e a h' they both slurred.

Penelope placed a large key into the casket's lock and everyone's eyes widened. As the heavy lid was opened Penelope turned her head away and a great gold and blue light shot from the casket. Penelope grabbed one of her dusty spell books to shield her eyes.

Cordelia and Mer were completely immobilised. Their eyes were stuck open with an idiotic expression upon their face. The sisters were utterly helpless and Penelope shrieked for joy.

'It worked...it worked!' she screamed 'Blimey, the Witches of Ice are going to be ecstatic with me!'

They would indeed. Penelope gazed at the girls' inanimate bodies, still transfixed by the blue gold light.

Walking to the opposite side of the table, so she could avoid the enchanting light, she knelt and picked up their brooms, tossed them into the air saying a few words of a charm.

The brooms immediately ignited, disappearing into a cloud of smoke.

'You'll have no need of those where you're headed!' she exclaimed. 'What a fortune they've promised me just for you idiots...can't think why. Anyway' she went on 'that's this new world of witchcraft for you!'

Penelope looked frustrated because the girls couldn't respond to her.

'Oh, if only you could hear me' she moaned. 'Never mind, you'll find out soon enough.'

From inside one of the books stacked on the table next to the spellbound witches, she pulled out a large sheet of paper covered with magical symbols and secret words. Then, Penelope sprinkled it with freshly plucked chicken feathers, and crushed beetles from a silver bowl.

'Now to summon the Witches of Ice!' cried the woman proudly. She was about to set light to the paper and all its contents, using a strip of crumpled paper held above the flame of her oil lamp, when the door burst open.

You don't normally get a storm cloud inside a house, or even a large mansion for that matter, but that's exactly what floated into the room.

The cloud was dark and thunderous, sparking with miniature lightening and two rotating whirlwinds. It was about the size of a floating armchair, though a great deal more dangerous.

Penelope hadn't seen anything quite like this before; and as it progressed into the room high above her, it sent chairs, ornaments, books, and an oil lamp, flying through the air.

The blustering whirlwinds caused the lid of a particularly nasty casket to slam shut as well. And straightaway, Cordelia and Mer were released from its charm.

They stood up, quite speechless at the wind and wreckage whirring about. Yet, before they could cover their ears from all the noise, the storm ceased and the cloud evaporated instantly, sending all the wind-borne objects crashing to the floor.

Equally as dramatic was the entrance of the witch Kaldre, head of a coven known as the *Five Witches of Gloom*. The woman was tall with an air of superiority about her. Even her dry voice commanded respect. Her clothing was long and flowing and as she walked, if you looked carefully, you'd notice her notoriously high heeled boots glinting whenever the front of her long coat opened and closed.

'Hello' she said addressing the girls 'my name is Kaldre, and I'm so glad you're safe!' Kaldre smiled with satisfaction at Penelope Plowright's present condition, which was completely paralysed, and turned toward the girls with a sinister looking smile.

Behind her lurked the other four of her coven; and similarly they were staring intently at the girls, rather like sadistic scientists observing a living experiment trapped in a sealed glass container; and about to add a deadly poison to see what happens next. Chilling indeed.

Kaldre, not receiving any deliriously excitable cheer from the rescued young witches, drew from under her cloak a tall blue-glass lantern and held it up for all to see.

'Five spells from five witches to quell the hopes and desires of one.' she muttered 'And the fifth spell being that she be cast into a bucket.'

Whilst Penelope's eyes glazed and her mouth refused to open despite much effort, Kaldre opened the glass door of the lantern and put her left index finger inside. A bright blue flame shot from her finger and ignited the lamp. She closed its glass door, muttered another few words, and the whole room filled with blue light.

Then the lantern dimmed returning the dungeon to the dingy yellow light of Penelope's oil lamp, which amazingly had repaired itself and now sat on the table beside the girls. Blinking their eyes adjusting to the light, Cordelia and Mer next heard a disturbing squelching noise coming from the corner of the room.

Peering through the gloom, they could just make out an old bucket wobbling slightly on the floor in front of where they stood.

'Stonking grief!' exclaimed Mer half in fright.

Cordelia walked over shaking her torch. She shone its

regenerated light to where her sister pointed. 'Blimey!' she cried.

What they saw wasn't pretty. Somehow, the witch had become liquefied. Now Penelope occupied the same bucket Cordelia had left behind at the cottage.

'Hang on, that's the bucket I cast a spell on to give us the brooms!' she confirmed.

Kaldre smiled sheepishly, but offered no explanation. It was cruel justice for Penelope and inside the old bucket, she fought desperately to keep her face at the surface; too slippery to remain on top and too liquid to cast any counter-spells. It was hideous, yet somehow amusing to watch.

Nevertheless, Cordelia became scared. She was fully aware that if Kaldre and her cronies had the power to do this to an immensely strong witch, who wasn't a white witch by any stretch of the imagination, what chance would they have?

'I'm warning you' yelled Cordelia arrogantly, 'I possess some powerful spells by none other than the great Melchior Fizz!'

Not knowing quite how to answer this rather diminutive threat from one so juvenile, Kaldre and her coven simply stared at her in disbelief.

After this they cracked up into uncontrolled laughter, which was so severe it caused pain in their strained stomach muscles. Even Mer, not wishing to demean her sister, couldn't help a polite cough or two.

Cordelia though, stood her ground, refusing to be

intimidated by their summary dismissal of her claim to hold extraordinary powers, even though it wasn't quite true.

'Dear Child' returned Kaldre now recomposed 'do you really think for one moment that we would waste our valuable time and effort to save you from certain death, only to kill you, ourselves?'

She had a valid point.

'Wouldn't it be easier to let the lady in the bucket do the hard work first and just take over when it suited us?' Kaldre nodded her head inviting Cordelia's agreement.

'I s'pose.' answered Cordelia reluctantly, though deep down she simply knew things didn't quite add up.

'So, what *are* you going to do with us?' urged Mer.

'Nothing!' she snapped 'We mean you no harm, we happened upon you by accident, thank goodness we did!'

Kaldre smiled, if one could describe it that way, and finished with 'No, don't thank us, just be off with you! Go on, shoo, get out of here before we change our minds!'

Cordelia and Mer needed no second invitation and ran with all speed up the stone stairway to freedom. Once more they were stood outside. It was pitch black except for the heavenly display of stars twinkling as they usually do against the black sky.

Not wishing to hang around, they both headed for home chattering incessantly about their narrow escape from death.

The thought of explaining their absence from studies to an angry mother seemed almost irrelevant.

'I still don't get it, how did that old bucket turn up just when Kaldre needed it?' puzzled Cordelia 'I mean, obviously it was conjured by Penelope to appear in our study, so how did Kaldre know of it? What's more worrying is that she must have got past mum's magic; and broken into our cottage to bring the thing to Penelope's hideout.'

'And, Penelope would've got rid of Meldrick too!' added Mer 'probably while we were still studying'

'It doesn't make sense' added Cordelia. Now they could feel the chill of the cold night.

Cordelia looked up at the stunning sky once more, but rather wished she hadn't. Circling high above she swore she saw five dark objects silhouetted against the delicate starlight. She nudged Mer.

'You're imagining things' she said. But quickened her pace. Without brooms, it was going to be a long, long walk home.

Chapter Three

Chapter 3: *Nightshade Ball.*

A few days later, close to witching hour to be precise, Mer was anxiously looking through the half fogged window of their den.

After their recent encounter with Kaldre and the nightmarish walk back home, and despite them inexplicably getting away with their absence from studies, she didn't feel so keen anymore on the hours belonging to witches, even though they were the most exciting hours to be had. But still she looked, staring through the sleety rain, and through the inky blackness.

Far off, Mer could just make out two dim distant lights flickering amongst the trees. Whatever they were, they were coming closer, no mistaking it. Furthermore, within a short amount of time they would whisk her, and her sister Cordelia, off to a very strange place indeed.

'How do I look?' asked Mer nervously, as if her whole life depended upon it.

'You'll do,' quipped Cordelia.

'It still seems murky out there' called Mer, deep in thought.

Cordelia nodded but wasn't really listening. She was lying on a huge sofa reading some more of the once confiscated and extremely dangerous book by Melchior Fizz *Out-Witching The Witches of Ice.* She didn't reply to her sister's murmuring, being glued to what Melchior was trying to tell her.

The door of the den creaked open and their mother, Mrs. Merryspell, carefully peeked around not wishing to make things tenser than what they already were. Cordelia quickly slipped Melchior's book out of sight.

'Everything OK?' she asked in a concerned sort of voice.

Just a 'Yep!' emanated from Cordelia, though nothing from Mer who was still tracking those ever-nearing lights.

'Don't worry, your carriage will soon be here,' she added. 'Oh Mer, my sweet, you look positively stunning!'

Mer turned from the window, and feeling a little more encouraged, asked, 'Do you really think so?'

Mrs. Merryspell rushed over to give her a big hug but Mer moved back a little; obviously concerned about creasing her dress.

'Careful mum!' she pleaded.

Mer had spent many months making this dress, months of patient designing, cutting, tailoring, and finishing. She'd even sewn in a few extra pockets as well to hold protection charms. Yet, the only charm she'd placed there was her mother's gift to her, the ancient Stone of Aberneth.

The result of all this work was clearly stunning. Even from a casual glance one could see that something rather special had been created, and it was all from Mer's own imagination; the other vital ingredient of course was the use of some rather strange magic.

And, it was this that she felt would attract the wrong kind of attention. Still, never mind, it was Mer's dress and she knew that its peculiar magic might just result in impressing the right people that night.

In all its strangeness the garment changed colour, shape and even appearance, as mysterious images that were captured within the very fabric itself moved around.

Mer's all-time haute couture favourite, Jemimah Silk of Paris, who uses a great deal of magic when making her gowns, would fall instantly in love with Mer's creation.

The fabric's colour is known as Black Malachite, and

its style would be considered as close-fitting with a high collar, long sleeves; its length allowing it to sweep graciously across the floor.

If you looked close enough, you'd swear you could see real stars glinting, even shadows of people's faces. The dress could be seen subtly going through the seasons too.

Cordelia and Mer had been invited to the most glamorous Witches' Ball in all of Witchdom. They knew this because they had received an invitation card, courtesy of Mrs. Glumm, a witch friend of their mum who lives in the tiny village of Mad. The card in itself was a true work of art. A grand crest featured at the top and all the writing was in gold script on a shimmering silver background. It read:

Drucilla Darkington & Herbert Von Pfirsich cordially invite Miss. Mer Merryspell & Miss. Cordelia Merryspell to attend their Annual Nightshade Ball. To be held at Nightshade Hall on the Third Saturday in February when the Moon has waxed full. Dress: Dressy. Brooms: To be provided. R.S.V.P.

Naturally, they were both thrilled, but for very different reasons. For Cordelia, creases in her dress were furthest from her mind. The only thing she could think about was the weird realisation that all was not well with the world of witchcraft. And tonight they may well find themselves involved in something they couldn't handle.

Nevertheless, in the soft light of the girls' den, Mer could only think nervously about the glamour and attention such a night would bring as what appeared as winter snow swirled about in the fabric of her creation.

'Cripes, your dress is snowing!' Cordelia shrieked in delight.

At last, there was a thunderous noise of hooves and

heavy wheels outside the Merryspell's cottage; the coach and horses had finally arrived. Maybe now Mer would calm a little.

'Ooh, it's here!' cried their Gran, Daisy, as she excitedly rushed into the den. 'You're going to have incredible fun my dears –any room for an odd one?'

There was definitely room enough for an odd one, as Gran put it, several to be honest. The coach was as grand as the ball they were invited to, incredibly spacious with masses of exotic refreshments for the journey too.

It was courtesy of their father Gawain Merryspell, who although separated from Mrs. Merryspell seemed to indulge the family more than ever. It even appeared likely to the girls that mum and dad might just get back together again. Gran certainly thought so.

'Don't forget to take some mischievous spells for games...I never forgot mine!' hummed Gran as she thought aloud about her childhood.

'Flatten the Lizard, Scare the Witch, and *Find the Poisoned Apple, oh and not forgetting Swallow the Black Frog,'* she mused, half expecting to be invited.

Cordelia laughed and wanted to know how to take part in these unheard-of games, but Mrs. Merryspell interrupted with, 'Come along, come along, there's no time for nonsense, there'll be plenty of that where you're going.'

That wasn't strictly true, for Drucilla Darkington and Herbert Von Pfirsich really knew how to organise a ball for witches and warlocks, even wizards, come to that.

The driver graciously helped the girls, in all their witchy finery, into the fine-looking coach. With a cheeky look he said, 'Bang on the roof if you think I'm going too fast!'

Cordelia asked 'What if you're going too slow?'

The driver winked and replied, 'No fear of that!'

In seconds, they were off, with the six strong horses galloping at full speed. As Mer looked through the rear oval window of their coach, she could just make out her mum and Gran waving them goodbye. In a flash, a rocket shot off into the sky from the cottage roof.

'Look, Cordelia!' she cried without even a hint of her previous nervousness. The sky lit up in a thousand colours. 'I bet that was Gran who let that one off!' she giggled.

The coach was soon tearing along at a phenomenal speed.

'If we go any faster,' yelled Cordelia, 'I swear we'll fly.'

How strange she would sense that. When the rumbling of the heavy wheels on the hard ground ceased, Cordelia sprang to the window and cried, 'We're flying!'

She slid down the window and reached out as far as she could to try and catch the leaves from the passing tops of trees. Alas, even they slid away beneath them as the coach rose higher and higher.

'That was stonking, Mer, I nearly grabbed a bunch of 'em!'

She stuck her head out of the window again and shouted to the driver, 'Brilliant, matey!' giving him a substantial thumbs-up.

Their journey was thrilling, especially passing through a low cloud, where they could hardly see each other –even from across the coach. That was thanks to someone leaving the coach windows down.

Before long, they had arrived above Nightshade Hall.

The imposing building looked amazing from the sky. All around the edge of its many roofs, strange beacons shone out in blue, mauve, and red. Neither of them could take their eyes off the spectacular scene below. Down the driveway was a procession of various cars, coaches, and limousines as many young people of all type, be they witches, warlocks or spell-casting people of all description, had arrived in style for the long-awaited ball.

Mer was becoming nervous once more and started straightening things that didn't really need straightening. Cordelia noticed this and said, 'Come on you; don't go all nervy like bloody Myrtle! Besides, if anyone can't see how obviously stunning you look, I'll weave a spell on them. They won't leave you alone after that; you might have to start practicing your autograph!'

Mer smiled warmly and stood up, a little taller Cordelia thought, and checked her hair in the mirror provided.

The coach and horses once more touched ground and slowly approached the grand hall along its equally grand driveway.

When they'd arrived outside the main entrance, their driver jumped down and opened their carriage door, helping them as they stepped onto the forecourt.

Cordelia looked up toward the dazzling lights of the hallway ahead, and couldn't ever remember seeing so many glistening chandeliers; they were glowing and flickering from inside too, as if each one was lit by a giant flame. The resulting sparkles from their cut crystals were scattering everywhere, which only added to the magic.

Mer, now looking very confident, strode forward into the main hall and stopped before an extremely mischievous looking host with a wide grin and bright adventurous eyes which darted this way and that as if

45

seeking out fun. It was Herr. Herbert Von Pfirsich.

'Velcome!' he cried, and warmly shook Mer's hand. When she brought her hand back though, she felt something moving about in her palm. It was a giant black spider, and Mer shrieked as it jumped up and turned into a puff of black smoke. Von Pfirsich burst into laughter.

'Splendid!' he yelled. 'Velcome to our little zelebration.'

Cordelia was next, but she kept her hands behind her back and curtsied instead. This amused Herbert Von Pfirsich. He sharpened his look.

'Oh, my dear, vhat's that on your head?' he enquired.

'My hat, silly –you can't get me with that one!' she answered.

With a loud whomp her hat sprang off and landed in front of her. A large toad appeared from underneath and jumped away into the crowd of guests, before it too went up in a puff of smoke. Cordelia choked a laugh, raised an eyebrow and winked with a knowing smile. She knew this was going to be quite a night.

'Very pleased to meet you both,' said Herbert Von Pfirsich, 'and I trust you'll have a fantastic time.'

Beside him stood Drucilla Darkington wearing an incredibly long black dress with magic stones set along its length. On her head was a very tall sort of pointed black crown, though it wasn't a crown. It had several spires of glistening black jewels linked by tiny arches, which looked breathtaking, like Drucilla. She appeared severe, almost unapproachable, but eventually she smiled at them.

'Welcome!' she said in a gentle voice. Cordelia smiled in return and whispered to Mer, 'She wouldn't want to take a bow with that tall thing on her head, or shake it too quickly!'

The two were then announced by one of the many courtiers. Well, they must have been courtiers, as they weren't dressed at all like wizards or warlocks.

'Miss. Mer Merryspell and Miss. Cordelia Merryspell,' he cried, and there wasn't an ear in the place that didn't know they had arrived. Mer felt embarrassed, Cordelia thought it was great.

Wild screams of 'You're kidding!' and 'Get out of here!' and 'I don't believe it!' ensued, and these happy cries stopped the two mid-step from walking further into the astonishing ballroom ahead.

'Delia...Meryl!' responded Cordelia.

'Persimmon!' yelled Mer just as excitedly. Their three great friends were standing in front of them, all dressed in their best outfits.

'I just can't believe your dress, Mer!' cried Meryl in her rich Irish accent, and reaching out feeling the fabric as if to make sure it was actually real.

'That is so sick, I love it!' admired Delia, whilst Persimmon just couldn't stop gaping. 'It's way above sublime,' she gushed.

'Yeah,' teased Cordelia 'Mer's mad tailoring drove the whole family up the blinking wall!'

There was an uncomfortable silence; then Cordelia burst out laughing. Everyone joined in.

'Hey, you might even win the Darkington Chalice this year!' added Delia. 'Doubt it,' moaned Mer awkwardly and she promptly changed the subject.

'So you got invites too!' she said. 'How stunning.'

'It wasn't easy' said Meryl. 'My Aunt Eloisa nearly scuppered my chances with a rather damming report on my escapade into *The Forest of Gloom*.'

'That wasn't the time when one of your potions blew up Gloom Castle?' quipped Mer.

'Well, it didn't exactly blow it up,' admitted Meryl, 'That's a bit of an exaggeration as it was only the kitchen that nearly burnt down. Besides, the place is falling to bits anyway. It was a good job actually there wasn't anyone home at the time otherwise I mightn't be here to tell the tale!'

Cordelia interrupted, 'You're right, you could've bumped into the five witches that live there. We met them, and they're pretty nasty, I can tell you!'

'Didn't meet a soul, thankfully. And it wasn't my fault even if I had have, someone gave me the wrong ingredients for the potion I was boiling.'

'Oh well,' said Delia sarcastically, 'No wonder your folks let you off.'

The others laughed.

During this chitchat there appeared upon one of the walls a cluster of crystal trumpets.

They blasted a loud fanfare to gain everyone's attention.

From a high balcony, Cordelia and the others could hear and see a very small witch make the following announcement through the same instruments. They made her tiny voice boom around the huge room.

'*Witches, warlocks and wizards all, gather please to take part in Drucilla Darkington's Grand Waltz Bizarre!*' she cried.

This was the moment Mer had feared the most, now her strange dress would be exposed to every critical eye of every critical witch in the ballroom.

More than that, the dreaded *Peter Hemsley* would see her too. She'd avoided him most of term whenever his school came for various contests.

He was bound to ask her for a dance. Even more horrific would be his boring conversation about the best spells to use for making pops, bangs, and explosions.

Sure enough, he was there, waving and signaling from across the ballroom. Mer smiled back at him, which she really ought not to have done. Peter Hemsley came running, running so fast he didn't notice a gangly slightly built lad near to Mer whom he accidentally sent flying to the ground in his rush to be with her.

The tall lad picked himself up and immediately apologised for causing any problems, though it wasn't any fault of his. Nervously, he adjusted his full dark costume that didn't quite fit, patted down his disheveled hair; and gathered up from the floor an assortment of books and notes.

'I've been keeping track of certain odd events and I think it's all beginning to make sense now,' he said edgily. 'Gosh, I'm sorry, Maxim Dashkov is my name, pleased to meet you under such strange circumstances.'

To say Mer was impressed would be an understatement; Mr. Hemsley could have evaporated into thin air for all she would've noticed. Mer smiled bashfully, Cordelia giggled.

'Mer Merryspell,' she added, and they shook hands awkwardly.

'Like to dance?' interrupted Peter Hemsley, quite unaware that he was hampering the start of a new and rather brilliant friendship.

'Er, no thanks, Peter,' replied Mer, wishing he'd perhaps succumb to a spell that would make him instantly disappear; *Cordelia could help with that!* she thought with a gentle smile.

Peter turned and looked up at Maxim Dashkov.

'Russian, are you?' he enquired smugly.

'No, born near here, but my father's relatives originate from Vladivostok.'

'Granny's bed-socks?' sneered Peter. 'Know any Russian spells on severe explosions?'

'Not me, I'm afraid, but try my sister, Aiyana; she's a wealth on dangerous stuff...she's over there.'

Maxim pointed to her and Peter's eyes lit-up.

'Have all your family got funny names?' he quipped, not waiting for an answer but rushing off to pester his newest victim.

'Sorry about that,' said Maxim. Mer smiled again, though not so awkwardly.

'Aiyana has been a bit of a drag lately, got me into heaps of trouble for having a copy of *The Forbidden Art of the Unilluminated* by Melchior Fizz, my personal mentor and all-time best magician!'

Mer looked surprised. 'Goodness, he's considered the best by Cordelia too!'

'Who's Cordelia?' asked Maxim.

'My younger sister...oh, oh dear, where's she gone? –She was just next to me!' Mer peered about. 'Ah, it's OK.' 'She's with the others.'

Maxim was still a tad nervous. 'Um, care for a dance?'

Outwardly, Mer simply nodded; inwardly it was a whole different matter.

Melchior's book *The Forbidden Art of the Unilluminated* is a dangerous volume to have in one's possession. Similar to another work; *Unseen Borrowing* by Edwardo Flynt, which by comparison is mere child's play, this strange volume is almost invisible to the naked eye.

A major reason for this is that it would be folly for anyone unskilled in the arts of deep magic to commence reading; even worse to actually initiate one of the simple spells in it like say, *the Inside-Out Spell,* or more severely, the infamous *Starlight Charm*, which if uncontrolled, could do some serious damage to the planet.

The other reason for the book's invisibility is simply that you have to be incredibly clever to cast enough magic onto it for the words, and diagrams, to become visible. Little wonder why Maxim got into so much bother from his overly protective mother.

Meanwhile, what happened next in the ballroom was quite amazing. Descending gently from the huge arched ceiling of this grand place, and accompanied by a flood of peculiarly discordant though oddly tuneful waltz music, floated a collection of large glasslike spheres.

They glistened exquisitely in the magic light, standing out against the charcoal-silver walls. There wasn't a soul there who wasn't caught by the moment, especially Cordelia and Mer, though for very different reasons, it must be understood.

Cordelia, who was with Meryl and the others cried out, 'Wow, I can't wait to ride on those!'

Meryl interrupted, 'Err...I don't think that's quite what they'd intended.'

Cordelia smiled wily. 'Perhaps you're right.'

As the music hushed, the guests cleared the dance floor. Two figures gracefully walked to the centre as one of the glistening spheres floated toward them. It was their hosts, Drucilla and Herbert Von Pfirsich.

Everyone watched intently as the two stepped into the sphere, passing through its glasslike shell as if they were ghosts.

They began dancing as the sphere rose into the air. Taking their lead, all the invited along with their choice of partner, which included a very happy looking Mer and her newfound friend Maxim, walked onto the dance floor, entering the nearest sphere to float and dance.

The translucent spheres probably weren't made for four, though Delia positively insisted they were; but she didn't have to convince Cordelia. All four of them bundled in having their own ideas as to the way they should dance.

Curiously, as they entered the sphere, it began thumping out their kind of dance music; it was as far removed from the traditional as possible –not at all gentle, not at all waltzy. Needless to say, their sphere looked decidedly out of place as it swerved and jolted its way to be amongst the others.

'Way cool!' yelled Delia above the noisy, energetic music.

Nobody bothered answering, mainly because they couldn't hear her, or because they were too involved in their dancing to even notice she'd spoken. It was a fantastic experience with the shimmering light and the mad swaying of the sphere.

Contrasting their sphere with some couples swirling and gliding to a slow waltz, others swinging to jazz, everything seemed almost comical. Each sphere was filled with the guest's choice of music.

Cordelia pulled at Persimmon's arm and mouthed, 'I'm heading out on top, coming?' She pointed upwards, but all she got was a frown from Persimmon, who hadn't a clue what she was on about. Cordelia reasoned that if there was a way of *entering* the sphere, then surely there must be a way of *exiting*; she wasn't wrong.

How she'd worked it out only Cordelia could say, but with arms stretched above her head and fingertips of both hands touching, a bit like when diving into a pool, she drifted upward like a balloon, passing through the sphere's glass-like skin without any resistance.

Wide eyed, the others looked on in astonishment, and at once joined her. The four were soon balancing on top, since the surface they'd passed through had become solid the second they'd passed through the sphere's skin. Holding onto each other, they rode the sphere like some kind of huge beach ball surfing the waves.

Mer was dancing with Maxim whilst all this was going on, and could only roll her eyes at seeing the mad antics of her crazy sister.

'Something wrong?' asked Maxim. 'Did I tread on your foot again?'

Mer smiled a polite 'no'. If the truth be known, and Mer had already discovered this, Maxim wasn't the best ballroom dancer in the world. But he was cute and incredibly intuitive in the ways of magic and mystery.

'So, you think something odd is about to take place?' she asked.

'Well, I've been trawling through the history of Nightshade Hall, and apparently it once belonged to a man that'd lost the manor in a duel,' answered Maxim who had now completely stopped dancing to sit down and go through the notes he'd been carrying.

Mer joined him as their sphere continued gliding through the crowded air.

'That was in 1783,' related Maxim, proud of his recently acquired knowledge, 'and the man he died at the hands of, Francis Sedgwick, was rumoured to be powerful in the secret arts, though nothing could ever be proven.'

Mer was fascinated.

'According to a book by a local historian named Ebenezer Longfellow,' enthused Maxim, 'he possessed rare Amazonian crystals from South America, which were rumoured to be used by him to conjure powerful spells and charms.'

'So, how does that connect with today?' asked Mer.

'Ah, it was commonly believed that because 'The Six Crystals', as they were known, were forged into a chalice, they'd always remain together...something about the stones' combined energies, you see.'

Mer blurted out, 'Don't tell me! You think it's the Darkington Chalice?'

Maxim beamed with pride. 'The very same...and what's even more enthralling is that I've sort of discovered through my mentor someone rather nasty has been sent to steal it!'

'Who? Pressed Mer.

'I'm not privy to that...yet!'

'Oh, I can't wait to tell the others,' replied Mer, now positively bubbling with enthusiasm.

She didn't have to wait long. The spheres floated gracefully to the ballroom floor allowing everyone to step out.

'Thanks,' said Maxim as he gave Mer a polite bow and a thoughtful look.

'See you again,' answered Mer. She walked, almost drifted, back to the others.

'Did you kiss?' enquired Cordelia mischievously.

'Certainly not!' protested Mer. 'We hardly know each other, besides, I'm not interested in boys at all.'

Mer, though, now sported a slightly red face. 'Anyway, just wait 'til I tell you what I've found out!'

'Do tell,' said Meryl with fascination; Persimmon and Delia eagerly nodded in anticipation.

'I know,' announced Cordelia, *'there's going to be a murder!'*

'No, silly,' answered Mer, and she broke into the history of Nightshade Hall and how the Darkington Chalice probably contains the Amazonian stones, and that it was likely to be stolen by someone that very night for something incredibly sinister.

'Well, I hope it's not tonight,' said Persimmon, 'I was rather hoping you'd win the chalice because of your stunning dress!'

Meryl added, 't'would be an awful shame if someone else got it, there's been nothing like your costume, Mer, ever!'

'I agree, but think of the adventure,' mused Cordelia brightly.

Their expectancy was softened as the hall became hushed and the light from the chandeliers dimmed. The crystal spheres had risen toward the arched ceiling and simply vanished into thin air.

Nightshade Hall was completely in darkness and silence. Everyone gathered around the perimeter of the ballroom floor awaiting the next event. In the centre of the pitch-black floor, a curious blue green light appeared.

At first it was a tiny orb of incandescent glowing, gradually becoming more intense. Everyone, including Cordelia and the others, watched with silent intrigue.

The orb of light became elongated and rose off the floor taking the form of a large chalice: the Darkington Chalice, no less. Beneath its blue-green glow, there was someone standing, holding the chalice above their head. It was Drucilla Darkington herself.

As the light brightened, her face could be seen bearing a roguish smile. She spoke, and her voice echoed throughout the hushed ballroom.

'Witches, wizards and warlocks,' she said loudly and rather dramatically, 'the time has arrived for the annual presentation of the Darkington Chalice!'

Her smile reappeared, though more roguish than before.

'I have six finalists on a parchment here,' continued Drucilla, 'and I invite the following to join Herbert and myself to the centre of the floor. The finalists will know who they are without me calling their names.'

After her announcement there came a forceful crackling noise, which rattled like thunder. From the six crystals of The Darkington Chalice emitted six twisting and curling beams of green-gold light. They reached out across the room. One by one, they located those lucky enough to be chosen.

Cordelia ducked as one of the light beams wavered above her, flickering from side to side. Soon, the others were ducking for cover, including Mer. But the light beam knew whom it wanted; and Mer was lifted into the air to join the five finalists now waiting beside Drucilla and Herbert.

Each of the chosen stood nervously on a stage that had risen from the floor. Overwhelmed but secretly relieved at being selected, Mer stood gazing at the Darkington Chalice whose curling beams had now retreated back into its six mysterious crystals.

'Good evening ladies und gentlemen,' spoke Herbert Von Pfirsich in his marvelous German accent. 'I vill now announce zer finalists from the six before you, vun of vich vill vin zis beautiful und mysterious chalice.'

He was quite correct in saying 'beautiful and mysterious'

as the powers and beauty held within the Darkington Chalice were to be found nowhere else in the world of witchdom.

Mer knew that whoever won this remarkable prize was surely in for a year of exceptional magic and good fortune; provided, naturally, the vessel wasn't used for bad purposes.

She stood almost dazed, pondering over the possibilities that may await. If she did win it, which was unlikely, she'd have to guard against it falling into the wrong hands. The chalice would certainly return itself to Drucilla if that ever happened.

Unless that is, she thought, *they were particularly evil; and possessed dark powers above and beyond acceptable skills.* Her mind raced. And, if they did, they'd really cause something horrifying to take place-something not even Drucilla would be able to put right!

Herbert's loud voice startled her mind back to the ceremony.

'Emelda Anwyl...please to stand over here vith me.' She was dressed in a stunning narrow fitting silver and gold flowing dress which continuously changed colours and shape. A buzz of chattering began filling the air as Herbert commenced calling out the final selection.

'Michael Grimr...please to join Emelda...Felizia Broussard...over here please.'

The three chosen stood nervously waiting as everyone held their breath. Herbert looked up stony-faced.

'Sadly, you are not vinners today.' He shook their hands graciously and presented them each with a miniature silver broomstick as a consolation prize. They then made their way back to their friends.

'Bernadette O'Reilly...Aravind Savarna...please come

57

and join me!' Mer looked gob-smacked, why hadn't he called her? Was it really over all so quickly, so bluntly?

She knew she'd obviously failed; and looking at the amazing costumes of the two admittedly clever witches remaining, one wearing an ensemble like it was made from a single piece of sparkling crystal, the other as a Peacock butterfly, complete with fluttering wings: Now she understood why. *Maybe next year, perhaps?* she thought.

Mer awaited Herbert's final words but could feel the tears beginning to well.

'This year,' he said, smiling at the two before him, 'your costumes have taken our breath avay, vell done and zank you for all your effort. But, as you know, zere can only be vun vinner...und to announce who zat is I velcome back my friend, my love, Drucilla. Bravo to you both!'

He raised his hands and applauded them, which caused the whole ballroom to erupt in cheering and clapping. The two young ladies stood almost motionless, except for their nervous jitters. Mer, not being told to depart the stage, stood apart from them in the shadows, desperately wanting to get back to the others. *Maybe I'm to receive a consolation prize like the others, perhaps a golden broom?* she fretted to herself. *But why didn't they do that first and save me all this embarrassment?*

'Thank you, Herbert,' said Drucilla, interrupting Mer's thoughts. She looked kindly toward the remaining contestants.

'The Darkington Chalice, as you know, is an incredible prize. It grants to the winner great abilities; and at the same time, even greater responsibilities. Normally,' she added, 'we not only award it for the most amazing

58

costume, but the maturity of the proposed recipient. That is very important to us when making our final choice.

Unfortunately, we can make no exceptions in this, and many outstanding costumes and their designer have had to go unrewarded.'

Mer's cheeks by now were flowing with tiny rivulets, whilst Bernadette and Aravind were both positively beaming, and couldn't wait for the result; each were certain they'd won over their opponent, despite giving out polite smiles through jealous clenched teeth.

'That's why,' continued Drucilla, 'this year, we've gone a little against the grain. Ladies and gentlemen, I give you this year's winner...'

Drucilla walked smartly toward the contestants whose eyes widened in anticipation. She held up the chalice, but walked straight past them and handed the prize to an absolutely stunned Mer, now illuminated by the light glowing from within the chalice crystals.

Mer instantly burst into tears and laughter at the same time.

Clumsily, she took the precious chalice with both hands and raised it high, well, as high as she could, into the air.

Drucilla looked at her and winked, so too did Herbert, who went on to present the other contestants with similar silver broomsticks, though these were festooned with tiny jewels as well.

'We can't believe what you've made, Mer,' said Drucilla, 'but we can believe the chalice will be going into good and safe hands!'

Herbert smiled and bowed graciously.

'Mind you keep it vell away from your young sister now!' he added cheekily.

Before long, Cordelia and their three great friends were beside Mer, who, it must be said, was beside herself with pride, humility, and uncontrollable excitement.

Her dress too had changed as images of beautiful flowers blooming drifted around the exquisite fabric.

'Crikey!' cried Cordelia, reaching for the chalice. 'Give us a go...only joking!' she added, though it was difficult to tell.

As Mer and company walked around the ballroom displaying the remarkable Darkington Chalice, all seemed to be going well.

That was until, out of nowhere, came racing a dozen or so witches riding brooms that were violently ablaze. They swept past each contestant brutally pushing them to the floor; their flaming brooms catching them alight.

Although the fire witch's brooms were burning fiercely, they weren't burning away. Each witch screamed and screeched as they sped along.

Cordelia, feeling it was all part of the show, believed they were awesome, and even screeched back at them as they passed trying to knock her and the others over. One of the fire witches began circling around Mer, isolating her from her friends.

Without warning, another burning fire witch swooped, reaching to grab the precious Chalice. Seeing this, Cordelia finally twigged what was going on and ran to help. But, a third fire witch dashed her to the floor.

In a twinkling, Mer was surrounded by a dozen or so of them, swooping and grasping at her prize. Maxim joined the fight, lashing out to pull the fire witches off their blazing brooms. Although he got burnt, it didn't prevent him from casting spells. Yet, the fire witches soon regained control.

Mer embraced the Chalice as close to herself as possible. Herbert and Drucilla, alarmed at the mayhem, flew to her aid. It was no use, the constant attack made it impossible for them to reach Mer.

There seemed no protection; and from out of a dark corner of the dark ceiling flew an extremely tall wizened witch riding a golden broom. As she reached a still-fighting Mer, she croaked a few words.

'Hello dearie, my name's Cragertha, that's Cragertha of Pain's Wood. Remember the name well, lest you challenge me again sometime.' At that, she kicked out with her long spindly legs, sending the Chalice high into the air.

'Say goodbye to your silly cup!' she screamed, grasping it mid-air. Cragertha speedily shot off with her prize.

The fire witches were close behind her.

'Quick, follow them!' screamed Cordelia. 'We musn't let them get away.'

The young witches and Maxim leapt over the many who were bruised and fallen as the fire witches and Cragertha made toward a small stone door at the far end of the ballroom. The stone door slammed shut after them, leaving their pursuers stuck outside.

Cordelia fumbled through her pockets for a powerful *undoing* spell, but Mer and Delia took the physical option, struggling hopelessly to pull the heavy door open. Persimmon and Meryl joined in.

'Don't worry,' called Maxim confidently. 'I think I have the answer.'

The girls looked up, unsure.

'The Entrapment Spell, that's what'll do it,' he called and began reciting a charm thatwas hundreds of years old, but just as effective today as the day it was first cast.

'What did you just do?' enquired Cordelia.

'Ah, one of many spells rediscovered by the famous Melchior Fizz,' he replied.

'Wow, you like him too?' she asked. 'He's got to be the best magician ever; my all-time favourite really.'

'I know, Mer told me,' answered Maxim, smiling. 'But, did you know that this spell comes from Fizz's book *Casts From the Past?*'

'Blimey, I didn't,' she replied, 'I've never heard of that one.'

Their impromptu discussion could have gone on much longer, but the once heavy immoveable stone door groaned its way open.

'Look, it's undone itself!' cried Meryl. 'Let's get after them.'

But Maxim and Cordelia hadn't quite finished talking about Melchior's book yet, and seemed in no hurry. Mer wasn't best pleased.

'Come on, you two, aren't we supposed to be chasing after Cragertha and her fire witches?' she yelled, maybe a little peeved at her sister's interest in Maxim's reading habits. 'We've just got to get that chalice back!' she barked.

'Oh, there's no hurry, really,' answered Maxim, looking particularly pleased with himself, 'they can't escape from anywhere. The spell I just placed has seen to that; sealed off all exits, this door is now the only way in or out! And, once we've passed it, I'll use one of Melchior's strongest spell-locks.'

'Brilliant!' remarked Delia who was decidedly impressed. They quickly bundled through the doorway. Maxim turned and charmed the door shut and spell-locked.

Leading the way, he called, 'By now, Cragertha will think she's got away with it; is she in for a surprise!'

The six fled further along without a second thought. They were in a narrow passageway with the darkness, the musty smell of undisturbed air, and the echoing screams of laughter from Cragertha and her fire witches far off.

They quickly found themselves lost inside its long twisting course. And, except for Cordelia's dodgy torch, there wasn't even a glimmer of light from anywhere.

'Which way now?' asked Delia.

'Not sure,' continued Persimmon. 'I s'pose keep following their voices?'

'Yeah, but there are so many different passageways, and their cries are echoing from all over the place!' added Mer.

'Mmm...what we could really do with is a *homing-glow* spell,' suggested Meryl. 'You know, a charm to light the way to where Cragertha and her mad witches have gone.'

'Not even my torch could do that,' remarked Cordelia. 'Besides, it's given up the ghost...yet again!'

It flickered out and she shook it in frustration.

'That's it, then,' remarked Delia, 'we're really travelling blind.'

'Guys, we absolutely need some sort of light to show us where to go,' complained Mer, 'and pretty damn quickly!'

'Problem is,' called Cordelia, 'the only homing glow spell that I know of is buried away in one of my books; and without my torch, I couldn't read it anyway.'

'Lytton O'Rourke's Spells for Lighter Moments –that's the book!' blurted Cordelia, and amazingly she pulled a copy from one of her many pockets.

'Yes,' said Persimmon, 'I seem to remember reading about that spell somewhere.' Persimmon went into deep thought. 'Now, let me see,' she drifted out loud, 'if I remember, his homing glowing spell goes something like this:

"By the glow of sun, moon and stars,
Guide us toward our enemies afar,
Show by light the shortest way,
Illuminate now a shining ray!"

Her words finished, there still came no light; and Persimmon was glad no-one could see her embarrassed red face. Happily, she needn't have felt self-conscious at all, as eventually the walls of the corridor to the far left of them did begin glowing.

'It worked,' yelled Cordelia, 'they're down that-away!'

They sped along the illuminated passageway passing a row of marble carvings on the walls. They featured witches and wizards from days gone by.

'They've probably all kicked the bucket by now,' observed Cordelia. Maxim and the others looked spooked.

'No threat to us then!' exclaimed Delia. Persimmon had paused to stare at one of the peculiar carvings.

'Mmm, it looks almost real,' she said. But, with a second look at the strange carved face, she let out a tremendous squeal. 'Ahrrrrgh! It opened its mouth!'

'Don't be daft,' said Mer, 'it's only a silly carving.'

'Never dismiss the mystery in carvings,' said Meryl.

Persimmon, being pulled away, agreed and kept looking back as if to catch it out. By now the screams of Cragertha and the fire witches had faded further.

'Maxim, are you certain they can't escape?' asked Meryl.

'Absolutely,' he answered, without a hint of doubt. 'They couldn't even squeezethrough a crack in the wall, or try and counter the *Entrapment Spell*...I know, I've attempted it myself, and failed miserably!'

64

Delia meanwhile had gone ahead without them, turning off down another twisting passageway. Curiously, it too had been illuminated by Lytton's homing spell.

'EVERYBODY...COME HERE!' she bellowed from halfway down the narrow passage.

Persimmon could just make out her shout.

'What was that?' she called to the others. 'I'm sure I heard something just then.'

'HURRY!' yelled Delia again.

'That sounded like...Delia,' said Meryl looking around for her. 'I never even saw her go.'

'Her voice was from down there, I think,' added Maxim, pointing toward the other passageway. They ran.

'You shouldn't go off without us like that!' scolded Persimmon once they'd reached her. 'For goodness sake, I thought we'd agreed it's best we stick together?'

'But look at this!' insisted Delia. She pointed to the floor where she stood.

'I can't see anything. Well, except for that glowing drain cover,' remarked Mer.

'You idiot, that's it, that's where they've gone!' replied Delia.

'Hang on, I think she's right, I'm sure I just heard whispering,' added Cordelia, kneeling down to listen. A strange noise was unmistakably rising from a grated cover. 'She's spot on, come and have a listen.'

Cordelia quickly reached over and grabbed Meryl's sleeve, pulling her toward the whispering. It was a very odd sound, somewhere between rustling sandpaper and muffled fox cries. Whatever it was, it was a fair way down.

'This must be a secret shaft,' suggested Maxim. 'It's far too wide for a drain. Hey, and yes, I can see an iron ladder.'

'Quick!' cried Cordelia, 'There's a ring in the centre of the grate, if we pull together, we could lift it.'

Everyone took hold of the rusted ring. It was no good though; the grating wouldn't budge an inch. So Cordelia began searching for another spell. No need, Maxim simply called *'Lift!'* and it shot up like a rocket, barely missing everyone's face.

'Sorry about that!' he said quietly, 'but I wasn't sure my spell would work.'

'How on earth did you do that?' quizzed Meryl, 'I mean, you didn't read out a spell! –We have to, otherwise nothing happens!'

'You can do it,' he answered 'just takes lots and lots of practice. Mind you, if the spell I'm using is very long-winded, it doesn't always work.' Mer looked impressed, the others nodded approval.

So, minus the heavy grate, they now stared down into the shaft and could see the iron ladder descending into darkness.

'Let's go,' called Cordelia; the others, not at all sure where they were going, followed her lead. As they climbed further and further downwards, gripping each wet rusted rung tightly, the whispering voices became easier to make out.

At last they reached the bottom and were standing on a wet slimy stone floor. Mer was doing her best not to completely ruin her incredible dress, but as she turned in the restricted space, she heard a terrible rip. She had caught her dress on a jagged piece of ironwork jutting out from a door right beside her.

'Damn!' she cried. 'What's a door doing here?'

'A door?' exclaimed Meryl. 'Now isn't that a lucky thing!'

'Nothing lucky about it,' complained Mer, 'Look what

it's done to my dress!'

Her design was now showing teardrops falling like rain.

'A door!' repeated Delia. 'Where does it go?'

'How would I know?' moaned Mer, analysing the huge rip. Maxim carefully opened the heavy door and peered around, signalling to the others to remain quiet. His eyes went wide, and moving back, he beckoned everyone even closer.

'You'll never believe it,' he whispered. 'There's a huge room behind here...and right in the centre...*I'm sure you're not going to believe this*...is the Darkington Chalice, sitting on a stone table just waiting to be rescued!'

'What?' cried Cordelia.

'Go on, see for yourself.'

Delia peered round first. 'Blimey, he's right!'

'Is there anyone about?' asked Persimmon. Maxim stuck his head back into the room, and looking cautiously, said 'No.'

At once they made a dash to grab the Chalice. Cordelia sprinted across the room, reaching out for the Chalice. Her fingertips were almost there, when disaster struck.

The girls and Maxim immediately began free-falling into a seemingly bottomless pit.

They were descending to *who-knows-where at who-knows-what* speed, and with no obvious way to stop their giddying descent.

Cordelia though, still reached out for the Chalice, and just managed to hook a finger around one of its handles, successfully pulling it along with her.

She desperately held onto the precious object, even though it felt like the Chalice was trying to pull her finger off.

Still free falling, Meryl cried out in desperation, 'I don't think the bottom of this tunnel is going to stay away from us much longer!'

Cordelia was onto the problem in a flash. With a firm grip now on the Chalice she managed to find a small book and recite the well-known spell *Falling Upwards* by Murgatroyd Upshott. With the pages of her small book fluttering in the extreme air current, Cordelia read the spell at the top of her voice. It didn't work.

'Anyone have a spare parachute?' called Delia. The rush of wind and dizzying descent was starting to overwhelm.

'For goodness sake, can't *anyone* conjure a broom, at least!' screamed Persimmon.

They were in trouble, seriously. On their way down to probably further than the fiery mantle beneath the Earth's crust, there was desperation to find the right spell. It didn't help with them colliding into each other either. But, it was at such a collision, that Cordelia accidentally let go of the valuable Chalice.

It shot upwards and all seemed lost.

Yet, regardless of Cordelia's anxious cry at losing the Chalice, somehow the loss of it immediately halted their terrifying descent. The G-forces involved in this sudden stop, though, were particularly painful; their loud groans were proof of that.

They eventually recovered, climbing off the floor and brushing themselves down. Before them, though they were now some way off was the same stone table seen previously, with the Chalice placed right in the centre.

'How could that have happened?' reasoned Meryl. 'Wasn't it all of us just now falling a thousand feet only to land back where we started?'

'I agree.' muttered Persimmon 'Surely we'd have known if we'd have just been standing in the same room all the time?'

She got no reply except for strange whispering that faded into the chamber.

As they peered at the Chalice upon the huge old table, instantly five veiled witches stepped out from the shadows to gather around it, whispering, whispering.

'Hang on,' said Cordelia, 'they remind me of someone.'

'Me too,' added Mer.

But, the five sinister witches didn't seem to notice the girls and Maxim; the women were far too deep in conversation.

'Is this some kind of collective dream?' quietly mused Meryl, 'or am I just going bonkers?'

'You're going bonkers,' whispered Delia.

'Thanks so much!' breathed Meryl sarcastically.

'Shh,' hushed Maxim, 'we must listen closely to what they're saying.'

At last, Cordelia and Mer twigged who the five were.

'Oh dear, we've definitely met them before!' sighed Cordelia softly. 'The Witches of Gloom –it's them, I'm sure!'

Mer agreed, nodding to the others, her face ashen for fear of being at their mercy once more. 'Cordelia's right,' she said as quietly as she could.

'Damn!' breathed Delia, 'Not that lot.'

Persimmon, next to her, gripped poor Meryl's arm like a vice.

'Ouch!' moaned Meryl.

'Shh!' returned Maxim. 'We must keep quiet. I can't even understand why they haven't seen us yet. But, before we try tackling them, we must know what they're up to.' It didn't take long. Kaldre, who'd positioned herself at at the head of table snarled, 'We'll soon have Nightshade Hall and its mystical treasure in the palms of our hands!'

Her cronies nodded their heads and cackled loudly.

'And that smug *Darkington* and her ridiculous puppy *Von Pfirsich* will both perish with what we have planned for them!' added Kaldre.

The coven was driven into a fit of spluttering at her pronouncement, their combined saliva fortunately too far to reach the young observers.

One of the Witches of Gloom, though, named Ulla, wasn't joining in with their spluttering, but was instead peering about. In a blink of an eye she caught Mer's curious gaze; and her black stare penetrated deeply. They locked their vision, Mer fearing to be the first to turn away.

'Greetings,' said Ulla at last. 'You took your time, we worried you might not make it.' The witch, with black eyes and cold voice, smiled cruelly. Kaldre turned and faced them all.

'Well, we meet again, don't we?' she aired in a sickly patronising voice. 'And, as you see, we now possess the Darkington Chalice; and like they say, possession is ten tenth's of witch law.'

Kaldre gurgled and spat in amusement at this, soon joined again by the coven.

'But, there's a problem,' she continued, her voice a little less patronising, and slightly more severe. 'Our coven not only owns this remarkable and soon to be extremely useful Chalice, but you lot as well...not bad for an evening's work, don't you think?'

No-one answered, but their minds were racing.

'Clearly, we don't need all of you for our deadly little spell; but as you're bound to make a fuss once we've got rid of Darkington and her cronies, not to mention gain possession of all their magic, then perhaps we do.'

The Witches of Gloom smiled knowingly at each other. 'You know, it's such a bore keeping prisoners...you have to feed and clothe them...keep them locked up, or in chains...and they cost money you know! Not only that, but some day, you have to let them go...which we certainly hadn't intended,' she said with all the airs of a cruel woman who'd lived most of her life in the Forest of Gloom. 'You can see where I'm going with all this, can't you...mmm?'

'It's an absolute disgrace,' she continued, 'giving a rare and powerful vessel like this to a mere child to play with! Anyway, I feel I'll be doing the world of witchcraft a great service by denying that silly carry-on.'

Mer ignored her and reached deep into one of her pockets for something her mother had given her weeks ago; and had almost forgotten about.

It was the Dark Stone of Aberneth. To most, merely a black pebble, but according to her mother, a family heirloom passed down each generation and said to contain peculiar powers for anyone in possession of it, especially those who might be in great danger.

'Um, excuse me?' called Mer with a certain amount of newfound courage. 'You say, possession is ten tenths of witch law?'

Kaldre looked put out by her arrogant interruption of this all-important speech. 'What of it?' she snapped.

'Well, I have possession of this!' She held up the minuscule looking Dark Stone of Aberneth, no bigger than a Brazil nut.

'Is that all you've got? Pathetic!' chipped Kaldre, obviously unimpressed and totally unaware of its tremendous abilities. The coven began spitting and mocking her once more. 'Throw it at us if you must, you silly little witch. Perhaps you'd like me to paint a target on myself...say like here, you think?' Kaldre pointed to her forehead.

Cordelia broke in, nudging her sister angrily. 'What do you think you're doing?' she urged. 'They'll make mincemeat of us if you're not careful!'

'Don't worry,' replied Mer in an undertone, 'When I won the priceless chalice, despite my uncontained excitement, I wove a spell to protect it –I just didn't want anything happening to my pize whilst I was looking after it! So, if I can land the stone inside the chalice...then hopefully, all hell will break loose!'

'Yeah, but what happens if you can't?' interrupted Meryl. 'Do these old witch-bags explode or something?' They all laughed.

'What are you lot muttering?' roared Kaldre, but the thought of five old 'witch-bags' exploding, as Meryl put it, had the girls in fits.

'Shut up, shut up, I say!' screamed Kaldre in a voice loud enough to scare her cronies into standing bolt upright. But, it had no effect on the girls.

Eventually Maxim interrupted them, he sternly whispered, 'Listen, we'll need to distract them if you're going to throw this stone of yours, otherwise, they'll simply catch it before it lands in the Chalice.'

'I could cast Melchior's *Confusion Spell*,' softly suggested Cordelia into Maxim's ear.

'Good idea,' he replied, 'but what if I were to use Gwendoline O'Bollerin's *Ridiculously Stupid Charm*?' he murmured, 'You know, the one that can send people stark staring bonkers?'

'Yeah, I know the one!' said Mer overhearing him and giving a knowing smile.

'They wouldn't recover from that in a hurry!' strained Delia. 'But remember, Gwendoline's charm has been known to backfire on perpetrators too, something we'll need to watch out for.' The five became silent at his whisper, and Kaldre appeared satisfied they were being obedient.

Maxim, nevertheless, wove Ms. O'Bollerin's spell. Unexpectedly, the Witches of Gloom started jumping up onto the table.

'GET DOWN OFF THE TABLE AT ONCE, YOU SILLY COWS!' screamed Kaldre to Rioghnach and Ulla. Meag and Wyn had joined in too. They had commenced dancing some kind of ritual and were screaming things at the top of their voices whilst pulling contorted faces.

It was quite a sight as the two eldest, being a stone's throw from decrepit, were almost falling over from loss of balance and co-ordination. The cracking noises from their ancient joints even reached the ears of Maxim and the others.

Yet, for some reason, Kaldre hadn't been affected. Perhaps she was far too powerful; Maxim wasn't sure. Instead, she busily tried containing her out-of-control coven.

With a hefty lob whilst Kaldre was distracted, Mer, trying to dodge their silly jumping, cast the precious Stone of Aberneth with careful aim toward the Darkington Chalice. They all watched the stone arc through the air. Luckily for them, Kaldre at last began developing signs of imbecility; and, against her will, had now joined the impromptu dance performance with the others.

Flaying her arms and legs about; she just caught sight of Mer casting the stone. Forcing herself away from her temporary madness, Kaldre athletically jumped to catch the object mid-flight.

As if watching some kind of sporting activity in ultra slow motion, they observed in horror as the stone spun toward her ever-approaching hand. It momentarily touched between Kaldre's two middle fingers as she violently commenced closing her hand to complete the capture. Everyone gulped. But the tiny, powerful stone amazingly passed between her fingers, and Kaldre's expression changed from that of success to failure.

Fireworks would be a slightly inadequate description of what took place. A jet of multi-coloured flames shot from the Chalice and from within them spewed a shower of tiny jelly-like snakes. Wriggling, twisting, and biting, the snakes immediately engulfed the Witches of Gloom. The old witches screamed and tore at the writhing menaces, as each snake sank its fangs deep into anything that would keep still long enough. The translucent creatures dove into ears, noses, and mouths, disappearing from sight.

One by one, each of the coven fell clumsily off the table to wrestle helplessly on the chamber floor. It gave the young witches and Maxim the seconds they required to escape.

The Darkington Chalice, embodied with a vast store of magic, floated expectantly before Mer; and her invaluable Stone of Aberneth simply flew out of it and back into her pocket.

Not sure of what to do, Mer simply grabbed the golden handles with both hands. She couldn't have taken a more appropriate action. As if her hands had gripped upon something charged with hundreds of volts, Mer wasn't able to let go of it and her whole body quaked in response.

'Oh cripes!' yelled Persimmon. She ran to help. But, as she made contact with Mer, she too became energised. At once Mer floated upwards.

'Grab my waist!' she screamed out to Persimmon, 'don't let me go.'

Yet, there was no stopping her from rising. The others jumped to her rescue. Delia managed to anchor her foot around a leg of the heavy stone table, desperately holding onto her friends.

'STOP IT!' shouted Cordelia in one of her eureka moments. But, no-one took any notice. So, one by one they too were lifted into the air.

'STOP FIGHTING IT!' she screamed once more. 'THE CHALICE WANTS US TO FOLLOW .'

'Just what are you on about, Cordelia?' cried Mer, struggling to hold on whilst staring in disbelief at the mad collection of friends keeping her grounded. 'I'm a bit caught up at the moment!'

'I know,' she replied, 'that's my point. Hang onto the Chalice, yes, but don't stop it from rising; it's trying to take us away from danger, that's all I'm saying.'

'Yes!' joined Maxim. 'She's right.'

Mer, at last, nodded a sort of approval whilst watching the comical battle between the coven and the tiny snakes.

Delia bit her lip. 'Man, this is going to be some ride...I hope you lot know what you're doing!' She released her foot from around the leg of the huge table.

Like a failed acrobatics team, the clumsy formation shot into the air, dragged upward by the power of the Chalice.

No sooner had they taken off, than from out of nowhere flew Cragertha and the fire witches. They were in hot pursuit, no doubt summoned by Kaldre.

But, the fire witches were no match for the speed of the Chalice. In no time, it exploded out of the shaft, whizzed along the winding corridors and burst into the grand hall through the stone doorway, all with Mer, Cordelia and their friends desperately holding on for dear life. Fortunately, the heavy stone door had simply crumbled to dust before them. Cragertha and her fire witches, though, weren't far behind.

Screams, flames and smoke soon filled the once-peaceful ballroom. Guests in all their finery dashed for cover under tables, chairs, even under a few refined looking witches in overly coutured gowns and dresses.

The blazing assail stormed around the ballroom, circle upon circle, not letting up for a second. The Witches of Gloom, now free of the wretched snakes, joined the desperate pursuit of the precious Chalice. But Mer, seeing no way out of this, steered the chalice toward a great leadlight window.

Despite the frenzied chase, Cordelia and her straggle of friends each held onto one another, fully expecting the inevitable earth-shattering shatter when smashing through the ancient stained glass.

Mer let go of the Chalice with her right hand so she could shield off the inevitable shards. She hit the window at great speed. Yet, at the moment of impact, the ornate window simply disappeared before her, allowing them all to pass through unharmed.

'Whoohoo!' screamed Cordelia and Meryl triumphantly as they embraced the outside cold night air. They were no further than a stone's throw when the ornate window reappeared as solid as ever. It didn't stay in one piece for very long. With a massive explosion of razor-sharp pieces in every colour, shape and size, Cragertha and her fire witches crashed through the reformed lead-lighted window.

Shards stabbed and dug at them from every angle. Looking back in dismay, Cordelia yelled, 'To the forest... and make it snappy Mer, they look pretty riled up now!'

This was their only choice as Nightshade Forest at least offered them some kind of protection from being seen and captured.

Above its dark and twisted undergrowth, and beneath the canopy of its over-large trees, they could easily duck and dive their way back to home and safety. Or, so they thought.

Outside Nightshade Hall, the rain was sweeping down hard. It was driving so hard that it became almost impossible for anyone to see in front of them. Mer guided the Chalice higher and higher toward the heavy clouds to avoid the rain, but it made no difference.

Looking down through the swirling raindrops, she saw once more how enchanting the hall looked from above. But, despite its inviting mystery, Mer realised that nothing as glamorous was going to happen again this year, at least.

The sudden reappearance of their pursuers speeding toward them reinforced that. *Goodness knows how, but they've even survived crashing through that flaming great window!* she thought.

Worse news still: the power of the Chalice seemed to be failing. Slowly and very definitely they were losing height.

'Why are we going down?' yelled Persimmon.

'I don't know,' answered Mer, '...but at least if we do, we can weave through the forest.'

'Well, we'd better hurry, look behind you!'

By now, the fast-approaching witches had gained on them and were no more than sixty seconds away. All they could do was to glide lower with fingers crossed for a safe landing and be more than ready to hide amongst the trees.

The flight to ground was agonising. During their rapid and steep descent they spread out whatever limbs or garments were free to catch the wind.

The terrified group whooshed over the treetops. The failing potency of the Chalice was only just allowing them to sweep and weave. A good landing place had to be found before it failed altogether. At last there was a small clearing.

Mer called for everyone to let each other go. With a rolling thump, repeated five times over, they made it to ground. The thick soaking wet undergrowth softened their fall. Cordelia was grateful to be on terra firma once more.

'That was a close one!' she said shakily.

Mer was still holding the Chalice and it had lowered her a lot more gently. Cragertha and her witches, though, weren't far off; and their landing was to be a shade more graceful than Maxim and the other four.

As Kaldre and her coven eerily and noiselessly floated down, the forest fell deadly silent. They snapped not one twig or voiced a single moaning cry in their pursuit of the young witches. All that filled the air was the splatter of heavy rain hitting leaves or thumping upon the already over-wet soil. It was dark too with the clouded sky, black, silent, and cold.

'Keep down!' stressed Maxim.

'What do we do now?' asked Persimmon, squelching in the mud, trying to regain her balance.

'Get far away as possible,' chirped Meryl, 'but, did those maniacs see where we landed? They could be right beside us and we wouldn't know.'

Persimmon read aloud her glowing spell, only to be rebuffed by everyone.

'Have you lost your marbles?' strained Delia in an undertone, 'we're trying to hide from them, we don't need a beacon light to help them find us!'

'Sorry,' said Persimmon softly. Her glowing quickly disappeared.

'We'll have to find a way out of here without them knowing. Any ideas?' asked Maxim. Before anyone could answer, the cold-wet silence was broken by the harsh voices of their pursuers.

'Come here at once, you fools!' echoed the rebuking cry of Rioghnach.

'It'll do you no good at all hiding from us,' reinforced Meag with acid in her voice. 'Our spells and tricks will surely seek you out!' continued Ulla. Her words had a sickly tone, rather like an overbearing grandmother soaked in syrup. Mer winced.

'Are they bonkers, or what?' she whispered, crouching lower into the slimy mossy ground. 'We're hardly likely to rush out with our hands in the air!'

'Let's move on,' urged Maxim, 'but carefully!'

As they awkwardly crept through the scrub away from the coven's beckoning, fronds of ice-wet bracken darted into everyone's face; and sharp thorns from bushes and thistles daggered into their legs. It was hard not to cry out.

'Spells and tricks, they said,' whispered Cordelia. 'Well,

what else would they be using?'

'And I suppose,' breathed Delia, 'if that doesn't work, they'll be telling us to trust them as they mean no harm!'

'As if we'd harm such young people!' coed Wyn. Ulla croaked half in laughter. 'Besides, you know we'll find you soon enough in this damp old rainswept wood, so why make it hard on yourselves?'

'Yes,' agreed Kaldre, 'wouldn't you much prefer to hand over that silly old mug now, so you can all go back home to dry off in front of a warm cosy fire?'

'Yeah, right!' thought Mer.

'It's this "silly old mug", as she puts it, that's keeping us all safe!' she added in a hushed voice.

'I agree,' replied Maxim. '...we'll make it impossible for them to get the thing back, too!'

They were now holed up behind a grassy embankment staring fruitlessly through the inky darkness.

There seemed no chance at all of seeing the hags, but each relied instead on listening out for their voices. It was thought to be easier to locate them that way, as no matter what magic they used, no-one had a clue where they were.

To their favour, though, it seemed the Five Witches of Gloom were further off than before.

'I don't think we'd do very well in a battle of spells with that lot,' confessed Meryl. Everyone felt the same.

'Yeah, let's put more distance between them...come on,' added Delia. With that, they gingerly crept away. Not far off, they came to a road.

'Hey, that could lead us back home!' Persimmon suggested, and frantically hoped.

'Hang on a sec,' said Cordelia. 'I've just remembered something. And it'll certainly help our navigation.'

She then took from out her pocket a very fine-looking compass. 'This'll do the trick.'

Cordelia flicked open the bright silver cover revealing a compass face that seemed to be glowing. Yet, on its face, rather than the usual North, East, South and West, it had Home, School, Witch Market, and Secret Hideout.

It was a remarkable device, which she could set to point to anywhere she liked. 'That's stonking!' mused Delia, 'where did you get it from?'

'My dad,' she answered proudly. 'He said he got it from India, fantastic place, I want to go there one day.'

'So, how does it work? I mean, there's no needle,' enquired Maxim, who just couldn't take his eyes off the extraordinary thing.

'Easy, it's the disc with the destinations that move. You turn with the compass until you're facing where you want to go. Um, that's as long as you first say or think of your destination of course!'

Cordelia held the object out and whispered, 'Home, please.'

When she brought it near again, they all watched the disc spin freely. It settled.

'There, I told you!' she declared rather smugly. Then, she moved the compass and herself to where the disc indicated "Home".

'See, home is that way, and it looks a good bet to take this road. It may meander a little, but as long as we follow the disc, we'll make it!'

They knew they were in for a long trudge being without brooms; and there still seemed no power in the Chalice either.

'Perhaps the Witches of Gloom have put another spell

over it,' suggested Delia. Maxim and Mer both agreed. They accepted that whatever they did, it was far better to move on, rather than just stand in the cold wet darkness hoping for something nice to happen –a bit like life, really.

However, in no more than a decent hop by a very athletic toad, their hike came to an abrupt end.

'Going somewhere?' asked a sinister-looking Kaldre suddenly appearing out of the darkness. Her dark sopping wet hair unflatteringly clung to her thorn-scratched face, and two fallen pointed leaves, a bit like horns, stuck out from her head.

She was arrogantly standing before them in the centre of the road; eerily lit by a slither of the moon now poking between the clouds. Her fellow witches surrounded her. The swirling heavy rain returned and although the moon once more fled from sight, Kaldre still glowed eerily.

The occasional flash and clap of thunder from an approaching storm didn't make the sight of the Witches of Gloom any easier to bear either.

'Home, actually,' answered Cordelia, pointing the bright silver compass ahead.

'I don't think so,' added Kaldre. She looked piercingly at the compass. 'And what have you there?'

'Nothing you'd understand.' With that, Cordelia whipped it back into her pocket.

'It's of little consequence,' mused Kaldre. 'I'll have it later, but for now, dear sweets, I think you have something else of ours.'

Her eyes were fixed to the glinting crystal and gold Chalice hanging from Mer's left hand.

'Actually,' butted in Maxim, 'I think the Darkington

Chalice rightfully belongs to my friend here.'

'Actually, whoever you are, as a matter of fact, I'd like you to shut your fat ugly gob!' retorted Kaldre.

Maxim lunged, only to be restrained by some spell cast over him. He snarled at her but it was no use.

'Resistance is futile,' she added. 'You and the Chalice will be coming with us to the Forest of Gloom, where you'll find a warm reception, very warm indeed.'

The sound of the five hags cackling simply strengthened Maxim and the young witches' resolve.

Above them, Meryl could hear a whooshing sound; and looking up, she could see the added threat of Cragertha and her fire witches swooping and circling for anyone attempting escape.

Noticing them too, Meryl tried moving backwards, but to her distress found she couldn't lift either foot off the ground. The others were similarly bound. Not one of them could move, even an inch.

What they hadn't seen, whilst talking with Kaldre, was two thin circles of smoking ground all the way around them. But now, these very circles had suddenly burst into flames.

Ulla, fully concentrating her sharp black eyes upon Mer, croaked, 'That's right, my dear, it's a *Double Witch-Circle*! Aren't you so very lucky to be probably the youngest witches and warlock ever to be trapped by such a thing?'

Mer rolled her eyes and said, 'You are just so uncool, we learnt all about *Double Witch-Circles* in fourth grade; and, I'll add, how to undo them too!'

Her bragging stopped dead though when Persimmon asked, 'Did we?'

Unfortunately, none of them had ever learnt about the

infamous Double Witch-Circle in fourth grade, let alone how to deal with them. That pleasure awaited them in ninth, that's if they should ever make it.

Whether or not Kaldre knew this made no difference, as by now, they couldn't even move their arms about. This paralysis stopped Cordelia from checking if Melchior Fizz had anything to say on the subject of Double Witch-Circles. All Kaldre had to do now was to simply walk over and take the precious Chalice.

And, all they could reasonably do was to cease being so stubborn, beg for mercy; and perhaps even offer to be servants of the five hags of Gloom Forest. At least anything would be better than being roasted alive.

Kaldre, Ulla, Rioghnach, Meag, and Wyn all moved back from the young witches. Instead of grabbing the Chalice, they simply began some kind of chant. It was so powerful that it even seemed to make the ground itself rumble. The Chalice began pulling away from Mer's stubborn grip.

Meryl felt the rumbling, as did the others.

'I just hope they can live with themselves!' yelled Cordelia above the noise, which was becoming louder and more disturbing by the second.

'Losers!' bellowed Delia frantically, straining against the circle's power.

'You won't get away with it!' cried Meryl.

'Oh, I think we will,' replied Kaldre coldly. 'We're witches!'

At this, the hags temporarily swapped their chant for a burst of crowing and hooting.

'Not if the Witches of Ice have anything to do with it you won't!' barked Cordelia above their annoying ridicule.

'Oh, that nonsense,' chortled Kaldre between chants. 'Do

you think for one second, witches of our power are worried by a bunch of frozen ice blocks?'

'Yes, I do, and if not, you should be, they're going to take over all of witchdom!' Kaldre and her cronies once again burst into howls.

It was difficult for any of them to fully describe the following sound, or even the sight of what took place for that matter, as they'd never experienced a coach and six strong horses slam straight into the five stupid Witches of Gloom, who, against all obvious rules of road safety, stood plumb in the middle of the road to Lower Wyshing.

The impact was as spectacular as it was thorough in removing the immediate threat to Cordelia and Mer and all their friends. By flattening and dispersing this evil coven, the coach and horses had broken the power of the Double Witch-Circle. Its demise also scattered the threatening circle of fire witches hovering over them.

A shrill pained screech from above indicated their immediate retreat, and not even the crag-faced Cragertha was to be seen.

'Blimey!' cried Cordelia, 'that's the coach that took us to the ball...great timing!'

Ahead, the coach screeched to a halt, sending a wave of mud and rainwater into the air. The carriage doors flung wide open. They ran like mad.

The driver greeted them with a beaming smile, giving Cordelia a thumbs-up. She smiled back, climbing aboard. 'What kept you?'

They both laughed. The coachman cried 'Home!' to the horses and in seconds the coach roared off into the sky.

Watching Nightshade Forest gradually disappear from view and grateful for their rescue, everyone started relaxing.

Mer tried desperately to disengage from the Ice Witch's hold upon her, but couldn't resist her last words.

'The world of witchcraft is changing', it said, *'and shortly, it will belong to us; and those who willingly do our bidding.'*

Understandably, Mer was shaken; everything Maxim and Cordelia had told her was soon to happen. It didn't bear thinking about, but she knew her and everyone she cared for must know the truth. Gone would be the fun and thrills of magic.

If the Witches of Ice weren't stopped very quickly, there would definitely be a price to pay; and not many would be willing to settle the cost.

Chapter Four

Chapter 4: *Witch School.*

Although the weather was fairly settled for this time of year, there was definitely something in the air that cold foggy morning. Though, just what that something was defied reasonable and sensible explanation.

It may have been due to both Cordelia and her sister suffering after-shocks from their previous encounter with Kaldre, not to mention the real threat of losing their amazing world of fun-filled witchcraft to the cold hearts of those Witches of Ice.

Mer had tried again explaining the horror of witchdom's demise to Mrs. Merryspell, but she simply dismissed it all with; *'Don't talk utter Pofflewaffle! If there was any gossip about this, I'd have heard it first from Valerie Pitheringae.'*

This rather dismissive response jarred Mer, who couldn't help but think how sorry her mother would be when bad things started happening to them.

The disturbance in the air could even have been due to Mer's chilling encounter with the Ice Witch who appeared through the crystals of the Darkington Chalice. What didn't help either was the energy emanating from the precious chalice whenever she passed the glass cabinet where it was safely kept under a spell-lock. Mer couldn't even bring herself to look at the thing anymore, despite her mother's praise —quite fearing another visitation.

Yet, despite all this, it was a school day like any other school day, and they had to *pull themselves together* as their mother often told them to do.

Across the landing from Mer's rather neat bedroom she could hear Cordelia manically laughing to herself.

'*Maybe she's gone mad*' thought Mer. This behaviour was certainly strange considering the danger they were no doubt in. So, she walked over to find out why, and soon found herself deep in discussion.

It turned out to be a subject that demanded utmost concentration, which Cordelia found very hard whilst searching frantically for school things to wear amid a pile of jumble in the corner of her room, which served as her wardrobe.

'Exploding bat bladders Cordelia...your room's in a total mess! Why don't you use a *Tidying Spell?*' shot a bewildered Mer. 'I've one that's really easy. You cast it on your room, and, over night, it tidies everything and puts it away for you! It's by Jessica Dolittle...*you know the one, surely?*'

'Not interested,' replied Cordelia in a blasé voice.

'So, what *is* going on, and why are you laughing so much?' pressed Mer.

'Well, it's simple really,' she said, sticking her head out momentarily.

'Why is it,' she began, 'that school teachers' names always make you laugh?'

Not waiting for an answer, she madly continued to ferret through her pile of tangled clothing.

'Is that what this is all about?' questioned Mer, expecting her sister to be in some kind of hysteria.

'Yes,' she answered in a muffled tone.

Mer, still uncertain about Cordelia's state of mind, responded; 'Well, I have to say, *I'm not really sure.*'

This was said in a patronising way whilst she once again unsuccessfully tried tying her school tie.

'But, isn't it enough?' asked Cordelia rhetorically. 'I mean, you're standing at your desk knowing full-well that the first rule you learn is *"No witches are permitted to laugh or cackle in class, unless granted permission to do so."'* (Cordelia used an authoritative voice here, as if reading from a rule book).

'Then,' she added, 'after that, in flies your teacher and you have to say *"Good Morning Miss. Plugbottle".'*

'I know!' sniggered Mer, now a little happier that her sister wasn't cracking up. 'Miss. Splosh-noddy, and Miss. Flurpkettle are two others.'

Cordelia choked a laugh from somewhere deep beneath her clothing, still desperately clawing through the mess for her school cloak. Eventually she emerged like some kind of peculiar scarecrow half-wearing the illusive garment. She stood up for a moment to dwell on such silliness.

'Why on earth don't we have teachers with sensible names like, Miss. Dennis or Mrs. Smith? It's beyond me!'

'Or, a *Miss. Cardboard,*' added Mer. They laughed some more as each of them added to the imagined list of acceptably boring names that wouldn't stir any kind of amusement in class. That was, until the suggestions of bland names became equally silly as the ones they presently had to deal with.

The young witches spent even more time deeply absorbed in further trivial matters rather than getting ready for school. It was at this point when their mother Mrs. Merryspell stormed into the room.

'LOOK AT THE MESS IN HERE!' she screamed. 'You haven't even packed your books or pens yet!'

'*Miss. Shrivelclang-snotpickle!*' declared Cordelia above her mother's annoyed voice. They both burst out laughing once more.

'ENOUGH!' shrieked Mrs. Merryspell, not enjoying the silly names at all. 'If you don't get a move on, you'll miss the school coach, then you'll have to stay home cleaning and tidying all day, *and that's without any magic!*'

With that the two suddenly sprang into action. In no time the pair were standing outside dressed, equipped, and ready for the journey to school.

They were both off to Miss. Emily Starch-Stiffington's School for Well Behaved Young Witches. Miss. Starch-Stiffington was considered by all pupils to be a real dragon in her discipline, and not always were the flames missing.

As regards travelling, some young witches use the cupboard method to get to school. They simply step into their favourite cupboard at home, cast a spell, then reappear in a convenient cupboard at school, hopefully a cupboard in the school cloakroom where they wouldn't be noticed by teachers.

Unfortunately though, and perhaps why most prefer not using this method, things can go horribly wrong.

Take, for example, Jennifer Sweazle's arrival. This poor young witch did everything right in her spell at home, but ended up in Miss. Starch-Stiffington's toilet cubicle. Alarmingly, the head mistress was about to sit down.

A few witches travel to school by various other means; one girl, Celestia Drift, being wonderfully lazy, often flies to school in her bed.

Most, however, prefer to take the strange old school coach, charmingly named Merg. It is clanking, smoky and clunky and quite weird at the best of times.

To travel this way is really an experience, as you

Merg awaits

never know which route Merg will choose, or what you'll encounter on the way. That's why it leaves so horribly early, 9.30am, to make sure pupils get to school on time.

Witch School begins exactly on the stroke of midday, and ends precisely when the large snake-like hand on the school clock touches the figure 12 with the smaller resting on the third hour of the afternoon.

All pupils are then expected to enjoy light refreshments before departing for home. There is strictly no homework –it would be far too dangerous.

As it happened, Cordelia and Mer were forbidden to fly to school this term, due to recent events, so they had no other choice but to travel by coach. The school coach merrily swerved down the narrow lane that led to their home and screeched to a halt just where the two sisters stood.

Their school bags, as usual, were invisibly wrenched from their hands, and without any request, the girls were bundled onboard by invisible arms amid much cheering from their friends. They pelted the two with anything from exploding paper darts to smouldering stink bombs.

Once onboard, they sat with their usual bunch, which included Meryl, Delia and Persimmon. They had a great deal to talk about, though amongst the usual chitter-chatter, it was impossible to broach the subject of the Witches of Ice and the impending doom upon everyone practicing magic. Understandable really, as the main subject matter of most students concerned newly discovered spells and incredibly awful magical jokes.

Merg was, like just about every day, in a peculiar mood. He'd decided his passengers would travel to school by way of the sea. He didn't have a driver or an engine that anyone would at once recognise, his overall shape was very old fashioned; and he could bend anywhere to get round the tightest corners, trees, or whatever needed to be got around.

The old coach weaved through the woods, swerving and creaking past obstacles, just like an overgrown snake. Smoke and steam jetted from every crack or split in his pipes and gauges. And, despite the pollution inside, each witch appeared to enjoy the ride. To those who weren't nervous, it was better than a day at the fairground.

All at once and with a deafening bang, Merg ploughed into a hillside.

'Bursting gooseberries!' yelled Cordelia above the thunderous noise. 'He means business today!'

Persimmon reached up to close the vent above her window to stop a bombardment of earth and small rocks.

Following another mighty bang, Merg eventually exploded out from the other side of the hill. They were now flying through the air, and all they could see in front of them was the sea. Huge crashing waves bashed under the coach, which seemed to help carry it along. With a dramatic plunge, Merg dived down into the sea.

As if by magic, which surely it must have been, none of the seawater flooded into the coach. So all of them had a wonderful lesson about what lives in the ocean without being drowned.

After quite a thrilling journey, the witches eventually arrived at the school gates. But, they weren't ordinary gates; their haunting countenance would send shudders through the toughest witch.

Between and around the bars of this tall structure clung fearsome dragons, giant spiders, and snakes. And worse, they weren't iron castings, they were alive, very much so, eyes piercing, bodies strangely wriggling and seething. They roared, hissed, and clawed at any who dared get near.

One false move and they would have you. It was wise to keep one's distance; a lost or injured limb would be no excuse to miss class. Cordelia though loved tempting fate, even though she was fully aware of the possible consequences.

'Don't even think about it, Cordelia!' barked Mer as her sister reached for the heavy latch. She ignored her completely. Even though Cordelia knew the only way to make the gates open was to call out the school spell, the thrill of disobeying school rules was well worth the challenge.

Instantly, a shrill scream filled the air.

A large metallic creature jumped from the gate toward Cordelia's outstretched arm. Despite her quick reflexes, its talons caught her school cloak and tore a huge rip in the garment.

'Blimey, that was close!' sang Cordelia cheesily.

Fortunately there wasn't much blood, which meant Cordelia had been very, very lucky.

'You're a bloody nightmare, you are,' scolded Mer. 'You could have killed us all!' Cordelia nursed her thankfully small gash, and smiled remorsefully.

'I have a potion for dragon injuries here somewhere,' offered Meryl. 'It was from my Aunt Eloisa after her new familiar had scratched her. It was *Tinkles*, her kitten that had done the deed. Not exactly gaping, but my Aunt has a tendency to overreact.'

Cordelia was grateful for the attention, but could see the rest of them hadn't quite forgiven her recklessness yet.

'Come on,' said Delia, 'Let's recite their stupid spell and get it over with.'

Even though everyone was reluctant, the school spell was very important, and once spoken, totally binding upon every student. Each stood ceremoniously to call out the spell in one voice, which didn't sound very enthusiastic at all.

"Open wide to Starch-Stiffington's school
On the hill,
And for any crimes, make us disgustingly,
And traumatically ill."

The witches recited the spell dry and dutifully, and at once the two old rusting iron gates, complete with the nasty looking creatures, shuddered and groaned their way open to let them in.

'Your Aunt's potion has worked!' beamed Cordelia, flexing and baring her arm for all to see.

'Great...better keep some of it for the next time,' moaned Mer as they commenced their trudge down the drive.

The imposing school building loomed dark against a threatening sky. Its foreboding appearance was preceded by rumours that the place at one time had been some kind of refuge.

It was further rumoured that past residents were actually eccentric and severely silly witches, warlocks and wizards. Magical mayhem like this would be unimaginable.

An interesting parallel today is that Starch-Stiffington's school seems to have no shortage of extremely eccentric teaching staff; *But should they be teaching young witches?*

asked some parents. *Mind your own damn business*, was the usual dubious response from Miss. Emily Starch-Stiffington, who lived there herself at some stage.

Upon arrival in the assembly hall, there was a real clatter of voices. A sharp hand clapping interrupted their racket. It was their headmistress ol' Starchy.

'Good afternoon, young witches.'

'Good afternoon, Miss. Starch-Stiffington,' replied everyone in a sombre but respectful tone.

Miss. Starch-Stiffington manifests a severe presence. The daunting headmistress is very tall and thin, has a particularly hooked nose, and bristly chin. She mostly dresses in shades of darkest grey and black, as these are her favourite spectrum of colour. Her odd-shaped glasses reflect whatever she looks at with a degree of magnification.

She disdainfully looked at her pupils, which is quite usual, and called out the school project for everyone to follow.

'Today, each class shall have a different project, that, when finished, will be used to compete against other classes.'

'Sounds wonderful!' called Cordelia to the others.

'QUI-ET!' screamed Miss. Starch-Stiffington, who Cordelia was sure turned purple in the process. 'The projects are; Class One –*Worst Brew*, Class Two – *Strongest Smell*, Class Three –*Vilest Smoke*, and Class Four –*Most Horrible Spots.*'

'WOW, I'M GLAD WE GOT THAT!' exclaimed Cordelia, which was followed by yet another *"QUI-ET!"* from Miss. Starch-Stiffington.

'THAT'S IT,' she hollered, 'now, take yourselves off to the library to collect your spell books, unless any of you have to report to me for punishment?'

There was a mad scramble. During the rush, Cordelia found it very hard to remain *"Qui-et!"* as the headmistress put it, chatting non-stop all the way to the school library.

Pupils are only allowed to use three reference books on "Most Horrible Spots". Naturally, there are many others written on the subject, but they, rather wisely, have been strictly disallowed due to the nasty results that frequently occur.

Of the books that are allowed, the first is Humphrey Bagwhistle's *Celebrated Guide to Causing Minor Bumps and Pimples*, the second is Eunice Screachfeather's *Itching to Have a Laugh*, and book three is Henrietta Spindlebury's *Fun With Boils*.

When they finally arrived at their classroom, they rushed in completely unaware of their teacher standing upright and asleep in the corner behind the door, which interestingly is the exact location where they usually throw their cloaks, hats, and scarves. Sadly, not all their garments landed magically upon the hooks provided, despite the witches learning the correct spell, many, many times over.

Not even their teacher's bizarre sounding snores alerted them to her presence. Though it must be admitted, she was buried under rather a lot of clothing.

The witches sat quickly and commenced searching through the pages of the three prescribed books, being careful to handle them properly. Some of them are known to be highly contagious.

Fortunately every desk was provided with a lantern, as the classroom was amazingly dark. This was mainly due to the walls of the room being almost charcoal black, and the other, was that the painter had forgotten to stop when he'd reached the windows. Well, that's what Meryl thought anyway.

The classroom featured a very, very high arched ceiling with many splendidly graceful cobwebs dangling, almost woven into place. It seemed that each wall too was lined with shelves of books. If not books, then various dust covered jars, bottles, and boxes of one sinister looking thing or another.

At the front end of the classroom, a huge old blackboard almost filled the entire wall, and protruding from the top of it were four gas lamps that flickered and spluttered.

Cordelia was impatient to get started and walked to the front of the class.

'Call them out,' she said, 'and I'll write down the first spell on the blackboard with this silly looking chalk. And remember chaps, once it's written on the blackboard, the spell takes place... so read it carefully!'

The silly looking chalk Cordelia had picked up was certainly not silly at all. It possessed a powerful magic, had an irritable nature and the name *Florence*.

'Ah, here's the very one,' called Persimmon. 'Itchy spots that move before you can scratch them.'

'OK,' said Cordelia, 'read it out.'

'It's one of Eunice Screachfeather's,' continued Persimmon, 'so it's bound to be potent.' At that, she read the spell precisely as written:

"Oh how itchy things we'd love to rid,
'Tis such pity when a spot is hid,
Much worse the pimple that runs around,
For today alas, it will never be found!"

'That could be quite a cool spell,' remarked Meryl. But,

as Cordelia began writing with the chalk named Florence, she wasn't feeling the task was easy. Actually, she felt almost as if Florence was forcing her hand to write something else.

This couldn't have been truer, for when she stood back from the blackboard, the last line had been changed. Instead of it saying; *"For today alas, it will never be found!"* it now read;

"For Emily Starch-Stiffington alas, it will never be found!"

Everyone in the classroom gawped at each other in horror. Their faces then changed to amusement.

'Come on,' cried Delia, 'let's go and spy on the old bag!'

'But, what about our teacher?' asked Persimmon.

'Oh, don't worry about Plugbottle, she's probably standing asleep somewhere,' repliedMer.

At that, they fled the class and ran down the twisting corridor to stand outside Miss. Emily Starch-Stiffington's office.

After much straining to get a good look, each of the witches peered through whatever possible opening there was.

The headmistress, as usual, was sitting bolt upright and writing things down on an official looking form. *Probably a nasty report about some poor young pupil,* thought Meryl.

Starch-Stiffington was using her darkest fountain pen with a very long black nib. The ink was blacker than usual too. And curiously, circling around the top of the pen as she wrote was a gathering of miniature storm clouds.

They were very dark; and if one looked hard enough, they would even see tiny flashes of lightening darting out. Whoever she was writing about, things weren't looking too good. Nothing seemed to be happening to her in the first few moments, but gradually ol' Starchy's right hand moved slowly up her left arm, attempting to scratch at something.

Not content with the place it found, it moved further up and scratched at her shoulder. Still not satisfied, her hand moved across to her long pointed chin covered in stiff bristly whiskers. Having no luck there, her other hand put down the black storming pen and joined the search. Things were really getting out of control.

At last, Miss. Starch-Stiffington stood up and began a thorough fit of scratching. The witches were finding it hard to balance in their precarious positions outside her office. One after the other, they fell away in fits of laughter which thankfully wasn't heard by the headmistress.

In no time at all, Starch-Stiffington was on the floor grabbing at an itchy spot that just wouldn't stay in one place. Laying on her back with her spindly legs kicking up in the air as if she was riding a mad motorbike, the observing witches could take no more. They rushed back to their classroom desperately seeking refuge from the ongoing comedy.

When they returned, Delia picked up Florence the chalk and said sternly, 'You'd better let me do it this time Cordelia, I'm stronger than you so I'll make sure Florence will behave herself.'

'How do you know the chalk is called Florence?' enquired Meryl. 'Is it your sixth sense coming through, or perhaps a voice from beyond?'

'No, 'cause it says so here on its side.'

Meryl walked over to look at it more closely. Sure

enough the chalk's name was beautifully carved into its side.

'No doubt some mischievous being is working magic through it,' reasoned a puzzled Meryl. 'We'd better be more watchful.'

Meanwhile, Mer had found a spell, this time in Henrietta Spindlebury's book, *Fun With Boils*.

'Get this!' she called excitedly, *'colourful boils and how to enjoy them with friends who have a very large sense of humour!'*

'Great!' exclaimed Jennifer Sweazle who'd arrived only moments ago in the classroom by using the Cupboard Spell. She dusted herself down and put her hat back on crookedly. 'Go on, Mer,' she said.

'Well, it says here, *"Boils no longer have to be painful and boring. Now, with my new spell, they can be completely pain-free and very colourful –perfect for your friends to enjoy at every witch party!"*

'Quickly, read the spell!' cried Delia enthusiastically.

"Firstly," read Mer, *"one must call out the name or names of friends to be 'em-boiled'. Then, you are to read or write the following words carefully and most precisely, lest you cause something really disgustingly horrible to happen."*

No sooner had Mer started reading out the following spell, than Florence began forcing Delia's hand this way and that.

This is how the spell was written in Ms Spindlebury's excellent book;

*"Grow my little beauties, and swell and swell and swell,
On every little face there to dwell and dwell and dwell,
Arise you tiny bumpies be you pink or slimy green,*

Bulge and stretch your sides out until your owner screams,
Lovely hot and rumbling as volcanoes spew the night,
Bursting splashing gushing over everyone in sight!"

On the blackboard however, there was a slight difference on line two. Instead of: *"On every little face there to dwell and dwell and dwell"* it now read:

"On every teacher and pupil to dwell and dwell and dwell!"

Straightaway, came a blood-freezing scream from under the careless pile of the witch's cloaks that had been thrown there earlier. The pile rose up revealing a horrified Miss. Plugbottle.

Having remained for sometime asleep, she'd been awoken to gasp and prod at a massive newly grown green boil. It hung like a huge sickly coloured balloon from the end of her nose, and was truly awful.

Without a second thought the witches rushed past the now hysterical Miss. Plugbottle, sped down the twisting corridor once more, up the main stairs and onto the balcony, where they could see the beginnings of a massive evacuation from the other classrooms.

The first teacher to emerge was Miss. Flurpkettle with two enormous boils, one orange, the other puce, hanging from each cheek. No matter what counter-spell the poor woman remembered and tried, she couldn't hide or get rid of them.

Miss. Flurpkettle was furious and became instantly surrounded by a gaggle of pupils similarly afflicted who pulled and prodded at her huge and beautifully coloured boils.

'Enough, leave me be, get back into class this instant!' she screamed at them whilst each giant boil bounced up and down with the movement of her mouth.

As she stood there waving her arms about in panic, fumbling for more spell books to put matters right, her boils, alas, continued growing.

With an almighty double bang both boils burst, sending out a shower of something best not described; suffice to say you certainly wouldn't want to be anywhere near it.

At once, Miss. Flurpkettle's face returned to normal, for a witch that is, and she stared blackly at the creaking old balcony where the young witches of Class Four looked down. Cordelia, Mer, and their friends fled back to their classroom at unbelievable speed.

Upon their return, Mer took up Florence the chalk and yelled at it angrily.

'This nonsense has got to stop!' she demanded. 'Pity you're the only chalk here. Never mind, perhaps my inner strength will make you work properly this time.'

She bravely gripped the errant chalk to write the spell. She was nervously hoping the chalk would thoroughly behave herself. Celestia Drift cast the spell this time from her bed at the back of the classroom where it was even darker and more conducive to rest. She did it exactly as written in Humphrey Bagwhistle's *Celebrated Guide to Causing Minor Bumps and Pimples*.

The description seemed quite innocent: *"A gentle and most playful bump that will appear on your face, arms or legs, or anyone you may care to tease."*

It went on; *"these little chaps are tremendous fun; especially good for tricking parents into allowing students to stay away from school due to illness."*

Though they were warned that the bumps last no more than one hour and cannot be repeated; *"spell casters best prepare with their finest act of illness and excuses after the bumps have gone."*

As soon as Celestia commenced her reading, the spluttering gas lamps above the blackboard jetted out long plumes of purple flame, which eerily lit the entire classroom.

Humphrey's spell was written as follows:

> *"Such lovely little bumps,*
> *Not even seen as lumps,*
> *Playfully rise where're I point,*
> *Defying all creams and oints."*

Florence worked hard on Mer as she rigidly scribbled away, and when they all looked up at the blackboard, everyone could see how well.

The spell was very different from the book and wove-in something extra that had at once caused problems. Their blackboard told the story, for it now clearly read;

> *"Such a lovely little witch school,*
> *So full of hags and frumps,*
> *Cover them all with bumps and lumps,*
> *The teachers, the school, the village & all."*

Class Four sat aghast, not knowing what to do. The flames in their lanterns became much smaller, the blackboard gaslights too, spluttering and spitting as they shrank. The classroom was unnervingly darker. Gazing at the dimly lit blackboard Cordelia noticed the chalk written spell had commenced glowing.

The surface of the board itself began rising and swelling with an undulation of vile lumps. These quickly spread from the board, down and across the walls, eventually landing to bubble up from the floor; rather like the swelling caused by fire, though there were no flames to be seen anywhere.

The heaving bumps, rising and falling, were on the move. Not only were they travelling toward the classroom door but to the desks the witches were now standing upon.

They were unquestionably disgusting too, a pustulation of the vilest content swelling and ready to burst. Persimmon could take it no longer and reached for a spell book to end the bumps revolting progress toward their desks.

Luckily for all of them she found a good spell and wove it just in the nick of time. The swelling torrent turned away at the last moment. Like a river of putrid boils fabricated from whatever surface they covered, they swept out the classroom door and onward to the schoolyard.

Seeing a way past, without being got at, the witches followed this awful tide. Delia, feeling brave, or perhaps idiotic, began jumping upon and bursting any disgusting heaving lumps that came too close.

Outside the plague was spreading quicker by the second, covering everything and everybody in its path. In no time all the pupils and teachers were infected with huge swellings.

The whole place was in a convulsive uproar, and by certain indications this giant rash was already making its way to the front gate and toward the nearby village of Drab.

There appeared no way to escape this curse, and Class Four could already hear the roaring screams of Starch-Stiffington bellowing for someone's head: they knew it was a good time to get out of sight.

This wayward spell would take some serious magic to stop.

Cordelia, Mer, and their friends fled, almost tripping down the twisting corridor that led back to the safety of their classroom. Or, so they thought.

As they crashed through the door, they noticed the classroom was filled with a blue haze, and it wasn't from the spluttering gaslights either. It seemed to hang in the air like a fog, silently waiting for everyone's attendance. Eventually, all of Class Four was present, standing as silently as the blue haze itself. Each tried to look as innocent as possible.

'We're in for a right scalding earful from ol' Starchy!' groaned Cordelia.

'Yes, we're definitely in for it this time,' added Persimmon.

'And it's all the fault of that damn chalk!' groaned Delia.

At last, even the school seemed peaceful. *Any moment now,* thought Cordelia, *old Starchy will fly in on a fiery broom and drag us off to the school dungeon.*

She was wrong. It was the blue haze hanging in the air before them that would do Starchy's bidding.

At once its shape became like a long ribbon that snaked around the classroom looking for victims. It didn't take much time finding any.

The blue haze lurched angrily around each witch in turn, including Cordelia and Mer, almost as if it were sniffing out their fear. Abruptly, all the suspects were held and pulled by their ears, forced to follow wherever the ribbon of haze would take them.

With ears tugged, the blue haze took them unwillingly out of the classroom and along the twisting corridor. It was a painful experience.

In minutes, Class Four was standing in a row outside Miss. Starch-Stiffington's office. The door opened with a sinister creak and before them, behind an impressive hand-carved desk almost in shadow, sat a severely dark and somewhat bedraggled head teacher.

She was holding a very large and very old book in her right hand, whilst writing something down with her left. At no time did either hand wander to scratch even the most wayward itch.

The pen Miss. Starch-Stiffington held was the darkest black fountain pen she owned. Even the black nib looked evil. And if there was some way possible to use an ink blacker than magic could conjure, she would have.

There wasn't a witch standing there who wouldn't have noticed the miniature storm clouds circling around the top of her black fountain pen as she wrote. It must be said as well that the pen's storm was greater than any that had occurred in recent years.

'WHICH WITCH IS RESPONSIBLE FOR ALL THIS MADNESS?' demanded the headmistress with a dark thunderous voice that seemed to match the blackness of her black fountain pen. Her black eyes, magnified by the lenses of her peculiar-shaped glasses, focused in on Cordelia, almost burning a hole in her head.

There followed a long uncomfortable silence as each witch looked at every other witch to see who might come forward.

'WELL?' barked Miss. Starch-Stiffington.

'Excuse me, Starchy, er, I mean, Miss. Starch-Stiffington, but no witch is the answer to your question, actually!'

The outspoken voice came from Cordelia, who everyone thought was incredibly brave.

Miss. Starch-Stiffington's reply didn't take long in coming.

'WHHHAAAAAT!' she shrieked unreasonably, causing the windows in her office to rattle violently.

'Well, it's obvious really, Miss.,' pleaded Cordelia amid the drama, 'it wasn't a witch, but a piece of charmed chalk that caused all this madness.'

The headmistress darkened her look somewhat and approached Cordelia with *"school dungeon"* written all over her face.

'Are you completely off your damn rocker, child?' she demanded.

'No, Miss., it's just that every time we wrote a spell on our blackboard, Florence the chalk changed it to something really terrible!'

'Yes, Miss. Starch-Stiffington, that's perfectly true,' added Mer, who was beginning to feel that being completely straight was perhaps the best way to get out of trouble.

'Well, if that's true,' snapped Miss. Starch-Stiffington, not releasing her doubts about the girls' story altogether, 'why didn't you tell your teacher...mmm?'

There was no getting around it, Ol' Starchy wasn't going to give up easily. And to be honest, she did have a point.

'Well, you see, Headmistress,' pleaded Delia, '...our teacher, old Pluggy, er, I mean Miss. Plugbottle, was buried under a boil at the time, and we poor scared witches didn't know what to do!'

Delia sounded unaccountably timid, and almost as convincing as Mer.

Starch-Stiffington sneered at this and opened her mouth wide. Her yellowing teeth, probably false, seemed to have been recently sharpened; and her oddly coloured tongue became flattened ready to let out a roar. Immediately, the pupils covered their ears.

'*MISS PLUGBOTTLE!*' screamed the Headmistress. '*COME HITHER AT ONCE, WOMAN!*'

Her screaming demand once again rattled her office windows, echoed along the twisting corridor to rattle the eardrums of old Pluggy.

With such a loud voice, there was simply no need for any sort of intercom in the school; for wherever you were, Starch-Stiffington's bellowing was certain to find you.

During this loud roar, Cordelia watched the headmistress's face with amusement, imagining how the two huge boils Miss. Flurpkettle once had would've bounced and wobbled at such an almighty yell. She couldn't help snort loudly at the thought.

'*QUI-ET!*' screamed the headmistress, and Cordelia did her utmost to prevent any further humorous visions.

The headmistress's office door eventually creaked open and their weak-kneed teacher entered looking fairly dazed.

'You called me, Miss. Starch-Stiffington?' said the diminutive Miss. Plugbottle in a scared and confused sort of voice.

'I screamed for you actually,' she pronounced. 'Now, please tell the court...er, I mean the class, were you at any time trapped beneath a large boil that prevented you from attending your pupils?'

Miss. Plugbottle, bless her, was a dithery loveable old witch, one that would help someone out at the best of times. For instance, she would often say something so badly, that it would come out sounding absolutely brilliant, even though what she said wasn't strictly true. This was one of those best of times.

'Err, pupils, yes err...that's right, big boil,' she jabbered, 'covered my face it did, and my ears too. Couldn't see or hear a bloomin' thing! Oh yes, I remember now...words on the blackbird...err I mean blackboard...not right, not right at all! Couldn't do anything you see...witches running around everywhere...probably frightened out of their wits I shouldn't wonder...but there you are, boils, that's what you get with boils...and big colourful ones too!'

At this, she pointed a finger at Starch-Stiffington rather like a Romani warning someone; and proceeded to gurgle. The witches knew they were winning.

The storm circling around Miss. Starch-Stiffington's black fountain pen seemed to be calming; there were certainly no tiny flashes of lightening to be seen.

Looking over her glasses and now fiddling with her apparently obsolete pen, she uttered sternly; 'I will of course be writing to your parents.'

In a much quieter voice, the headmistress added, 'And, it's such a pity that I haven't been able to tell them something that would have made me extremely happy, like how much punishment I'd given out, and how much punishment you required at home!'

At this, her voice began to rise once more. 'Still, there's always tomorrow, isn't there my dear witches...mmm?'

She leaned toward them again, searching for their answer.

'Yes, Miss. Starch-Stiffington!' they all said together, obediently, like a chorus of choirgirls.

With that, she wagged her index finger in a way that said, *"leave my office at once"*, which they did happily. Using another wag of her finger she banged her office door shut after the girls left; and surprisingly, not one pane of glass fell out.

It was time for school tea before home, and Cordelia, Mer, as well all of Class Four was feeling proud of themselves.

After they'd sat down at one of the many circular tables in the cavernous dining room, the kitchen witches flew in with their hard-earned tea. It was a welcome sight.

'I could eat a mountain, I swear it,' spluttered Cordelia as she dived into a plate stacked high with delicious-looking sandwiches.

Delia and Persimmon had their eyes upon the multi-tiered trays of cakes oozing with thick icing and cream. They too soon had their faces stuffed full. Meryl and Mer on the other hand were a little more genteel, preferring to take tea or a glass of the school's extraordinary fizzy pop; a potion drink with a recipe known to only a few witches.

There couldn't be a more fitting end to a perfect school day. Or, so they thought. Instantly every witch from Class Four started coughing and spluttering out everything they'd just eaten or drank. It was a ghastly sight.

Somehow the sandwiches had begun tasting like rotting rats, others with the texture and taste of slimy fish entrails. Everything Class Four tasted in fact was vile and disgusting. Even the soft drinks and tea were salty.

The witches from the other three classes sat obediently at their tables staring at Class Four in amazement, and the dining room floor.

Rather too timely, Miss. Starch-Stiffington flew in and landed at the head of their vomit-covered table.

'QUI-ET!' she screamed at the top of her voice.

'What on Earth is going on?' she demanded. 'Are you witches never grateful, I ask myself?'

Well, on this occasion, they definitely weren't.

'The food is revolting!' choked Cordelia, who immediately gagged on what she thought was a decaying something or other, pulling its withered tail to remove the rotting object from her mouth.

'Yes, it's disgusting!' retched Mer, doing her utmost to avoid being sick all over Starch-Stiffington's highly polished boots.

'Oh dear,' replied Miss. Starch-Stiffington, looking rather pleased with herself, 'I am sooo sorry. I can't imagine what you're going through; I wonder what's gone wrong? I can assure you, this has never happened here before; believe me. I shall question the kitchen witches immediately. I will make it my business to get to the bottom of this sickening situation. We seem to have a serious health and safety issue here!'

As she turned to go and investigate, Miss. Starch-Stiffington looked back at Cordelia and the rest of the class once more. They were still coughing and spluttering, and feeling distinctly wretched.

'Oh, and something else that delighted me greatly,' she mused, 'I did find one thing beside the school's kitchen blackboard. How it got into the school kitchen, I'll never know.'

With that she pulled something from one of her pockets; it was Florence the chalk.

'*Oh dear, naughty Florence!*' she said, and flew off cackling at the top of her voice.

It was finally time for everyone to go home. Celestia Drift, still feeling very ill, had unquestionably the perfect vehicle to travel back with, but she wouldn't be allowing any other witch to join her, no matter how desperately bad they felt.

And perhaps Merg the school coach wasn't the best way to travel home either. Especially since he'd planned a particularly bumpy ride for them all to enjoy.

The trouble was, Cordelia and Mer had no other option as they staggered toward the school gates, occasionally and urgently wandering off into the bushes as they did so. After the gates rumbled open, Merg screeched to a halt in front of them.

The two couldn't help notice that he'd changed colour; a kind of sickly sea green this time, which perfectly matched the colour of their faces.

One by one, the witches were invisibly wrenched onboard soon finding themselves firmly planted in a seat, and not of their choosing either. Cordelia now had her face pressed hard into a window, whilst her sister pressed into her out of sheer weariness.

They both felt incredibly and utterly nauseous. Merg's unkind engine burst into life with an annoying thumping that shook everyone onboard. As usual, smoke and steam filled the air, but this soon abated, much to the girls' relief.

Looking out the coach window and high into the sky, far off Cordelia could see the school witches flying behind Miss Starch-Stiffington in a single obedient line. They were going somewhere in a hurry, weaving their way higher and higher into the dark assembling clouds.

But, just before they disappeared from sight, five dark objects joined them to circle and circle about.

Cordelia had a bad feeling about this. She nudged Mer, who groggily peered through half-closed eyes. In alarm, Mer sat bolt upright and wrenched a small folding telescope from an inside pocket.

'It's them!' she proclaimed; and Cordelia snatched the glass to see. They stared at each other. "Oh no, The Five Witches of Gloom!" both yelled at the same time.

From the cloud the teachers and the evil coven disappeared into, a flash of lightening briefly illuminated the beginning of the young witches' storm-filled return home.

With a jolt, Merg roared along the rough road leading from the school; swerving to flatten several fence posts on the way.

Mer frowned deeply. *Seeing the Gloom witches* she thought to herself *has to be the worst possible omen.*

Chapter Five

Chapter 5: *Market Daze.*

A thousand boiling cauldrons filled the spring air with a perfume of many amazing mixtures and potions.

As usual, the witch market was abuzz with noise and excitement from countless folk buying and selling the most wonderful collection of magical things ever to be seen.

Small tents and stalls in a mixture of colours and designs were spread along every ally, filling every available space. Business was brisk and the voices of witches, warlocks and wizards announcing or singing out their wares produced a cacophony of choral splendour.

There hadn't been a day like this for many a year. The sun was full, the rain for the time being had departed, and no-one wasted a second trying to sell whatever they'd conjured, connived or perhaps stolen from other witches.

From all the smiles and skulduggery about, the awful truth about the demise of witchdom at the hands of the evil Witches of Ice could have been a thousand miles away from this busy market. For Cordelia and Mer, probably the next planet would've been a better option.

But, for the sake of their Gran, the girls had buried their concerns about this fast-approaching event, and were intent on just getting through for the time being.

Cordelia and Mer's Gran, Daisy Asteroi, sat back in her market tent admiring the market's entire goings on, whilst amply filling her favourite and rather spindly Wicca chair.

Gran's market tent really stood out from all the others. It was bright green and featured rich golden brocade sewn along all the edges, especially the opening. Above that sat a handsome-looking scroll with the name of her tent *"Warts & All"*.

She was cackling and waving her arms about with great happiness. Gran was to meet Tobias Trumpworthy again after numerous years, and this marvellous event seemed almost beyond her belief. She hadn't clapped eyes on him since she was eighteen. That was nearly seventy years ago, when the two of them were very much in love.

Lamentably, life has a strange way of changing things. By a series of curious happenings, none of which were planned by either of the two young sweethearts, they were to be separated from each other all this time.

Happily for Cordelia and Mer, their Gran went on to meet and marry the witch's grandfather, Orbilus Asteroi. Their first daughter, Hepsibah, went on to become the girls' mother. So, for Cordelia and Mer, at least, things worked out pretty well.

But for Daisy, since Orbilus had passed away, life had become quite lonely. And even though she enjoyed immensely the fun she had with her family, and naturally the mischief of her magic, she always yearned for something or someone to put a spark back into her life.

Enter her old flame Tobias who was renowned for being a little left of totally bonkers.

At the very least, even at his grand age of eighty-seven years, Tobias was considered to be the biggest daredevil in all of the witchy world.

So, this was Gran's big day. And, as a special treat to her gorgeous grand-daughters, as she often called them, she left the running of her market tent –brimming with the most brilliant collection of potions, spells and magical objects –utterly and completely to them. Wrong move.

Gran looked a proper picture. Exactly what kind of a picture, most couldn't say, though some might unkindly suggest abstract. She wore a bright pink witches hat, an orange and blue thickly woven jacket, a dark mauve top embroidered with pink dried frogs, matched with a long velvet skirt in richest bright green, bejewelled with beads and stones that painted a host of magical symbols.

And, although she wouldn't show them, Gran sported a pair of blue and white spotted bloomers as well as canary yellow stockings hooped with purple rings; she might show you the stockings.

Daisy indeed loved being colourful. And she finished the whole outfit off with the biggest, brightest, brownest boots she could find.

There would be absolutely no way anyone could miss seeing her, especially Tobias, even after such a very long time. She'd always been eccentric, especially in her choice of clothing; it was one of the first things that caught his eye, and probably everyone else too.

Cordelia and Mer beamed as Gran did a somewhat awkward little curtsy and offered them her special key and a metal box for them to keep all the money they may earn.

'Thanks Gran,' said Mer, 'you can trust us!'

Gran smiled with a hint of doubt.

Cordelia gave her a wink and said, 'You're stonkingly brilliant, Gran!'

At that, Gran commented, 'Well as long as I'm not *stinkingly* brilliant!'

She cackled loudly at this, grabbed her bright red leopard-spotted handbag, and waved the girls an eccentric farewell.

Cordelia and Mer watched her fly off out of sight. It was only seconds after this that an old witch by the name of *Chantress the Wise* butted her way into Gran's tent and asked, 'Where's Daisy?'

'She's out,' replied Cordelia, 'taking some bloke on a date.'

'On a date?' questioned the old woman, 'at her age? She should be ashamed of herself –what's the world coming to!'

'Never mind,' she continued, 'give me some more of my usual.'

Neither of them knew what Chantress the Wise got as usual, so Mer asked her politely, 'What is it that you want, good lady?'

'Good lady?' she snapped back. 'Have you gone potty? There's nothing good about me dear, I'm a witch!'

At that she lifted up a small but still-hot cauldron she'd brought in with her 'til it was just under Mer's nose and said, 'Smell that! Does it smell good to you?'

Mer choked a little.

'No, I didn't think it did, so you can hardly call me good, now can you? Pentacle Berries!' demanded the 'not-so-good' witch. 'I want Pentacle Berries!'

And she pointed toward a dusty-looking chest at the back of Gran's tent.

'She keeps them locked up in there,' she added, 'and be quick, I've a broom to catch!'

Cordelia dragged the chest before her, inserted the key Gran had entrusted them with and opened the lid. Inside were a dazzling display of bottles, jars, bags, and boxes, all clearly marked.

'Here they are,' cried Cordelia. 'How many would you like?'

'Oh, just a handful dear,' answered Chantress the Wise.

Cordelia poured them out from a beautifully embroidered silk bag into her own hand and held them up for the old witch to see.

'Is that OK?' asked Cordelia.

'Lovely, dear,' she replied with a grin.

'And how much do you usually pay?' pressed Mer helpfully.

'Oh, I really don't know about things like that, dear. Go on, you girls make me an offer.'

'How about sixty pence a handful?' offered Mer.

'Sixty pence a handful –that much!' she screamed. 'You want me to pay sixty pence for a handful of silly Pentacle Berries!'

Mer had no choice but to make amends, though Chantress kept on moaning. 'They're only for this 'ere soup you know?' she added, whilst pointing at the still-hot cauldron that smelt so awful. 'They add a little flavour, that's all. I'm not made of money, poor little old lady like me.'

'Alright, ten pence a handful?' suggested Cordelia in her kindest voice. Whereupon, Chantress the Wise wisely grabbed the small black and very bitter berries, tossed a ten pence coin into the air and fled Gran's tent without so much a *'goodbye'*, or *'it's been a pleasure doing business'*.

And what a business it was, for nearly every witch or warlock knows Pentacle Berries, deeply charmed berries from a rare bush that only grows in the most inhospitable places on Earth, are valued at about two hundred pounds each. That's everyone excepting these two evidently; and they were now in total control of Gran's market tent.

Before their next customer, both of them had a good sniff around.

'Blimey!' yelled Cordelia, 'what have you there?'

Mer smiled mischievously as she pulled down a large dusty old box from a particularly high shelf. Obviously it was placed well out of reach so that it couldn't be easily got at.

The box appeared to contain nothing more than junk; a deflated football, an old broken teapot, an ancient-looking camera, a few dented thimbles, the odd reel of cotton, some decrepit books with no spines, and a piece of folded parchment to name but a few.

'Cripes, I love the camera,' said Cordelia as she excitedly reached in and took it for closer examination.

Mer thought the parchment worth investigation so she unfolded it on a nearby table. When it was spread out, she wasn't sure what she was looking at.

It was inscribed, *"Montgomery Lamplight-Worthington's Only Way Out –A guide map for the witch in peril."*

Apart from its title, and the word *"exit"* scratched on using a broken pen nib, there appeared nothing else except for a few grubby stains and discolouration due to its age.

'Bloodstains if you ask me,' piped Cordelia. 'Yes, and very old stains at that. Probably caused by injuries sustained by the one-time holder during a nasty fight for their life –that's if you push me for an explanation.'

Mer wasn't pushing, but it certainly added to their speculation.

'Why aren't there any instructions?' she asked.

'Because you're not in peril, you idiot!' answered Cordelia smugly.

'I'll ask Gran if I can keep it, but 'til then, I'll hold onto it so I won't forget to ask,' said Mer as she rolled the document and slipped it deep into an inside pocket.

Without warning there came a very loud noise from someone clearing her throat at the entrance to Gran's market tent.

'Are we to stand here all day to get served?' asked a tall, gaunt-looking witch angrily. Her hands arrogantly rested upon her hips as she looked impatiently at them.

'Well?' she continued.

'Yes, we're both well and healthy I'd say, apart from having a dreadful lack of really exciting things to do,' answered Cordelia. Her cheek didn't impress.

'Look!' shouted the irritated woman, 'there's a whole queue of people waiting outside, are you going to serve us, or what?'

'I'm most dreadfully sorry for my sister,' butted in Mer with a falsely apologetic voice, 'what would you like?'

'Pentacle Berries, how many have you?'

'Oh, there's been quite a run on these today, only a couple of handfuls left I'm afraid,' replied Mer dutifully.

'How many would you like?'

'I'll take the lot,' she snapped.

'I'm afraid they're ten pence a handful, is that alright?' advised Mer. The woman coughed.

Still pretending to be shocked, the woman said; 'Oh dear, *that much?*'

Smiling sheepishly, she promptly held out both hands.

'That'll be twenty pence thank you very much,' said Mer, feeling rather proud of herself.

The woman handed her a pound coin and said, '... and mind you give me the correct change young lady, I

I know all about you kids of today.'

Mer scraped up the correct change from Gran's money tin and handed it over politely.

The witch scoured the coins closely, moaning an ungrateful, 'Mmm.'

Before she left, Cordelia quickly took a picture of her using the ancient dusty old camera, which probably didn't work, or had any film in either.

The vexed, though scheming, witch brushed Cordelia aside dismissively and whooshed off on a rather smart-looking black scooter. The two had been done again, and they didn't even know it.

'Next!' shouted Cordelia, walking up to the entrance. But, upon peering round to see how many more customers there were, her jaw dropped with shock. There was a queue stretching from their tent and way, way out of sight.

'What the...' exclaimed Cordelia.

'What's what?' enquired Mer as three new customers barged through, ready to buy. Ignoring these three impatient customers who were already nosily poking around in the boxes and drawers behind Mer, she walked to the entrance to see what Cordelia was on about.

'Blimey!' she cried. 'Gran's going to be well pleased with us, we'll have sold out in no time.'

'Service...I want some service over here, and now!' croaked one of the customers who'd just entered.

'Alright, alright,' barked Mer, who looked at the bent-over old lady with a certain amount of suspicion; something definitely wasn't quite right about her. She felt the same about the old lady's two companions as well.

One was a skinny warlock, not very tall, wearing an odd-coloured beard, the other a frail-looking witch that was doing everything she could to avoid showing her face.

Mmm, curious, thought Mer as she approached.

'What's this used for?' demanded the decrepit bent-over witch. She was holding up as best she could a tall, arched and clear crystal box emitting what appeared as wispy strands of gold and blue light with words written upon them.

'It's a Fortune Box and it tells your future,' stated Mer confidently.

'No it bloody doesn't!' croaked the witch in a voice that was beginning to break-up and definitely sounding younger than someone supposedly ancient.

'It's just telling me what I've already done!' she snapped angrily.

'That's 'cos you haven't given it any money, you silly... er, I mean, madam,' replied Mer impatiently.

'Money...money, who gets the money?'

'Well, our Gran, Daisy gets it, actually.'

The witch, still trying to hide her face, yelled back, 'So, let's get this right, I pay you for this, then I have to keep paying someone else to tell me my fortune?'

'That's right,' continued Mer, 'Just like you pay every time you visit a fortune teller.'

This didn't please the old witch one bit, who quickly slammed the crystal Fortune Box back on the shelf again muttering something like, 'Someone's making a greedy fortune...flipping rip-off!'

Cordelia's customer was just as rude. The skinny warlock wearing the odd-coloured beard asked her to go and fetch down a very large heavy bronze cauldron from the highest shelf in the tent.

Using her broom to levitate up to the shelf, Cordelia

barely managed the task, nearly letting the thing slip from her arms as she landed.

'No, not that one, stupid,' shouted the warlock impatiently, 'it's the copper cauldron beside it...for goodness sake!'

Struggling to lift it up, Cordelia was sorely tempted to let it fall out of her grasp onto the warlock's foot, but thought better of it. Once more she strained and flew down from the high shelf with the cauldron barely balancing on her broom.

With the copper vessel before him, the warlock rubbed his chin deep in thought '...mmm, perhaps the other one was better after all.'

Back at the shelf again, Cordelia struggled to swap the cauldrons over.

The customer seemed to be enjoying the bother he was causing and, noticing she'd now finally got a firm hold of the bronze pot, called out, 'Actually, on third thought, I think you're right, the copper one does have a certain appeal.'

Cordelia was spitting mad and, forsaking all her skills of tolerance, screamed out, 'Listen, sludge head, any chance of you using a few more brain cells so you can MAKE... UP...YOUR...FLAMING...MIND?'

All three of the awkward customers they'd been dealing with immediately swooped toward Cordelia; and she knew she was in trouble.

Without warning, one by one the three irritating customers inexplicably burst into an explosion of soot and smoke.

'Squeaking bats!' yelled Cordelia.

'I know I'm rude, but not that rude!' she complained, waving away the haze.

In seconds, the three clouds of soot reformed to become three sinister-looking beings, fuming with rage before a shocked Cordelia and Mer.

'I told you to be nice to people, didn't I?' reprimanded Mer, and they both staggered backwards expecting the worse.

In a whoomph, the dark beings reshaped into their true identity. Cordelia and Mer gawped in disbelief.

As the creatures' faces and bodies transformed in the gloomy half-light, they realised they were no less than... Meryl...Delia and Persimmon. It was a shocking trick, but, played brilliantly.

'You creeps!' yelled Cordelia.

'Well,' defended Delia, 'we came to give you a hand, and, by the look of things you damn well need it!'

'We're doing alright,' defended Mer, 'we've made nearly a pound so far.'

'Oh, that's wonderful! And, like my Uncle Dermot, lost yourselves several hundreds in the process,' added Meryl, 'and wasn't he the same as my Aunt Oonagh? For sure it was herself that sold their donkey to buy a cart!'

'Very funny,' snapped Mer.

Persimmon added her penny's worth too. 'It's all around the market, you know. Everyone's saying *"Oh, you must get to the bright green tent, there's a couple of loonies selling off Daisy Asteroi's stuff cheap...obviously they haven't a clue what they're doing!"*

'Shut up! What do you mean by loonies?' asked Cordelia angrily.

'OK, how many Pentacle Berries have you sold today?' asked Delia.

'All of them!' announced Cordelia proudly.

'And how much did you get for your troubles?'

'Er...mmm...about thirty pence, I think,' she replied cautiously.

'Thirty pence? Oh, well done!' Cordelia smiled smugly. 'Well, your Gran's going to be amazingly pleased with you two, I don't think. Pentacle Berries sell for hundreds of pounds...each!'

'She's right, you know,' added Meryl, 'have you not heard the *Pentacle Berry Charm*? *"Place them well as five points of a star, then command for thee rewards afar."* I mean, just five Pentacle Berries could bring someone a great deal of good fortune, you know!'

'Blimey!' cried a stunned Cordelia, quite unable to say anything more. Mer frowned at how Gran might react. 'But, not to worry,' continued Delia, 'we're here now, so you're day's about to get a whole lot better!'

'And, I've got something that could pull you from the very flames of tragedy,' said Meryl with a gleam in her eye, 'it's Rosemary Befuddling's A Merry Ol' Time.'

At that she held up for all to see an old book, which was perhaps one of the most sought after and coveted volumes in all of witchcraft. The tatty book was close to falling to pieces, being held together by nothing more than string, glue, and sticky tape.

Rosemary Befuddling is one of the jolliest wizards in the world. Her book is a feast of frivolous nonsense that to the everyday eye would be nothing more than a complete and utter waste of time.

Not so for younger wizards, witches and warlocks, who love the sheer pottiness of her ideas. As Meryl read through some of Ms. Befuddling's subjects of interest, Cordelia and the others quickly got a taste of what the decrepit looking volume was all about.

'Here's a good'n,' said Meryl, delighting in Rosemary's

wacky sense of humour, 'How to be in two places at once –have you ever heard of such a daft thing?'

'Could come in useful,' mused Persimmon, 'especially if you've been grounded for the umpteenth time!'

She looked sarcastically at both Cordelia and her sister.

'Or, how about this,' continued Meryl, *"Thirty-six Ways to Become Invisible"* or, perhaps, *"The Fools Guide to Climbing Into Mirrors"* would be of interest?'

'I wouldn't mind that,' piped up Cordelia, 'that's until the mirror gets broken though!'

The old book soon captured everyone's imaginations as Meryl in her rich Irish accent continued her brief journey through several faded and worn pages.

As she read, Meryl noticed a few teacup stains and cake crumbs. They weren't there because of a previously sloppy reader; they were Rosemary's. She'd had left these to allow the reader to see where she'd come to a natural pause, especially on particularly silly subjects.

Rosemary often went to the extent of taking refreshments whilst developing spells; it would allow her to properly think things through.

Meryl flicked page after page of amusing charms and incantations. Eventually, she came to the greatest spell Ms. Befuddling had *ever* created, and one that had led to international recognition.

In no time, Rosemary became something more than simply a wizard who devised countless daft spells. It was her all-time mega hit, the *Averting Spell*. This was, and is, a spell of staggering importance throughout witchdom.

Page one hundred and thirty seven features this madly simple spell. *Anyone could have thought that one up*, accused many jealous wizards. But in truth, it's brilliant.

The *Averting Spell*, now commonly used by witches, warlocks and wizards everywhere, enables spell-casters to appear or disappear at will, without being seen to do so.

'How?' demanded Cordelia, who seemed to speak for everyone in the now-crowded tent. It was crowded because countless witches and warlocks of all description had somehow got in whilst the girls were understandably distracted; and they were cramming in to grab some insanely hot bargains.

'Simple,' explained Meryl, continuing above all the commotion, 'upon reading Rosemary's spell, any casual onlooker is unknowingly made to avert their eyes the very moment the witch disappears.'

'So, you mean they're never actually seen disappearing,' stated Delia rather obviously, '...so cool!'

'And,' continued Meryl, 'they read the spell once more to re-appear again, completely un-noticed.'

After a while, Gran's tent had become impossibly full with bargain hunters waving their finds in front of the witches, vying for a knockdown price.

'This is getting ridiculous!' yelled Delia, 'can't we get this lot out of here? Shoo... shoo!' she screamed, spreading her arms out as if rounding up a gaggle of geese.

Whilst Delia did this, Meryl cast a 'homing-spell' upon everything the uninvited intruders had hold of. The items were tugged from their greedy grasps and returned to their rightful place in Gran's tent.

It wasn't long before the place was rid of the disgruntled customers and Cordelia yelled a final *'Clear off!'* to the queue outside. She speedily tied the door strings together.

'We'd better get out of here right now,' urged Meryl.

'What, and leave Gran's tent to the mercy of that bunch of thieves?' replied Cordelia. Mer added, 'Our lives wouldn't be worth living if Gran found out we'd been chased off like cowards.'

'She's right,' agreed Persimmon, 'but what else can we do?'

It was a fair question, and needed an answer there and then. But as Meryl glanced back at the door, she noticed something quite peculiar taking place. The door strings Cordelia had just knotted were now untying themselves. Even worse, Gran's tent was becoming uncomfortably cold–freezing actually.

'Mer...Cordy...guys?' stuttered Persimmon. 'Look at the tent door!'

When they did, all of them shrieked. Between the canvas openings, the all-too-recognisable face of their most feared nemesis pushed through.

With an evil sickly smile, Kaldre spoke. 'How wonderful to find you all together amid this den of iniquity!'

'Blast my spell books, it's her!' shrieked Cordelia. 'Quick, let's get out of here... we can take Gran's tent with us...warts and all!'

Without a moment's hesitation, everyone charged at Kaldre, pushing her outside. It must have been powerful magic surrounding the place, for no matter what Kaldre and her cronies attempted, the Five Witches of Gloom couldn't get back in.

It was at that moment Cordelia had a brainwave and read aloud the *Transportation Charm* by Melchior Fizz, changing some of the words to accommodate a very large tent along with some very strange merchandise indeed.

Just for good measure, Meryl read the Averting Spell. They both worked, and in blast of purple smoke, the young witches were gone, leaving the Five Witches of Gloom standing around in no more than an empty smoke-filled space where Warts & All used to be.

The girls felt a tremendous wrenching sensation, which ended with a shuddering thump as they and the tent hit the ground once more. Amid the smoky haze, even Mer was impressed with her sister.

'Wow...I like it! How did you do that?' she asked.

Cordelia, just as stunned as the rest of them, simply smiled, hiding her shock yet at the same time trying to look very clever indeed.

Persimmon worriedly peered through the canvas opening.

'Oh, so sick!' she cried. The others ran to see a sight that brought instant smiles to their faces. Cordelia untied the door strings to open up Gran's amazing tent to a very different world of people. They had landed slap bang in the middle of an ordinary market day in the village of Staunch, just down the road from the town of Snobb-on-the-Rise.

'Oi, take a look at this lot!' she yelled, staring at a crowd of everyday market shoppers.

'Bor-ing!' cried Delia.

'How can they bare to look so plain?' continued Persimmon, so used to dressing up in the most bizarre costumes.

'Yeah, but there's loads of mugs...er, customers buzzing around,' added Cordelia. 'Think of all the money we could make out of them! And, none look like trouble to me, not like that bunch at the witches' market.'

'You could be right,' said Meryl, closing her eyes for a

confirmation from beyond.

Not far off, a young lad, noticing their weird green tent and standing for a while gawping eventually walked up and asked if they sold computer games.

The girls looked at each other, not sure how to answer such a question.

'What's a computer?' asked Mer genuinely.

The lad spluttered, 'Yeah, right!'

'Certainly, matey,' called Cordelia, promptly taking charge. 'Computer games, mmm... I think I've the very thing over here.'

The boy joined her with a look of excited anticipation. As he strolled, he had a quick look at all the fascinating things on offer in Gran's extraordinary tent.

'Wicked, and well evil!' he exclaimed with delight. 'Some of this stuff is seriously mind-blowing!'

The unsuspecting youth pulled his laptop from under his arm and placed it on a rickety table in the centre of the tent. Opening its lid, the girls looked bemused at the bright screen showing a picture of a dragon.

'Got any dragon games?' he asked and Cordelia smiled knowingly at the others. The kid was clearly obsessed.

'Oh yes, indeed we have –violent or playful?' she asked coyly.

'Violent, what else! None of those wussy gutless games for girls!'

'OK,' offered Cordelia, choking an amused cough and trying her best to be as responsible as possible, 'but I do have to warn you that any player has to be...er...very careful with this game; it could be harder for you than you think...like, *actually dangerous!*'

'Bring it on...the meaner the better,' said the lad coolly.

Reasonably, this gave Cordelia little choice in the matter,

so she promptly climbed a nearby stepladder to bring down one of Gran's more obscure devices; *Halloran's Celebrated Magical Compendium of Dangerous Games.*

This title was printed in large bright green lettering on its black pentagonal box with a glowing red warning label; which meant there'd be no excuse for anyone who falsely claimed they thought they were opening a box containing tiddlywinks.

To most, apart from the glaring title, the container would look almost whimsical. Not so for witches; the very sight of it would make their pulses race. Naturally, Cordelia already had one of these.

But, although Gran had generously given it to her for her twelfth birthday, her mother, Mrs. Merryspell, decided to confiscate it incase she, or anyone else, suffered a disaster. Her mother was furious at her Gran for being so irresponsible.

'What's that, and where do I plug it in?' he wanted to know as Cordelia placed the compendium box before him.

'Er...you don't plug it in,' she replied, frowning.

'Oh, so it's Bluetooth?'

'Well, there are some blue teeth in it I s'pose,' answered Cordelia.

The kid just grunted a confused 'Eh?' as she moved it next to his laptop.

'Now, you want to play a game with dragons, do you?' she asked politely.

'Yeah, that's right... like I said, the meaner the better!'

'Happy to oblige,' replied Cordelia, smiling wryly at the unsuspecting kid who in turn smiled back in a smug know-it-all kind of way.

Cordelia placed her hand on top of the box, uttered a few

Playing with Dragons

words under her breath, and with her left index finger invisibly wrote the word *"dragon"* on the lid of *Halloran's Celebrated Magical Compendium of Dangerous Games.*

Although it was bright and sunny outside, rather cheerful for this time of year as a matter of fact, the boy was sure he heard thunder rumbling not far off.

It wasn't thunder at all, something more solid in fact. Instantly, a long thick spiny tail shot through the opening of Gran's tent, wrapped itself around the now screaming kid; and kid; and shot back out again with him wound inside.

'He's gone to play with the dragons,' said Cordelia toothily.

There settled an embarrassed quietness in the tent, followed by a roar of nervous laughter from the witches.

'Don't worry,' Cordelia added, 'he'll be back in about twenty minutes; a little shaken and bruised maybe, but would've had the time of his life!'

She smiled ingratiatingly. Soon, a few more interested villagers wandered by, sticking their heads through the tent door, and nosing around.

'Charming, absolutely charming!' called out one lady who sort of reminded Cordelia of Mrs. Pitheringae, though a little more gentle in appearance perhaps.

'You've done a beautiful job, so entertaining, well done! Are you organic?' she wanted to know.

'Oh,' answered Meryl, 'much more than you'll ever know, Missus.'

The woman smiled and walked further into Gran's emporium of magic.

'I'm not sure if your name *Warts & All* is strictly appropriate though, you might find there's a government ruling on it somewhere. Call my solicitors, *Oily, Smyle & Grabbe*, I'm sure they can advise you. Speak to Mr. Oily, he's very good at getting into places where others can't!'

Meryl didn't know what on earth the woman was talking about, but choked a discrete laugh anyway.

'Do you perchance have any organic make-up? Umm, vanishing cream would be nice,' she asked. The eyes of every witch lit up immediately.

Mer put on her poshest accent and strode over like someone out of a fashion boutique. 'Yes, *Modom*, actually we do,' she assured her customer. 'Perhaps *Modom* would care to try this?'

She held up a large tub of what appeared to be face

cream and unscrewed the lid. It was a jar of the most powerful disappearing cream Gran had ever kept.

'It's Chareese Broussard's *"Illusive Label"*,' she said. 'I can promise *Modom* that it is the *original* Pre-Charmed Vanishing Cream, made only with freshest Windberries. And, I know for a fact, Miss. Broussard clambers the highest hills to gather the cleanest and wildest Windberries to be found!'

The woman looked convinced.

'Go on, try some on,' urged Mer, pushing her finger into the cream and attempting smear some on the lady's face.

'No, no, that's all right, I can do it myself,' she said, brushing Mer's willing and overly keen hand aside.

The woman then tried it out for herself and seemed to fully appreciate the vanishing cream's delicate smoothness.

'Oh goodness,' she remarked, 'that feels wonderfully clearing.'

'Yes, *Modom*,' added Mer, pushing her luck, 'it will make even the tiniest blemish completely disappear.'

'I'll take two tubs then, thank you,' she cooed whilst rubbing the creamy potion well into her cheeks and brow.

Almost at once Chareese Broussard's Pre-Charmed Vanishing Cream went to work on the unfortunate woman. Firstly, her face disappeared, and if it weren't for her silly hat and neck-scarf, no-one would have known where her head was. It was just as well she wore gloves too, as it made it much easier for Mer to take the twenty pounds she charged and to hand over the bag containing the two tubs.

There was, in fact, enough vanishing cream to last her for several years of disappearances. As the good lady left Gran's emporium, Cordelia rushed out after her with the camera she'd found earlier.

'Oi, lady, smile please.' As the lady turned, well her clothing at any rate, Cordelia pressed the shutter.

Obviously, she couldn't see her expression, nor for that matter could anyone else, and maybe even the camera wasn't working either.

Chareese Broussard's *"Illusive Label"*, the original Pre-Charmed Vanishing Cream.

The woman continued walking, but she must have been looking in Cordelia's direction, for she walked slap bang into a porter carrying a huge tray of fresh fish above his head. The resulting collision sent the lot scattering to the ground.

One look at the headless woman was more than enough to make him scream in terror. Not bothering to pick up the fish, he ran screaming into the crowd never to be seen again. Cordelia just shrugged her shoulders at such odd behaviour and stepped back into the tent.

By now, the tent was quite full with eager customers. Though, surprisingly for the girls, they were a lot more civilised and calmer than the greedy grubbing witches at the witch market. There was a lovely hum of busy browsing, and no pushing or shoving so often encountered at that other place.

The general feeling was that maybe they should come back again. Away from main hustle-bustle, Cordelia admired the old camera; intrigued to know whether or not she'd actually taken any pictures. That moment, a middle-aged man with an exquisitely shaped silver moustache, wearing a posh tweed jacket and trilby hat, interrupted her concentration with a gentle, '*Uh hem?*'

'Yes, matey?' she replied brashly.

'I'm interested in this yard broom,' he said, holding up one of Gran's best brooms for her to see.

'Yeah, great isn't it?' assured Cordelia.

'Can I try it out?' he said.

'Sure!' she replied.

With that he began sweeping the huge rug covering the tent's floor.

'No no, not like that, matey! It's a special broom. You have to sit on it to use it!'

'Sit on it?' he exclaimed.

'Ang on,' she said. 'Let me explain outside; there's more room out there'.

Cordelia led the puzzled gent outside to demonstrate.

'But, surely,' he complained, 'if I'm sitting on the damn thing, I won't be able to use it for sweeping, will I?'

'Trust me,' assured Cordelia, 'you won't be disappointed.'

With the brush in place, he nervously leant on the upright broom handle, not exactly seated, but near enough for Cordelia.

'*OFF!*' she yelled. At once the poor unsuspecting man, holding the broom for all his life, immediately shot way into the sky bellowing for help. In his wake, he left a worrying trail of smoke.

Dusting her hands together, Cordelia walked back inside saying, 'Don't worry, just a test drive, he'll be back in a mo.'

Fortunately, no-one had noticed his extreme departure, and the gentle hum of contented customer browsing continued unabated.

'Where are your lanterns?' croaked an odd-looking woman with pebble-thick glasses and a tiny yapping dog continually attacking Delia's ankles.

'Up there, above your head,' answered Delia, stooping to try and make friends with the offending pooch. The dog, not at all interested in making friends, simply snapped at her hand instead.

'Friendly little blighter, isn't he?' said the woman who could either not see due to bad eyesight or knew full-well what her dog was up to.

Whatever it was, Delia removed her hand quickly and continued pushing him asidewith whichever leg was under attack.

The woman peered upwards with her right hand above her forehead as if trying to shield her eyes from sunlight, which understandably, there wasn't any. Her dog was steadily becoming more of a nuisance. Delia knew she had no choice but to do something very quickly –its bites were becoming rather painful.

Obviously, she wouldn't want to cause a great kerfuffle, so any magic had to go unnoticed.

Probably, the Averting Spell will come in useful here, she thought. And, as the woman seemingly had trouble in seeing things, Delia felt she might not even notice if her yapping biting pest was temporarily transformed into something less aggressive.

So, whilst her customer gazed up at the ever-evasive lanterns, which to most were as plain as the bulbous nose on her face, Delia recited the Averting Spell under her breath, along with a little something extra.

With a stifled yelp and a small puff of white smoke, the troublesome yapper had now been turned into an off-white small dog-sized hairy slug. Certainly a sight more docile and maybe a teeny bit harder for her to drag around. All the same, the lady hadn't noticed the change at all, still pulling at its lead gazing and pointing at the blur of lanterns hanging above her head.

Cordelia noticed the newly formed thing with amusement. *Perhaps we could call it a pug-slug?* she mused to herself.

'I'll have that one,' the woman said, pointing to the main chandelier hanging from the centre of the tent.

'Sorry,' replied Delia, 'you can't have that; it's the tent's only source of light. How about this large brass lantern with the shining blue light hanging right before you?'

The woman, with those extremely powerful glasses, moved her face up close bumping the lamp with her bulbous nose.

'Oh, that one,' she said, quite startled, 'Mmm...I do like its pretty blue flame, I have to say.'

'Well, why don't you open the lantern's door?' asked Delia and she did. There was a sudden rush of wind and before the poor lady could do anything about it, she was sucked into the lantern, pug-slug and all. The door snapped shut after them.

'Crumbs!' yelled a surprised Cordelia from the other side of the tent, and she immediately took a photo of the offending lantern with the ancient camera. The old thing gave off a loud rusty click as she called out, 'Smile please'.

Fortunately, apart from the witches, no-one had seen what had just happened to the lady with the pug-slug.

Mer was halfway between a look of amazement and total amusement, mystified as to how a whole person could disappear into such a tiny space.

Cordelia returned to serving her customer, who'd become

greatly interested in a small wooden container curiously named a *Lightening Box.*

'We'll have a play with it,' smiled Cordelia. They did.

Almost immediately, with a loud crack and bright flash, the tent and everyone in it shook violently. Cordelia and her loyal customer, both holding the Lightening Box, were gone. Just a pall of smoke rose up from where they once stood.

'She's really done it this time!' cried Meryl. Mer tried calming everyone.

But there was no need as the witches could see that their customers now appeared in some kind of daze.

Persimmon tried waving a bottle of Camilla Phume's *Industrial Grade Smelling Salts* under a few noses whilst Delia had fun pulling bizarre faces in front of them to get a reaction. But, it was most peculiar; whatever they tried, no-one could bring them out of their stupor.

In an instant, the tent was again shaken with another thunderous crash and flash of lightening. Cordelia and her devoted customer reappeared, both singed and completely frazzled. Their hair and clothes smoked from the flash and their astonished faces were blackened.

'And that's how the Lightening Box gets you from one place to another in an instant,' confirmed Cordelia.

'Shall I wrap it, or would you like to take it as it is?' she asked politely. There was no response from the woman apart from a dazed smile. She took the box from Cordelia without a hint of emotion.

'Well done!' praised Cordelia. 'That'll be two hundred pounds, thank you.'

The lady automatically opened her purse and handed her a few crisp new notes, which Cordelia took hurriedly in case the woman changed her mind.

Strangely, all the remaining customers in the tent were still in a similar dazed condition, each accepting their purchases with the same wan smile. The young witches were delighted with their trades, because it seemed no matter what prices they suggested, everyone was agreeable to pay.

So, with a weird assortment of magical purchases clutched closely and a vacant gaze in their eyes, one by one the satisfied customers departed Gran's tent.

The witch's impromptu visit to *Staunch Market* had been a huge success and they stood there hardly able to believe their good fortune.

'I can't help thinking Gran had better order a few more of those Lightening Boxes meself,' suggested Cordelia.

'Did you know that Signor Benito Flash was responsible for this remarkable invention?' she went on. Mer and the rest of them could only offer blank faces.

'Yes,' she added with a very knowledgeable voice, 'Flash & Co. make the best Lightening Travelling Box to be had. No wonder people still use the phrase...as quick as a flash!'

'Please shut up, Cordelia!' yelled Mer, watching her sister, who was still smouldering from travel by lightening.

'Yeah, I think we get the point,' added Delia.

Cordelia could feel it was time to go, especially looking around the now empty tent once full with blank expressions.

So, with their stock all but sold, and new customers eagerly trying to push and prod through the just tied tent flaps, everyone felt it was the best time to leave the village market and head back home.

'They're getting as pushy as those nutters at the Witch

Market!' remarked Mer.

'Yeah,' added Meryl, 'once they understand there's something on offer that's too good to be true...'

'...They all want to steal it,' finished Persimmon.

Meryl beamed as she held up Gran's money tin with the day's takings. Although large, she had difficulty closing its lid. Hardly surprising really; it contained over two thousand pounds in notes.

'Oh, I nearly forgot,' said Cordelia, 'that daft old camera, where did I put it? There's something quite intriguing about that thing.'

'Yeah,' chimed Delia, 'like, it doesn't work!'

Strangely, as she picked it up, screaming voices could be heard from within its workings.

'Hey, there's someone in there!' exclaimed Mer. 'Quick, open it.'

Carefully, Cordelia undid the latch on its side and opened the cover. She couldn't believe what she was looking at, neither could they.

Circling around inside, were miniature people. In fact, they were the very ones she'd thought she'd captured on film. But instead, Cordelia's camera had actually been capturing them *inside* the camera; and their screams of horror were only too real.

As she stuck her face closer to examine the goings on, the back of the camera sprang fully open and her captives shot out. They landed in the middle of the tent; and amazingly each returned to their normal size almost at once.

Those troublesome *Pentacle Berries* did the same, spinning freely out of the old camera. Floating in a single line, they quickly made their way back to where Gran had kept them safely spell-locked.

The stunned customers soon surrounded the girls with a babble of arguments, each demanding to know what on Earth had happened to them, and more importantly, why?

To make matters even trickier, the poor lady who'd used the vanishing cream had now returned to Gran's tent demanding her money back.

Cordelia appeared aghast.

'I thought you were trapped in my camera,' she said holding it up.

'What? Are you quite sane, child?' the woman asked. 'Now look, this cream is dreadful stuff. Everywhere I go, people take one look at me and run off screaming!'

Cordelia pointed her toward Mer.

Mer did her best not to laugh hearing her story, trying to show a concerned face.

'And I can't find a mirror anywhere to see myself,' moaned the woman. She felt someone bump into her and looked down to see a pair of pebble-thick glasses staring up at her.

'What are you gawping at?' she shot accusingly to the lady who'd previously attempted buying a lamp. 'And what's that strange slimy thing attached to the end of your dog lead?'

The old woman ignored her and instead strained to get a closer look. Even with her bad eyesight, she knew something wasn't quite right about her.

'I can't see your stupid face,' she barked, 'that's what I'm staring at, you fool!'

'You really need stronger glasses, either that or a larger piece of brain,' quipped the other lady sharply.

Upon hearing this, the old woman set what she thought to be her dog upon the irritable lady. 'Go on boy, get her, don't let the old bag insult me like that!'

Sadly, the slug-pug just bounced up and down as she pulled on its lead. The worst the invisible lady suffered was a coating of disgusting slug-goo over her legs and shoes.

'You're bloody mad!' said the invisible lady who immediately stamped on the poor creature, popping it and splattering its remains all over the floor. World War Three was about to erupt, and the girls didn't want to be around to see it.

Meryl and Delia quickly and perhaps unfeelingly ushered their irate customers, including these two, from the tent, not daring to give them any kind of explanation. But, after they'd gone, despite the witches feeling somewhat relieved, they soon realised that their afternoon of drama wasn't altogether done with.

In an effort to make a fast exit, Cordelia once more read out The Transportation Charm by Melchior Fizz, this time to take them and Gran's tent back to the witch market, though nothing happened.

'Why isn't it working?' asked Persimmon.

The reason was soon evident as the inside perimeter of the tent began freezing. Slowly, ice crystals crept up the canvas walls.

'What on my poor Uncle Sully's black crow is going on?' said Meryl as she and the others watched the ice forming before their eyes.

The canvas doorway then became unfastened; allowing a large gilded cage to float through. Stuck inside the cage was a large exotic bird. It distressfully flapped and squawked for a way out. The girls stared at this strange-looking macaw. It was as gold as the golden cage. Every feather was gold, its eyes shone with gold;

and even its giant curved beak appeared to be made of highly polished gold.

Yet, despite appearing to be made from this rare metal, the bird flapped and moved like any other large macaw. The cage, with its brilliant gilt finish, glinted even in the soft light of the tent. Persimmon, looking as distressed as the poor bird, yelled, 'Quickly someone, help me set it free!'

So, they rushed over to the cage, now settled on the carpeted tent floor, and undid the latch on its door. The bird let out a squawk, but refused to escape.

'Perhaps it's too frightened,' said Mer. As the cage was very large, she suggested going in herself to coach the macaw out.

'If it won't leave, I could try a couple of spells.'

'Yeah, I might have a few for that,' added Cordelia helpfully.

Mer stepped in, but no matter what she tried, the bird obstinately refused to climb over to her waiting arm.

'Here,' said Delia. 'I've got some peanut brittle, maybe it would like that?'

So she stepped in to join Mer, waving her peanut bar under the macaw's dangerously large golden beak. It didn't seem to like peanut brittle, turning its head away in disgust whilst continuing to squawk in distress.

So, in stepped Cordelia, searching her countless inside pockets for a bird spell. Meryl and Persimmon joined them, making funny chirping sounds, whilst beckoning the tormented creature down from the top of the domed cage.

The birdcage door then snapped shut. Alarmed, the young witches looked around in horror. The tent became darker and even colder.

'We're trapped!' shrieked Persimmon.

Whilst the girls tried unsuccessfully to escape, a rasping, unfriendly, unfamiliar voice croaked: 'I cannot believe how dopey some witches are!'

The cold utterance belonged to the deadliest form of witch ever known; a Witch of Ice; and this time there appeared no escape for any of them.

'Let me introduce you to Belladonna,' it rasped, floating into the tent and circling around the cage.

The look of this Ice Witch, called *Estoriah*, that's if you could bear observing her long enough, was dark; and even her sickly grin contained no humour.

'Belladonna,' she added, 'was once a young witch, much like you. Pretty...carefree...and ridiculously stupid.'

The witches tried not to listen. Like the wretched macaw they simply wanted to escape from the Ice Witch's trap. Sadly, no matter how much they tried to force apart the cage's bars, the bars remained in place.

Spells worked neither, as Cordelia soon found out; her precious volume by Melchior Fizz, *Spells All of a Flutter —The Best 100 Charms & Chants to Use with our Feathered Friends* simply went up in smoke the very moment she started reading.

'What a silly girl Belladonna was,' continued Estoriah, 'she actually thought she could trick me into giving back her freedom; even after everything I'd done for her!'

Once more the face of the witch darkened.

'Nonetheless,' she continued, 'I know she's delighted to be the world's first and only golden macaw!'

Belladonna squawked louder, ferociously biting at the cage bars.

'And, I have to tell you, a worse fate than this awaits you five! You see, all the rumour-mongering you've invented about our so-called deadly plans for witchdom, which

I must add is a complete nonsense, hasn't gone unnoticed. Understandably, we *have* to put a stop to you, don't we?'

No-one answered. 'Oh dear, what brainless young witches you are, especially not knowing how lethal we powerful Witches of Ice can be!'

Ah,' snapped Cordelia, 'why don't you go climb a ladder and get over yourself!'

'Yeah,' agreed Delia, 'we've really got to do something about her, she's bloody barking!'

Persimmon nodded shyly.

'Once we get out of this mare's nest, you mean!' said Mer.

Regrettably, a few more Ice Witches entered Gran's tent and circled around, causing an even deeper frost inside. The cage bars were coated in ice, and by now the light too had darkened, hardly bright enough for any to see.

'This is becoming an invasion!' yelled Delia. Persimmon began to fret, her eyes darting everywhere.

The Witches of Ice drifted around the gilded cage; their beady eyes beadier than ever, their frozen garments catching on the bars. This caused an unnerving sound of grating as the frozen fabric dragged and plucked each bar in turn, shaking away any ice crystals. All the Ice Witches then commenced a peculiar chant as they glided. It was loud enough to allow the gang to talk to one another.

Cordelia restlessly searched her pockets. 'What are you doing?' asked her sister impatiently. 'I'm searching for that old camera.' she replied

'What!' whispered Mer keeping he voice low incase their frozen enemy could still hear them. 'This is serious, we haven't time for silly photo snaps...our lives are in danger!'

'I know that!' strained Cordelia just as impatiently. 'But, I've an idea.'

'What idea?' Meryl questioned.

'Shh, keep your voice down,' cautioned Cordelia. 'Look, the flash on that camera catches people I aim it at, right? —You've seen that, and this might give us enough time to cast a deadly spell while they're imprisoned inside it!'

'Yeah, but you how do you know if the silly camera and its wonky flash still works, even you said the thing was an old wreck!' chided Delia as quietly as possible for her. 'And, we won't be trying to capture just ordinary people either!'

As she said that, the camera Cordelia was searching for tumbled from her inside pocket and bounced to smack the edge of the cage. Estoriah's raven sharp eyes immediately fixed on it. The Witches of Ice immediately ceased their noisy chant.

'What have you there?' she snapped. Both the Ice Witch and Cordelia lunged for it at the same time.

But the witch's magic worked against her this time; the cage preventing her from grabbing the dirty dented camera away from Cordelia.

'Smile!' she yelled, picking it up. One by one, Cordelia snapped Estoriah and each of her cronies. This time there was no flash with any click of her camera, though there was something even better; the Witches of Ice had actually gone, exactly as hoped.

Peering around the tent, there was nothing to be seen of them, anywhere.

'What happened?' asked Delia 'Are they inside the

the camera?'

'I'm not sure,' said Cordelia. 'There's a good chance, I mean, one second they were in front of the lens, the next, completely vanished...so, let's hope they are!'

As she was saying this, the cage began shaking violently, causing its door to spring open. Everyone, including Belladonna the golden macaw, fled from their temporary prison.

Before their gawping gazes, Belladonna instantaneously changed. Her transformation from a beautiful golden macaw into a *not-at-all* macaw-looking young witch stunned them into silence.

Eventually, Mer walked over to her; and not knowing what to say, simply dusted away some remaining gold flakes from her clothing.

'I'm Mer,' she said.

'I'm Belladonna,' the girl at first squawked, though her voice promptly returned to normal.

In no time, everyone was chatting excitedly with Belladonna, wanting to know all about her, how long she'd been held captive, the pain she must have suffered being cruelly duped away from her parents, and did she actually have to eat macaw food? The latter was Cordelia's daft question, but she wasn't being unkind... just curious.

Belladonna smiled, but as she did, Cordelia let out a sharp squeal; immediately throwing her camera to the floor. It was suddenly freezing cold; so much that it actually hurt. The camera rolled to a stop and was so frigid that it began freezing Gran's precious hand made carpet.

The frost caused by the camera spread alarmingly, making anything in its path crack and splinter with ice crystals.

'Quickly!' yelled Delia. 'Get it out of here!'

With that, she ran and kicked the camera through the narrow tent doorway.

'Crikey!' exclaimed Cordelia. 'The camera did trap the Witches of Ice inside as I said it would. Wow, not bad magic to do that to a bunch of ice crystals haha!'

'Well, it's frightening, actually!' answered Persimmon. 'And we'd better leave fast, before anything worse happens, like freezing us too.'

'Let's go now!' cried Mer and she hurredly read out Melchior's Transportation Spell.

Instantly they were lifted up by a swirl of freezing wind, and shot back to the witch market.

A cloud of green-blue smoke was all that remained to signal to the people of the ordinary little village of Staunch that their world of comfortable normality had returned.

Fortunately for them too, the Witches of Ice had fled the scene after the camera had burst. It was raining when they got back, cold and damp.

Twilight had replaced day and every single witch, warlock or witch-thief had long ago packed up and gone home, wherever that was, leaving the place deserted, quiet, and decidedly creepy.

'I can't say enough to thank you,' said Belladonna. 'I mean, I can't believe I'm going home!'

Mer and all of them smiled. Belladonna turned to wave and in an instant faded into a purple haze.

Feeling good about things, they left Gran's market tent, tied the charmed door strings, read the Locking Spell to keep intruders out, and trudged down the path to he market entrance.

'What shall we do now?' asked Delia. 'C'mon, doesn't anyone have any ideas at all?'

'I s'pose we could head home,' suggested Persimmon meekly.

'Or visit the *Madhouse!*' yelled Cordelia with widened eyes.

There was an eruption of whoops and cheers; they all knew *Esmeralda Peabody's Magical Madhouse* is the only place to go for really going bonkers.

'I can try out my new *Loony Moon Spell*,' enthused Persimmon, appearing brighter. 'Esmeralda's not going to worry if a few things disappear, will she?'

'Or, explode!' chimed Mer.

'Hey, what about that new *Wicked Witch* dance – that's to die for – come on, let's break some bones!' sparked Delia.

'Yeah, you probably will, it's just the place for total brain-cases!' laughed Cordelia. 'I bet the place is already rocking to it!'

'But I just think,' dreamed Meryl, 'I may spend a little time in the *Turvy Room*.'

'Oh, wicked,' cried Persimmon, 'but make sure you come back the right way this time!'

'Yeah,' joined Mer, 'it took us an age to transform you into Meryl again!'

Amid their laughter, the five now had a spring in their steps as they passed under the huge witch market banner just before the main gate exit.

Recognising them, the gate reluctantly and rather miserably groaned open to let them out. Despite the fun of going to Peabody's Madhouse they couldn't help but recap on the day's strange experiences.

From above though, there came a voice; one they'd

hoped never to hear again.

It was the cold rasping, decidedly ghost-like voice of Kaldre, well that's who they thought it was.

What it said was: *'If the Witches of Ice can't find you, I certainly will!'*

The dreaded words floated and wailed through the air several times. Maybe, it was simply a gust of wind playing tricks on their ears and minds, or perhaps a chorus of rustling springtime leaves in the high trees above.

But, one thing's for sure, it didn't take long for them to mount their brooms and soar high into the night sky, turning instantly toward Esmeralda Peabody's extraordinary Madhouse.

Chapter Six

Chapter 6: *Holiday Haunts.*

As Cordelia swept back the heavy cobweb curtains of her and Mer's den, the bright sunlight of a perfect summer's day streamed through. Her head was still pounding from the noise of Peabody's Madhouse, which didn't help with what she saw either.

The sky was as blue as the rare *lapis lazuli* stone, the trees like precious emerald. Butterflies awkwardly and playfully fluttered and skipped from plant to plant, whilst every bee nuzzled deep into each available flower beneath the golden sun.

'If this ridiculous weather doesn't end soon,' spiked Cordelia 'mum will definitely call off our witches' holiday. We need gloom and storms, not sunshine and silly outdoor games!'

Cordelia shook her head in disappointment. The more she thought about it, cancellation was a distinct possibility; and that would hardly be fair after all they'd been through. The sisters were desperate for a holiday.

'What we want is a great big fat thunderstorm.' sighed Mer

'Yes, we do,' agreed Cordelia, and she added more to the imaginary disaster, 'Whopping flashes of lightening, huge dollopy raindrops.'

'...And hail!' chimed Mer as if she was already inside Cordelia's storm.

But it didn't look like it was going to happen. The sun, clear sky, and warmth obstinately refused to go.

'Pity we don't have a spell to conjure dark heavy threatening clouds,' said Cordelia hoping that Mer would say she had.

'Prescilla Flashington had one that would make steam,'

replied her sister, trying to be helpful, 'but I think it got confiscated.'

They both stared some more at summer.

Breaking their *wishing-for-a-storm* concentration, the den door bumped open and in stumbled their favourite Gran.

'Oh...it's far too hot dearies.' she complained fanning her face with a handful of motley ostrich feathers. 'Even, I think, for my two grandest granddaughters!'

'Yes Gran,' the two moaned. Gran smiled and mopped her sweaty brow with the same moth eaten feathers. She wearily stepped over to observe the depressing blue sky from the un-cleaned lead-light windows.

'It's sooo dreadful out there,' she added shaking her head with deepest disapproval.

Dramatically, she threw her arms into the air, and asked 'How about a black thundery storm with thunder-claps loud enough to shake your boots off?'

'Yeah, bring it on!' they both yelled with renewed excitement in their eyes.

'Oh,' she sighed 'I'd love to be able to do that!'

She cackled uncontrollably. Both their hearts sank as they realised their loveable old Gran was only trying to cheer them up.

Just then, their mother strode into the den, and floating behind her was what seemed to be a large and extremely scruffy shipping trunk.

She also brought with her some extremely good news. 'Come on you two, and you Gran, we haven't got time to sit around gossiping, there's loads of packing to do yet.'

Their mother was in one of her fidgety moods again and reminded them of a chicken strutting around pecking at everything in sight.

'Does this mean we're going?' asked Cordelia half expecting her to say no.

'Obviously we are!' returned their mum. 'Why on Earth shouldn't we?'

'But it's so hot and sunny,' protested Mer, 'it won't make for a very good witches' holiday, we need rain and storms.'

'Utter Pofflewaffle!' called their mother 'summers are well known for being dreadful here, and the same's true of where we're going. Now, come on and get packed, we're leaving by first moonlight.'

The family were off to Dragon's Head Castle, run and owned by Mr. & Mrs. Pilchard. The castle was built on a huge granite ledge, which perilously hangs over a roaring and crashing sea some several hundred feet below.

Dragon's Head Castle is near to the little holiday village of *'SunnyPleasington-Next-the-Sea'*, a name that was totally opposite to everything about it. Interestingly, as Cordelia had recently found out, SunnyPleasington-Next-the-Sea is neither sunny, nor close to the sea, or even at all pleasing.

There was even a newspaper article on the place that Gran had told her about. It blamed the scurrilous Lord Mayor, Ian Gratiate, and his cronies, for trying to fool gullible tourists by simply tacking on the letters *'SunnyPl'* to the town's original plain-old name of *Easington*.

"Shameless move!" screamed the headline of the local rag, *"And just to make the place sound more attractive."* it went on. Not according to Daisy, though *"The locals think it's a brilliant way of trapping holidaymakers and no doubt robbing them blind! Why,"* she'd continued, *"the town's coffers are already brim full, and, I dare say,*

the pockets of those greedy councillors too!"

SunnyPleasington-Next-the-Sea lies roughly, very roughly, five miles inland from a coast so dangerous and rocky, no-one in their right mind should dice with their life to be near it, unless they're going to the castle.

As described, Dragon's Head Castle sits on top of a three hundred foot high cliff. There's just one dangerous road to it, and certainly, no one would dream of fighting their way to the castle via the cliff.

There's not even a way up from the miserly two-yard wide stretch of sand below they call a beach either; assuming you'd get to it safely, and in one piece.

And, would one ever risk standing on this calamitous beach, even during an extremely low tide? No, not in their right mind, unless they were a witch or wizard – there's a lot of extraordinary magic that can be done at this spot, especially when standing on the *Wishing Rock* near the crashing waves.

Still, despite all the bad press, many people flock to the place each year, including the Merryspells.

The whole family would travel by umbrella this time for two very good reasons. One; you can see all the sights below you, and two; they keep the rain off.

You don't even need to keep hold of your umbrella's handle to fly. Many witches hook them under the backs of collars or belts. Sometimes a witch will attach a small seat for added comfort, hanging it from the umbrellas by rope. This is precisely how their Gran travelled. But, Myrtle, being totally awkward again, insisted on bringing her bike. She said she would simply stick the handle of her umbrella under the bike's handlebar.

Cordelia had pointed out to her sister many times that this was pretty daft to do. She'd even tried helping her with some spells that would allow the bike to fly by itself. But, as usual, Myrtle ignored her.

The shipping trunk their mother presented them with was unusual. It was about the same length as Mer's height, and around half Cordelia's in depth. It glowed too; and would probably require a few umbrellas to lift once fully packed with all their rubbish, which is how their mother described most of their belongings.

The trunk was dark brown in colour, and covered in loads of paper stickers of various shapes and sizes from places it had visited in the past. It possessed a strong magic, a will of its own, and the name *Gradimir*.

As soon as Mer opened Gradimir, she heard it moan *'Here we go again!'* sighed a voice within.

'Hey...did you hear that, Cordelia?'

'Yeah, there's probably some kind of spirit trapped in it I'd say' she replied.

'A ghost?... really, Cordelia!' replied Mer sarcastically 'like, how did you work that out?'

Cordelia pulled a face. Both of them watched the trunk as it unbuckled itself, unzipped covers, and snapped open clasps; revealing drawer after drawer needing to be filled. And Mer didn't miss her chance to clumsily stuff one drawer with a handful of potion bottles either.

'Oi, they're my drawers, you know!' protested the ghost within Gradimir. 'OK, OK We know!' tutted Cordelia.

There was one drawer though that did have something in it, an old dusty manuscript. And, as it turned out, it had the title *Useful Spells for Difficult Holiday Situations* by Miss Victoria Station, 1875. It was a bit out of date, but Mer and Cordelia beamed at each other.

'This is just the sort of thing we need!' exclaimed Mer 'Are there any others?'

There were, as quite a few witches had used this trunk during many past holidays.

How their mother had missed these books they'd never know. But there they were, as bright as gold and worth every ounce. Amongst the spell books were *Juliska Fogg's Holiday Ruins* and *Haunting for Pleasure* by Clarissia Strange.

Cordelia and Mer's den was filled with a mist of dust by the time they had finished packing. Even the summer sun was having trouble getting through or, so they thought. But, instead, dark clouds had begun moving across the sky.

Mer gazed out of the window and yelled for joy.

'Whooooohooooo!' she cried and Cordelia jumped up to see what all the fuss was about. She wasn't disappointed.

After a few hours the moon had risen high in the sky, and although being only half moon, it was bright enough for everyone to see despite the thickening clouds.

'And you two had better behave yourselves this year!' snapped their sister Myrtle who was, rather stupidly, still trying to attach an umbrella to her bike's handlebar.

'We don't want a repeat of last year's debacle.' she said sharply, testing her bike's bell with a couple of sharp rings. 'Those poor witches, it's a wonder they're still friends of mine!'

'That's precisely what I think,' muttered Cordelia under her breath.

'Oh, don't pick on them.' chimed Gran trying to sit comfortably in the armchair chosen for her flight.

Cordelia and Mer's mother was using one of her special knots to tie extra strong ropes from the chair to the twenty-six umbrellas being used for Gran. Twenty-six, because Gran had put on a lot of weight lately, and it had a great deal to do with the spell book her beloved granddaughters had acquired for her eighty sixth birthday.

It was Marjory Thin's stout looking book on spells for delicious treats called *Piling It In –Seventy Unearthly Spells to Send Your Taste Buds Wild*. The book was a huge success with many witches and warlocks, as well as the accompanying volume *Keeping Fat*.

'Lift off.' cried Cordelia jokingly, and their mother gave her one of those looks.

Hepsibah turned to Gran, gave her a reassuring pat on the back, and read the *Umbrella Charm*.

With that, the witches, including Gran (waving her arms about in excitement as if conducting some great orchestra), and all their clobber, were whisked off into the storm-gathering sky toward Dragon's Head Castle.

Myrtle peddled furiously, which there was absolutely no need to do. Cordelia shook her head.

'You can't tell that woman anything' she muttered.

Both Cordelia and Mer had their umbrellas hooked under their collars. It was the perfect way to read anything by torchlight, especially the spell books they'd found in Gradimir. Strangely, their collars weren't choking them. The umbrellas seemed unaffected by their weight. All the family seemed to float along as light as feathers, even Gran – her extra umbrellas must've helped though.

Every so often the girls, using a spell discovered by Cordelia, swept down for a closer look at something that seemed particularly interesting; much to the displeasure of their mother and Myrtle, who still persisted with her peddling.

By the time they'd arrived at Dragon's Head Castle the storminess had really set in. Surprisingly, Gran remained fast asleep during the thunderclaps and vivid flashes of lightening, which seemed to miss her by mere inches.

As they circled high above the sinister-looking castle, a rain soaked Mr. Pilchard could just be seen, leaning over the battlement waving an old oil lamp attached to the end of a long wooden pole.

'Ahoy there!' he cried as if he was the captain of some ancient galleon.

'Ahoy there, back!' screamed Cordelia through the driving rain and roaring wind. Cordelia's cry awoke her Gran who perkily called, 'Oh, 'ello dear!'

Gathering her whereabouts, old Daisy peered onto the castle below. 'Oi, why's that peculiar man down there waving a big pole at us for, what's he want?'

Gran hadn't realised it was Mr. Pilchard doing his best to show them where they should land. When she eventually touched down, if they're the right words to use, Mr. Pilchard did his best to get her out of her armchair.

'What have you been eating, eh Gran —cream mountains?' With that he burst out laughing. It didn't last long though; one black look from her was enough.

Soon, they were in from the storm and sitting by a huge fireplace in front of a mouthwatering feast. The lovable Mrs. Pilchard had magically prepared it for them with her usual charm. Which one precisely, couldn't be said.

Roast chicken, roasted, and creamy mashed potatoes, peas, stuffing and thick, rich gravy. For pudding there was inevitably the delicious *Mrs. Helena Plumbstuffer's Celebrated Sticky Sweet Surprise Pudding for Witches*.

The surprise in the pudding this time was quite amazing, leaving everyone stuck to the ceiling for a while.

Needless to say, after they'd floated back down again, they soon finished off this delicious treat.

'That was extraordinary, Mrs. P!' said an overfull Gran 'I won't ask for seconds, as I'm watching my weight dear.'

Cordelia and Mer grunted; Gran winked back. By now the girls were quite restless to leave the table and settle into their room.

As they got up to go, followed by Myrtle looking as miserable as the weather, a stern faced Mr. Pilchard had a few choice words to say to them.

'Now, I want you three to be very careful as we have some holidaymakers staying with us this year; and in case you'd forgotten, they're not witches or warlocks like us, so behave yourselves.' Cordelia and Mer's eyes widened.

What luck! thought Cordelia, and her sister no doubt thought *What fun!*

He turned to Hepsibah and Daisy as if to explain himself over this incursion of holidaymakers into their world of spell weaving and potions.

'Well, our visitors simply couldn't get a place to stay in town, I'm afraid. Fully booked they are.' said Mr. Pilchard a little warily 'I can't believe people can be dumb enough to stay in a place like Easington in the first place to be honest.'..

'Oh, don't mind us, Mr. P,' reassured Gran 'the more the merrier, I say!'

'Thanks Gran,' he piped 'Anyway, they were happy to find us, something about staying a while in a haunted castle, they said.'

Cordelia and Mer were positively bursting by this revelation. Mr. P turned his attention back to the girls.

'So, I'm warning you three young'ns, stay out of their

way and don't cause any trouble –you hear me?'

To be included with her two younger sisters made Myrtle furious, and she aimed a sharp kick at them. It missed and hit Mr. Pilchard instead.

'Ouch!' he screamed 'Look what you've done, girl!'

Glaring sharply at Myrtle, he squinted as if focusing all his attention 'I'll be keeping an even closer eye on you for that, Myrtle!'

He rubbed his leg, 'and another thing, don't you dare go anywhere near Easington either!'

He was angry now, and there was more to come. 'Remember, there's a curse on all witches from the castle who perform magic outside of the grounds, the Dragon's Head Curse –it'll come back on yer, you see if it don't. Now be off with you!'

Mrs. Merryspell looked suitably impressed with his *telling-off* ability, smiling warmly at both him and Mrs. Pilchard.

Cordelia and Mer meanwhile had never heard of the Dragon's Head Curse before, and were sure he'd made it up, or, at the very least, the curse didn't mean much at all. Instead, they spent all their energies trying to stifle their sniggers at Myrtle being hotly chastised by their mum for kicking their host.

'I would have expected that kind of behaviour from Cordelia, not from someone entering young womanhood!' she jabbed rather stuffily.

Mr. Pilchard, although prone to these sudden bouts of extreme grumpiness, was actually a very nice man. Gran had often told the girls this *"He just purrs when his guests are peaceful and quiet, especially witches, he knows how easily a rough bunch like us can give a place a bad name!"* she'd once said *"The trouble is, who's heard of a well-behaved witch?"* she'd added *"Apart from your mother, I don't think any exist at all, certainly not me!"*

At that, Gran had burst into fits.

When the girls arrived in their bedroom, waiting for them in the middle of the room was Gradimir their well-travelled trunk; and without any hesitation, he un-buckled himself. *'Now, be careful this time.'* he moaned.

'Oh, shut up!' snapped Cordelia 'Whoever you are, you shouldn't be so blinking miserable.'

The trunk huffed and shook arrogantly. Mer and Cordelia simply ignored him.

One by one they removed the precious contents, quite sure there would be a use for everything the umbrellas and Gradimir had strained to carry: Clothing, including socks, clean *and not so clean*, crystal ball, several pairs of boots, magic mirror, string, potions, hand bell –*you should never be without a hand bell,* frogs, emergency witch-sweets, soot, magnifying glass, hats –lots of them, torches, fountain pens, brooms, oil lamp, and without doubt, their vast collection of spell books.

'What d'you want a flaming bell for?' wailed the voice from within Gradimir.

'Mind your own business!' shot Cordelia 'Trunk ghosts, what would they know? Anyway, I think we're ready now; we seem to have all the all the spooky things we need.'

'Ready for what?' quizzed Mer

'Don't act dumb, woman; scaring the guests of course! You brought all the haunting stuff, and they did sort of say they wanted to see some spirits during their stay, right?'

'Oh, that,' she answered 'but, what about old Pilchy -he'll be on the prowl tonight for sure.'

'Well, we'll have to be extra careful, won't we?' urged Cordelia 'Oh, come on Mer, it wouldn't be a holiday if we didn't do something crazy!'

Mer agreed reluctantly, not keen on facing their mother's wrath if found out. 'OK, it'd better be one scare and straight back here,' she said 'and I mean *one*!'

After witching hour, the two took their brooms and crept from their room. It wasn't going to be easy finding the guests; the castle had a myriad of passageways and hidden corridors. As the storm continued to rage, the sound of waves pounding on the rocks below the ancient castle echoed from every wall and floor.

The castle was dark everywhere, only occasionally lit by strangely glowing lanterns. Eventually, they'd reached a junction of passages. Cordelia came to a halt before a small doorway with stairs spiralling up to another floor.

'Which way now?' she wondered.

Possessing an uncanny sense of direction, Mer pointed toward the steep granite stairway Cordelia was standing in front of. 'I don't know why, I just feel they're up there somewhere'.

When they'd reached the top, she had another strange feeling; she felt sure where the guests were sleeping too.

'I can definitely feel someone up here' she added 'and I'm certain they're down that way'

Mer pointed confidently along yet another dark passageway. Her sister shone her torch, but couldn't make out a thing. 'Nothing, not a sausage!'

'Shh...did you hear that?' whispered Mer in alarm. She grabbed Cordelia's arm like a vice.

'Ouch' yelped Cordelia 'What are you doing?'

'I heard a weird *whoosh*. There it goes again!'

In the near darkness the whooshing sound was all the more worrying.

'Maybe a real ghost?' suggested Cordelia under her breath.

'Or, Pilchy on the prowl like I said,' answered Mer. 'I

think we'd better get a move on'.

Without thinking, Cordelia mounted her broom and shot off into the darkness toward the strange noise, leaving Mer standing by herself. Mer wasted no time joining her impulsive sister.

Upon rounding a particularly tight corner, they slammed smack bang into three dark objects that promptly began screaming.

The girls were instantly knocked to the ground.

They shrieked with fear, so did the strange objects. Cordelia nervously shone her torch at the monsters they were up against; fully prepared to deal with them without mercy.

'Persimmon!' shrieked Mer '...And Meryl ...and you Delia!'

She removed someone's foot from under her chin. 'What on Earth are you lot doing here?'

'We're with my Aunt Eloisa.' replied Meryl picking herself up and retrieving her snapped broom 'We've only just got here...wonderfully brilliant weather, don't you think?'

'Yeah,' added Delia 'Our parents thought all three of us should go on holiday together – but only if Aunt Eloisa came along as chaperone, that's because she's very hard and strict.'

'Cripes, you poor things!' exclaimed Mer.

'No, not at all,' continued Meryl, 'Aunt Eloisa's as soft as butter really, just have to keep her occupied, that's all!'

'Wow! I love your nail polish Pers,' sparked Mer 'that's sick you can get it to sparkle like that.'

'It's one of Melissa Murksome's charms,' she replied with delight. 'Glad you noticed it...look, you can have faces and things appearing too.'

Mer stared at each of Persimmon's nails. 'Blimey, you're right! I can see that good looking Justin Blackthorn you're always on about!'

Pers blushed. Eventually she recovered to tell more. 'The polish changes colour to suit your mood too. It will even change if there's anyone nearby you need to know about.'

'Like who?' urged Mer.

'Well, say someone jealous is nearby; my nails will flash green. Or, if there's a boy standing close with a crush on me, they'll glow pink.'

'What about danger?' asked Cordelia 'Oh, well that's usually black, but a dire warning can turn them red.'

'Stun...ning!' gasped Mer.

'Oh, oh' cried Pers 'they've just gone brown.' 'What does that mean?' shot Mer.

'Either trouble...or a ghost.' answered Pers.

'Oh dear!' called Meryl 'I do hope it's my late Granny Thistle coming to haunt us, I did so like her!'

'Shhh,' whispered Delia 'I think someone's definitely headed our way.'

'Yeah, that'll be old Pilchy.' said Cordelia.

'Who?' Asked Meryl.

'Mr. Pilchard, he runs the place,' answered Mer 'he's OK really, a bit touchy as we've got holidaymakers staying here.'

'We have!' shouted Delia, forgetting the approaching Mr. Pilchard. 'Sorry.' she added.

Mr. Pilchard's hobnailed boots echoed heavily on the stone floor, everyone looked around for somewhere to hide.

'H E R E!' strained Delia.

Before them, with the light of Cordelia's torch, they could just make out a very small old door set in the stones of the corridor wall.

'What is it, a broom cupboard or something?' asked Persimmon.

'Who cares?' hollered Delia, kicking it open. The door gave way with a mournful groan and everyone bundled in. Immediately they were slipping and sliding on a shiny stone floor to hurtle down some kind of steep tunnel.

The stone surface was so slippery and wet their descent was completely uncontrollable. Even reaching out to grab something wasn't any help; the walls seemed to be lined with a slimy moss too.

With an amazing clattering thump, and an understandable arrangement of panic-driven screams, the witches arrived on the cold paved surface of what appeared to be the floor of an inner sanctum. There was little doubt it was hidden deep in the bowels of Dragon's Head Castle.

At least they'd held onto their brooms. Meryl's though was still badly off. And somehow, Mer had lost grip on the bag she'd been carrying.

'It must be somewhere,' she sighed, feeling around.

Meanwhile, back at the small door they'd just fallen from, which was probably a hundred or so feet above them, Mr. Pilchard had arrived.

He stood there puzzled in his heavy hobnailed boots and long brown tartan dressing gown. He was certain he'd heard a strangled cry for help. Or, was it perhaps, merely the howling wind mingled with crashing waves outside? It could've even been his overactive imagination on such a wild night.

At any rate, Mr. Pilchard would never know. And, being none the wiser as to what was happening to the five witches below, he simply closed the creaking door;

locked it and shuffled back to his bedroom, his big boots clacking with every step as he went.

Still affected from the ride down, the girls began peering through the gloom by the dim light of Cordelia's torch as she waved it around this way and that.

'Bursting bat brains, just look at all them *coooool* things everywhere,' cried Delia. 'Sick, aren't they!'

Indeed, the room they'd ended up in was certainly full of peculiar objects for one mysterious use or another. Intriguing old brooms, cauldrons of solid gold and silver, crystal balls glowing in a variety of colours; and stacks of witch hats in all shapes and sizes, some centuries old. Above these were shelves upon shelves of old books, and countless jars of glistening sparkling whatnots.

But, apart from all of that, there was one thing that caught everyone's eye. In a dusty old corner stood a hand carved chair, which kind of glowed and looked a bit like a royal throne.

'Blimey!' cried Persimmon in awe.

'Double that,' added Meryl.

They'd all stared at it for a while. Cordelia said, 'Shall I sit in it?'

'*NO!*' replied the others in one voice.

'You don't know what it'll do, you idiot,' snapped Mer.

Cordelia, though, smiled and said; 'But, on the other hand, we'll never know if someone doesn't give it a try, will we?'

Before anyone could object, she promptly sat. With a breathtaking rush of wind both her and the chair disappeared from the room in a swirling cloud of smoke and sparks. 'Stonking thunderclaps! Where's she gone?' cried Delia.

'I hope she's OK, we did warn her!' worried Pers.

'Wherever she's gone, that's a strange chair,' pondered Meryl. 'Maybe it's from the spirit world?'

Mer fumbled around in the dark for her bag of things that had also disappeared. It contained the oil lamp for emergencies. A light would be pretty handy to her right now, if only to see if her rash sister was anywhere in the room.

'Ah, here's the bag, and my lamp too!' she called. 'I knew I could hear something rattling down after us!'

She soon lit it so that everyone could see.

'Yes, I'd have to say, Cordelia's definitely gone,' confirmed Mer, waving the thing about. 'Though knowing her, she'll find her way back pretty soon.'

She noticed several ancient candlesticks placed around so Mer obligingly lit them. They began searching through all the treasures of this inner sanctum. And, after a few minutes of going through every bit and bob they could get at, a loud wind again rushed into the odd dungeon-like room; and in a swirl of sparking smoke, Cordelia was back.

'Whoa!' was the first thing she uttered, followed by, 'Unbelievable!' in a shivering sort of voice.

'So, where'd you go?' asked Delia who couldn't help notice her friend looking a tad scared at the experience.

For some reason her hands seemed to be firmly gripping the arms of the chair, her knuckles distinctly white.

'I'm not sure,' confessed Cordelia in a trance-like voice. 'I just remember the place we're in spinning and dissolving into smoke. Before I knew it, I'd landed in another room, but this time with drawers covering every inch of its walls.'

'Drawers?' questioned Mer.

'Yeah, old, dusty and covered in cobwebs.'

'What was in them?' pressed Delia.

'Well may you ask!' she exclaimed. 'Each drawer was labelled, I remember that much. The first one though really caught my eye, it was marked *"Home"*. I carefully walked over and slowly pulled it open.'

'And?' urged Mer as Cordelia paused.

'Well, inside was our home in miniature.'

'What, you mean like a model?' said her sister anxiously.

'No, not a model, real! I could even see smoke coming from the chimney, and the trees around it were moving in the wind!'

'Spiritual,' remarked Meryl, thoroughly caught up in the unfolding mystery.

'What did you do?' urged Persimmon.

'Well, naturally, I knelt down to have a closer look, then jerked back in shock!'

'Why?' asked Mer.

'I saw *ME* peering out at myself from our den window!'

'Other world...totally other world,' breathed Meryl, shaking her head.

'Well, I immediately shoved the drawer closed and stood there getting my brain around it all. As I looked about the small room, lined with every conceivable type of drawer you could imagine, I caught sight of a drawer marked *"Holidaymakers"*.'

'That's daft!' said Delia.

'No, not really, when I pulled the drawer open, sure enough there were two holidaymakers, snugly snoring away in a miniature bed. And I thought, blimey, they must be Ol' Pilchy's guests!'

'Crikey,' said Delia. 'Did you prod them awake? ...I would've!'

'No,' replied Cordelia, 'as by this time I was beginning

174

to feel really strange about the whole place.'

From her description the girls were beginning to feel a bit weird about it too.

'Is that why you returned so quickly?' asked Mer.

'*Abso-blinking-lutely,*' gushed Cordelia. 'I jumped straight back in the chair and was instantly whisked here before I knew it.'

'Well, at least you got back,' said Persimmon.

'Trouble is,' continued Cordelia, 'I wouldn't mind having another go, I think my nerves would be up to it now!'

'Even better,' added Delia. 'Why don't we all go together?'

'Yeah, I'd love to see what's in the other drawers,' breathed Meryl dreamily.

'Alright, let's do it!' replied Cordelia, 'but are you lot ready for something more than a bit disturbing?'

She didn't need an answer, everyone, including Mer with her bag of junk, charged toward the peculiar chair with brooms tucked under their arms; landing in one big heap and somehow hanging on without losing their grip.

Once more came a tremendous rush of wind. Before the witches' eyes, the stone-walled sanctum spun and disappeared into smoke. Sure enough, just as Cordelia had described, they ended up in an odd-shaped room with a high ceiling, and the walls panelled with drawers.

This time, Cordelia noticed a small fireplace before them. She viewed with intrigue the motto inscribed into the arched opening.

"Everything is Here." it stated. *That's curious*, she thought.

They flew about reading the labels of various drawers.

'Ah, here's the one marked *"Holidaymakers"*,' called Delia. 'And I've got one marked *School*!' replied Cordelia.

'By all the ghostly witches!' sighed Meryl, 'haven't I got a drawer marked Sunny-Pleasington?'

'That's nothing,' cried Mer, nearly at the ceiling of this tall strangely glowing room, 'I've found one labelled *"Forest of Evil"*.'

Delia swooped up to take a look.

'Who's for going there?' she cried. None volunteered.

'C'mon you lot, where's your spirit of adventure?' she urged. No-one seemed keen.

'Well, what if we tried the drawer later?' Delia pleaded. Mer nodded reluctantly. 'Mmm, maybe.'

'Actually,' chimed Cordelia, 'how about we haunt old Pilchy's holidaymakers? After all, it wouldn't be a complete holiday without scaring somebody, and Mer, you do have your bag of tricks with you!'

'Yes, I do, and you literally pestered me into bring the required candle, silver and soot for summoning ghosts,' added Mer, waving the offending items in the air.

'Well then, it would be a crying shame not to use them. You've even got your trusty hand bell to wake them up!'

Agreeing, they approached the drawer in question, opening it slowly so as not to disturb the sleeping occupants.

'Aw, would you look at that now, they're all so beautifully tiny,' said Meryl, peering down on the miniature Bracknells lying peacefully asleep.

'Well, we're obviously not going to climb in!' answered Pers. 'So, why doesn't someone reach in and get them out, if they're only miniatures, no-one will come to harm, will they?'

She was as unsure as the rest of them.

'Go on,' urged Delia.

Meryl, with great delight, delicately pushed her hand into the drawer before anyone else had a chance to object. What followed was simply amazing, taking the witches completely off guard.

The magic chair they'd been using flew from behind with great speed, gathered them, and somehow pushed the witches into the open drawer. It appeared to be shrinking them in the process. In a split second, the two sleeping holidaymakers had company.

The shock for the witches continued as they soon realised the room they were in now wasn't the one filled with drawers, they were either inside the drawer they'd just been staring down at, or actually inside the Bracknell's bedroom.

'How on earth did that happen!' exclaimed Cordelia, awkwardly trying to get to her feet. The chair in its rush to capture them had caused everyone to become entangled, and she was lucky not to have strained anything whilst extricating herself from the knot of arms and legs.

'I mean, how could we just shrink like that into this stupid drawer?' she asked whilst extricating her left leg. 'We didn't,' answered Meryl, wrestling with Pers to try and free herself as well, *'We were transported!'*

'She's right!' added Delia. 'We're now in the holidaymakers bedroom, if you want to know.'

'Well, straighten my wand,' enthused Mer, 'who'd have thought it? Well, I 'spose, as we're here, we may as well get on with the haunting.'

Mer and Cordelia laid out a silver spoon, a candle, and poured a palm full of best-quality chimney soot. They did this on a small bedside table close to the snoring holidaymakers.

Mr. and Mrs. Bracknell had come from the village of Unwary, a twisted road away from the hamlet of Alert, and some three hundred miles south of SunnyPleasington-Next-the-Sea. They didn't stir. Both witches continued the enchantment with a series of high-pitched chants whilst Mer rang her hand bell. It was truly enough to awaken the dead, let alone the Bracknells.

Delia, Pers, and Meryl looked on, amused.

But, despite their racket, the Bracknells remained soundly asleep. So, Cordelia opened a book she possessed on haunting, and under the chapter *"Terrifying With Ghosts"*, she read out an *Evocation Spell* –well, at least she tried to.

The charm was not easy to read. It was far too dangerous for someone to use the spell casually, as it could invoke spirits who probably wouldn't appreciate being woken at such an unsociable hour. Especially just to perform like spirits in a bizarre circus act.

Trouble was, for her, nowhere in this tatty old book did it actually explain the enormous risks of using these spells. Furthermore, it never covered the likelihood of severe injury or even death resulting from annoying any already deeply disturbed ghostly beings. And that was a near hundred percent possibility too.

Cordelia, nonetheless, looked at the instructions for the Evocation Spell. It plainly read: *"Under no circumstances should anyone attempt reading this tongue-troubling nightmare of words, even just to see whether in fact it can be actually read in less than the prescribed eight seconds, as stipulated by the author, who, for safety reasons, shall remain a mystery"*.

So, at last Cordelia now fully understood that if the spell

weren't read in under that time it just wouldn't work.

"A third of a silver filigree spoon of soot,
An upturned candle uncertainly stood,
A thrice-trod step thoroughly good,
A painful shrill shout petrifyingly put."

'A third of a silver filigree spoon of snot' was incorrect, so, Cordelia failed her attempt. Mer took the helm, pushing her sister away, clearing her throat and commencing with, *'A third of a silver filigree thpoon of thoot...'*

She broke away in laughter and fought her sister with barrage of equally tongue-troubled renditions, which resulted in all the witches butting in to be the first to finish the wretched spell. Yet, still the Bracknells snored happily in their sleep.

Eventually, it was Persimmon who completed the task successfully, in 7.6 seconds; though soon enough, she'd rather wished she hadn't.

It was already very dark in the Bracknell's room even with lightening from the storm outside momentarily illuminating their surroundings with occasional stark blue-white flashes. Nevertheless, it quickly got darker.

'I think it's time to shout and awaken the ghosts,' said Cordelia. '...And the Bracknells.'

'But, what do we shout?' asked Delia.

'Would you want something petrifying?' suggested Meryl wryly. They laughed and in one voice shouted five different words, more than loud enough to wake the dead.

Their discordant chorus had a direct affect upon the Bracknells too, who awoke with a start; though the kind of sleep they awoke from wasn't exactly what the girls expected. It was the sleep of the dead: Mrs. Bracknell and her husband, Charlie, were ghosts already, and therefore hardly required haunting.

A tremendous crash rattled the air, a bit like a huge bell tower crumbling and falling to the ground right in front of the girls. It silenced them. More ghosts had arrived, and they certainly weren't there for fun and games. The room became even darker and a few degrees colder.

Persimmon was the first one to scream out, followed by the others in unison.

Out of the walls came several translucent spectres, quite unformed. None of the witches could make out their faces, probably because they hadn't any, yet the ghosts howled a loud terrifying moan all the same.

The ghost of Mrs. Bracknell stood and pointed directly at Cordelia.

'She's the one, Charlie!' Then she scowled at her. 'you be warned, witch. Terror awaits you all. The book will not save you, neither the spells inside!'

With that, Mrs. Bracknell, Charlie, and the host of translucent spectres charged toward the witches shrieking at the top of their ghostly voices. The girls turned to run but were overtaken.

Something like a wave of misery and utter darkness overcame them. It was mixed with a feeling of terrible despair, which swept them into temporary unconsciousness. With a rush of wind they were once more back in the room of drawers.

'What the screaming turnips was that about?' stuttered Persimmon, awakening from a daze.

'Don't know,' choked Meryl. 'I didn't even have a clue the Bracknell's were ghosts! They certainly fooled old Pilchy.'

"Terror awaits us?" mused Cordelia, who, for the first time in ages seemed greatly worried. 'It's a warning from the Witches of Ice, I'm sure of that!'

'I'm afraid she's right,' said Mer to the others.

It wasn't nice coming to terms with this realisation, and the musty darkness of the room didn't help. The four walls and ceiling, covered in labelled drawers, somehow appeared more ominous than before.

'Well, we'd better carry on, I s'pose,' muttered Pers.

'Yeah, maybe the next drawer will be a real bag of fun,' added Meryl ironically.

'You mean, you guys still feel up to this?' asked Cordelia.

'Definitely!' cried Delia. 'I'm not going to let a bunch of half-dead ghosts give me the creeps!'

A degree of laughter returned, and there seemed renewed enthusiasm.

They began searching the drawers once more with many suggestions floating across the room from one witch to another. Drifting higher and higher upon her broom, Meryl decided to join in. Without tape or a decent broom-mending spell to mind, she held together her recently snapped broom handle. At least it allowed her to move about.

'How about this,' called Delia from near the tremendously high ceiling. *"Starch-Stiffington's School for Well Behaved Young Witches"*.

Everybody laughed once more.

'Would you not think this a little odd!' called Meryl. 'I'm not believing what's written up here; *"The Home of Melchior Fizz"*,' she announced.

'It's a trap, don't you dare open it!' snapped Cordelia.

'Alright, alright...' called Meryl. 'Will you just keep your wig on now...I'm only telling you!'

'Sorry,' apologised Cordelia, 'it's these loony ghosts and the Witches of Ice; they're making me flaming nervous –you never know where and when they'll appear!'

She smiled guiltily, and charmed her hat to bow respectfully to Meryl who grinned back.

'Yeah,' added Mer. 'I want to meet this wizard too. But, whoever's running this place would hardly be friends with him. So, I'm afraid, like Cordelia said, it's definitely a trap!'

'Hey, here's one marked *"SunnyPleasington-Next-the-Sea"* –Now that's a lot closer to home than where Fizz probably lives,' interrupted Persimmon.

Everyone shot up to see the drawer she was staring at. Delia was the first one to reach over and slide the drawer open.

Inside the drawer Meryl held open, they found themselves staring down at a sinister rain-swept building illuminated by occasional flashes of lightening.

'What the heck's that place?' said Delia.

'I don't know, maybe a prison?' answered Meryl. 'My cousin Shaun is in prison and he's being saying for years that he possesses a spell to escape, which is daft actually as now he's only two days from release!'

They leaned in to take a closer look.

'Well, SunnyPleasington doesn't look very pleasing to me, that's all I can say,' moaned Persimmon.

Mer grunted an agreement, adding, 'Yeah, there's not even a fun arcade or anything.'

'OK, what are we going to do?' urged Persimmon. 'Shall we go, then or what?'

'I vote yes,' confirmed Delia. Meryl agreed.

'Could be a lot of fun,' added Cordelia. Mer charmed the chair to rise closer to them this time; and as they all took hold, she reached her arm into the drawer. In an instant they were spun from the room in a mist of smoke and dust.

Curiously, as they now stood outside the ominous looking Victorian building, its tall windows stirred a feeling of awe. So too did their metal bars reaching from top to bottom of them. The dark stoned bricked walls were just as uninviting.

'Is it a factory or something?' asked Pers, climbing out of the magic chair.

'Not sure, but whatever they've got in there,' remarked Delia, 'must be very precious. I don't think anyone could get into that place!'

'Or out,' shot Cordelia, walking over to the stern-looking outer wall.

As they peered up, their attention was drawn to a heavy metal sign hanging over the large foreboding door, which was as daunting as the rest of the building.

The sign read, with the help of Cordelia's torch, *"Mrs. Emily Killkipper's School for Bullies"* with the school motto written just below in a beautiful scroll; *"We'll teach them a lesson or two!"*

'How do we get into this place?' enquired Meryl eagerly.

'You could try bullying your way in!' suggested Delia.

'Ha, very funny, not,' she answered.

'Maybe with a few powerful spells, no doubt,' continued Mer.

Yet, to their surprise, the main door unlocked itself with several clanks and a grating noise of rust upon rust.

Slowly, as the giant door opened before them they could see a darkened entrance hall. Beyond that past a narrow stairway awaited another door, which appeared to lead out onto a courtyard.

The witches, with trepidation, walked through holding their brooms close to. In seconds they'd walked across the hallway, avoiding the temptation to take the stairs. They passed through the second door, which had been magically opened for them, and nervously stood at the edge of a massive quadrangle.

With the huge dark stoned walls of the Victorian-looking school looming each side, all five stared at the centre of the square where they couldn't help notice an ominous square tower that seemed to reach up into the very clouds.

From inside came the curious sound of snoring.

'Who'd be sleeping in a place like this?' asked Pers.

'Idiots?' suggested Delia.

'No, I think it'd have to be bullies, as we're in the middle of a bullies' school,' answered Meryl.

'There's a thumping lot of 'em if that's true,' said Cordelia, 'shall we take a look?'

The five ran to the perimeter of the tower, looking for a way in. They found the main door. It was made from thick oak, heavily barred, and bolted, rising to a Tudor style stone arch.

'We're not going to get through that in a hurry,' said Persimmon. She was wrong; Meryl had just the spell already, beating Cordelia to the task by a fraction. She'd found a spell by an extremely clever witch, Ryszarda Dietrich from Bavaria.

Her book, roughly translated, *Keys, Locks & the Whole Silly Business*, has a charm to undo just about anything, right up to bank vaults. Meryl read Ryszarda's elegant *Unlocking Spell for Heavy & Ancient Doors*. With a clunk and several grinding sounds the old door shyly opened with predictable creaking.

What they saw was quite a shock. Rising up over two hundred feet was a tower of single bunk beds, one on top of the other with people sleeping in them. There must have been over a hundred beds at least, probably nearer two hundred.

Attached to the side was an equally long ladder for the kids to climb with. And, because this single, very tall, vertical dormitory reached so high, the beds disappeared into a mist; plausibly low cloud.

The whole structure appeared unstable as it wavered and twisted slightly to every move the bullies made. Nightmares, or simply turning over, would not be ideal, as every movement affected the peculiar tower. Its wooden frame groaned unnervingly with their constant restlessness.

'I think I know why everyone here has to be a bully,' said Delia.

'Why?' asked Pers.

'Well, because if so, they'd have no-one to pick on, excepting each other. Which means, there'd be no bullying anywhere in the school!'

'Yeah, right,' said Cordelia, unconvinced.

As the witches craned their necks, Delia spotted an old dusty cobweb-covered enamel sign; it was screwed to the nearby brick wall. She nudged Cordelia, who had to wipe off the grime before she could read anything; obviously, no-one had bothered to look at it for years.

The others gathered around as she read the sign by the light of her flickering torch.

"Notice To All Bullies" it read. *"The most desirable bunk beds are nearest to the ground as they require less climbing to get to. If you're sleeping at the top, and fed-up with climbing all the way up there every night, you'll*

have to 'bully' your way down, won't you? Just remember though, only pick on someone less advantaged than yourself, otherwise, you won't be a bully anymore. And, I dread to add; you'll have to go back to normal school to finish your education. Signed Emily Killkipper, Headmistress."

'Well, that sort of puts them in their place, don't you think?' asked Delia.

'It does,' agreed Cordelia, 'which makes me kind of think that these kids could be desperately in need of some amusement...maybe we can help?'

Just as she finished saying that, the girl on the lowest bunk, which would probably mean she'd be the head bully, snorted awake with a start. Upon seeing the witches standing around gawping at her, she screamed: 'Quick!...Everyone wake up...Invaders!...Let's get them *–ONE HAS RED HAIR TOO!'*

The moving creaking tower of bunk beds erupted into an explosion of activity. The whole tower wavered dangerously as countless kids clambered down the ladder like ants, throwing and catapulting anything to hand at the five witches.

But the witches whizzed off into the air. Meryl could at last join her friends as she'd wound a piece of her deliberately torn dress to mend her broken broom, casting a holding spell over the binding just for good measure. They flew, spiralling up the tower of bunk beds, laughing, and weaving between each of the narrow bed openings.

The head bully thought flying was something she could do. Not having a witch's broom to hand, she instead reached for the school's dormitory broom.

Her flightless jumps were no more than a couple of feet

186

high. Embarrassed in front of her underlings, she tried to save face by climbing up the ladder into an oncoming rush of kids climbing down, pushing them out of the way punching and swearing at them as she went.

Getting to about twenty feet off the ground she attempted once more. It was a painful failure and she was lucky not to break her neck, or worse, someone else's.

Seeing this, Cordelia thought that maybe they all needed a little help with flying; and summoned every broom in the school, casting a flying spell over them.

As soon as the rabble of ratty half-broken sweepers arrived, weaving through the air this way and that, the kid's eyes lit up with excitement. Balancing precariously off the bunk bed tower, they reached out to grab whatever flying broom they could.

To try this was a big mistake. A few, holding on for dear life, quickly realised that they were in deep trouble. Most crash-landed, some traumatically; and some even ended up wedged into the sides of the bunk tower. If it were possible, they were angrier than before and baying for the witches' blood.

Cordelia and the others couldn't help but laugh. As she zoomed down, she suddenly saw a tall, thickset woman of obvious authority, standing at the base of the tower holding a large megaphone. Her voice boomed aloud.

'You there, stop this nonsense and come down here at once, you nasty little brats!' she roared at the young witches.

'Not a hope, lady!' yelled Cordelia.

It was at this point that Mrs. Killkipper decided to set her bullies to work on bringing the witches to book.

'Come on you weak-kneed bunch, don't just gawp at

them, throw something...hurt them, bring them to me. I want to see bruises, blood and broken bones!'

Without much thought at all, the bullies at the top of the bunk-bed tower, commenced ripping and tearing at the wooden frame, breaking off handy lengths of wood; and using them like javelins to throw at them.

Regrettably, with even less thought, so did the kids on the lower bunks. The whole bunk bed tower soon became dangerously close to collapsing.

'I can't bear to watch!' yelled Persimmon.

'Me neither,' added Delia, 'I think I'd die laughing!'

All feeling the same, the witches immediately flew back to the magic chair still waiting outside the school, hotly pursued by an avalanche of long spears of freshly snapped pine as well as a megaphone-screaming headmistress.

As the five jumped onto the poor creaking chair to escape, they could hear the clatter of falling timber from the now collapsing bunk-bed tower. In a spin, the chair hurtled them back to the room of drawers.

After a dizzying arrival, the girls, still hanging onto the seat for dear life, were sped up to the drawer marked *"Dragon's Head Castle"*. Cordelia, again tangled amongst her friends, managed to pull it open and reach in. 'Come on, let's get back before we're missed!'

Another spin, another gust of wind, smoke sparks and dust, and the magic chair sent them inside the strange drawer. But the sides of the drawer once more quickly disappeared and they were at once outside and beneath a storm-filled sky. Like an out-of-control wheelbarrow, they were shooting along the rain-swept road beside the castle.

The witches' untimely and untidy arrival back at Dragon's

Head was certainly dramatic. The battered chair continued to skid down the wet driveway that led to the main gate, only just stopping and falling to pieces right before an angry-looking Mr. Pilchard.

His face was angry dark and above him mauve-blue flashes of lightening forked through the sky, making him look almost wizard-like and scary. But somehow, it didn't work with him standing there in his tatty dull brown tartan dressing gown and matching soggy slippers.

'Pull yourself together, you silly old chair!' he cried and the chair did as it was told.

'Been out all night, have we?' he shouted to the five witches as the wind billowed out his old moth-eaten dressing gown, revealing striped pyjamas and those ludicrously large slippers.

The gale force wind seemed powerful enough to sail him off into the threatening storm above, but it didn't.

'Look at the mess you're in, what will your parents say, eh? Bet you didn't think about that, did you?' he yelled above the howl of the rough weather.

The rain pounded the ground harder and all of them stood there getting ridiculously drenched.

'Oh, and where did you find Sarabeth?' he demanded. The witches were about to ask Mr. Pilchard who this *Sarabeth* was, when a sound like an approaching wind-borne tree or something filled the air.

It wasn't a tree, but several lengths of broken bunk bed timber flying like javelins seeking a target.

'I told you to remember the Dragon's Head Curse!' he cried, unaware of the coming danger, '...things will come back on yer, you see if they don't!'

Naturally, the witches, being quite experienced from

"Sarabeth"

190

recent events, ducked for cover. Happily for them, the wood whizzed past but, unhappily for Mr. Pilchard, found him instead. Battered to the ground, he eventually emerged from under a pile of snapped and twisted timber.

He was even angrier than before.

'That does it!' he bellowed. 'Your parents will hear about this, right away!'

They began to snigger at the sight of a dishevelled and soaked through Mr. Pilchard standing in his comical soggy nightwear.

Their amusement never lasted, however, as each felt a pulling at their ears. Mr. Pilchard possessed much mystical ability, and they were led into the castle with the strange chair floating behind.

'Who *is* this Sarabeth?' pressed Cordelia, wincing at being invisibly dragged by her left ear.

'I don't know!' answered Mer, in similar discomfort. This was followed by more pain-induced murmurings from the others who hadn't a clue as to whom Mr. Pilchard was talking about either.

'Sarabeth is my magic chair!' he boomed indignantly, putting their minds but not their ears at rest.

'Oh dear,' sighed Cordelia.

'And you had no business taking her without my permission...that alone will earn you a week in the castle dungeon!' Mr. Pilchard seemed to brighten a little at the thought of this, even to the point of sniffing a kind of laugh.

Eventually, their ears were lowered and they were in front of Mrs. Merryspell, Myrtle, their Gran Daisy, and an astonished Aunt Eloisa.

Myrtle was so happy about her sisters being in trouble

she couldn't keep still. Her face was just as busy, not deciding whether to smile, frown, appear manic, or even smug.

'These little wretches have been up to a whole lot of no good, Mrs. M...' said Mr. Pilchard in a growling voice. '... and you indeed, Aunt Eloisa; being that you're guardian to the other three.'

Aunt Eloisa smiled in a dazed sort of way.

'Firstly, they got into my secret basement and took Sarabeth to the village. Not content with that, they had a go at the poor kids residing at Emily Killkipper's magnificent prison... er, establishment. Ask me how I know? Look at the mess I'm in!' he said, plucking large splinters from his wet and tatty dressing gown. Pointing to a couple of worrying bruises on his face he added, *I'm damn lucky to be alive!'*

Aunt Eloisa Foolhampton fully appreciated Mr. Pilchard's angry sternness; as well the need to teach her charges a few lessons, but really, she hadn't the first idea on how to punish them.

'What do you recommend, Mr. Pilchard?' she asked coyly.

Mrs. Merryspell joined with Aunt Eloisa's request, but much firmer and added a little extra.

'Better make it nice and severe, otherwise they'll think they've got off lightly!'

Myrtle was overjoyed and started fidgeting once more.

'Keep still, dearie,' said Gran. 'I'm sure they were all innocently led into this, how could anyone think they're to blame!'

Gran's comments made no difference to Myrtle who knew, at last, her sisters were in serious trouble.

'Well, Mr. Pilchard, what do you think?' asked their

mother.

'Normally,' he offered, 'I'd suggest sending them straight back home, but that means you grown-ups would miss out on your holiday, and that ain't fair as I see it.'

'Quite right!' added Aunt Eloisa 'Why, I haven't even had a chance to dip my toes in the sea yet.'

'Lucky old sea, I say!' said Delia in a whisper.

'That's why I feel they should spend a bit of time in the castle dungeon, meself,' said Mr. Pilchard with a smirk of revenge.

'What a thoroughly good idea!' agreed their mother, 'why not make it for the rest of their holiday?'

At that, Aunt Eloisa smiled and nodded in agreement. Myrtle was ecstatic and burst into a manic cackle. Gran scowled at her.

'But mum,' pleaded Cordelia, 'it'll be dark and horrible down there!'

'You should have thought of that before you started playing with magic, shouldn't you?' she said.

There was no answer, just a remark from Mer warning everyone that there could be monsters in the dungeons, and they probably wouldn't survive.

Mr. Pilchard denied this.

'There are no beasties in my dungeon,' he said, 'but there is a light and a little food, if you deserve it. You'll find a few books to read as well.'

Cordelia's eyes lit up.

'No, not spell books, good learning books by that lovely Prunella Primm on how to behave yourselves,' added Mr. Pilchard as he watched their smiles disappear.

It all seemed rather bleak for the five of them as they were led down the twisting stone stairway. Mr. Pilchard placed a large, thoroughly charmed key into the lock of the heavy dungeon door. Slowly and noisily the door creaked open.

Before them was a dimly lit stone walled room. It had rough-looking wooden beds and benches, several cupboards and long shelves of *"Primm's good learning books"* for them to read. Their prospects were as bleak as the dungeon they'd be in for the rest of the week.

As Mr. Pilchard pulled the heavy door closed behind them, he whispered something to the witches. 'Oh, and by the way, you can make as much noise as you like down here...nobody will hear you, screams or otherwise!'

With that he began to snigger as he locked the door. It was spell-locked too for good measure.

'What on earth are we going to do now?' asked Delia.

'Read those terrible books I s'pose,' replied Meryl.

Cordelia immediately searched her pockets for a spell to help them out. 'Blimey...they're gone!'

'What's gone?' said Persimmon.

'My stupid spell books, and everything!' Hardly had she finished saying this when a strange whooshing sound filled the air. There was a bang and thump, and before them spun Sarabeth, Mr. Pilchard's precious chair.

Meryl was the first to reach it in the scramble, but held the others back from sitting. 'Wait a mo,' she said, 'isn't there something a weensy bit odd about our little chair of wonders?'

'Like what?' enquired Delia.

'Don't you see it? Isn't Sarabeth a shade bluer than usual, and does she not have a kind of glow about her now?'

'Oh my spotty socks! ...She's right!' cried Mer. 'I wonder

what it means?'

'Could be that old Pilchy fixed her so well that she's up to speed and raring to go!' added Cordelia.

'I'm not so sure about that,' suggested Persimmon 'Maybe it's a trap.'

'Nonsense!' protested Delia. 'I think Cordy could be right. Besides, maybe Sarabeth has a spirit trapped inside her and it sensed we needed help. Hey, that's why she's glowing!'

It took them a while to decide whether they should use the chair or not, but eventually settled on giving it a try. Persimmon was still pessimistic; and, although reluctant, eventually agreed to go.

Cordelia was the first one brave enough to sit, and alarmingly, as she sat it shook with a violent shudder. Delia was delighted by this and followed her. Meryl closed her eyes for guidance, eventually drifting over to join them; more nervously, Pers followed her.

As they held onto the chair tightly, the dungeon and everything in front of them soon went into the expected spin, causing an explosion of smoke and sparks.

They arrived back in the room of drawers in one piece, and, with dismay, saw their brooms leaning against the wall, waiting for them.

'Wow, my broom's been repaired!' exclaimed Meryl.

'Fortunate,' remarked Delia.

'Fortunate, but not likely,' suggested Persimmon.

'Oh, don't be a doubt-monger,' snapped Delia.

Mer flew high up, and could see there was something different about the room. She called down, 'Hey, everyone, who's noticed the drawers are missing labels this time?'

'Yep, I have. None here,' confirmed Cordelia.

'I wonder why?' reasoned Pers. 'It just doesn't make sense. How are we supposed to know what's in them?'

'Ah, here's one with a label!' yelled Cordelia. *"Forest of Evil"* it says.'

Delia swiftly moved in alongside her.

'Oh, wow!' she cried. 'That's where I wanted to go first time around!'

She beamed widely at the others; and, presuming their agreement, summoned Sarabeth.

Delia reached into the opened drawer. As before, each held onto their brooms as they were wrenched into Sarabeth's strange dimension.

The room spun before their eyes and everything turned to smoke.

In a fraction of a second they were thrown from Sarabeth, and, in the nick of time, managed to mount their brooms. All of them swooped and swerved between the giant pine trees of the strange forest, trying to regain control.

'Where did Sarabeth go?' yelled Pers. No-one knew.

Fear painfully coursed through through Persimmon's brain and body; it was almost consuming. Yet, there was worse to come. Racing into the dark and nightmarish Forest of Evil, they had their first encounter. It was a giant apparition of Kaldre's alarming face. It seemed like a cloud of smoke when first spotted. The witches couldn't avoid it either as they were forced to fly right through her giant screaming mouth.

Without warning, the second encounter was the disappearance of their brooms; and in mid-flight too. They instantly spiralled helplessly to the forest floor.

The screams from Kaldre and screeches from the witches of her coven reached their ears.

Only the small limbs of trees below slowed the witch's rapid descent to ground. Snap...snap...snap went the branches one after another as they hit them. At least it broke their fall, not their bones. This crisp branch-breaking sound mingled with their terrified moans, and echoed across the cold, silent forest.

Amazingly, the girls kind of landed safely. As they did, the forest instantly fell silent. Except, though, for the dull croaks from hundreds of frogs and toads along with the hoots of countless annoyed owls.

'What now?' urged Persimmon, scared and shivering, barely able to stand upright.

'Find our way back, I 'spose,' answered Mer.

'Crikey!' broke in Cordelia. 'Look, over there...I can see a light in the distance.'

She was right. Far off, a soft green-blue glow could be seen glinting through the trees.

'What is it?' asked Meryl.

'Just a sec, and I'll tell you,' replied Cordelia, reaching into her pocket and pulling out her small brass folding-telescope.

All of sudden, she realised her pockets were full again.

'Blimey! I've got everything back! And guess what?' she cried peering through her telescope '*It is Sarabeth!*'

'Another trap, you mean,' urged Persimmon. 'Like the first one I warned you about and nobody took any notice of!'

'Well, there's no mistaking this time,' added Cordelia, still looking, 'it's Sarabeth, alright.'

Despite their differing opinions, they realised they hadn't much choice in the matter but to make for the chair; they wouldn't find their way back without Sarabeth.

'Come on,' said Delia to a reluctant Persimmon, 'Let's

make a start at least.'

The first steps were difficult: they hadn't any light, magic, or even a broom. It took them nearly an hour to reach it, and what a surprise awaited them when they did.

There Sarabeth sat, almost translucent; the chair's magic nearly depleted. Cordelia, a lot more familiar about the Witches of Ice since reading Melchior's valuable book, knew exactly what this meant and what to do about it.

'Jump!' she screamed to everyone, 'jump on Sarabeth, we haven't much time!'

Without disagreement, they leapt straight onto the chair. Thank goodness they did.

As they spun away, desperately hanging onto Sarabeth, the Forest of Evil behind melted into an overwhelming whiteness.

Twisting and turning, the young witches spiraled into a whole new and very disconcerting experience. Their ears thrummed to the clang and clatter of church bells, singing, and voices; voices that were cold, hard and unforgiving.

'Almost time...almost time...life almost drained away,' said one, repeating it over and over.

'Death,' said another, a little more sweetly, *'death is like closing your eyes, gently losing all feelings, and dreamily giving away hope.'*

Her words were followed by something even nastier.

'You're in our realm now, the new realm of witchdom. There's no more fun and games...this is deadly witchcraft.'

Several grey whips of mist-like beings glided and wove around the witches as they spun, reaching out to grab at them as they swept past.

The beings never said a word, but the witches heard their deadly thoughts and felt their icy presence.

Illustrations
by Maxine Gadd

Delia   Mer   Cordelia   Persimmon   Meryl

Drucilla & Herbert await their guests

1205

The extraordinary "Darkington Chalice"

Starch-Stiffington's School for Well Behaved Young Witches

Miss Emily Starch-Stiffington, *Headmistress*

"Warts 'n All" Gran Daisy's Market Tent

213

Dragon's Head Castle

The peculiar Room of Drawers

217

Chapter Seven

Chapter 7: *Wedding Belles.*

It was like waking in hell. Everything around blazing hot, though Cordelia felt frozen to the core. The heat and flames gradually disappeared and she felt normally warm once more. Above appeared an endless pattern of glinting silver specks set against an eerie blackness.

Cordelia jerked upwards and realised she was awake and staring at the starry Heavens. The scent of a pine forest filled her nostrils. As she looked about she could see the others awaking. But, there was another transition. Now, they were no longer in the Forest of Evil, and the black sky had changed to stone, an arched stone ceiling. Somehow, they'd all been returned to Pilchard's dungeon, but only at the appointed moment.

Mr. Pilchard was a stickler for timekeeping, and this was near their exactly appointed time to be released from imprisonment. Standing outside the dungeon door waiting, he looked intensely at his shadow clock. When it pointed precisely to the ninth hour of the new day, he reluctantly placed his huge charmed key into its equally huge lock. What he saw once the door opened simply amazed the man.

'Get out of it!' he grated in disbelief. 'What...all of you, still here? Blimey, you just wait 'til I tell your parents!'

With that, he pointed to the door and motioned them to leave, still shaking his head in disbelief.

'Obedience... I never thought I'd see the day,' he muttered whilst following them up the stone stairway to freedom. He held his lantern, fixed to a long pole, high enough for everyone to see through the darkness.

After they'd been reunited with their respective guardians, seemingly cured of the desire to provide gushing recounts of all they'd endured, and how sorry each of them was over their crimes, the five, almost trance-like, bid farewell to the Pilchard's, Dragon's Head Castle, and each other.

Once back home, Cordelia and Mer slowly began to recover from their experiences in the Forest of Evil, especially their shocking encounter with the Witches of Ice.

Neither was able to unload any of this onto their family, even Gran. It was just too powerful to come to terms with. They'd grown much older over the past week, well beyond their years.

It took many weeks and much healing from friends, books, even school to put them both back on track again. Needless to say, it was the same for Meryl, Pers, and Delia.

But, at last, there came a welcome distraction for the girls, taking them right out of their malady; *Myrtle, their crackpot sister, was to be married.*

The announcement, whilst shocking to some, principally considering whom the groom was, provided a great distraction. Immediately, the sisters poured their efforts into this very big occasion.

In due course, the day of this remarkable wedding dawned. As the dark of early morning gave way to an unenthusiastic light, Cordelia and Mer managed, with little difficulty, to outshine all as the brightest wedding belles ever, definitely, much brighter in fact than the dull greyness outside.

Nevertheless, this was their older sister Myrtle's wedding day and its miserableness was exactly what she had always dreamt of for the perfect witch wedding.

Her sisters, despite many conflicts in the past, sort of

loved their older sister Myrtle. Many though would find that hard to believe, especially with all the wrangling between them.

Still, the years had flitted past and Myrtle stood proudly in her silver-spun wedding dress that seemed to match beautifully the heavy clouds that hung low in the sky.

Rain wasn't foreseen by anyone, although Gran did predict a stormy future, but that had nothing to do with the weather.

Myrtle's heart's desire was none other than Colin Mistook, a shy, soft-hearted kind of warlock who really didn't like making his mind up over anything much at all.

It was commonly rumoured that Myrtle had made up his mind for him over this fast-approaching event.

And, to add to the woes, their wedding appeared to be going off-course. Not because of any mismatch, Myrtle just wouldn't allow anything like that. It was because someone at the Registry Office, where they were to be officially married, had double-booked the *'Merryspell – Mistook'* ceremony with another party of eager-to-be newlyweds.

So, instead of the ceremony being at three o'clock, it was changed to the earlier time of eleven o'clock, this very morning in fact, and it was already past nine o'clock.

This inexcusable change to scheduling didn't please Mrs. Merryspell much at all either. No, not one bit. And that's why this morning, of all nerve-wracking mornings, everyone's nerves were even more wracked than usual.

'Stop fidgeting girl!' cried Mrs. Merryspell, irritably. 'How do you expect me to cast this finishing spell properly on your wedding dress if you keep moving about?'

'But we're going to be late, and it's too loose on me,' complained Myrtle, who'd been "off her food lately with nerves," as she put it.

'That's precisely what the spell will do,' continued her mum, 'tidy up all the seams. And please, don't keep worrying about the time, we'll do it easily!'

Mrs. Merryspell didn't believe this for one second, but would do anything to keep Myrtle from fidgeting even more.

Mrs. Merryspell had ordered and received perhaps the finest wedding spell book a mother witch could ever want to own. In fact, she had already promised to loan it to at least seven other desperate mothers who were having trouble finding suitable grooms for their particularly difficult daughters.

The book was the highly sought-after Ms. Delicia Curvington's *Hook, Line & Clincher* –an inspired volume that set out the spells for hooking the unwary groom, the fashion lines expected at a typical witch wedding, and as a bonus, featured all the trappings necessary to *"clinch"* the magical day.

'Tying the knot, eh?' asked Myrtle's uncle, Wistar Asteroi, knowing full well she was, otherwise he wouldn't have been there to ask silly questions in the first place.

This was especially so because he was dressed from head to toe in a stylish grey top and tails, sporting a flock of the reddest hair; whilst handing around a ginormous plate of freshly fried *friggle-chips* and *charmed-chicken-egg fritters* for the guests to nibble on.

Uncle Wistar was a devilish load of fun; both Cordelia and Mer adored his childish pranks, and he wasn't about to let them down.

Seeing his mother, their favourite Gran Daisy Asteroi,

sitting by the window with many adoring fans and putting on quite a show, Uncle Wistar walked over to offer her something from the plate he was holding.

'Mother, my dear,' he said, 'care for a *Charmed-chicken-egg fritter?* They're very 'frittery' today.'

'Ooh, you lovely boy!' she said, 'I really shouldn't as I'm watching my figure.'

At this, she cackled, saying to her gathering, 'I'm probably the only one who would be watching it!'

She burst into a bout of giggles. Politely, so too did her small audience. Gran then reached over to the plate offered by Uncle Wistar. He was using one hand placed underneath the centre, like one of those fancy waiters in a very posh restaurant. With his other hand he whipped out a white napkin for her to use. It all looked very impressive and Gran smiled graciously as she chose a particularly flat and crisp Charmed-chicken-egg fritter.

The first man on Earth to charm a chicken egg was none other than the revered Gregory Peck, a West Country warlock and part-time amateur thespian.

To charm a chicken egg is relatively easy. Providing, importantly, you posses the right spell and a few peculiar ingredients to sprinkle on them.

Once a hen's egg is charmed, the recipient tastes whatever food they most desire. Naturally, the downside is that they can be charmed to do many other things too. Hence, Uncle Wistar's seemingly generous offer to his unsuspecting mother.

Licking her lips in anticipation of the exquisite taste she may encounter, Gran opened her mouth wide to accept the incoming treat. With the fritter in-between her jaws, she took a healthy bite.

At once, she jerked back in her chair as the fritter turned

into a bat, flying off with her false teeth gripping it firmly. The whole room burst into laughter as Gran chased after her teeth, waving her broom as if it were some kind of butterfly net.

'WISTAR!' screamed his sister Mrs. Merryspell, 'PUT THAT PLATE BACK AT ONCE, I TOLD YOU BEFORE; THE FOOD IS FOR THE RECEPTION AFTERWARDS.'

'Oh, is it really, Hepsie?'

'You know very well it is, so stop mucking about, and don't call me Hepsie, my name is Hepsibah if you don't mind.'

Cordelia couldn't help a stifled chuckle. Uncle Wistar winked at the two young witches whilst ducking beneath Gran's broom and returned the offending plate to the table.

Outside the Merryspell's stone cottage, there echoed a sound not unlike thunder. It wasn't thunder, thank goodness, it was the arrival of Gawain Merryspell; Cordelia, Mer, and Myrtle's father.

He'd simply floated down by magic from the murky sky in his precious and very old bi-plane. Its engine was roaring madly, and although he didn't need it running at all, he couldn't resist doing so for the sake of the racket it made. He didn't need a runway either, because it could easily drift between the trees to land safely in their garden.

Mr. and Mrs. Merryspell, although separated, still saw a lot of each other, and so too their children. In fact, everyone was the best of friends, for now, anyway.

Gawain stepped out, magnificently dressed, to be greeted by his three loving daughters. Naturally, he'd bought everyone a present from the various places he'd visited.

After giving Myrtle a big hug, he presented her with a most exquisite silver tiara. It was breathtakingly beautiful and encrusted with precious and magical stones of every variety.

Myrtle's face couldn't have been more glowing if she tried. Not even one of Cordelia's more bizarre spells could have done a better job. After hugging her dad again, she took the precious object and placed it upon her head. All the guests gasped at the transforming effect it had on her.

Even Myrtle's silver-spun dress glistened almost to the point of being dazzling. Her mother joined them in the garden, and Mer was sure she could see a teardrop gently rolling down her mother's cheek as she walked toward her soon to be married daughter.

'Oh, my sweetheart,' she said, 'you've made us all very proud. Today, you have become a woman, and in a little while a wife as well as a very talented witch!'

Mer choked at that last comment, whilst Cordelia developed an artificial cough. 'Talented?' she called to Mer under her breath.

Then, she raised her voice and eyebrows, calling out in laughter, 'I hardly think so!'

For this she got a sharp dig in the ribs from Mer who could see the frowning stare coming from their mother.

'And for you, young Mer, I've brought you something, well a little exotic, let's say,' called her dad.

If Mer's eyeballs hadn't been firmly held in place, by now they would be stuck to the stunning purple, gold and silver bridesmaid's gown that Gawain held up proudly. None other than the legendary dressmaker Jemimah Silk of Paris had created it.

Naturally, the dress was enchanted. Mer was as stunned as Myrtle now, and held it across both her raised arms, almost expecting it to float off into the heavens due to its precious and almost ghostly quality.

'Shall I wear it, Mum?' asked Mer keenly, despite the time she'd spent designing and making the bridesmaid's dress she already had on.

Mrs. Merryspell nodded a smile. 'You can always show off the dress you're wearing at Cousin Rachel's wedding next month.'

Mer didn't hesitate, rushing into the house, even forgetting to thank her father, but he just smiled at her enthusiasm.

He turned to Cordelia next, with a smile so cheeky no-one would have any doubts as to where she inherited hers.

He presented her with an odd-looking box, hexagonal in shape, almost wider than Cordelia could stretch her arms apart and taller than the average witch's cat.

She could hardly carry it but did so out of sheer determination. Thanking her dad with a wink, she fled the garden and rushed toward her and Mer's den.

As Cordelia hurried through the den door, Mer was performing a pirouette in her new dress.

'What do you think?' asked Mer.

'Who are you, and where are you hiding my sister?' replied Cordelia jokingly.

'More importantly,' continued Mer, 'what's in your fantastic-looking box?'

It was fantastic-looking as boxes go, and on the lid was a superbly painted bumblebee with bold white and blue lettering that read *Bumble Bee's Best Quality Spoilers*.

Below that was the motto: *"Everyone is spoilt for choice!"*
Cordelia lifted the lid. What they saw inside made their mouths fall open. Bumble Bee's Best Quality Spoilers are sort of like ordinary party-poppers, only bigger and stranger –much stranger.

By now, everyone was ready to depart for the Registry Office to make Myrtle and Colin legally married.

Obviously, it wouldn't do for the wedding party to travel to the Registry Office by broom or even Gawain Merryspell's bi-plane.

So, Mrs. Merryspell had arranged for a fleet of very expensive-looking cars to pick them up at the Wary Traveller Hotel in nearby Lower Wyshing. It was wisely decided the cars avoid driving up to the witch's cottage.

'Can you imagine the rumours the drivers would spread upon seeing our place?' defended Mrs. Merryspell to her friends.

Following an uneventful broom ride from the Merryspell cottage, and a short walk to the Wary Traveller, everyone stood outside waiting for the wedding cars to arrive. There was a real buzz of chit-chattering about everything from wedding spells to wedding belles.

'They're here!' called Mer at last, and the first car, the largest, drew up and stopped beside Myrtle and Colin.

The driver, dressed in a rather smart grey top hat and tails, got out and courteously opened the door for Myrtle and Colin to climb in.

This procedure was repeated at all seven cars, and the grand-looking procession drove off with the happy, excited guests discussing the wedding, and the reception afterwards.

Cordelia and Mer shared a large Rolls Royce with their

Gran and Uncle Wistar. It was splendidly sumptuous inside with plenty of room.

'What does this red button do?' enquired Cordelia.

Uncle Wistar looked up with a gleam in his eyes and provided the required information.

'It sets off two honking great sirens that pop out of the roof.' Then leaning closer to Cordelia and speaking in a whisper, as if he feared anyone might overhear him, said 'They're to warn people to get out of the way because there's an emergency wedding taking place.'

'Wistar!' snapped Gran, 'don't tease them so.'

'Sorry,' he said making an attempt to amend his behaviour, 'it's actually an ejector seat button for when passengers get bored and want to escape!'

Cordelia grinned dubiously, and still curious, slowly and carefully reached over. Quite unseen, she pushed the red button very hard and closed her eyes in dire expectation. Her seat immediately jumped up and Cordelia at once opened her eyes in shock as she bumped her head on the car's roof.

She had only risen a couple of feet, but was sure she was going to go through the roof. Uncle Wistar burst into a fit and cried, 'Got you!'

The intercom then snapped on.

'Yes, madam?' came a rather refined voice. It was the driver, evidently, who wanted to know what the passengers required.

'I do beg your pardon,' said Gran in an unusually respectable tone, 'my family were playing about... so sorry.'

'Thank you, madam,' said the driver and the intercom speaker gave a little click as he switched off his microphone. Cordelia narrowed her look at Uncle Wistar and gave him a smile, which said; *You'll keep 'til later!*

Sweeping along the beautiful country lanes, the fleet of wedding cars headed for town and the awaiting Registry Office. Just past the village of Little Hope, Cordelia knew it was time to get back at Uncle Wistar. She pretended to burst into a short bout of coughing so as to take out one of her forbidden spell books.

She held the book cupped in her hands. Not even her sister noticed; Mer was simply gazing at the countryside gently passing by.

The tatty and well-used book was Edwardo Flynt's *Deep Magic*. This volume, of all deep magic works, was not one to be trifled with, especially for an inexperienced witch. If her mother ever discovered her with it, well, it wouldn't be worth thinking about.

Gran was chatting away to Uncle Wistar as if there were no tomorrows. Naturally he'd heard all her exploits many times over, though he smiled politely, taking graciously what seemed to Cordelia as 'just-punishment' for his mischief. If any time was a good time, it was now, as Uncle Wistar was far too occupied with Gran's repetitive exploits.

Eventually, her constant chatter took hold and his eyelids began closing, readying him for a well-earned sleep. Cordelia, reading a spell she thought would be perfect, muttered the words in a low voice.

Without warning, Cordelia's, or should that be, Edwardo Flynt's, spell, began affecting Uncle Wistar. Awaking from a not yet full-blown sleep, his body started to change shape. At first, his bright red hair grew longer and longer, eventually covering his entire face.

Reaching his arm up to investigate, his hand missed his face by more than a foot, hitting the seat behind; his arms had grown by a full foot in length.

His trouser legs appeared to shrink, or so it seemed. But, Uncle Wistar now had long hairy legs, which pushed him up out of his seat. He jumped up and down squawking just like an orangutan.

His first act was to knock poor Gran's beautiful flowery hat from her head and attempt eating it. Still jumping up and down, he reached over to Mer, tugging her cloak, trying to feed her the remainder of Gran's once flowery hat.

Gran snorted out of control like a tickled pig. Their merriment was only interrupted by the sound of the car's intercom snapping on again.

'Is everything OK back there?' asked the very sober-voiced driver who was obviously unaware of just what was going on behind him.

'Oh yes, couldn't be better!' reassured Cordelia, as Uncle Wistar changed back to his normal self.

Throughout the remaining journey, many spells and tricks were played on each other, much to their amusement, and much to the puzzlement of the poor driver who found it hard making sense of his odd passengers.

Their car eventually arrived at the Registry Office and everyone followed Myrtle, as she appeared to be pulling Colin through the main door.

Traipsing up a narrow wooden stairway, they arrived in a large office with oak panelled walls and an awesome arched lead-light window that took up most of the wall facing them.

The official, who had developed an annoying tickle in her throat, beckoned the couple, their parents and witnesses to step up to the rather grand table she stood in front of. She didn't actually say any words, as she was too busy spluttering.

Cordelia and Mer couldn't quite hear everything the woman eventually said between coughs, but it did sound very proper.

As Myrtle leaned over the table to sign the legal document, Cordelia received a nudge from Uncle Wistar who was holding a small cardboard box for her.

'Come on, then', he said, 'best hurry if we're to make the guard of honour, and don't worry, your Aunt Eunice has the brooms.'

He tapped his nose knowingly at her and Mer.

'I now pronounce you man and –kerrrrrrstrife!' sneezed the official in a loud explosive snort. Well, that's what Cordelia thought she'd screeched as the three hastily exited to join the guard of honour.

Outdoors, along both sides of the short pathway that led from the Registry Office to the High Street, the Merryspell and Mistook families, with the help of Uncle Wistar, formed an archway of broomsticks, with Cordelia and Mer at the end.

Both had their pockets stuffed with things to shower the happy couple. Several passers-by looked rather oddly at them, one even took a photo; and Cordelia put on a deathly expression especially for him.

'You all look like witches, if you ask me!' he returned sarcastically.

Gran heard this and leaned toward him saying, 'And you look like you'd make the perfect husband, come here dearie!'

With that, she attempted kissing him whilst winking with both eyes. She only just prevented herself from falling on top of him from laughter. The man ran off in quite a hurry.

The huge Registry Office doors eventually burst open and out rushed a triumphant Myrtle, and a fairly washed-out Colin, followed by Mr. and Mrs. Merryspell. A bewildered but proud and happy Mr. and Mrs. Mistook followed.

Uncle Wistar guiltily nudged Cordelia with that small cardboard box shown earlier. He tapped his nose again and said deedily, 'This *confetti* will help!'

Cordelia's eyes lit up as she lifted the lid to see a collection of *Bumble Bee's Best Quality Spoilers* inside.

'Where did you get these?' she asked her uncle.

'Never you mind!' he answered with a grin.

'What d'you think, shall I throw them now?' urged Cordelia.

'Yes, now!' cried Mer, and in no more that a few seconds, the whole place turned to complete pandemonium as the sisters let off a volley of Spoilers.

Myrtle literally dragged poor Colin through the rapidly falling-apart archway of shakily held broomsticks, diving for refuge into the waiting Rolls Royce.

Sadly for them, a few Spoilers, including a couple of real shockers from Uncle Wistar, managed to whizz past into their car for the romantic, or maybe not-so-romantic journey to the hotel. As the newlyweds sped off, the remaining guests were still fending off a barrage of those wayward Spoilers.

After quite an eventful journey, the vehicles again drove majestically along the Wary Traveller Hotel's broad lavender-bush lined driveway. The air was thick with summer's perfume. Heavy grey clouds hung even lower in the sky as the cars arrived outside the front entrance.

The chauffeurs climbed out and courteously opened the doors for their odd customers, even though they thought the lot of them were completely barking mad. It had been a job they wouldn't forget in a hurry.

'Oh, you're so polite, young man,' called Aunt Eunice as the driver reached down to grab the end of her unnecessarily long dress. It had become trapped under the car door as he tried rushing her out in an attempt to get away quickly.

'*Sorry Ma'am,*' he offered.

Myrtle and Colin stood, well kind of stood, as they tried ridding themselves of the last of Uncle Wistar's Spoilers. The rest of the family and guests soon joined them.

It didn't take long for the drivers and their fleet of grand-looking cars to speed away from their mad guests, promptly disappearing into a cloud of exhaust smoke and tyre screeching dust.

Somewhere way off, a loud horn interrupted the guests' excited chatter, and each looked round sharply to see Merg, the school coach, approaching at some speed. But Merg looked different today. He was clean and respectable, and brightly sporting a warm yellow paintwork with a charming twist of green and mauve ribbons, terminating at the front in a spectacular arrangement of flowers of ever-changing colours.

Mrs. Merryspell had arranged to borrow the coach from Miss. Starch-Stiffington just for the journey home.

She thought Merg would be a sensible choice after such a lot of celebrating, mainly based on advice given by Cordelia. Soon, everyone had bundled aboard, sitting happily in their designated seats, which too had been transformed into things of beauty.

Their positions ranked from the most grown up at the

front seat next to an aloof Mrs. Pitheringae, with varying degrees of friends and relatives placed behind them.

Naturally the children, Gran and Uncle Wistar filled the rear seats.

All seemed to be going well as the driverless coach made its way gently and peacefully down the driveway.

In no time, it joined the tree-lined main road leading out of the village, and smoothly rode along just like any other respectable-looking coach. This very much pleased Mrs. Merryspell, and her snobbish friend Valerie too.

But, once they were out of sight of prying village eyes, things changed dramatically. Merg became more like his old self and swerved violently off the main road, snaking past every tree he could find, or so it seemed to Mrs. Merryspell who by now was holding onto whatever handrail she could find.

Her knuckles and face both shared the same shade of white. Embarrassed, she smiled helplessly as her guests bounced around in their seats. Mrs. Pitheringae's ridiculous hat slid off under her seat.

Mer, Cordelia, Gran and Uncle Wistar, on the other hand, had begun playing "coach-football" with Valerie Pitheringae's now rather bedraggled and badly torn hat.

Gran, as expected, cheated by flying on her broom, strictly not allowed by the rules only just invented.

Spinning the hat toward the back window, or goal, as they called it, Uncle Wistar dived at it with a saving header. The hat lodged itself firmly on his head.

It was at that moment that Merg began ploughing into the ground, sending him sprawling to the coach ceiling. He soon came down though. Merg was getting deeper and deeper as they tunnelled through the earth.

234

Perhaps this was the coach's way of saving Mrs. Merryspell from suffering those nasty tree-twisting turns.

With a brain-shattering bang, Merg shot out of the ground and into the daylight once more. They had landed right outside the Merryspell cottage.

Sadly, the front garden now had a tunnel feature, though Cordelia was sure she had a spell somewhere to fix that... Not that she would be suggesting anything to her mother for a while. Mrs. Merryspell's clenched hands still appeared firmly affixed to the handrail at the front.

A shaken Colin, and an acutely angry Myrtle were the first to leave, followed by the rest of the wedding party in a similar condition.

Except, that is, for Gawain, who was nattering about the experiences of their coach ride with his daughters and Gran. Uncle Wistar, who strangely still wore bits of Valerie's poor hat, occasionally joined in with his re-enactments of various diving hat saves.

Eventually, everyone was decanted from the coach, including a still shaking but fortunately placid Mrs. Merryspell, much to Cordelia's relief. The agitated guests were then herded as gently as possible into the main room of the Merryspells' home, which had been decked out in an amazing display of magically changing decorations and illuminations. There was plenty of food for them to stuff themselves silly with too, including those bizarre charmed-chicken-egg fritters.

As far as Cordelia and Mer could tell from being at the reception, for no more than fifteen very long minutes it must be admitted, receptions are all about a lot of people standing around with glasses of champagne and either toasting someone, eating nibbles or talking about absolute drivel. Except for Gran and Uncle Wistar, that is.

Their conversations were wildly entertaining, covering things like their maddest adventures, the most disgusting spells they'd ever cast, and how close they'd ever come to being found out for doing something they shouldn't, or being trapped and completely lost somewhere incredibly scary.

According to the sisters, these were real conversations. And, not even a *"May I introduce you to..."* or *"Goodness me how she's grown..."* in any sentence whatsoever.

Spending just twenty minutes discussing things with either Gran or Uncle Wistar, felt to them like they'd been talking for mere seconds.

So, sadly, when they were both dragged away to mingle with other guests, Cordelia and Mer developed an instant attack of utter, utter boredom.

In fact, if it wasn't for the large brown and gold spell book loaned to them by Uncle Wistar, with a nod and a wink it must said, the poor things would have gone into a coma.

The book was quite remarkable, as it happened, being the one and only spell book by a very gifted wizard. It was Hector Springlock's *Marvellous Spells for Marvellous Machinery*.

What attracted Cordelia particularly were the excellent and finely detailed drawings on the front cover featuring several precisely interconnecting cogs and gears in a simply amazing-looking machine.

This, she thought *is definitely going somewhere.*

And she rather hoped that it would take them along.

Just what connected to which, and why, fascinated

her greatly.

"A cog is a very peculiar thing," Hector once said. And as all this was running through Cordelia's mind, she caught sight of something invitingly red in the garden. In an instant all feelings of boredom evaporated into thin air.

'Mer!' she cried, 'Look what I see.'

With a furtive look, Cordelia pointed directly at their father's bi-plane.

'NO!' shrieked Mer. 'No way in this whole wide world, are we going to take Dad's bi-plane! Definitely not! Not now, not ever, not anytime. And it's no use you asking, either'.

Five minutes later they were both seated in the cockpit. Even now, Cordelia was buried in Hector Springlock's masterpiece of working magic upon machines. She had already located the relevant chapter on aeroplanes and had skipped through the various headings until finally settling upon *"Propeller Engines –Spells for both Single and Bi-planes"*.

It must be added, that even to Cordelia, Hector Springlock's spells are strange to read; and highly mystifying as to how they come to work on mere machinery, but they do.

Once the first verse of this spell was read, the whole aircraft became covered in a sort of blue glowing plasma gas with green sparks shooting out of the prop-engine's exhaust. There was no noise, except for Cordelia's loud exclamation of *'Whoa!'* as the propeller blades silently whizzed into life.

Cordelia was thrilled with Hector Springlock's amazing spell. They even found two pairs of goggles on the rear seat of the cockpit.

'Strange, that, I wonder if Dad knew we might be tempted to fly?' asked Cordelia ridiculously.

Mer shook her head. Quickly, they pulled on their goggles and were ready to go.

'None, but the brave!' cried Cordelia.

'...or the mad,' added Mer.

Silently, the bi-plane lifted and quite slowly weaved toward the trees. They were away.

Staring nervously across at the house, they were relieved no-one noticed their departure. Even the window overlooking the front garden was strangely unattended.

In fact, it seemed not even a small explosion would have distracted the huddled gathering. All their attention appeared to be focused on the family table.

But why? wondered Cordelia. Then she saw it.

Occasionally, through the window she spotted the tops of various witches hats, and the odd leg or pointed boot rising up and down to some kind of tune.

The person at the centre of this attention quickly gave their identity away to her by completing a giant leap above the crowd. It was Gran dancing on the table, and everyone was gawping at her bright yellow poker-dot bloomers in shocked amusement.

Cordelia couldn't have hoped for a better distraction, and seizing the moment, she and Mer together cast a particularly strong floating spell. With the plane lifting further away from the squeals and gasps of Gran doing her little number, the two secretly wished they could be there cheering her on.

Eventually, with the witch's cottage only just visible below, and a strong fresh breeze blowing, they decided to give the sparking, glowing engine the power to move them forward.

Cordelia, positioned in the driving seat behind Mer, held up Hector Springlock's *Marvellous Spells for Marvellous Machinery* and began reading his *areoplane-thrusting* spell.

In no time, the girls were holding onto their hats as the bi-plane shot forward to the demand of the now roaring prop-engine.

'THIS...IS...STONKING!' shouted Cordelia as they swept through the fog of a large white cloud.

'YES...IT...IS,' yelled Mer. 'GOOD...JOB...WE'VE...GOT...GOGGLES!'

Cordelia and Mer had never flown an areoplane before, but they had seen their dad flyit on several occasions, and it appeared that all he did now and again was to *'waggle that stick in front of him about a bit'* as Cordelia put it.

With the help of that stick, they were diving and weaving just as good as when using their brooms, though it was somehow a great deal more fun.

The two certainly weren't as careful about being seen in the bi-plane as they were with their brooms. In what seemed like no time at all, they had flown several miles. The witches were flying over a place they were quite unfamiliar with.

It was *Bishops' Stocking*, a village they'd never been to before. The place was a charming collection of normal-looking houses and cottages huddled around a grand Norman church, and beyond that, a few fields, and very thick woodland.

'SEE...THE...WOOD...AHEAD?' screamed Cordelia above the wind and noisy engine.

'YEAH, GREAT!' cried Mer. 'CAN...WE...GO...DOWN...NOW?'

Cordelia nodded with a broad smile. At once she

adjusted the various controls sending it into a dive. It was a bit odd not using spells for this.

With a flurry of panicked pushing and pulling of the same controls, the plane eventually swept along gracefully. She smiled smugly, almost as if she'd been doing this sort of thing for years.

At last, Cordelia gave the command for the engine to stop. Without its power, they glided smoothly over the treetops of the dense woodland.

Presently they could speak without screaming, and both chatted about the things they'd noticed below, making a mental note of where to go upon any return visit.

'Yikes!' yelled Mer, 'Look at that over there!'

'That, over there' wasn't a particularly good instruction for Cordelia to follow, so naturally she replied with *'What, where?'*

Mer then thrust her arm toward something that was very dark and pointed, and not so far ahead.

Cordelia glided the bi-plane closer. This thing she'd noticed was sticking up a little higher than the surrounding trees. It looked decidedly strange too. But what seemed even stranger to Mer; she was sure it wasn't there when she'd looked a few moments ago.

'Hang on,' called Cordelia, 'we're going in.'

With a few deft movements of the plane's controls they drifted toward the tall object. When they'd got close enough, they both realised what it was, and were quite dumbfounded.

'Fancy putting a thing like that up in the middle of a place like this,' puzzled Cordelia. 'And to make it visible only to witches when it suited them as well,' pondered Mer.

It was in fact a witch's tower, made of wood and mud

and rope and things. How it stood up at all was amazing. Obviously, it was charmed.

Nevertheless, there it was wavering even in the fickle afternoon breeze. They swooped past the tower several times, barely missing it with the end of their bi-plane's wings.

'Ooops! I forgot about them!' exclaimed Cordelia as she swerved violently away just in the nick of time.

They turned once more for yet another look. As the witches swept by, a loud cry of '*HELLLLLP!*' echoed from the tower and across the wood.

With a shocked look at one another, Mer used a strong floating spell to make the bi-plane glide to a slow stop outside the top of the tower beside a small barred window.

'Help me please!' said a voice from inside.

'Who are you?' asked Mer.

'My name is Nevara Applewood, and I'm supposed to be marrying my true love at three o'clock this afternoon.'

Before them and held captive behind some rusty old iron bars was a beautiful young witch dressed in a long flowing gold and black wedding dress with a stunning gold tiara upon her head.

'The only trouble is,' she continued in a very distressed voice, 'I'm being held prisoner by two ugly old witches.'

'But, they can't keep you from your wedding day!' insisted Mer.

'Oh, but they are!' she cried.

'Surely not, how could they do such a thing?' continued Mer.

'Because I'm young and pretty and too useful around their dirty crumbling tower.' With that, the poor witch started howling bitterly.

She was exceptionally pretty, this Nevara Applewood, her hair was almost green-blue black, like a raven, her face finely featured, and she had the deepest purple-blue eyes the girls had ever seen.

'Don't worry,' exclaimed Cordelia, 'I'll throw you a rope and we'll pull these bars away.'

'It's no use,' replied Nevara Applewood, 'the witches have cast a spell on the place; so I could never escape –you'll have to forget all about me.'

'Don't panic, we'll get you out eventually!' yelled Cordelia.

'Thank you, I'm sure you mean well,' she continued through streaming tears, 'but I have to be at the Registry Office in Lower Wyshing by three o'clock, so it's probably too late already.'

'No, it's only just two PM now,' chirped Cordelia, looking at her pocket watch, 'we'll get you out. And we know where the office is as my sister Myrtle and Colin were married there earlier.'

'Colin?' quizzed Nevara, not crying as much, 'he wouldn't happen to be Colin Mistook by any chance?'

'The very same,' replied Cordelia, 'why, do you know him?'

'Oh no, not really, who did you say the girl with him was?'

Butting in, Mer answered proudly, 'Our elder sister, Myrtle, actually.'

'So that's the girl?' blurted Nevara.

'What makes you say that?' asked Mer.

'Oh, it's just that I used to go to school with a girl named Myrtle, that's all.'

Nevara was interrupted by a shrill cry from within the tower.

'Get away from here!' the voice screamed.

Sure enough, it belonged to someone offensively ugly. Pushing Nevara aside, the hag leaned toward the barred window. Between the bars she poked her long crinkled old nose followed by a very decrepit looking broom, sharpened at the end. Her nose and the sharpened broomstick were remarkably similar in appearance.

After this, she lanced at them with both, though her nose seemed more effective in keeping the girls at bay.

'Excuse me,' cried Mer in defiance, whilst avoiding each jab of the old girl's nose and sharpened broom handle, 'you've no right keeping this beautiful bride from her wedding, just look at the state her dress is in.'

At that point, another witch, just as old and revolting as the first screamed, 'She's no bride, she's a menace to society and our prisoner –so clear off and mind your own stinking business!'

Quickly, she joined in with the first witch, thrusting something at the young witches between the iron bars.

At first, Mer thought it was a sword or lance, but it was a murdered dragon's tail dried and bound to a pole. She maliciously swept it from side to side; certain to annihilate anything that came into contact with its razor-sharp scales and central frill.

'Don't worry, Nevara, we've a plan and will be back soon to set you free,' assured Cordelia.

'Have we?' puzzled Mer.

'No,' confided her sister honestly, 'but we soon will have.'

Cordelia started the engine with Hector Springlock's spell, and they flew off.

High above the tower, Cordelia put the bi-plane Into a

dive, which panicked Mer to say the least.

Over the once quiet, but now noisy engine, she cried, 'WHAT...ON...EARTH...ARE...YOU...DOING?'

With a broad smile, Cordelia yelled, 'TRUST...ME... IT'LL...WORK!'

This was understandably of little value to Mer, being very familiar with her sister's madcap ideas and outrageous risk-taking.

The closer the plane got to the witch's tower, the more the colour drained from Mer's face. Interestingly, the reverse was true for Cordelia's.

At full speed, the bi-plane headed toward the witch's tower, levelling off a little so that Cordelia had more of a side-on view. Its engine's buzz hummed warmly through the summer air.

But this did little to make her sister feel any easier, as she didn't even know Cordelia's plan or indeed whether it would be wise, let alone dangerous.

'PLEASE...TELL...ME...WHAT...YOU'RE...DOING!' she demanded.

Cordelia replied with something Mer really didn't want to hear.

'I'M...GOING...TO...DRILL...A...HOLE!'

Before Mer had a chance to scream out, *what, are you mad?* the bi-plane's propeller ripped through the top of the witch's tower, and Nevara flew out upon the old crone's dried dragon's tail, free at last.

'Look what you've done!' cried Mer as the plane's engine spluttered to a halt. At once, Cordelia peered at the twisted and mangled propeller.

'I see what you mean, we'll have to find a spell for that.'

She hardly had time to open the cover of Hector Springlock's brilliant book on spells for mechanical marvels, when they heard a large thump on the plane's upper wing.

'Lead on!' cried Nevara Applewood triumphantly.

Cordelia and Mer strained from their cramped cockpit looking up to see her standing mid-wing and angry.

'Crikey!' exclaimed a surprised Mer.

Peering down at their alarmed faces, Nevara added, 'The thing is, Applewood is only one of my names, the name that is truest of all is, *The Mad Witch of Arageth!*''

'O...K...' drawled Cordelia slowly.

'Trouble is,' cried Cordelia, hoping it would strongly deter Nevara flying with them, 'although we want to get you to your wedding, we've sort of lost our propeller, which sort of means we might not reach the Registry Office for a long...long time.'

Nevara leaned over the wing to get a better look at the witches, and with a particularly crazed look said, 'We'll get there alright, I'm not called mad for nothing!'

A mighty roar, a bit like a hurricane-force wind, filled the air and the plane carrying one stark staring crazy passenger; standing ridiculously strident upon the top wing, shot off at lightening speed.

Cordelia, still looking up at her, could see that her gold and black wedding dress had now become fire red.

She called out urgently to Mer. 'Can you smell something burning?'

Alarmed, Mer leant out of her seat sniffing vigorously. At once she caught sight of the wing above; it was definitely on fire. In seconds it produced a trail of flames reaching all the way to the tail of the bi-plane.

'Quickly!' she yelled to Cordelia, 'give me your spell book on putting out fires.'

Even if Cordelia could find a spell book on putting fires out, which she couldn't, it would have been far too late anyway as the skin covering the top wing was almost burnt through. Only the frame of it remained; and strangely, that refused to burn. Even stranger, the plane was still flying perfectly.

'Can we really be flying fast enough to burn like this?' cried Mer. Then she noticed her sister furiously pointing up at Nevara. Mer strained to look.

The mad witch was herself the cause of the fire as sparks and sheets of flames coursed from her body. The blaze was rapidly engulfing the whole plane, but amazingly, not one person was affected, not even Nevara.

Deep magic from the mad witch was all that kept them flying, and the girls were now sitting and bitterly holding onto their still-remaining seats. A mere skeleton of their dad's once-majestic bi-plane surrounded them.

The flames had done their worst; Cordelia and Mer could only hope for a safe landing, as even their precious brooms had gone up in smoke. Still, at least they weren't burnt to a crisp as well.

There was no need for the girls or Nevara to strain to see each other anymore; there was simply nothing much left to obstruct their view. The remains of the small aircraft's frame was still just holding together but enough to carry them forward at tremendous speed. Nevara turned completely around to address them.

'No longer a pretty little plane flight, is it?' she snapped. 'Fear not, though, young idiots, you'll soon be where I want you.'

'And where the hell's that?' asked Cordelia. The witch simply turned ahead and completely ignored her.

A few miles ahead, bathed by a now persistent moon-glow in early twilight, arose the highest hill in the region. It was hard to miss, even in near darkness, which could be a problem when travelling in a tattered uncontrollable plane driven by somebody completely bonkers.

Yet, despite all this, the craft glided beautifully up the steep hillside coming to a graceful landing upon its rugged crest.

'Right then,' sparked Cordelia brightly to a burning Nevara, 'thanks for that, we'll catch up with you again some time.'

Mer smiled agreeably as she too clambered from the smoking remains to make their escape. 'Good night,' she added, 'hope you get better soon!'

'Not so fast!' cried the witch as she sent out a ribbon of fire, which crackled and circled around the girls preventing any escape.

'I told you I was mad, didn't I?' she announced; and the girls in horror tried every which-way they could to free themselves from the captivating flames.

Nevara smiled patronizingly. 'This ribbon of fire is inescapable, so it's futile trying, and you see that huge unlit beacon beside you?'

The two could, it was so huge no-one could miss it. The dry wood was dripping with some kind of oil too; ready and waiting for a stray spark or magic flame to complete its purpose in life. Reluctantly, the witches nodded.

'Well, I've only to point at it to set it ablaze!'

'So what?' yelled Cordelia. 'We've some dire magic ourselves to call upon!' Nevara laughed madly.

'You silly, stupid young witches!' she roared. 'Where on earth do you think all your magical fun and games come from?'

Mer and her sister both looked blankly at each other. 'What's she on about?' grumbled Mer.

'I'll tell you,' replied Nevara angrily, 'the world of witchdom –that's where you get your silly magic. And, you little fools, it's changing; there's a new deep magic now, newly created and shaped by the Witches of Ice, and vile corrupt practitioners... like me in fact!' Nevara stifled a laugh. 'That my dears, is because greed is the only thing people really care for!'

'No it isn't,' protested Mer, 'what about friends and family?'

'To hell with them!' snapped Nevara.

'Or having fun with magic!' added Cordelia.

'Huh!' she yelled, 'you've happily taken all those things for granted and soon they'll end. So too will you! Look about, can't you see? For goodness sake, start growing up, *magic isn't your play-thing...it's powerful and power-giving!'*

Once again, as had happened a lot recently, Cordelia and Mer were alarmed and vulnerable; and they had good cause to be.

'The second I ignite this beacon,' cried Nevara, 'which will announce to every witch in sight and thought that I've bound and shackled, by flame, two young witches ready for the taking, the sky will become clouded with selfish spell-casters desperate to have your souls.'

Mer gulped. 'Why would you do such a thing?'

'Why, child? Why?' enquired Nevara, quite bemused, 'Because I'm a witch and I'm from this exciting new realm of witchdom, that's why!'

After that she violently pointed at the waiting beacon and it burst into red flames. Nevara, still ablaze herself, jumped from a ledge in front of them, disappearing into the waiting darkness with a muffled roar from the flames engulfing her.

'Crikey!' exclaimed Cordelia. 'I told you Melchior was right about witchcraft...it's becoming full with absolute dire evil. Somehow, we've got to get out of this!'

But, they remained trapped by the ribbon of flames, and seemingly had no practical or magical means of escaping the nightmare.

Mer at last was beginning to understand the true significance of the wizard Fizz and his troubling book *Out-Witching The Witches of Ice*. Cordelia had certainly used every opportunity to tell her everything she knew.

Perhaps it was time the two of them realised that the magic they so flippantly practiced now came at a dreadful cost.

Both of them were far too brave and strong-minded for tears, though somehow the thought of crying provided small comfort. Mer tried strengthen her resolve. Still, it was no use. Try as she may, her emotions welled up inside.

Looking up, they saw with horror the prophesized cloud of witches covering the twilight sky. Mer couldn't control her grief and she turned from Cordelia with even more tears streaming from her eyes. She really didn't want her sister to witness this momentary lapse in bravery.

The thought of not seeing her parents, Gran, even Myrtle anymore, was almost far too much to bear.

As the cloud of witches drew nearer, screeching and wailing, the night air filled with a thunderous roar. But, it wasn't from these evil beings.

Unexpectedly, the engine of their dad's once grand bi-plane burst into life. The remains of the plane turned toward the helpless girls, sweeping in at frightening speed.

One end of its skeletal wings then ploughed into the roaring fire, scattering the beacon, sending blazing wood everywhere. The witches were immediately released from the unmerciful ribbon of flames that had trapped the two victims.

'STONKING GRIEF!' yelled Cordelia again, 'How did that happen?'

But she didn't even give herself time to reply.

Mer sighed, 'Thanks, Dad.'

Cordelia immediately reached into her cloak to find a spell book from one of her hidden pockets. 'Melchior's *Get Me Out of Here Spell*, that'll do it!'

'Are you sure it's safe to use?' asked Mer uneasily, 'you know, a lot of people who've used it have never been found again... please be deadly careful.'

Cordelia pointed at the approaching danger. 'I don't think we've any option!'

Without delay she shouted the spell's words over the whoosh of just-landing witches
who'd come to claim their prize.

The spell took hold with alarming effect and Cordelia hurriedly grabbed Mer's arm. In a flash of green light and puff of mauve smoke the two evaporated into the night.

Chapter Eight

Chapter 8: *Underground Spells.*

Escaping Nevara's evil trap to end up in one of the world's greatest cities as if nothing had ever happened is beyond simple explanation. Suffice to say, Melchior's *Get Me Out of Here Spell*, despite its inherently dangerous drawbacks, managed to do just that. OK, so they had to endure some pretty vile and life-threatening diversions along the way, but at least they'd escaped.

"At least we're alive," was one of Cordelia's reassurances to a slime-soaked and battered Mer. *"And, at least that Swamp Witch didn't make you eat all of her 'pâté en croûte des entrailles' for being so rude to her."*

Mer gagged over Cordelia's unhelpful reminder of when they'd landed in *The Black Swamp*. For, in plain English, what she'd been forced to eat, by way of a rather nasty charm, was simply a 'Pie of Entrails'; animal entrails baked in a shortcrust pastry jacket.

Swamp witches, despite being unforgivably *mega-gross*, possess a form of snobbery too, which embraces the use of posh French titles for various homemade items, including potions, charms and exotic food creations.

'Yes, granted we're lucky to be alive,' answered Mer, still not accepting they should be full of gratitude for being saved by such a flawed spell, even one by the great Melchior himself, 'but at what cost?'

Mer then gagged again at the thought of the awful pie she had been made to eat, mouthful by vile mouthful.

Cordelia had no immediate answer, and still none as they trudged dispiritedly through their cottage door, passing their acutely suspicious and ever-cynical cat familiar,

Radmila, and falling into their respective bedrooms for a bath and overdue change of clothing.

Strangely, not one member of their family enquired how they'd returned home in such a disgusting state. Even more curious was their father's complete indifference to the demise of his much loved bi-plane.

It was if someone had cast a deep spell over the lot of them.

So, after several days and many reflections upon what was happening to their cherished world of magical fun, the two had joined their family for a previously planned big day out in the city of London. It was as if the strange encounter with Nevara after Myrtle's grand wedding had never even occurred.

"London possesses such an unnecessary clatter of noise and pollution," barked Ms. Starch-Stiffington once during one of her disdainful lectures on great cities. But Cordelia & Co. loved the bright red buses, colourful taxis, amazing curios and peculiar people filling the streets, all adding to the city's din.

Though, older witches hated the mayhem of thousands of people rushing this way and that, not caring a tinker's cuss about how they got to their destination, just so long as they did. Occasionally, by not paying attention, some of these city people actually bumped into complete strangers in their rush.

On this particular day, Cordelia and Mer's strange family –a singularly odd bunch of witches– joined the throng.

And predictably, Gran had just collided with a group of innocent pedestrians; an accident that could've been avoided; and altogether quite unnecessary.

'*I'm so sorry, madam,*' apologised a distinguished looking gentleman with grey hair and grey suit to match. 'Allow me.'

He knelt to pick up a large basket of finest sun-dried frogs and crushed spiders.

'Oh!' he said in shock, politely hiding his disgust whilst holding up the old lady's moth-eaten basket. It was one of Daisy's most beloved baskets, once given to her by a secret admirer. She snatched it from him and held it close to her, clutching it like rarest treasure, which to her it probably was.

He bravely attempted a smile, but it didn't quite develop, unlike Daisy's, which was embarrassingly wide. He hurried on, refusing to look back.

The witches were making their way from a popular eating establishment to a pre-arranged departure point.

This seemingly unending stream of bumpy confusion, though, was a welcome challenge for Cordelia and Mer after tangling so recently with such dire evil, but not so for Mrs. Merryspell, their Gran Daisy, newly married eldest sister Myrtle and her husband Colin, who were all in London for the day trying to enjoy themselves.

'I wish everyone would stop barging into us,' complained Myrtle, shooting a stare at Colin as if he could put a stop to it with a spell or something.

After all' she jabbed, 'You are some kind of wizard...or so you say!'

Colin pretended not to hear. The noise, colour and sheer excitement was wonderful for Cordelia and her sister though.

Added to this gathering of witches was the two sisters' good friends Delia, Meryl and Persimmon, accompanied by Meryl's Aunt Eloisa, who was kindly asked if she would oversee these young ladies so they wouldn't get up to anything bad.

Meryl was once more delighted with her mother's choice

of guardian; Aunt Eloisa was not renowned for her parenting or spell-casting abilities at all. And, it was probably for this reason that Aunt Eloisa walked zombie-like, frozen upright, staring blankly into space, quite terrified.

'Do cheer up, Eloisa dear,' chipped Gran, 'it's not as though you're going to an execution!'

By overseeing these five, she may well have been. Gran's encouragement had no effect except to cause a slight twitching in her nerve-wracked face.

No-one could blame her for remaining somewhat apprehensive about the daunting task ahead of her. But, she never objected to the job, not wishing to let down Meryl's mother, or anyone else for that matter.

They'd all just finished a giant burgery meal, which included ice-creams and thick shakes for everyone, and were walking off some of what they'd just eaten.

'If I see yet another ice-cream,' confessed Gran, 'then, I'd have to eat it!'

The young witches smiled at her remark and in a few steps this odd bunch were stood outside a very busy Covent Garden Underground Station, on the Piccadilly Line; about to separate into very different directions, for very different reasons.

Cordelia looked up in awe at the splendid arched windows of the shiny red-brown tiled building. To her, it seemed like some kind of museum, preferably a museum of witchcraft where she could go and discover many deep spells and enchantments.

Gran and Mrs. Merryspell were 'off shopping', Myrtle and Colin planned on seeing some scary movie called *"Dark the Woodland Deep"*, which was all about an evil witch, whilst the girls were expected to gain much education from visiting various museums in South Kensington, and they certainly had nothing at all to do with witchcraft.

Hence, the lot of them being outside Covent Garden station and ready to set off to realise their incompatible objectives.

'Now, you behave yourselves, you lot!' snapped Myrtle. 'Just remember the trouble and punishment you received for your last misadventure here.'

'Last misadventure, indeed!' echoed Mrs. Merryspell.

'Oh, I'm sure they didn't mean anything bad,' chimed-in Gran, protectively. Colin, who knew the awful truth about Cordelia and Mer's London incident, gave them a wan smile of approval, which from Colin was equivalent to a hearty cheer. Mrs. Merryspell, still frowning at him over this, ushered everyone into the station entrance to see the girls and Aunt Eloisa off safely.

'Good luck, Aunt Eloisa!' she said, knowing full well she'd probably need every ounce of it just to survive.

'Thank you, Hepsibah,' she replied, smiling in a decidedly optimistic way, though there did seem to be a tiny flicker of fear in her eyes.

'Ooh,' said Gran, 'If I had my broom, I wouldn't worry about those silly ticket barrier thingies... I'd be over them and off swooping down the tunnel before anyone could shout stop!'

Gran spluttered, cackled and staggered backwards over this. It was only Mrs. Merryspell's quick reaction that prevented her from falling to the ground in one mischievous heap.

The unfortunate Aunt Eloisa waved a pathetic farewell as her and her young charges successfully navigated through the ticket barriers.

'Come along girls,' she yelled, feigning authority in an effort to impress Mrs. Merryspell. 'Stick together now, that's the idea.'

Soon, they were travelling down the escalator.

'This is way too slow,' remarked Cordelia, itching to look up a go-faster spell from one of her many forbidden spell books. Mer gave a look that said *don't even think about it.* Cordelia smiled and placed her hand back on the moving handrail.

All the witches, except perhaps for Aunt Eloisa that is, absolutely adored the idea of doing things underground. Delia reasoned that the person who thought up this *underground railway thingy*, was a very clever witch or wizard.

'I'd have to say, there's something totally spiritual about tunnels, don't you think?' remarked Meryl who, like the rest of them, had been caught alight by the dark adventure that seemed to be calling out from these railway tubes.

'Exciting I'd say!' replied Cordelia.

'It's such a pity we can't conjure our brooms,' she added, waiting for someone to take the bait.

'That's it!' cried Persimmon, sounding unusually adventurous.

'That's, what?' interrupted Aunt Eloisa, just catching the last thread of their conversation.

'Er... that's our train coming!' said Cordelia quickly rushing for the platform, hoping to divert her from what they were chatting about. If Aunt Eloisa had even a clue they were planning anything, their day would surely be doomed.

'No, dear, it isn't a tube train, its simply a wind coming

through, it happens now and then.'

Cordelia winked at Persimmon and they stood patiently waiting.

Distant rumbles from far off trains echoed from the blackness of the tunnel approach as the young witches stared with excited expectation.

Aunt Eloisa, being ever-practical, stared unflinchingly at the train indicator board hoping that their train would soon light up. *At least*, she thought, *they'll all be confined to one place in the carriage.*

Beneath the streets of London, just like many great cities, much happens that couldn't possibly be noticed by ordinary people or those without gifted sight.

All sorts of strange entities occupy the dark places below your feet, some good (some even good fun), others not so good. And, when you encounter those not so good, it would be better if you had stayed above ground.

As they hung around for their train, sure enough, another of those *"winds"* that Aunt Eloisa referred to earlier wafted in, and the girls felt its freezing chill on their faces. Meryl swore she heard some kind of ghostly sigh as it blew from the tube tunnel they were facing.

There was also something else that came along with it. It was hard to perceive at first, but Meryl felt she could just make out some kind of dark grey shape ahead, and travelling at speed as well.

'That could be a lost spirit,' she whispered.

Cordelia agreed and nudged Mer, who in turn nudged Persimmon, who in turn very nearly nudged Aunt Eloisa thinking it was Delia. But they had no need to worry about Eloisa seeing anything, for, like all the commuters waiting with her, she really hadn't developed her seeing abilities in the least.

So, whatever was coming their way would come and go completely unnoticed. As indeed occurs everyday in tubes and tunnels around the world.

With a collective gawp of disbelief Cordelia and the others were suddenly staring at an old-fashioned underground steam engine blasting steam and smoke everywhere, and chuffing urgently toward them.

They could see clear through it as well. Another odd thing was that it made absolutely no noise at all. They couldn't see anyone driving it either. Whether that was because of lack of light couldn't be said for certain, though they were about to know for sure as it and its ghostly carriages glided onto the platform.

A blast of ghost-like steam shot out from one of the engine's pipes blowing off Aunt Eloisa's ridiculous hat, as well as scattering some poor office worker's papers across the platform. But, to the unsighted, it wasn't a jet of steam at all, just another pesky wind from the tunnel.

Only the five young witches noticed the drama as the train came to a silent halt in front of them. Aunt Eloisa continued to fumble around for her hat, the office worker scrambled to retrieve his papers, whilst everyone else continued to look vacantly, as one usually does when one is waiting for something to arrive that hasn't.

Cordelia was positively frowning at how nobody seemed even the slightest bit aware of the exciting event that was currently taking place right in front of them.

The transparent train, which stood silently before the witches, was made up of old wooden carriages that likely belonged to the Edwardian era. At the head, still hissing and smoking, was the steam engine they'd first noticed. Its hissing seemed as if it was impatiently demanding they get onboard.

A carriage door in front of them sprang open, and the witches felt obliged to get on. Once inside they couldn't help but notice the floor beneath was see-through too, yet it seemed quite strong enough to take severe stamping from Cordelia, who was driven to *'testing it out'* as she put it.

Peering through the smoke-grimed windows, the girls stared at everyone on the platform with great amusement. Aunt Eloisa was still gawping at the train indicator board, completely oblivious to their absence.

A few businesspeople remained with their heads buried in newspapers, and an old lady continued rummaging through her bags for something she thought she'd lost. Most, though, avoided any activity at all, preferring to remain vertical and disinterested in anything. *If only they knew!* thought Cordelia.

Without warning, her sister screamed. Not from horror, but delight. It was Maxim Dashkov; the lad Mer had made friends with at the Nightshade Ball, standing not far off down the platform. He'd been waving furiously at them trying to catch their attention.

Aunt Eloisa had noticed him, but thinking he'd flipped or something, moved further back in case he demanded money or valuables.

'How cool is that?' yelled Mer, 'How can we get him on, this door seems jammed!'

Cordelia attempted an opening spell and the door unlocked. Annoyingly, it only opened partially, but enough for Maxim to get his hands through and get a grip on the doorframe.

A huge jolt pushed the ghostly train forward. Maxim desperately tried to squeeze through the narrow opening.

Not quite onboard, he began walking along with the moving train, refusing to give up his attempt to get on. His pace quickened as the narrow tunnel entrance loomed ever nearer.

Aunt Eloisa, oblivious to the train's presence, stared at his peculiar antics, convinced the boy was being totally and profoundly ridiculous.

The door at last gave way to Maxim's efforts, but still holding onto the outside of it; the thing swung dangerously outwards ready to smash him into the approaching tunnel wall. Mer reached and grabbed his arm, pulling the lad safely into the carriage with only seconds to spare.

The girls and Maxim stared, amused, at Aunt Eloisa and the others left behind on the platform. As they disappeared into the darkness of the tunnel, the last they saw was of her anxiously looking up and down for her charges. The girls couldn't hold back their laughter, explaining everything to a delighted Maxim.

Instantly, the carriage unexpectedly lit up as a central row of old incandescent light bulbs flickered to life. For the first time all the fittings seemed solid. So much so, that Mer and Delia sat down on the plush seats nearby.

They were covered in salmon-pink velvet with large buttons sewn deep into the cushioned surface. The middle of where they rested their backs was proudly embroidered with the intertwined letters "*D.R. & Co.*"

'Cool!' admired Delia. 'And, whoever "D.R." may be, they must be well rich!'

Just then, the door at the end of their carriage burst open and an oldish train driver entered carrying an empty metal bucket, swinging it happily.

'Anyone have any coal?' he asked.

'What you want coal for?' quizzed Cordelia as he approached unsteadily to the sway of the train.

'To run the damn engine obviously...why do you think?... *What do I want coal for, I ask you?*' he mumbled.

The driver seemed most put out that someone would actually question his need, and shook his bucket in front of them, once more asking for donations.

Cordelia pretended to pour some coal from an imaginary sack into his bucket. Maxim smiled.

'Whoa,' yelled the driver, 'not too much now, what d'you think I'm holding, a flaming coal tanker?'

Cordelia looked astonished at him and sniggered to the others as the driver staggered off with a seemingly heavy bucket back to the engine, still moaning.

'What do you want bloody coal for!' he jibed once more before leaving. When the carriage door slammed, they all burst into fits.

'This is so weird!' said Maxim.

'And wonderfully bonkers too,' added Mer.

'He could well be a lost soul drifting between here and the beyond,' mused Meryl.

'More like lost his silly marbles,' chipped Delia.

Yet, whatever imaginary thing Cordelia had given him, it plainly had some effect; the train picked up enormous speed. After a while, they felt a sinking sensation as the train plunged deeper into the ground.

At once they realised they were no longer in a London Underground tunnel, but travelling through solid ground instead.

'This doesn't make sense,' quipped Persimmon. 'I wonder if the driver's heard of Merg, our old school coach?'

Perhaps he had, including its propensity to dive into

the ground and burrow its way to their school with them onboard. This strange inclination by Merg was a regular event on school days, and something the witches were quite used to by now. But somehow, this felt rather different. Meryl suggested that it might be a good time to go and ask the old driver what on earth was going on.

So, the six, with great intrigue, made their way up to the connecting carriage door that the driver had used. Opening it was quite a strain, as if they were pulling against some invisible force, which they were.

A quick spell from Meryl did the trick and the witches went swiftly through to the following carriage. Unlike the one they'd just left, this was full of people, and the male occupants were all oddly dressed, wearing overly tall smokestack top hats and tails too.

The dour-looking women accompanying them weren't much better. They all wore long flowing dresses with bustles and each lady held a folded little white parasol. Not one of them uttered or stirred at the sight of the witches.

That was until they'd reached the connecting door where one of the strangely dressed gentlemen enquired 'Are we there yet?'

Cordelia, biting her lip to avoid gasping with amusement, said 'Nearly,' and passed through the door with the others.

'Who are they?' asked Persimmon, but no-one knew.

'I think they've been sitting there for ever,' remarked Delia.

'Very odd,' added Meryl, 'a little like ghosts if you ask me.'

She wasn't far from the truth. Leaving the carriage, they faced climbing a narrow iron ladder that went right to the top of the engine's coal tender. It was the only way they were going to get to the engine and its driver to find answers as to where they were going, and why.

'Who's climbing first?' said Maxim. 'I'm not good with heights.'

Cordelia pushed through and clambered up without a second thought. 'Don't worry, I love danger! Follow me, I'll look after you!'

Maxim smiled dreamily at Mer; Cordelia stared at them impatiently, 'Come on then!' she called.

At the top, the jagged rocks of the tunnel roof were flying past missing her head by mere inches. The others soon joined her. To everyone's surprise, as they looked down the tender below was completely empty, not a scrap of coal in it.

'Beats me how it chucks out so much smoke and steam,' said Delia.

'Ah, the wonders of everlasting mystery!' answered Meryl.

With the engine lurching violently, they slowly made their way across the shaking tender over to the ladder at the far end. Once again, Cordelia began the climb first.

Shortly, all of them had reached the engine's cab, and staring down into it, they were surprised to see the old driver and his fireman sitting at a small round table.

Curiously, it was set with a large pot of tea and a plate of delicious-looking cupcakes.

The crockery was precariously rattling and lurching with the swaying of the train.

'That's bizarre!' exclaimed Cordelia.

The driver, who 'til then had been so focused on their tea party, looked up startled and yelled, 'What are you lot doing here?'

Stunned into silence, no-one answered.

'Well,' he reasoned, 'I s'pose now that you've found us

you might as well make yerselves useful. *Come on, get shovelling!'*

'OK matey,' fired Cordelia.

'Don't you think it's a bit cramped in here for all of us?' interrupted Persimmon. It was true, eight people in one small cab was a bit much.

Cordelia, squashed up beside the driver and fireman, reached out to grab one of their tempting cakes covered in thick icing.

"Get yer mucky 'ands off!" yelled the fireman. His long coal-blackened face appeared angry as he muttered some odd words. Promptly, a lengthy and fairly battered looking shovel appeared in his right hand and he shook it at Cordelia.

'Well...start working!' he commanded. Un-amused, and convinced he was utterly bonkers she took the battered shovel and winked at her friends.

Upon kicking open the firebox door though, Cordelia didn't see a roaring fire, just a black emptiness.

Barking, she thought, *absolutely barking bonkers the pair of them. But, I'll go along with this nonsense for now.*

Comically, she attempted to fill the firebox from the tender. Obviously, with the coal tender being empty, Cordelia had nothing to shovel. But, strangely, although her shovel was devoid of coal lumps, as she brought it back to fill the waiting firebox, it felt remarkably heavy to her. So much so that the task became hard work as she strained to carry the invisible load to and fro.

'This really is bizarre!' she yelled pushing past her friends. They laughed. Yet, what was really puzzling was that smoke and steam still belched from the chimney. It jetted from various poorly maintained gauges and connectors around her too. Obviously, whatever she was doing was having an affect.

Cordelia slavishly continued to shoot the invisible but heavy load into the firebox, if only to find out where all this madness would lead. And, as she shovelled, the faster they went.

'More tea, Morris?' enquired the driver to his fireman, who was sitting back holding an empty mug with one hand whilst feeling the imaginary heat of the empty firebox with the palm of the other.

'Don't mind if I do, Dudley,' he answered.

Naturally, they were well pleased with Cordelia's effort.

'Now listen, you two,' interrupted Delia impatiently, 'what the screaming toadstools is going on around here?'

The men, planning to tuck into yet more cupcakes, and washing them down with tea from the large battered mugs they held, were surprised at Delia's no-nonsense question.

Ignoring her for the moment, Morris prepared to stuff his mouth with a particularly delicious cake. This time a *Chocolate and Strawberry Cream Surprise* with a large candied strawberry on top. But, his teeth had hardly bitten into the cake, when another visitor climbed down the small ladder and into the cramped cab, booming out a question with some authority.

'You chaps, what on earth is going on with this train?' he barked.

All looked up to see the same strangely dressed gentleman Cordelia had briefly spoken to earlier, still wearing his over-tall top hat. With great purpose he pushed past Maxim and Meryl to lean over the fireman with a threatening look upon his face.

Morris stared helplessly at his driver Dudley, hoping he'd have the courage to tell the bloke to go away, or at the very worst tell him the destination they were headed.

'Go on, man' he commanded 'I insist you tell me this instant!'

The gentleman removed his top hat; he revealed a balding head and somehow looked less dazed than Cordelia had remembered.

Dudley though tried to deflect answering by asking how they had all managed to *'escape...er, get out of the carriage'* and *'didn't they know how dangerous it was to climb over the tender when they could so easily have had their heads knocked off by the flying rocks above them?'*

'It's strictly against railway regulations,' continued Dudley in a more official tone.

But, Cordelia wasn't having any of it 'Tell ol' matey with the tall hat where we're headed for, right this moment!'

Dudley's eyes bulged with more resolve 'If someone doesn't start shovelling soon, we'll come to a grinding halt, then where'd we be?'

'You tell me?' quipped Delia.

'Look, missy, passengers are forbidden to question company drivers or their firemen as to destinations,' barked Morris. 'It's official see?'

He held up a grease-smudged and coal blackened rulebook and waved it in their faces. 'Go on you,' he commanded Cordelia 'get back to stoking.'

Strangely, she did exactly what he'd asked. But, Mer cast an instant *jamming spell* on the firebox door.

Cordelia really wished Mer hadn't done this. Or, at the very least *tell her first she intended doing it.* Upon kicking the now jammed firebox door open, her right foot slammed into it causing her enormous pain.

'Jumping coal sacks!' she shot, hopping and holding her foot 'You could have warned me woman!'

The heavy but invisible coal scattered from her dropped shovel making a rattling sound as it went. But no one could actually see anything.

Mer gushed an apology 'Cripes, I'm sorry.'

'It'd better be worth it!' snapped Cordelia.

Delia, seeing things were getting out of hand, yelled to the obstinate driver 'Go on, tell us now, matey; no coal means we'll go no further.'

'Alright,' snapped the driver warily, '...but you aint going to like it!'

Although Dudley and his fireman, Morris, had worked together on this bizarre underground train during many equally bizarre journeys, which had made them tougher than the rocks their engine now burrowed through, a hint of fear was noticeable in the old men's eyes as they both realised that telling their uninvited guests the awful truth was inevitable.

'You're all heading for *death* at Deathwytch Halt' said Dudley blackly. 'I'm sorry, I can't say it any nicer than that, death is death no matter how many lovely flowers you throw at it...and for you lot, there's no way out!'

Despite the roar of the engine's relentless burrowing, Persimmon clearly heard herself gulp at the possibility of imminent and unavoidable death.

The panic is she thought *not even a spell by Melchior Fizz, or one from Cordelia's unending library of books will get us get out of this mess...but there again...*

She looked with a pained expression toward Cordelia, who at once seemed to read her mind.

'Let's see what Melchior has to say about all this' she quipped with a knowing look to Persimmon, who in return gave a slightly more hopeful smile 'He'll get us out!'

Morris and Dudley grunted, slowly shaking their heads in disapproval over Cordelia's audacity. The driver simply reiterated 'There's no way back, I tells yer.'

'I'm afraid it's all true' assured Dudley nodding slowly 'Deathwytch Halt is not a place any witch would care to visit...with or without all their marbles!'

'Yeah, he's right,' mused Morris between licks of his cup-cake icing 'even if the railway company produced one of them lovely glossy travel brochurey books –yer still wouldn't wanna go, unless yer bonkers!'

'Yeah, cos you'll end up as dead as a squished toadstool!' roared Dudley, and they both began laughing.

'Why us, why should we die?' questioned Maxim.

'Don't blinking ask me,' barked Dudley as he picked up the shovel dropped by Cordelia. As he stood, he stuffed yet another delicious looking cake into his mouth.

'You're the flaming idiots who boarded the train, can't think what made you do it!'

'Wasn't our fault you didn't have a sign on the front of your ridiculous train reading *"All aboard for Certain Death"* now was it?' piped Cordelia 'and, for your information matey, were about to get off it anyway; and we're taking our new friends with us!'

At that, the engine began slowing, which immediately prompted Morris to throw down his half-eaten cupcake, grab hold of a nearby shovel, and, along with Dudley, push past them all to commence stoking the none-existent fire.

The train responded, picking up speed once more.

'See,' yelled Dudley 'there aint anything you can do about it...you're all going to die at Deathwytch Halt, so accept it and deal with it!'

A blast of very thick coal smoke and steam filled the cab and they all started choking. It seemed things couldn't get any worse for them.

Even Mer's *Door-Jamming Spell*, as well as everyone else's attempts to stop their doomed progress, were made useless. Defeated for the moment, they stood helpless, swaying and shaking with the motion of the engine.

After a short while, the strange underground train slowed. Curiously, neither Dudley nor Morris seemed the least bit perturbed.

'Almost there, Morris.' smirked the driver nodding toward the witches with an expression that sort of said, *Told you so.*

With a roar, the train exited the tunnel into a palatial cave of soft blue green light glowing from crystal walls and cathedral-like arches.

'I knew it, I knew it!' cried Maxim excitedly. He jumped down from the cab onto a crystallised platform twirling about amazed over the station's cavernous size.

'This is what I've just been reading about. It's exactly as Nathaniel Silverspoon predicted in his stunning book *Something Nasty Below.*' Maxim walked off to explore the place as the others disembarked with equal amazement.

Soon, they were all stood on the platform of the astounding looking railway station. Smoke and steam from the engine swirled and swept around. None of them had seen anything like this in their lives.

Meryl, quite overcome with curiosity, ran over to the

nearest wall. It was smooth and translucent. 'I can hear spirits talking from within the crystal itself, I'm certain!'

'It's as hard as diamond,' squealed Pers 'and I can see right through it like glass!'

To her dismay, even the platform signs were made of the same stuff.

'Can you believe it Mer, this is the legendary *Crystal Palace of Death*' called Maxim 'I'm amazed!'

'Oh great, just what we need, *a palace of death*! How can you be so sure, anyway?' she said remaining just as transfixed by the place.

'Well,' answered Maxim eagerly 'understandably Silverspoon couldn't come straight out with where the place was, or who ran it, probably from fear of being bumped-off. The Witches of Ice would have taken care of that straight away. Nevertheless, his book did set out its purpose, as well as a lot of details for people to follow.'

'Blimey!' said Cordelia joining the discussion 'I think Melchior was onto that too.'

'And precisely what is its purpose?' added Persimmon with concern.

'Simple, but awful,' said Maxim 'to take the souls and magic of very powerful witches and warlocks; and kill them off; they're not formidable enough to tackle wizards, *yet*. That's probably why none of them have gone missing!'

'So, what can we do about it?' asked Meryl, butting in. 'I mean, my father always hung garlic in the bedroom to avoid dying in his sleep, but me mother soon put pay to that. He's still alive' she continued 'and the house smells a lot better too!'

In no time, Delia joined them. Maxim continued: 'Silverspoon did hint of a way, but even a wizard would have difficulty succeeding.'

'Isn't that *the Black Conjuration?*' asked a confident but somehow smug looking Cordelia.

'Don't tell me,' said Maxim with excitement 'I know, you've got the *Conjuration* somewhere, haven't you?'

Cordelia was beaming as she held up Melchior's translucent and highly dangerous book *'Out-Witching The Witches of Ice'*.

'You wolf, you never told me that you kept his deadly book actually on you!' exclaimed her sister. Normally, Mer would've been angry, but in light of their terrible circumstances, she felt quite proud of her rebellious sister.

'Trouble is,' pointed out Cordelia 'we need a wizard to help us, I'm sure none of us could do it on our own. I mean, you do know that if your power fails during the conjuration, you'd be consumed by black fire and lightening, don't you?'

No one looked keen anymore.

'Got it!' cried Maxim 'Individually, perhaps we couldn't, but what about *collectively?*' His eyes were shining with excitement.

'Brilliant,' added Delia 'but when?'

'Well, we'd have to read Melchior's notes first, then the conjuration, that's if you don't mind Cordelia?' he asked. But, before Maxim had a chance to breath in again, the book was in his hands. Cordelia winked.

'Looks as though we're going to get out of this, after all' she added. Her enthusiasm, though, was short-lived.

A cold, commanding voice, echoing throughout the cavernous station from several speaker horns located between every archway, demanded attention. But, it wasn't the rasping icy voice that chilled them so much; it was what it said.

'Uh hum...attention, attention please!' went the echoing announcement 'All passengers, accompanied by any baggage, including magical paraphernalia and especially any written spells, enchantments, and incantations, must make their way to the end of the platform. Upon arrival, they will each meet the end of their life...Thank You for travelling with the Deathwytch Railway Company.'

The cold voice ended with a click, and the speaker horns disappeared back into the crystallised arches.

'End of our flaming life...that's what they think!' snapped Cordelia.

Just at that moment, a huge barrow rolled past pushed by a thin lanky station porter. 'Ere, where you going with that, matey?' she demanded.

The young man, shabbily dressed in a railway uniform that was shiny from wear and neglect, as was he, moved his slouched head upwards making his rounded shoulders appear more upright and less tired.

He turned his head toward her.

'Are you speaking to me, Miss.?' he asked in a thin, subordinate voice.

'That's right, matey,' she replied.

'Actually, miss, I'm taking it to the baggage compartment at the end of the train to collect all the confiscated materials of witchcraft.' With that his head slouched morosely, ready to move on.

'But wait,' she pressed 'Don't you realise what they're doing?'

'Yes,' he replied 'it's *dark magic*, and I'm a slave to it, can't break the spell, you see.' Cordelia couldn't help notice the porter's face; it was anguished and tearful.

By now, a line of confused passengers from the train

slowly shuffled forward. Trolleys and barrows of their baggage, wheeled by dumbstruck porters, accompanied their obedient progress toward the end of the platform.

'Come along... come along, hurry everyone, we haven't all day, you know!' barked the same insensitive voice from every re-emerged speaker horn in the station. It echoed off of the crystal walls and seemed to have the desired effect upon all the doomed passengers who were now marching quite quickly.

Cordelia couldn't take her eyes off them. Without exception, each looked vacant, showing no emotion whatsoever.

The men still wore tall top hats and tails, the women long flowing dresses, carrying tiny parasoles; some rolled, some held up as if shielding them from imaginary strong sunlight or light showers.

There was certainly none of these elements this far down.

'Have you our tickets?' fussed one of the ladies to her gentleman partner.

'I fear I have, Victoria,' he replied courteously '...and to that end, my dear, we shall make our connection perfectly for the next train home.'

Meryl couldn't hold back 'What's a matter with you people? There isn't any train home, that's the truth, this is your last stop before you die!'

The woman was thrown by Meryl's audacity in speaking to a lady and gentleman of such high breeding, and unannounced too. So, she stared blankly at her. Meryl followed them as they walked quickly, ignoring the snobby woman's constant stares of disapproval. Nevertheless, she continued pleading with them, but it was no use.

The woman's face remained unmoved. She turned to her husband, raising her eyebrows, and rather haughtily said; 'Tell her to go away, Albert, we're not buying anything today thank you.'

'What?' said Meryl angrily 'I just said they're going to kill every one of us with dark magic at the end of the platform, wake up!'

Her husband, Albert, squinted at Meryl as if he was looking for some kind of diseased spot or irregularity growing upon her face. He wasn't.

'I'm not convinced, Victoria' he said, staring hard into Meryl's eyes, 'I think she may have a point.'

'What would a mere slip of a girl know about railway timetables, I ask?' snapped the woman 'Furthermore, the girl's attire and demeanour are utterly outrageous... has her mother no shame?'

Meryl bit her lip.

'Sorry,' the man said, apologising, 'but we must keep going, we've a train to catch'.

'Blimey, can't help this pair, they're really off their trolley!' whispered Meryl under her breath striding off without even a flicker of success.

'I'm afraid they've all gone loopy,' she confirmed, rejoining the others.

'Perhaps they're charmed by something maybe?' offered Cordelia '...have you noticed they're all holding tickets?'

'Yeah, shuffling along like zombies!' sighed Mer.

'Don't worry,' said Cordelia, 'they're not zombie-like, Mer...they're definitely being charmed, and I feel the charms are actually inside the tickets they're holding, it's the only answer! Just look at the way they're grasping them.'

'Gosh,' gasped Persimmon 'you're right Cordelia. So,

holding those will kill them with dark magic.'

'Surely, we'll have to do something, and quickly, there's only a hundred or so yards left of platform!'

'Yes,' agreed Delia 'Once they reach the platform end, that'll be the *end* of them alright!'

'Well, then it's vital we undo the magic somehow.' urged Meryl. 'And afterwards we can herd them like a gentle flock of sheep back onto the train.'

'Which will give us a chance to carry out *the Black Conjuration* to finish this place off forever!' added Mer.

'I wish it were that simple,' worried Maxim 'whatever powerful magic that's being used, it isn't going to be undone so easily'.

'Then we must destroy the tickets themselves,' urged Cordelia. 'Wait, I'm sure I have something on tickets... well, somewhere here anyway.'

At that, she furiously rummaged through her pockets.

'Sorry about my sister,' said Mer looking at Maxim with a half enthusiastic smile. 'Sometimes though, she does come up trumps'.

What Cordelia was no doubt searching for was Jacob Slott's *Tickets & Ticket Machines –Making Sense of Them.* After a speedy search for the handy volume, and upon miraculously finding it, Cordelia instantly flicked to the introduction, where Mr. Slott explained, quite openly that *"tickets are somewhat loathsome things"*.

He went further by suggesting they're often viewed in various circles as being: *"Made by people who like nothing better than to make life difficult for everyone by actually charging them to go somewhere or do something!"*

Mr. Slott advocated that anyone having problems with tickets should read Hugh Plugg's magical and somewhat derogatory book *Death To All Tickets!* Naturally enough,

Naturally enough, Cordelia happened to have an overly dog-eared copy of this small thin publication too somewhere, and, quickly putting Mr. Slott's book back, exchanged it for Mr. Plugg's masterpiece.

"Hugh Plugg," she read in the introduction *"is a self-effacing man who lives a fairly simple and blameless life for a magician. The only reason he ever bothered to write this work in the first place wasn't out of ego, but to help those who likewise suffer at the hands, or should that be the card or perhaps paper, of tickets."*

What followed required a strong degree of sympathy from Cordelia, as Hugh never stood a chance with tickets.

"From a very early age tickets bothered him. He remembered as a boy saving all his pocket money to purchase one for a movie.

"After presenting it to the lady at the darkened entrance of the cinema's auditorium, was told, upon closer inspection and admittedly with a particularly dim torch, that the ticket he held was a fake.

"Despite Hugh kicking up a rumpus over not seeing 'Strange Mad Dragon's' –his and many other's all-time favourite movie– the cinema manager became involved; and eventually the local police, whereupon, he was unceremoniously ejected from the theatre. Cruelly, Master Plugg was additionally threatened with criminal charges for fraud: rather a lot to bear at the painful age of just nine years."

Cordelia, engrossed in Hugh's story, was rudely interrupted by her sister. 'What on earth are you doing woman, haven't you finished reading the instructions yet?'

'Just a sec' replied Cordelia 'nearly there.'

With that, she read more of his sad story.

"But your sorrow shouldn't be directed to him for just that event. Later his misfortune for ticket failure extended to football games, trains, buses, and even airline tickets.

"It was after this last tragedy, where he was to fly to New York to receive an award for the person most ejected from any venue or method of transport in all of history, that his problem was duly compounded. He was accused of fraudulently acquiring the very ticket he was about to use for travelling to the ceremony, even though his hosts paid for it.

"And, to add further insult to injury, that this prestigious award itself was gained by him as a result of cheating and therefore void.

"Following that dark moment" the book concluded "he decided at last to seek absolute revenge over every ticket in the world. Hugh Plugg is famously quoted as saying that: 'The best thing anyone can do with tickets is to blow ones nose on them and throw them away".

Now, that's bitterness thought Cordelia. However, she did find something else in his little ticket-sized book. That something was the very thing they *urgently* needed to save everyone on the platform at that very moment, especially as they were walking so busily toward their deaths.

Casual readers were invited to use the *Ticket Vapourising spell*. It was by none other than the famous Dr. Basil Smallcard and to be found in his diminutive book *Nasty Horrible little Things & How To Deal With Them*, which is exactly what Cordelia would do the very moment she found a copy.

'COME ON, WILL YOU!' blasted Mer 'there's nothing to grin about, they're all going to die!'

Luckily, Cordelia found it and turned straight to his

Ticket Vapourising spell. It worked. After several puffs of orange smoke each harmful ticket simply vapourised into thin air.

At once, the passengers, previously dazed and confused, stopped marching. Mer and Persimmon immediately began ushering them back onto the train. The others eagerly helped.

'What the hell do you think you're doing with my passengers?' shouted an extremely incensed stationmaster, racing toward them. He wore a long plaited beard, a ridiculously ornate and twisted moustache, a dark official-looking uniform, and tiny circular glasses that were barely able to balance upon his fat squashed nose due to their small size.

'Taking them to the seaside, what do you think, hairy?' answered Mer.

'Why you little...' he said, not finishing what he really wanted to call her. 'I've never been so rudely spoken to like this in all my life!'

'Oh, come on, surely you must have' replied Mer with a snigger.

The stationmaster did finish calling her something this time. Mer politely and sarcastically curtsied continuing to usher the now un-charmed witches and warlocks back onboard the underground train.

Infuriated, the stationmaster clumsily tried some magic of his own. He either got the spell the wrong way round, Mer countered it, or that he was quite simply crackers.

Any of these explanations would suffice as he at once commenced growing smaller. Oddly, his tiny spectacles remained the same size, gradually becoming as ridiculously large as they were once small by comparison.

'You won't get away with this' he screeched from under the now huge-rim of his glasses, his voice reducing with his size. His final mouse-like squeak could barely be heard but Mer just made out what he said.

"There's someone coming who's going to really deal with you lot," he squeaked threateningly.

Eventually the stationmaster wasn't to be seen. Though his once proudly-worn cap did make a hasty retreat.

'I'm just *soooo* tempted to jump on it, even if only to scare him!' laughed Mer.

With the un-charmed passengers now safely back on the train, Maxim and the witches strode halfway down the hauntingly beautiful crystal platform to commence the planned conjuration.

The blue-green mineral that everything seemed to be made of, including the platform they walked along, was stunning to look at; so sad the place was the legendary subterranean Crystal Palace of Death.

The group stopped and prepared to set about the *Black Conjuration*. They started with casting a circle, and held hands within it, about to chant the deadly incantation. It was scary stuff. But, Just as they were about to commence, Persimmon yelled '*WATCH OUT!*'

Toward them came rushing two familiar figures wielding handy-sized shovels that seemed to be designed more for warfare than shovelling.

'Thought you'd got away with it, didn't you?' cried Dudley. Morris repeated his words as they both stood before them.

Whether it was commendable bravery or sheer lunacy will never be known, but Maxim broke from the circle and menacingly strode up to the two of them, reciting a charm.

"BANG, THUMP, CLANG" came the sound of shovels ringing against a puny if not courageous warlock, felling the lad to ground. Mer screamed and they all ran to Maxim's aid.

'Get back!' warned Dudley and Morris, still shaking from what they'd just done.

'Get back, or you'll get some too!' they cried together.

Fortunately, Mer still had the spell in her mind she'd used on the stationmaster. Fighting her drive to rescue Maxim, come what may, she spouted out the spell instead. Nothing happened.

'Right, that does it!' she yelled, running and screaming toward Dudley and Morris, who immediately began swinging their shovels viciously.

"BANG, THUMP, CLANG" came the horrible sound once more. It was shocking, but this time their blades had landed on each other, rather than Mer.

Amazingly, they'd begun shrinking, and were already half their original size.

'Cripes, the spell worked!' she gushed.

'Well done!' yelled Cordelia. Maxim groggily laughed at the sight of the now tiny driver and fireman brandishing nothing bigger than matchsticks.

Outrageously, he conjured a cat to play with the shrunken enginemen.

'That'll keep them busy for a while, how long will your spell last?' he asked Mer who could now afford to smile a little.

'Until we carry out the conjuration, I hope' she said.

The opening lines of Melchior's Black Conjuration are extremely difficult to read, let alone say. Doubtless Maxim and Mer, sharing the task, would have completed the job though. Would have, because unexpectedly there appeared to be what seemed as a smoke-black featureless shadow. It spread quickly over the group engulfing them in a strange and intense darkness.

'Has someone put the lights out?' asked Persimmon.

The shadow that covered them was much darker than nearby shadows in fact.

'Odd that' observed Meryl 'but I think the answer's above us.'

They all looked up.

What they saw was dark, cloudlike, and swirling. By squinting their eyes, the ominous object revealed strange shapes drifting in and out of it. Upon straining their eyes further, all was revealed. There were five shapes, five human shapes, flying and occasionally, pausing to stare at them.

Not one of the girls could budge. Meryl was the first to try running from this strange cloud of swirling spirits or whatever they were, but the resulting pain of her attempt to escape immediately made her stay put.

Peering down at her feet, she could see they were now physically part of the crystal platform itself, and not simply attached by some spell or peculiar glue. Worse still, whenever a foot, or the leg pulling it, was moved they stretched like a piece of elastic.

The pain was excruciating; and soon experienced by all the witches when attempting escape. At last, one of the five beings swirled down and stood arrogantly in the middle of their disorderly circle.

It was Kaldre of the Five Witches of Gloom.

'Never look a gift-horse in the mouth, say I' said Kaldre cruelly 'I mean here are the five witches I've been attempting to capture all these many months!'

But you saved our lives the first time we met!' shot

shot Mer.

'Seriously? Hasn't it occurred to you yet? Well, let me enlighten your dumb brains. We're taking you as an offering to the wonderfully cruel Witches of Ice –*there's something about you lot that they really, really want!* I can't see that myself, obviously, ¬you're totally worthless! Naturally, they'll reward us too in a most spectacular fashion!'

'You'll not take us!' yelled Cordelia arrogantly as she lunged toward Kaldre. At once she felt the sharp pain of her bodyweight stretching her legs against her stuck feet.

Kaldre laughed and continued. 'Not only that, but I've caught you in the very place where soul stealing takes place – I couldn't have planned it better myself!'

She laughed vulgarly this time, so too did her four coven companions floating above. It was mockery their victims could well do without.

Spells are word-specific. And everyone who weaves them knows how vitally important it is when writing or conjuring that they stick to the words used exactly. Otherwise, things can get quite messy. That's particularly why Maxim at that moment had a well-developed smile spread across his young face.

The Five Witches of Gloom, especially Kaldre, should have known better when casting the spell that held the witches to the crystal platform. They omitted to include warlock in this charm, enabling Maxim, even though he stood seemingly motionless, to remain unstuck; and free to cast whatever counter-spell he desired.

Naturally, he never signalled this freedom to them; as he knew they would quickly, very quickly indeed, have him under their power. The only reason he afforded himself a great big smile at that moment, was that under his breath, he'd just completed a potent but temporary immobilising charm upon Kaldre and her floating cronies.

In microseconds, Kaldre and her coven became speechless, staring blankly at their victims. It was simply was awe-inspiring.

Maxim burst out laughing and walked toward Mer, Cordelia and their friends to help free them and explain what he'd done. They had no idea Maxim had such ability.

'How long will your charm hold them?' fired Mer urgently.

'I can't be sure,' said Maxim, 'but first, let's get you lot free from this awful crystal. I'm sure I have a charm somewhere!'

Too late, Cordelia found it in a book by Quirien Leave. It was at the dog-eared page *"Disassociation Techniques"*. Cordelia carefully read out the sixth spell down the page, *"Unkind Stones"*. Eventually, with splintering crackles and snaps, their feet were freed from the crystal platform.

Wasting no time, the six, retaining a wary eye on the Witches of Gloom, reformed their circle and composure. Once more Maxim and Mer recited the *Black Conjuration* between them.

The result was short in coming. Thunderous rumbles shuddered everything around. The speaker horns in the archways reappeared barking, *'Don't panic...all is under control...Stay where you are...the witches of death are finding whoever is responsible!'*

They weren't; like every selfish person employed at the Deathwytch Railway Company, the first thing they did was to look after number one.

The whole crystal palace shook some more, this time sending giant shards of broken crystal from the high vaulted ceiling. They roared like a thousand smashing windows as each piece crashed into the solid mineral surface below.

The sound was deafening, the air thick with crystal dust. Maxim and his friends ran like hell, dodging between the deadly missiles raining down.

'Let's hope the train doesn't get hit,' yelled Cordelia, 'it's our only means of escape.'

The very second she said that, a huge chunk of blue green crystal roared in front of her, wedging itself between the engine and platform.

'You idiot, you should've kept quiet,' moaned Pers, lying flattened on the platform, shielding her head from debris.

'Sorry!' stifled Cordelia, knowing it wasn't her fault.

Nevertheless, she held back from saying she hoped the carriages would be OK too.

'Don't worry,' said Maxim, 'I can fix this.'

Again, he surprised all the witches with a spell which sent the huge chunk flying off to land just inches away from Kaldre, who was still standing motionless in the middle of where they'd circled her.

'Ouch,' said Cordelia as she boarded the footplate of the engine, 'that chunk would've really hurt her!'

'Pity it didn't,' quipped Delia, jumping in after.

They were safely aboard and their last hurdle was to get the engine steaming.

'I knew Uncle Wistar was right in giving me this,' smiled Cordelia, holding her valued copy of Hector Springlock's *Marvellous Spells for Marvellous Machinery.*

'Don't you mean loaned?' reminded Mer.

'Yeah, I know, don't rub it in!' she replied, turning to the section on locomotives. Hector's *Spell No. 354b Steam Tank-Engine (Medium to Large)* was quickly found and initiated.

The welcome roar of the engine bursting into life was hardly audible above the catastrophic destruction going on around them, but it was enough to cause everyone to shout a resounding '*YES!*' in one loud voice.

'I really hope the tunnel remains open!' cried Cordelia. Persimmon frowned at her, Cordelia bit her lip. 'Well, I'm not predicting the future, you know, just hoping, that's all!'

Persimmon appeared relieved as the underground engine and its battered carriages rattled safely into the tunnel ahead.

'Phew,' called Meryl, 'wasn't that the closest thing ever?'

They had done it. Not only that, they had done it in style. Even the witches and warlocks travelling with them in the carriages behind had remained alive. But before everyone became too smug, Delia reached over to grab a shovel.

'It may have escaped everyone's notice,' she called out, 'but, we're slowing down; and I don't think it's all to do with the steep climb!'

She was right.

'Don't all look at me,' snapped Cordelia, 'I stoked the firebox last time. I swear my arms are a few inches longer.'

She partially transformed herself to appear as a primate, including the noises they make. They broke out laughing, and Maxim grabbed the shovel from Delia.

'How gallant,' called Mer.

'Not gallant,' answered Maxim, 'just plain old lazy!'

With that, he cast a *Working Spell* over the shovel; and with a series of finger pointing directions, got it stoking happily from tender to firebox.

'Now, why didn't I think of that,' complained Cordelia.

''Cos you're not as smart as him?' smirked Mer.

By now they were making good progress, so good, in fact, Maxim reasoned they could be back on the main line within minutes. He was wrong, not from his estimation, but from an unseen force which was about to become deadly.

'We're slowing again,' yelled Delia as the hard-working shovel flew past her head on its way back to the tender.

'What do you mean?' questioned Meryl. 'I'm fully aware now the silly shovel's quite empty each time it clangs into the firebox that has no fire, but it's been working up 'til now.'

'I know, but look for yourself, we're slowing even as I speak,' confirmed Delia.

'I feel a presence,' said Maxim in a worried kind of voice.

The witches looked at him, knowing he was right.

'Kaldre?' asked Mer, coldly hoping he wouldn't confirm her suspicions.

'Afraid so,' he returned, 'and I know I've got to do something about it, and on my own.'

'Are you mad?' barked Delia.

'If one goes, we all go!' added Cordelia.

'No, please,' he continued, 'this is altogether different. I've been reading about this, trust me; it's something only one soul can do, providing, importantly, that they have a particularly powerful patron, one steeped in deep magical abilities.

'Who is he, how do you know him? pressed Cordelia.

'Trust me, I will let you know, here or another place. But there simply isn't time to explain, I have to leave right now!'

In an instant, Mer was talking to no more than a large swirl of smoke where Maxim once stood.

'Blimey,' cried Cordelia, 'that Maxim means what he says!'

'Either that or he's a raving loony,' added Delia. Mer didn't smile, and in seconds had climbed the tender ladder after him. It didn't take long for the others to join her.

At the door on the end of the last carriage, Maxim stood gripping its handle, quaking with the fear of opening it. Sweat covered his face.

He'd never done what he was about to do before, mainly, at his own admission, because he wasn't ever brave enough. Additionally, up 'til now he hadn't possessed the dark knowledge that was coursing through his brain.

There was another quality that ran through his brain too, an overwhelming desire to protect and save his friends from dying along with him. With that powerful thought, he wrenched the door open.

Before him, sure enough, was Kaldre flying toward the train, followed closely by her coven.

'*YOU DIDN'T EXPECT ME, DID YOU?*' screamed Maxim viciously toward her far-off dark face and dark bead-like eyes. 'That's one force you never reckoned, a warlock with the heart of a white wizard!'

At that, he leapt to take them all with him to the bowels of the earth. Yet, he moved no further than the length of his body.

'What magic is this?' he questioned madly.

Looking back he could see the hands of Mer around

his ankles, then the hands of Cordelia, quickly followed by the hands of all his friends clambering to complete his rescue.

'NO!' he screamed at the limit of his voice, 'LET GO, YOU DON'T KNOW WHAT YOU'RE DOING!'

But, their desperate struggle continued and there was nothing, even in magic, that Maxim could do to stop them.

However, there was something Kaldre could do. She could pull him and the witches toward her; thus perversely accomplishing her task to kill them all.

'They certainly won't let go you,' she cackled aloud, 'they care for you too much.'

To everyone's surprise, Kaldre's arms began lengthening and lengthening until her hand had a vice-like and freezing cold grip upon Maxim's arms.

Slowly, her force overcame the witches, and Maxim turned with tears in his eyes to mouth a final goodbye.

With a terminal kick, he shook off Mer and his friend's desperate grip, thus releasing a bond that once attached him so deeply to them. Like a slow motion sequence they watched as he collided with the Five Witches of Gloom, sending himself and all of them into a maelstrom of rocks and magic fire.

Mer screamed and uselessly strained her arms to reach after him.

'MAXIM, MAXIM,' she yelled over and over again. Tears ran down everyones' faces.

It was no good; he was gone, a life-full soul given to save them.

There's an ancient mournful song from witchdom that belongs to another world. Its long undulating chorus is the very meaning of sadness. In many ways, it captures the essence of the soul it's being sung for.

And, if it were now to fill the empty air around these young witches, staring so blankly from startled grimy faces, it would surely cause such an outcry of anguish so deep, not even the kind voice of a parent or friend could reach them until all tears were spent. It sings like this:

"O cry me no pity my soul dashed asunder,
Gone 'neath rainy downed hill.
To lie with thunder,
I caress death's harshness,
As but some long-missed friend,
Once truant of life's silly mischievous end."

It was a shallow victory. Kaldre was vanquished, yes, but at the cost of someone good, someone loved.

The deep rumbling jerk of their train rejoining the metal rails of the London Underground System was of insignificant comfort.

Maxim was lost. Gone to a molten grave where no soul could reach him, not even to drape the finest flowers known to grow.

'What is the point of all this?' bawled Cordelia, tearstained and angry, wringing her hands, not able to sit stand or do anything because of the pain inside.

Mer and all their friends uttered not one word though deep down each of them knew the answer, and it was tearing them apart.

Chapter Nine

Chapter 9: *All Hallows Eve.*

The precious memory of Maxim still haunted everyone. Though, damaged souls do repair as the days and months weave through the year, rising and falling with expectations, hope, and happiness. Just like, in fact, the fresh shoots of an eager sapling once trodden down.

At last, All Hallows Eve was here and with undying spirit, Cordelia and Mer were determined to carry on. They'd done with crying and enduring hours of empty pain. There was after all something still to be settled, something within witchdom that had to be put right. That's why they felt the night, despite its bleakness, had some answers waiting for them.

The venture they were now embarked upon, albeit through some quite lonely and dark-covered places, was most appealing as it would help take their minds off the loss of Maxim. It was to prove strangely beneficial for them as well

Snaking ahead, like a bright silver ribbon, the road before them disappeared into the ever-blackness of Haegeth's Wood.

The moon was reflecting off of its mirror-like surface of freshly formed ice. Its mirrored luminescence allowed the two witches to see the way forward more easily, albeit cautiously. But when the eerie lunar beams became obscured by heavy cloud, their guidance became less clear.

Devoid of light and, because the two were forbidden the use of brooms, the lonely journeyers could only inch along, careful not to leave the road and trespass upon strange ground.

To make matters worse, it was *All Hallows Eve*; a

dangerous time with a heightened chance of encountering an Ice Witch upon their journey, especially by foot; their vulnerability being naturally greater. For the moment, fellow witches and white witches hardly presented a threat to the Witches of Ice, so the girls hoped against all hope they wouldn't encounter a sinister Ice Witch, especially tonight of all nights.

Cordelia and Mer had little choice but to scurry along at speed whenever the moonlight permitted. It was during one of those shadowed moments, though, that something very strange and ghost-like silently shot past like a grey shadow.

It was unquestionably a witch, as the hunched over figure and long tailed brush of a riding broom was still evident whilst it quickly and noiselessly glided away from them in the rapidly fading moonlight.

Their worst fear though was soon realised.

'It's a Witch of Ice!' shrieked Cordelia, dusting off ice crystals that had covered everything in its wake; nothing other than an Ice Witch could cause this. The two of them were petrified.

They immediately jumped into a hedgerow at the side of the ice-bound road, landing straight onto a briar bush. Within their prickly surroundings, they stared and stared as the being moved away.

'She's going, thank goodness!' spilled Cordelia with a gush of relief as she spied it through her folding telescope.

But its progress only continued so far. The hardly-visible creature stopped; and turned back toward them.

No matter that Cordelia and Mer were witches wise beyond their years, they weren't willing to tangle with a Witch of Ice, despite some recent successes; as, for certain, by her very presence, she wouldn't want to talk to them about the weather or indeed how exciting Halloween is.

'Keep...very...still,' whispered Mer, though Cordelia needed no such advice.

'I don't even want to breathe, but I have to,' she whispered back.

They hid low, as low as they could in the hedgerow as the soft-lit sylvan rapidly approached them.

'I knew she'd seen us,' breathed Mer, 'all we can hope for is that either she gets distracted somehow, or loses interest.'

'Hardly likely,' muttered Cordelia, who'd now developed a tickle in the throat. She tried convincing herself that it wasn't there.

Too late to do anything about it now, right above them hovered the deathly Witch of Ice. She peered down, her black frozen eyes scouring every twig, every thorn, and every gap between every branch below her for a sign of life.

Her meticulous search seemed to go on forever, and Cordelia's itching throat wasn't getting better.

"Tickle not, fickle be, itch depart, and set me free" strained Cordelia in thought.

Mer had other thoughts though...her eyes had locked contact with the Ice Witch's. She gasped inside and daren't blink; knowing only a slow unnoticeable eye movement away from the witch's gaze would work.

"I can't do this...I can't do this!" she strained inwardly. Meanwhile, Cordelia's foot developed cramp and she knew she'd have to stretch somehow.

"Moon, for goodness sake stay hidden behind the clouds" agonised Cordelia as very, very slowly she attempted her stretching.

A distant cracking noise from the woods then caused the Ice Witch to move her head violently in its direction. At last, Mer was free of her penetrating stare as the being peered intently toward Haegeth's Wood. But, her rough frozen gown became caught in the leafless twigs sticking out from the hedge.

As she slowly began moving off, it tugged and pulled the briar twigs apart, thus exposing the two girls sheltering underneath. Cordelia instantly ceased her unseen stretching. *If she glances down, then we're done for!*

The huddled witches knew this could well be their end. The frost from the Ice Witch began affecting them too. How they stopped from shivering cannot be known.

Another snap and crack from the nearby wood made the Ice Witch jump. At once, she jerked her iced body toward it, snapping the caught fabric away from the twigs. She sped off at blinding speed to hunt down whatever had made that sound. A further spray of ice crystals was all that remained in the witch's wake.

Dusting them off, Cordelia and Mer daringly climbed from the thicket hideaway and back onto the icy road.

'*EXPLODING NEWT BRAINS!*' strained Cordelia 'That was a close one!'

Mer heartily agreed, and they took a well-earned deep breath, blinked several hundred times and Cordelia cleared her throat that no longer tickled.

As they hesitantly walked another few steps toward their longed for destination, another whooshing sound approached from the road behind.

'QUICK!' yelled Mer, 'HIDE, SHE'S BACK!'

'Not this time, not on your worst nightmare, NO!' replied Cordelia indignantly.

Cordelia stood unafraid and fully prepared to face the oncoming horror straight on. Whatever was approaching was very large, which they could both see by the dim moonlight.

'That's more than just a witch on a broom!' warned Mer 'Look Cordelia, I won't allow this. Get back here now!'

But, her sister took no notice.

'Close your eyes Mer, this isn't going to be pleasant!' she called, even though she had no idea what to do.

The oncoming threat loomed larger by the second, and, with a gulp of fear, Cordelia saw that it wasn't the Ice Witch as before, but several monstrous looking witches on a single broom. Mer grabbed at Cordelia's arm, trying to pull her out of the way. Cordelia resisted. With a final tug Mer managed to rescue her sister just as they whooshed past.

Her attempt was only partially successful though, as Cordelia in defiant retaliation, managed to stretch out her leg and kick at the handle of the passing broom, which she could now clearly see supported seven young witches; and not at all monstrous as previously thought.

'Cripes!' yelled Cordelia as she realised what she'd just done.

THUMP! TWANG! CRACK! came the sounds of the out-of-control broom's forward-facing handle as it first hit a fence post on the side of the road, smacked against the next post to almost breaking point, and with a loud crack sent the seven unfortunate riders into a ditch.

'*STONKING GRIEF!*' cried both Mer and Cordelia rushing to help. 'Awfully sorry, awfully sorry you guys,' offered Mer. 'My sister's a bit of an idiot I'm afraid, thought you were some kind of monster chasing after us!'

'Not to worry,' dragged a voice that Mer instantly recognised.

'Meryl!' she exclaimed, pulling her friend from the mud.

'Yes, 'tis me, for sure. And, I'm still in one piece. So too, I think, Delia and Persimmon. They're buried under here somewhere,' she added brushing the mud from her once very grand looking witch costume.

'Don't worry, I may have a spell to fix that. Your costume could look as good as new!' said Mer reassuringly. But she wasn't actually sure she had such a spell.

'W *h* *e* *r* *e* *o* *n* *e* *a* *r* *t* *h* *a* *r* *e* *w* *e* ?' called Pers in a stunned long wailing moan.

'In a ditch!' replied Cordelia rather unhelpfully. She then went to pull her from the mire. But, Pers was pulling Delia too, so it made her task harder. Cordelia groaned under the strain.

Delia stepped from the ditch.

'I suppose we should've conjured some kind of light before us to see if any lunatics like you lay ahead' she said angrily in her water and mud drenched costume. 'This is hopeless, I need a drying spell...and quick!'

Meryl obliged with her mum's *Pixie Drying Spell*, but it sort of got carried away, covering Delia in a cloud of steam.

'Help!' cried poor Delia in a muffled and hard to hear voice, whilst flapping her arms attempting to disperse the steam. More stifled cries ensued, but the cloud of steam became so thick and sound absorbing, no-one noticed her panic, just the cloud.

Meryl, oblivious to Delia's predicament, nattered on whilst her drying spell, or should that be *dying* spell, did its worst on a gasping Delia. 'You know, Delia seems to be actually enjoying this,' she cooed, 'listen to her singing! *Aw, isn't that nice now!'*

Cordelia nodded and Meryl went on chatting. 'We heard that Ice Witches are out tonight during Halloween, so you'd better watch out – that's one of the reasons we searched for brooms.'

'I know!' piped Cordelia, 'we've just had an encounter with one!'

'What?' exclaimed Meryl above another desperate gasp from Delia; the hissing steam though, helped drown out her pathetic cry.

'You actually saw a Witch of Ice? Shut up!' she added. Meryl then at last stopped her drying spell.

'Delia's probably done now, if not over-done,' she chuckled 'can't have too much of a good thing you know!'

'There you are,' she called, ending the charm; and the cloud disappeared leaving a steam-baked Delia crawling feebly on the ground.

'Thank the wizard's exploding feet for that!' she cried, steam wafting everywhere 'didn't you hear me shouting, woman? You could have killed me!'

'Oh dear, sorry!' offered Meryl, 'so sorry, I thought you were shouting for joy!'

She helped Delia to her feet.

'Oh, really?' sighed Delia sarcastically.

'Did omeone say they saw an Ice Witch?' butted in Pers rushing to fan the steam away from Delia.

'We did,' nodded both Cordelia and Mer.

'Whoa!!!' sighed Pers.

Delia adjusted her newly over-dried dress and continued looking daggers at Meryl for her absurdly enthusiastic attention. Meryl, still embarrassed and apologetic, introduced the four other witches that had ridden with them, who were also drenched in mud.

'That's Petunia Woodleigh,' she rattled quickly avoiding any continued rebuke from Delia '...she's bonkers, but cool.'

Petunia bowed, curtsied, threw her tall hat into the air, set it ablaze, then made it reappear under Mer's arm.

Everyone applauded.

'Mmm' sighed Petunia, 'I could have done that better... maybe not so many flames!' Mer agreed, patting a few of them out whilst handing the hat back to her.

'And the shortest but strongest,' continued Meryl, 'is Celessia Poffleton; she loves moving things...with or without magic. Trouble is, her family can never find their home!'

'Hi,' called Celessia sweetly, still straightening her near-ruined costume.

'She's brilliant at accessing many strange secrets by the way; and this is Fenella Poppleweed who's stonking at making up excuses and the spells to go with them; and lastly, here's Briony Everstone, our best mate 'cause she's a classic at charming school teachers; even Starch-Stiffington thinks she's brilliant!'

'Wow!' added Cordelia, noticeably impressed.

'So, are you lot going to the Halloween contest too?' she asked.

'Wouldn't miss it for the world!' piped Briony with enthusiasm.

'How come you've got a broom?' asked Cordelia. 'You know the contest doesn't allow brooms, or any flying objects come to that!'

'Ah, well it's quite a story,' answered Petunia. 'The drama all began with a mad hermit and ended in a short, controlled explosion.'

'What?' quizzed Mer.

'Take no notice,' offered Celessia, 'she goes like that sometimes.'

'More importantly,' enquired Persimmon, 'who invented this daft Halloween contest anyway?'

'Ah, that was Haegeth Oakwood,' replied Mer. 'Story goes, she started it about thirty years ago, after an argument with another witch over who'd played the meanest Halloween tricks of the night.'

'Sounds crackers,' said Delia.

'Well,' continued Mer, 'Haegeth thought the challenge would be the perfect way to settle any future Halloween dispute between them. The contest grew from there, and today there's not a Halloween-loving witch around who'd miss it!'

'*But no brooms!*' reiterated Cordelia, 'otherwise the locals will get a bit suspicious, seeing us lot flying about everywhere!'

'Oh, and don't forget,' urged Mer, 'we could win a *Golden Broom* this year!'

'Yeah, I've heard about those,' said Celessia, 'isn't there something not quite right about them?'

'If that alchemist Cillian Smolder has anything to do with it, then yes,' quipped Cordelia. 'Hey Petunia, you never did tell us how you got that broom, did you conjure it with old Wickham's *Come-to-Me Spell*?'

'No, no magic at all! It was just meant to be, that's all I can say,' she replied dreamily. 'We'd just been bundled out of Fenella's mum's place, with a stinking long walk ahead of us I might tell you, when I spotted this large old broom leaning against her dad's potting shed.'

'So, we had think about who would use it, even tossed

a coin, but Briony said to me jokingly, *"why don't we all fly it?"* It took us several goes, nearly destroying the potting shed in the process, yeah, but we got this far!'

Cordelia smiled guiltily. 'Sorry about that!'

Whilst they'd been talking, the clouds had thickened once more, blocking out the precious moonlight.

'We'd better get a move-on,' urged Delia, 'otherwise we'll miss the joining-up ceremony!'

'Don't worry, it's not far now,' called Mer as her breath steamed forward into the frosty darkness. 'Just over this hill, I think.'

'What hill?' asked Celessia.

'The steep one we're climbing, you nut,' choked Fenella, 'Like we're on it and it's over a hundred feet high!'

'Oh...yeah, right,' she vacantly replied.

The night was pitch black without the moon now, so it was little wonder nobody could make out a thing. All they could do was to walk as best as possible 'til the clouds thinned again.

Sharp vixen barks, and occasional hoots from owls perched high, ready to strike their prey, provided at least some dimension to their journey.

They had eventually made it over the hill and all along the winding roadway without being bothered further.

Strange as it seemed, the sky ahead seem to be glowing green and mauve, a bit like when approaching the *Unfair Funfair* they went to each year – a place of unbelievable mystery and profound danger. There was a high risk of injury and possible death at this fair. No wonder witches and all sorts of spell-casters couldn't keep away from it.

At last, in a large illuminated clearing in the wood, they could see a host of young witches and warlocks dancing and milling around in a buzz of activity.

Despite having trudged a fair way, there seemed enough energy in them to run down to where the action was. The clearing, grandly encircled by small marquees, showed off hundreds of magic wares: foods, clothing, books, charms, potions, and a dazzling array of mysterious objects; it was truly breathtaking.

The entire arena was well-lit by burning torches, candelabra stands, and oil lamps stuck on poles. There were some huge glass vessels too, full of strange glowing insects. The resulting light was pure magic, which of course it would be.

Through a megaphone, the Head Witch made an announcement:

'Welcome to the thirty-third annual *Haegeth's Halloween Contest!* Gather around please. Quick, quick... that means all of you! And, don't forget, you need to register your name with one of the ten witches seated in the middle of the arena.

'When you've completed this, you'll be handed a special Halloween bag and, *most importantly*, a Halloween wreath, don't lose them – you won't be given another!'

By this time, Cordelia and Mer were bursting to get going. Once more the Head Witch raised her megaphone into the smoky and increasingly foggy air to tell them further important instructions.

'You will also be given a hand-written list of witch houses to call upon. Under NO circumstances are you to knock at any house other than those on your list. You are forbidden as well, under pain of most awful death, to even get close to ordinary children taking part in their Halloween! DO YOU UNDERSTAND?' she screamed out..

A slow, unenthusiastic 'Yes' warbled from the gathering.

'I can't hear you! Do you understand?' she repeated with a lot more threat in her voice. This time their 'yes' was a little more encouraging and so the Head Witch continued with the rules.

'When arriving at any witch house on the list,' she barked, 'your first task is to show the Halloween wreath; this will identify you as a real witch. Once the niceties are over though, your job is to trick the witch into giving a treat, using your own spells, naturally.'

'The more witches you trick, the more treats you win. You will place these treats into your special Halloween bag. *"Why is my Halloween bag so special?"* I hear you ask.'

She didn't actually hear anyone ask, but continued anyway.

'The bag is special, because it will only accept the treats you win from the witches, no other treats, either stolen or conjured, can enter. The bag will just not accept them, end of story, finished, that's it, full stop. *SO DON'T CHEAT!'* boomed the Head Witch.

Quite bemused by the stunning effect her booming voice had upon everyone, she chortled loudly into her megaphone. Gaining her composure once more, she added, 'The winners of the gold, silver and bronze broom trophies will be announced after every bag has been returned for the count.'

'If you've cheated, you WILL be found out. Furthermore, you'll be changed into a slimy big worm and placed in the middle of a Casting Circle!'

'WHAT!' shrieked an alarmed Persimmon. At that the mischievous witch burst into a roar of spluttering laughter.

'Only kidding, only kidding!' she added. 'The bit about

a magic circle is a fib!'

Again she laughed ridiculously.

'Now, you have three hours from the time the starting gong sounds – good luck!'

The head witch lowered her megaphone. But she raised it again quite quickly, ready to add a little bit of rather important information she'd carelessly forgotten to include.

'Oh, and by the way, the old witches you fail to trick, will, I'm sad to say, trick you by taking any treats you may have stashed inside your Halloween bag, and that means ALL the treats you've won at the time!'

With that, she went into a rage of crowing.

'That's hardly fair!' protested Cordelia. 'I wonder whether she knows our headmistress?'

The others couldn't help wondering either.

'I don't trust her,' added Pers.

The girls stood in a long line of witches waiting to register, joking and sharing stories with everyone they met. It seemed to take absolute ages before they reached the sharp-looking woman now sitting before them at a very splendid desk.

In the middle of it was a large old leather-bound book and she was writing things down with a fine black and silver fountain pen.

'Name?' she asked in a dry, no-nonsense voice.

'Cordelia Merryspell.' Cordelia grinned, which didn't go unnoticed. From a huge leaning pile by her right arm, the witch handed her a piece of hand-written paper listing the houses they could visit. From a bucket sitting on the ground to her left, she reached down and pulled out a small hand-sized wreath.

'Don't lose it!' she snapped.

Cordelia felt it was somehow glowing, but couldn't be certain because of the light from all the lamps. The sharp-looking woman, dressed in a dark green dress with silver lace featuring deep mauve mystical designs throughout, looked kindly, though had obviously led a hard life.

With her right arm she reached down again and produced a rather tatty and sad-looking cloth bag, which presumably was the Halloween bag.

Cordelia fully understood why the wreath was considered worthy of not losing, but certainly not for the moth-eaten bag she was handed.

Her sister stepped up.

'Name?' said the woman in the same dry, no-nonsense voice.

'Mer Merryspell.'

'Sisters, eh?' she asked, not really interested if they were or weren't. Still, it probably made her job fractionally more interesting by making these observations. Mer stared at the pile of addresses each listed by hand, or more than likely by a charm, and realised the woman would be sat there for quite some time yet.

'Don't lose it!' she snapped, handing Mer a wreath. Quite automatically, she reached down and gave her a bag that was even tattier than Cordelia's.

'Don't lose this either!' she added in the same warning tone.

Mer's look of disdain at the bag's condition didn't escape the witch as she watched Mer promptly stride over to her sister.

'I can't be seen with this! Please swap Cordelia, you know how you prefer to have cruddy unfashionable things, don't you?' she pleaded.

The old woman overheard and barked, 'No swapping! It has your name.'

'Where? I can't see it,' protested Cordelia.

'It's not written,' barked the woman, 'it knows your name, and what you put in it. Next!'

Delia, Pers, and the other four joined them.

'Where's Meryl?' asked Mer.

'Over there somewhere, I think,' answered Pers, and she pointed toward a crowd of people who seemed to be chanting and dancing to something.

'Well, she'd better hurry, according to this list, we're off to the village of *Wart*, once the gong goes,' she announced.

'Village of what?' quizzed Briony. Her three friends looked puzzled too.

'No, not *What*, Wart!' corrected Cordelia.

Without warning, Meryl suddenly arrived, almost falling into them. She was as white as a ghost.

'What's wrong with you?' snapped Delia, watching her standing as if mortified. Meryl couldn't move a muscle. Mer and Petunia tried helping her to sit down, but she was as stiff as a board. Her face was ashen and she was muttering something unintelligible.

'Speak up,' said Delia.

'She can't, you twit, she's in shock,' reproached Mer.

'What's wrong, what is it you want to say?' she enquired more gently. Meryl's eyes told the story, but somehow she couldn't get the words out.

'Are you ill?' enquired Celessia. Meryl at last managed a reply.

'*No,*' she simply said.

'So, what is it?' urged Fenella.

There was a long pause and eventually she spoke. 'I've

just seen him!'

'Seen who?' pressed Mer, though she wouldn't like the answer one bit.

Meryl shuddered as to what she had to say next. 'Maxim!' she said with great sadness '...and, appearing like a ghost!'

Mer gasped as she still somehow believed he hadn't actually passed-over, even though she watched him fall into oblivion.

'Don't be so cruel!' snapped Mer with tears welling into her eyes. Understandably, she wasn't over the grief of recently losing a good friend; especially one she had a crush on.

Still taken aback by her sighting, Meryl could only offer Mer a blank look of 'sorry', though insisted she wasn't mistaken. 'I don't mean any harm... but I *did* see him, and as clear as day.'

Everyone was stunned by Meryl's revelation, yet knew she wouldn't lie like this, especially to Mer.

Mer wiped the tears away from her eyes. 'Ok, ok, let me have time to get my head around this.'

She smiled distantly at Meryl, suggesting she believed her. Mer needed to know more. 'How can you be so sure it was Maxim?'

Meryl told how she'd first recognised his tall shape, though, not certain, had moved in closer to where he stood.

'Well, he turned and looked me straight on, there was no mistake – it was Maxim! He wasn't a ghost either, I've seen them before! I shivered, not knowing whether to scream or call his name. His face didn't react at all on seeing me; he just stared blankly. With that, Maxim disappeared into a group of people. That's all I can tell you.'

'Weird, really weird,' pondered Fenella. Meryl nodded.

'Yeah, but now, I'm wondering if my mind was playing tricks on me' added Meryl, appearing just as tearful as Mer. 'Perhaps I didn't see him at all! Maybe I'm going crazy.' Meryl glanced at Mer half expecting an angry glare; instead she smiled in a way that said 'it's ok'.

The loud echoing sound of a very large gong, struck by a very large and intolerant witch, filled the freezing fog-bound air, helping to diffuse their emotions. The noise bounced off the surrounding trees in the forest, and even a few far away hills.

Celessia, cupping her ears against the racket, offered, 'Perhaps we'd better get going.' But they were immediately pushed aside by a stampede of excited witches and warlocks determined to win the precious trophies.

'If only I had my broom,' yelled Briony.

'Yeah, but so would everyone else,' added Cordelia.

'Just imagine how much worse it'd be than now!' she complained, fighting against the growing body of shoving, barging contestants.

The trek to *Wart* wasn't as far as the nine of them thought it would be, and soon they traipsed into the unsuspecting village, ready for the usual Halloween madness.

'Can't wait to scare the pants off this lot!' sparked Celessia. Petunia, like Persimmon, seemed nervous.

The village centre was now bristling with both ordinary Halloweeners and witches. 'Where do we start?' asked Briony.

'Let's split up, you three against us,' said Fenella.

'Celessia, Petunia, and Briony could join me, we're bound to do better than you lot!' she added, smiling at Cordelia and friends.

'OK, the challenge is on, then! Good luck... and may

the best team win!' cried Cordelia as they marched off.

Except for the occasional squeals of delight and screams of horror from various villagers facing the real witches, the village at last became quieter. A few distant barks from lonely dogs echoed through the night air.

Above, a spray of glittering stars filled the heavens, though no-one would have known with all the fog. The accompanying frozen air forced them to walk on in haste, searching for the first witch house to visit.

The list of houses started with number forty-five Lampblack Lane.

'Having a map would help,' suggested Delia.

'Follow your mind,' echoed Meryl in one of her humorous haunting voices.

'No, seriously though,' she added, 'mum taught me how you can train your mind to see everything from above'.

All of them strained their minds.

'Nope, not a thing,' blurted Delia.

'I did!' cried Persimmon excitedly.

'What was it?' asked Meryl.

'Honestly, it was a row of roofs.'

'You're imagining things,' doubted Delia.

'No, I'm not, I'm sure I saw us lot too, standing in a group just like we are now beside a street lamp.'

'Yeah, right,' returned Delia.

'Like, how did you get that one,' she added, leaning against the street lamp beside them. She laughed mockingly.

'And, if we go that way,' continued Persimmon, ignoring her and pointing toward a narrow and unlit lane, 'we'll pass a pony and trap, with no-one in it. Two houses down will be number forty-five.'

Once again, Delia sniggered. 'All right, just to prove

you're wrong, why don't we try? If you're right, Pers, I'll eat my Halloween Bag... and all the contents!'

A wave of smiles eased the tension. But soon, a look of shock upon Delia's face said it all as they edgily walked past an unattended pony and trap.

'Scary,' mulled Cordelia as the swirling fog became a little thicker. 'She got that bit right.'

Tentatively, Delia looked up at the wall of the first house. Set into it was a blue enamelled street sign with Lampblack Lane printed boldly in white.

'Disappearing donkeys! How did you do that Pers?' asked Delia, not really wanting an answer but patting her on the back anyway.

'It's no good being nice now, Delia,' chimed Mer, 'I'd get that bag ready for munching straight away!'

'Yeah, I've got a spell somewhere that could change her disgusting-looking bag into toffee if you like!' sparked Cordelia. Delia gave her a sharp stare.

'Just wait... just you wait!' crowed Delia smugly. 'It ain't over 'til the big wizard sings!'

But, sure enough, at the second house down the lane, as Pers had predicted, and huddled amid an overgrown garden, stood number forty-five. It appeared old, dark and forlorn from the outside; and even the front gate squeaked and groaned as Delia pushed it.

'Are you sure it says forty-five on the list?' enquired Persimmon nervously.

'That's what it says,' replied Mer and they began walking along the path toward its front door.

'OUCH, THAT HURT!' screamed Meryl.

'Don't scream like that!' spiked Persimmon in alarm. 'You scared the living wits out of me.'

'Well, I couldn't help it,' replied Meryl, nursing a badly

scratched arm. 'Those stupid rose bushes jumped out at me! Old Mrs. McKenzie has a bush like that, it's why she wears chainmail when gardening.'

'Yeah, I saw it attack you, Meryl,' affirmed Cordelia, 'a branch was trying to get me too. And its thorns are like claws, in fact they are claws... look at them!'

Meryl nodded and peered back toward the front gate, and couldn't help but notice the bushes had moved even closer together.

'Now there's no room to make a hasty retreat,' she sighed, 'and by every indication so far, one will definitely be required!'

'I'm not actually liking this,' grumbled Pers, 'do you think maybe we should leave?'

'It's a bit late for that,' said Delia, 'the bushes have now become entwined.'

'Which forces us to do one thing only,' observed Cordelia, 'knock on that silly door in front of us.'

At the gloomy and ancient oak door before them, Mer stepped forward and hesitantly knocked. The rusting knocker groaned as she lifted it up, so she banged it down hard a few times because it was nearly seized. Mer stood back, but there was no reply.

From a small half-oval leadlight window above the knocker, Cordelia was certain she'd seen a flash of light. It was also accompanied by what sounded to her as a fluttering of wings and squawking.

She strained to look through. The place was still blacker than coal inside and not a hint of that light she'd glimpsed. Though something or someone was certainly flapping about.

'Maybe the witch is out?' said Persimmon.

'I don't think so; I definitely saw a flash of light and

heard some kind of noises. They only lasted a few seconds, but someone's home for sure.'

'Look, why don't we try the other house on the list,' said Pers, 'this one gives me the creeps if you want me to be honest.'

'Well, we don't want you to be honest, actually,' said Delia, 'if you're feeling jumpy now, just wait to you get inside!'

'Trouble is,' pointed out Meryl, 'we have to go in as there's no chance of going back anyway, we'd be torn to shreds by those deadly biting bushes!'

'Yes, much better to get torn to bits inside,' shot Persimmon. Cordelia shone her torch around to see if there was another way through, but there wasn't. She was about to reach into her pocket and grab one of her trusty spell books, when the front door of the cottage unexpectedly creaked open.

In front of them appeared a figure silhouetted against the yellow candlelight from the room beyond.

It was a tall feathery figure. Well, that's how it seemed. It screeched something at them, but nobody could make out what it was. Whatever they were faced with was weird at best, terrifying at worst.

The figure loomed large in the hallway, and ruffling its feathers to make it appear more threatening didn't help matters either.

Without warning, there came an almighty screech as though someone had just trodden on the clawed foot of this very large creature. At once, Persimmon hid behind Delia. Meryl and Mer hid behind her, which left Cordelia standing out in front.

At last it croaked something intelligible.

'Persis! Persis!' came its squawking voice. 'That's my name! Have you something to ask me?'

'Um, is this forty-five Lampblack Lane?' asked Persimmon shyly.

With a wave of its hand, the hallway became bathed in a warm glow; and the air felt distinctly warmer.

They were shocked to see a gaunt, elderly woman dressed from head to toe in a witch's costume made entirely of feathers and dark silks. Meryl was certain her arms were wings. Yet, she had a kindly face and her house smelt of honey cakes and strange potions. She smiled at them and her face deeply creased as she did so, though it didn't make her expression look ugly, rather the reverse.

'Come in!' she insisted with a very welcoming tone, then turned to rustle her way forward, eager to get the witches into her kitchen. 'Follow me!' she squawked.

Mer held out the required wreath to which she dismissively said, 'Oh yes, I see.' Whereupon, Delia asked loudly, 'Trick or treat?'

Persis, seemingly ignoring her question, walked ahead down the long narrow corridor lined with framed pictures of exotic birds. But, she stopped, turned, and focused upon Delia.

'Ah yes,' she trilled, 'that's right, it's silly Halloween, isn't it? *Well?*'

'Well, would you like to give us a treat, or face a diabolical trick?' asked Delia boldly.

'Oh, I don't think I could stand the shock of a trick this evening –you youngsters of today! I can't imagine where you get all your ideas!' She chirped. '...So it'd better be treats for all of you. Besides, I wouldn't want to counter your tricks with any of my nasty surprises, now would I?'

Persimmon gulped at the thought of nasty surprises, especially from her, which was still very, very possible.

At the end of the corridor, they were ushered into a large dimly lit room with a huge steaming cauldron in one corner. A grand open fireplace piled with burning logs blazed nearby, and a table in the centre of the room featured plates of freshly baked honey cakes.

From a tall dark cupboard Persis began taking out a lot of small objects and stacking them upon the table.

'I expect you'd like some of these treats then?' she asked. 'Take as many as you will!'

Cordelia wasn't sure about her motives and asked the others under her breath, 'How come she's doing all this?'

Mer shook her head. 'Maybe she likes us.'

Cordelia frowned and murmured something like, 'Beware of a trap.'

Pers nodded and the well-lived-in witch's face creased into a smile once more, though her eyes looked darker, piercing even, and there was definitely an air of something or other.

Reluctantly, they wandered over to the table. Delia, the first one there was shocked at what she found.

'Bursting Broomsticks!' she cried '*a Forget Everything potion*... I've been wanting this for years, can't wait to try it on old Flurpkettle at school –picky old windbag!'

One by one, each of them began rummaging through the pile of treats. Their enthusiasm soon replaced any trepidation they once had.

There followed several more exclamations with a particularly loud rendition from Cordelia.

'*Weeeeeiiiiirrrd*,' she sang, waving a small translucent sickly-green book above her head just in case no-one could see it.

'It's only one of the strangest books on the planet,' she declared, 'written by none other than *Nevenka Kosovskaia*, I mean, blimey, she's brilliant. I've tried so hard to get this... wow!'

The work she was holding, and not likely to let go of was, *Between the Meanings –An Essay on Weird*. It was translated from the original Russian text, and perhaps one of the hardest books on magic a witch could obtain; and now, it was all hers.

Not one of them failed to find something extraordinary or indeed what they'd always wanted but dared not ask for. It was like Yuletide but several weeks before due. Another odd thing; every time a treat was placed into their Halloween bags, they glistened with a remarkable sheen of blues and mauves.

This strange glistening lasted precisely five seconds, the bags soon returning to their previous dull and shabby appearance.

'What a shame!' said Meryl. 'They were beginning to look quite cute for the moment.'

Cordelia, though, had begun returning to her previous suspicions. She smiled graciously at Persis, well as graciously as possible for her, and suggested it was time to move onto another witch's house and find more treats.

'Not so fast!' barked Persis coldly, her face darkening, eyes piercing. Cordelia immediately thought she was right for being concerned. Persis turned to them and harshly squawked; 'You haven't eaten any honey cake yet!'

'Here comes a trap!' warned Persimmon under her breath.

'Come, my lovelies, the cakes aren't enchanted or anything. Imagine all the fresh honey, butter, eggs, and flour Persis has used to make them, there are some with chocolate icing too!'

Delia had succumbed to her charms and was already taking a second bite through the creamy sweet icing and into the firm fluffy cake, which gave off the deepest aroma of honey she'd ever smelt.

The others looked at her aghast; waiting to see what hideous creature the cunning witch would turn her into.

'Tea or coffee anyone?' asked Persis, holding a full teapot in one hand, and a coffee jug in the other, as if she were serving at some local café.

Whether it was the sweet aroma and delicious appeal of her honey cakes, or indeed some enchantment that both Persimmon and Cordelia had previously feared, they were all now biting into the freshly baked delights, which Persis generously handed around.

There was the smell from some kind of elixir wafting past their noses too, which lowered their resistance to leave. This intoxication lasted a while and, to Cordelia, surprisingly her friends suffered no harmful results –no hideous transitions to their shape, extreme growth of hair, dire alterations to voice or mental alertness.

What had happened in fact was that they'd enjoyed a delicious meal of cakes, prepared by someone who really only wanted their opinion as to her culinary skills, especially in the art of cake making, that's all.

'Well, what do you think?' she asked with an uncertain look, as if being judged by the finest panel of patisserie chefs in all of France.

Speaking with her mouth full, and taking a further bite at the same time as she did so, Cordelia's reply by that action alone, was the biggest compliment Persis could've received. 'De...li...ci...ous!' came her muffled crumb-spitting reply.

'Ten out of ten for effort and result!' said Meryl with cheek, whilst from the others came a mixture of nods, mouthful smiles, and thumbs-ups.

'Thank you, everyone,' said Persis genuinely, 'you've been very kind! Oh, and I just hope you win the contest, that's what I say!'

Eventually, they bade Persis farewell, almost weighed down by the meal, and those brimful bags of treats they lugged. Happily, the narrow pathway was clear of threatening rose bushes, so they made it safely to the front gate. They couldn't have been more exhilarated by this first Halloween success.

Turning round to wave goodbye, Persis was gone, the front door was rudely slammed shut, and the house, to all intents and purposes, appeared empty and forlorn once again.

'Oh,' said Cordelia, 'so much for *"bye"* and *"see you later when you need more treats if you lose this lot, which you probably will"*!' she moaned.

The night air had become even colder, as demonstrated beautifully by Meryl and Delia each sculpturing their steamy breaths into a variety of odd shapes and creatures. Persimmon joined in as they walked along laughing. Mer consulted her list once more to find the next house on the list.

'Ah, 51 Lampblack Lane, it says here.'

'That's just up a bit,' remarked Delia.

'Do you think we even need go there?' asked Persimmon. 'I mean, our Halloweenbags are almost full, they probably wouldn't hold much more, anyhow, what if we were tricked out of our winnings by the next witch?'

'She's got a point,' added Meryl, ever the pessimist. Though optimistically, Delia couldn't help wonder that

317

collectively, with all their magic, spell books and knowledge, they'd be in a far better position to win treats than lose them. Her optimism won the point, so they continued.

Before long, they'd reached their destination. Unexpectedly, the gate of number 51 sprang open even before touching it, and they found themselves confidently walking toward a rather grand well-lit house.

The front door was remarkably different to number 45's, it was newer and well looked after. Meryl reached for the knocker but the door swung open before she could use it.

The interior had a fantastically decorated hallway with an impressive twisting stairway at the far end, lit by burning torches.

Their flames of blue, red and green burnt wildly, spreading licks of multi-coloured light everywhere.

'Something *über* suspicious about this place,' murmured Persimmon as she hesitantly followed the others. 'Far too inviting, don't you think?'

No-one answered.

In spite of this, the hallway seemed bright and welcoming.

'Look, the torches lead right up to the top of the stairs,' called Delia, 'could be some great things up there to trick for!'

As the five climbed, Persimmon couldn't help but notice the rather interesting effect on the walls. In the strange light it seemed almost as if they glimmered and sparkled with each step taken.

'I think the walls are covered with diamonds,' she called. Delia reached out and dragged her finger across the surface. 'Not diamonds, these are ice crystals!'

They all stopped in their tracks.

'Ice crystals!' sighed Meryl, fearing the worst. 'You know what this means? ...By my Aunt Oonagh's saintly shoes, it could be...'

'One of those horrible Witches of Ice?' gasped Persimmon, hoping she'd say no.

'Definitely an Ice Witch,' confirmed Mer, 'that's the only explanation.'

'Well, do we run, or tackle it head on?' said Delia urgently.

'I knew it,' added Persimmon, 'and we had the chance to turn back as well!'

'Well we didn't,' replied Delia indignantly.

'So, what shall we do then?' urged Persimmon.

'No disrespect Mer, but I think we should see if it really is a Witch of Ice first,' offered Cordelia, 'otherwise we could be missing out on some real treasures. Besides, even if there is one waiting up there for us, surely we've plenty of magic between us to take care of it.'

'I agree with Cordy,' added Delia, though deep down she was uncertain.

'I'm picking up that you two aren't you sure about this,' drifted Meryl. 'I've heard you say, Cordelia, that the Witches of Ice are semi-supernatural beings far above evil witchcraft, so clever and heartless, they can't even be considered fully human anymore. Which is what my dad says too, and he doesn't even believe in them!'

'More than that,' whispered Mer, hesitating to climb further, 'Cordelia herself insists that the great wizard Melchior Fizz reckons they live in a frozen realm surrounded by sinister evil magic... hey, and you guys still want to go up there?'

'No!' joined Pers in a panic. 'They could be powerful enough to freeze any one of us into a solid block if ice!'

'Alright, alright, but we could check first. And, as a caution,' Cordelia said, removing from her pocket one of her most prized books on deep magic, '...we could use the power of this!'

It was Melchior Fizz's *Dark Moments, Lighter Outcomes.*

They still had doubts, though the book she held was particularly dangerous-looking by anyone's standards, and to the others it seemed remarkable how Cordelia had hidden such a large volume from sight.

'Well maybe, yes then,' said Mer. '...But I'd like to know where are you getting all these books by Melchior Fizz, Cordelia?'

'The school library, actually!'

'Well, I've never seen them,' she protested, 'what section?'

'The teacher's section, near old Starchy's office if you must know! And don't worry, I will return them... *eventually.*'

'You'd better, Cordelia, I'm not getting into trouble for you again!'

Cordelia gave everyone an aloof sort of stare and opened yet another recent acquisition of Melchior's books, *"The Witches of Ice – A Hundred Ways to Defrost their Spells"*, going straight to the relevant section. But before she had time to look for and read the most appropriate spell, a voice called out, *'Don't worry about Mr. Fizz and his completely useless spells; they'll be of little value here!'*

The remark was cruel, and to make matters worse, Cordelia's book slammed shut by itself. No matter how hard she tried, she couldn't open it.

'Come here, young witches, 'I have need of you,'

echoed the cold, sharp voice.

Strangely, and without knowing why, they felt compelled to do as the witch requested. It was as if their legs were being made to continue climbing the stairs.

Soon they'd reached the top balcony and were being forced to walk toward a half-open door at the end of a gothic arched hallway. No longer was everything brightly lit and cheerful, in fact all of them were feeling disgustingly cold.

'Feels like we're in a freezer!' exclaimed Mer, dusting a layer of ice crystals off the balcony rail. She attempted to grip it with all her strength to prevent her involuntary walking. It made no difference.

Persimmon, like everyone else, was having the same problem. They were being marched against their will toward the door before them; 'I tried warning you,' she said in a smug voice, 'I knew there was something especially weird about this house, but, like always, none of you listened!'

The frosting on the walls was becoming thicker as they moved upward. In seconds, their spellbound legs had taken them through a half-opened door and into a dark room. They were standing there stiff with fear and coldness, staring at something they didn't want to see.

In the gloom, they made out the hunched figure of someone hovering above a large chest. Cordelia, still wrenching at her Melchior Fizz volume in a vain attempt to pry it open, cried, 'Who the hell are you?'

In all horrors, the being suddenly revealed herself as the Witch of Ice they'd all feared. And, spying them enter, she'd quickly turned her attentions toward someone in particular.

Although unnoticed by her, the witch's frozen black eyes were staring unrelentingly into Meryl's.

'I know you've seen someone, child,' she said, pointing at her. Meryl moved back in shock. 'And I know you're bursting to tell me who it is!'

Meryl attempted turning her head away from her gaze, but it was of no use.

'Don't be afraid,' continued the Ice Witch, 'just give me his name!'

Meryl was trying hard not to reveal her thoughts.

'I understand your reluctance,' the Ice Witch added sourly, 'you've never seen the likes of me before, have you?'

'Oh yes we have!' blurted Cordelia, interrupting her concentration, 'we saw one of you lot on the way here. You're not very good at finding people either, are you? One of you was no more than a couple of feet above me and Mer, and still missed us!'

The room became sharply colder.

'I think,' said the figure, turning to Cordelia, 'you don't know what you're dealing with. Otherwise, you wouldn't be so damn arrogant.'

The Witch, crackling with splintering ice as she moved, swirled through the air to hover more closely. Once again, both Cordelia and Mer noticed the frozen garments. They were the same as the Ice Witch they'd previously encountered along that deserted road to Haegeth's Wood.

'Soon,' rasped the frozen creature with great conviction, 'it will be the time of we Witches of Ice'.

Whereupon, she floated down and settled above Cordelia to penetrate into her eyes and brain.

'A new witchdom,' she continued, 'with power and reward

for those like you, if you choose it.'

Cordelia sneered. The Ice Witch re-focused, saying; 'A realm that crushes and disintegrates obstinate people like you and your cronies!'

Regardless of her spiteful proclamation and fearful appearance, Cordelia moved her head to try and see her hooded face. She wasn't successful; all that could be seen was a black emptiness where a face should be. So, Cordelia bravely leant closer for a better look. She immediately wished she hadn't.

Cordelia could only remember, after waking coiled and frozen on the floor before her friends and sister, falling into this terrifying witch's void and being drawn down to the bottom of a black pit. After that, she'd felt something like a frozen hand grasp her round the throat, throwing her further into the darkness.

She was still choking when she awoke; and no matter how much comfort Mer and her friends gave, she was flooded with fear.

'Perhaps now, you've learnt a little respect?' hoarsely rasped the Ice Witch. Her name was *Zylphoriah*, though no human would want to remember it, unless they inexplicably desired a visitation from her during the fearful witching hours past midnight.

No amount of spells or enchantments or magic circles would prevent the likes of her from coming either. An invitation by name would be enough for any one of the Witches of Ice to appear in all their frozen evil.

Mer and the others were still concerned whether Cordelia was OK.

'*Smouldering eyeballs!*' she moaned groggily, 'What on earth happened then?'

As they began telling Cordelia how she'd kind of

fallen into *Zylphoriah*, then reappeared laying on the floor in front of them, Meryl, without warning, screamed at something that had fleetingly passed in front of her.

The others looked up to see a tall ghostly figure, quite different to an Ice Witch, dart across the room.

'IT'S HIM AGAIN!' squealed Meryl, 'MAXIM!'

Mer believed her this time; the figure's shape was unmistakable. Shocked, she looked toward Meryl and nodded slowly. The figure abruptly evaporated into the wall furthest from them.

'That's odd,' said Mer, 'I can move about again!'

Everyone could. Delia leant down to help a stunned Cordelia stand. 'Come on, you can't lay there and sleep all night, we've an Ice Witch floating about somewhere!' Cordelia found it difficult, but managed half a smile.

Persimmon interrupted with, 'It's like we've all been together in some kind of nightmare,' quite convinced nothing about anything was real anymore.

'No, 'fraid not, it did happen,' answered Meryl, turning to go, 'though I've often wondered if my eyes are telling me the whole truth!'

As they were about to run off, something bounced off Mer's shoulder. Then came another object, and yet more. They were small chunks of ice; and had a lot to do with the recent apparition they thought was Maxim.

She peered up to see where the pieces came from, and was totally shocked.

Zylphoriah the Ice Witch had begun disintegrating, *splinter-by-splinter, shard-by-shard*. Fragments were falling like pieces from a giant jigsaw puzzle; and, it seemed, there wasn't anything she could do to stop herself from wasting away.

'Crikey!' yelled Cordelia. 'How did that happen, Mer? It's impossible... I'm sure no-one's ever made an Ice Witch smash into pieces like that before... that's amazing if you have! Well done, which spell did you use, was it one of Melchior's?'

Her questions shot out in quick succession, not leaving her sister any chance to answer.

The others joined in the tirade, but soon moved back to avoid being struck by ever-larger chunks of a broken, splintered Witch of Ice.

'I didn't do a thing!' called Mer. 'It just sort of happened.'

In a short space of time, after the clatter of Zylphoriah smashing to pieces on the hard floor had finished, all that remained was an icy mist hanging in the air, which finally faded from sight. Zylphoriah was dead and gone, no mistaking it. Not one of the witches could understand it either.

'I can't say for sure,' said Meryl, 'but my Aunt Oonagh did once tell me that spells can sometimes be cast from beyond the grave to help those in the living world.'

'Just what are you saying?' frowned Mer as they speedily fled the room, picking up their almost-forgotten Halloween bags on the way.

'Well, and perhaps maybe, the spell that shattered the Ice Witch, could have been cast by Maxim?'

'So, you really think he's dead after all?' replied Mer, looking distressed.

'Sorry,' answered Meryl quickly, 'I'm not meaning any hurt, I just don't know, it's a possibility, that's all.'

'But, equally,' argued Cordelia, 'he could still be alive, keeping his distance, afraid of the Ice Witches capturing him.'

'You've a point there,' reasoned Persimmon, 'perhaps

to use such powerful magic, you have to be kind of *out of this world* anyway.'

'My head's spinning with all this,' sighed Mer as they at last reached the front door and ran toward the awaiting and appealing normality of Lampblack Lane.

'Don't know about you, but I've had enough of trick or treating for this year!' said Mer as they huddled under an unlit streetlamp.

'Me too,' agreed Delia, 'let's get back to Haegeth's Wood...with this lot, we might even win a golden broom!'

'Yeah,' added Cordelia. 'I wonder how much the others have managed to bag?'

'Don't know, and I don't even feel like finding out,' said Pers, looking very shaken by their ordeal. 'Is our lovely witchcraft really coming to an end as Melchior says?'

'Not if we have anything to do with it!' reassured Cordelia.

The streetlamp above them dramatically burst into light, as did the others along the lane, almost as if signifying that some great evil had departed. The freezing fog had lifted too; and feeling braver, the witches strode more confidently, deciding to return to the gathering at Haegeth's Wood after all. Their burgeoning Halloween bags could easily win them that golden broom.

As they walked away from Lampblack Lane, they never looked back, even once; they didn't want to. Yet, if they had, they might have caught sight of something to their advantage.

Though it could be argued whatever this thing was, it belonged far too much to the world of shadows than the one they currently occupied.

326

Chapter Ten

Chapter 10: *Unfair Funfair.*

Rain had been sweeping down all the gloomy day. Early evening had begun with the light fading fast, and still it swept down just as hard.

Cordelia and Mer were soaked to the skin, but didn't mind at all. They were standing in a long, long queue to enter *Horace Brill's Magnificently Unfair Funfair.*

It's the most desirable funfair any young witch warlock or wizard worth their spells could go to. Each year, from far and wide, they'd ride their brooms, or whatever they liked flying with, toward the fair, days before it opens.

Nearly everything about the Unfair Funfair is totally unfair; and, that's the appeal. The blindingly exciting challenge to overcome these horrors, are exactly what keeps Cordelia and everyone else coming back each year for more.

No wonder there was such a queue stretching way back from the main gates. No wonder there was such a buzz of excitement in the air. Even the stupid rain couldn't dampen that.

Countless spell-casters stood or sat upon specially conjured seats, armchairs or even beds, patiently huddled against the weather waiting for the magic moment when Horace Brill's Magnificently Unfair Funfair, would finally open.

Naturally, Cordelia and Mer had journeyed with Meryl, Delia, and Persimmon. For such an amazing event, there'd be no way any of them would miss being together for this.

Having arrived a day earlier, and enduring a night of torrential rain and howling wind, they'd earned their place near the front to be within a stone's throw of the entrance. But, almost at the end of this very long queue, a tall warlock had started a *witch-whisper*.

As previously mentioned, a Witch-Whisper is a way of whispering secret magical messages that are immediately recognised by the person they were destined for. They are whispered along witch-by-witch and warlock-by-warlock, until reaching tbe right one.

The Witch-Whisper on this occasion belonged to Mer; and, she knew the whisper was hers, because her ears literally glowed and buzzed, so it went no further.

The message contained within the whisper was as follows: *"pmaws s'aicileb fo ertnec eht ni ruoh gnihctiw ta thginot em teem rem"*.

There's no profoundly complicated cipher involved in the encryption of the whisper; actually it's very easy to understand once you know how. As long as the listener is conversant with the way witches do things, they'll have no problems at all. But, bear in mind, words do get mixed up when messages are passed from one witch to another, and can end up very different to what they started. Still, because Witch-Whispers are wrapped in a spell, they nevertheless do eventually make sense.

Mer understood the message at once, being the rightful owner. It concerned her greatly though, and after sharing it with the others, was strongly advised not to carry out the instruction. So, forgetting all about the bizarre witch-whisper for the time being, she waited patiently for the opening.

Although the daylight had nearly gone, the dazzling fairground lights from hundreds of rides and sideshows more than made up for its gradual disappearance. Added to this was the tantalizing cacophony of fairground noise and music thumping from every corner of the fair.

'We can't even trick our way in!' complained Cordelia.

'I know,' replied Mer, not offering any hope other than to hang around until the great moment.

'Apparently, they've put *Spell-Locks* on the gates and fences –spoilsports.' she moaned.

'Worse than that,' added Meryl, who was dreamily standing with Persimmon and Delia under an invisible umbrella, 'you can't even conjure a ticket this year.'

'Have you tried?' asked Delia.

'Absolutely, but as soon as you make one appear, they burst into flames.'

A few flashes of lightening lit up the sky and their following rumbles of thunder added to the weird atmosphere. The rain thumped down harder and the brims of most witches' hats now sported tiny waterfalls.

'Crikey,' cried Meryl above the roar; 'Perhaps it's best I avoid the *Slime-Slide* this year after all!'

Meryl didn't even get a smile over this. Even though no-one was talking about it, they still felt the acute sting of losing Maxim. None of them had told their parents, even after it'd become known that he'd been missing from home for some time. His mum and dad were naturally beside-themselves with worry, fearing the worst.

However, the girls knew they had to keep quiet about poor Maxim, as there was a distinct possibility that he was still alive, especially after Mer and Meryl's experience on *All-Hallows Eve*. If the Witches of Ice got wind of this, they wouldn't waste any time finding and destroying him. According to Melchior's book *Out-Witching The Witches of Ice,* that's *exactly* what they'd do.

So, although it was heart rending not to do or say anything, it was imperative they didn't.

At long last, a fanfare of trumpets blasted through the

air and everyone covered their ears to avoid the enormous sound.

'That was stonking!' shouted Delia 'I love the opening of this fair.'

A great volley of magic firework shells shot toward the heavy clouds, bursting with a shower of witches flying upon brooms. It was a truly magnificent sight as they swooped down waving long flaming banners displaying "*Welcome to Horace Brill's 53rd Magnificently Unfair Funfair.*"

Huge charmed padlocks holding closed the main gates finally snapped open with a puff of green smoke. These amazingly tall iron gates rumbled apart to a roar of cheers. The long queue began shuffling through and there was a decided hum of excited chitter-chatter as it progressed.

Each entrant held out their by now soggy tickets to an equally soggy ticket inspector. In front of Cordelia, a trickle of rainwater ran down the seated inspector's nose to form a large droplet.

This dolloped unfairly upon her already wet lap as she checked her ticket.

"*Pass,*" she croaked miserably, and Cordelia raced in waving her arms screaming 'Yes! Yes!'

She was in, and couldn't wait to begin the adventure.

The others soon joined her. Naturally, the first thing they decided to do was to stuff themselves silly with the best *witch-sweets* available to witches; and that meant finding the finest confectionary at the Unfair Funfair. But at this place it pays to be on your guard, as most conjurers of *witch-sweets* are crookedly dishonest, if not downright evil.

Some witches have eaten such innocent-looking vile

candies, only to turn into a hideous old crone, or some vile-smelling pustule-encrusted creature for the rest of their lives. So, obviously, they had to be very careful.

About the only thing that's fair at Horace Brill's Magnificently Unfair Funfair is the price of the ticket. It actually does include *everything* on offer in the funfair, no more to pay. Whether it's rides, snacks, drinks, or even *witch-sweets* that appear highly suspicious; by merely presenting your ticket, soggy or otherwise, it won't cost you a penny more; and you can use it as many times as you want.

It could well be the main reason why even the meanest witch warlock or wizard is always agreeable to pay the reasonable cost of getting into the fair.

'*Spiderfloss*...get your lovely *Spiderfloss* here!' came an important-sounding voice from a rather unimportant -looking barrow stall. 'Come on girls, over here... every witch loves *Granny Black's Tasty & Completely Unforgettable Spiderfloss!*'

Out of pure curiosity, and nothing else, the five of them approached the barrow.

The man serving this strange confection, looked quite normal as normal warlocks go, except for the damp -looking and very crumpled green velvet suit and tails he was wearing. His over tall green velvet top hat didn't look quite right either.

Still, thought Meryl, *he is wearing green after all.*

The others stepped closer.

'Well,' he said 'I can see you're interested.'

'Not really,' replied Mer 'So, what have they got in them, these "*Spiderfloss*" things, and why on earth would anyone want to eat one? I mean, are they really made from spider webs?'

'Ah, don't you worry about that, Miss.,' he replied confidently. 'Once you've tasted one of these, you'll never want another sweet again!'

'Or anything else,' quipped Cordelia '...*you'll be dead!*'

'What's it to be, young witches?' he asked.

'Well,' replied Cordelia 'you haven't told us if they're really spider webs yet?'

'Oh, for goodness sake,' he snapped angrily, 'damn right they are!'

The girls jumped.

'Sorry,' he chimed, 'It's just that I've had a lot of worries lately, and I know you're going to love Granny's treat'.

'Now listen,' he whispered closely. 'I'll let you into a trade secret. *Spiderfloss* is really quite different from any other candy in the fair, and you won't want to miss out on the amazing effect it'll have on you either!'

'You see' he went on 'it's made with only the finest hand gathered and most delicate morning spider webs, lightly spun onto a stick, just like candy-floss. And, during this spinning, Granny Black cleverly weaves in some tasty little treats all the way through. The result is a completely unforgettable taste experience! Go on, try one, they won't bite...you know you want to.'

The witches looked at each other and looked at the warlock in his daft crumpled green velvet suit. Whether or not they were simply being gullible, or whether it was because they were at this strange unfair funfair, can never be known, but they each took a tempting candy-pink Spiderfloss from the smiling warlock, bit and swallowed a whole mouthful.

Instantly, their confections changed to a mud-brown tangle of old matted webs, dried insects and droppings. The result of coughing and choking, as well as their overwhelming desire to vomit, cheered the warlock no no end as he rolled about on the rain swept ground laughing at the top of his voice. Now they realised why his green velvet suit was so crumpled and wet; he'd done this more than once.

'Oi!' shouted Cordelia indignantly, and between chokes, 'you said after tasting these we'd never want another sweet!'

Still laughing, the warlock sat up and said 'Yeah, I know I did…so welcome to the Unfair Funfair!'

Eventually they saw the funny side of it and threw their almost uneaten Spiderfloss into the air. They cast a spell to set them alight. Each *Spiderfloss* burned and sparked as they floated off into the thunderous night sky.

'So much for something *über* special!' moaned Pers, rather disheartened.

'No, not really. Look over there.' cried Meryl, pointing at a very grand well-lit tent, striped in countless bright colours.

The sign outside said it all for just about every witch or warlock at the Unfair Funfair; *"Mrs. Boyle's Celebrated Honest to Goodness Sweet Emporium – Nothing Boyled Sweeter or safer for over 100 Years!"*

The sight of the colourful tent displaying a host of treats in every shape and hue would be enough to draw in even the staunchest opponent of witch-confectionary. As they entered, they were handed a large red and white twirled-striped box to fill with a selection of their favourite sweets.

A delicious aroma of a thousand candied inventions filled the air inside the tent. Every time they walked over to a new stand of amazing ideas, they were overwhelmed by their novelty taste and smell. Many witches had spent many hours of magic to produce such a huge supply of confection.

Pers looked up to read some of Mrs. Boyle's supposedly *spell-safe* but eccentric ingredients, from an enormous board hanging just inside the tent door.

'I think we can trust these' she enthused. Mrs. Boyle's list included;

The Witch's Hat

Contents: *Soft Brazil nut fudge in the centre, covered with coconut ice, followed by honeycomb crumble, a marzipan coating, and a layer of thick, thick chocolate decorated with icing sugar spider webs.*

Problems: Tries to sit on your head, hard to remove.

The Wayward Broom

Contents: *Thick chocolate covering over a liquorice and barley sugar handle, dark rock candy brush, dusted with sweet ginger powder.*

Problems: Will attempt flying off whilst being eaten, can take you with it.

Toffee Bombs

Contents: *Secret, well guarded, recipe for the centre, which is thickly coated with a cherry fudge, a layer of roasted almond truffle, thick creamy toffee and an outside covering of toffee nut crunch.*

Problems: Explodes if it feels like it, which is more likely than not. Best eaten behind a shield.

Poisonous Snake

Contents: *Hard chewy windberry flavoured jelly body, patterned with chocolate shapes, boiled sugar head with delicious fruit drops for eyes, and barley sugar fangs.*

Problems: Can bite if you're not quick enough, but will only hurt a bit. Not poisonous at all, though the name makes everyone want to have one.

Marshmallow Pillow

Contents: *Softest marshmallow in a choice of flavours including strawberry, lemon, and caramel, vanilla or chocolate. Dusted lightly with icing sugar.*

Problems: Very big; and despite their size, never last long enough to be used as a pillow as they're eaten far too quickly.

Cordelia was first to order. 'Two *Toffee Bombs*, one *Poisonous Snake,* a *Wayward Broom*, a *Witch's Hat,* three *Stupid Monkeys*, oh, and a *Stinky Lizard.'*
'You'll need an extra cardboard box for that lot, dear.' said the witch behind the counter with an approving smile 'How about a *Deadly Toffee Apple* to go with it? But her look was shifty as she said the word *deadly*. This worried Cordelia who reluctantly waved her unfair funfair ticket before the lady.
Mer, not feeling at all worried, chose a *Sherbet Volcano,* three *Spinning Lollypops,* a bag of *Crawling Liquorice Spiders,* a *Wizzle Stick,* and a dozen *Laughing Bon-Bons.*
By picking different things they could share them around. It was a great way to discover new treats and surprises.
Leaving the huge tent of *Mrs. Boyle's Celebrated Honest to Goodness Sweet Emporium*, they went in search of their first amusement, carefully trying their confections along the way; wary of any changes to them that may occur. Sweet-witches should *never ever* be trusted.
The walk through the narrow lanes of sideshow amusements was dark and threatening. Odd-looking characters lurked within many dubious looking tents and

stalls. A thin spiky-faced man with long nose and a long flowing cloak lunged toward Persimmon.

'Wanna test your luck?' he demanded thrusting a black dice with constantly changing dots under her nose.

'No thank you' she said haughtily.

'Win lovely prizes...or lose everything you've ever owned' he said slimily. They moved on quickly.

Cordelia led the way; and passing another stall, she flippantly pulled open its strange mauve glowing curtain. There was a terrific bang throwing all the stall's contents into the alley.

'I'M NOT BLOODY READY YET!' screamed an annoyed voice. Once again the girls fled quickly.

Hurrying around the nearest corner, Delia stopped abruptly and cried, 'Wow a real *Dangerous Coconut Shy*!'

It was too, and the shies, run by Sergei Molotov were renowned for being particularly hostile.

'What's a *Dangerous Coconut Shy?*' asked Pers.

'Oh, just a lot of crazy fun I suppose' answered Meryl being deliberately obtuse. She winked at Delia, who knew well what to expect.

A gaunt-looking man, standing behind the counter of Sergei Molotov's *Original Dangerous Coconut Shy,* reached over to Persimmon holding out an ordinary looking coconut.

'Roll-Up! Roll-Up! -And all that nonsense.' he said in a dry, uninterested voice. 'Come on, take a coconut, throw it at the target and win yourself a lovely prize.'

Persimmon smiled at him nervously and asked 'How dangerous is it?'

'Not dangerous at all if you're a good shot and you can dodge things, Miss,' he said, a little brighter whilst waving the coconut at her more insistently.

Persimmon couldn't help but notice the dazzling array of prizes to be won. From costumes to charmed jewellery, to spell books and magical potions, it all looked too good to be true. There was a reason for that.

'Come on Pers,' encouraged Cordelia, 'it'll be loads of fun.'

Delia nodded the go-ahead to the attendant, and, smiling wickedly, he gave each of them a large bag of coconuts.

'Hang on, don't you normally throw something at the coconut to win something?' asked Pers

'Not at this stall' answered Delia 'it's far more adventurous!'

Just as Pers hesitantly took her bag, the stall opposite closed its shutters. She looked a bit worried by this, even more so when the attendant said, 'Oh, and here's your shield.'

Rather timidly, she asked 'What do I need a shield for?'

He smiled sympathetically and replied, 'Just take it, *please*.'

Their shields, naturally, weren't ordinary. Although they gave the impression of being made from glass they were almost jelly-like. In fact, Delia easily passed her finger through hers.

Yet, they were tough enough to withstand even the hardest objects, as they were about to find out. The five of them stood facing the various coloured targets on offer in the stall, and immediately began throwing their coconuts.

Delia was the first with a powerful lob. It didn't hit the bull's eye though, as the target swerved to miss the incoming nut. Instead, the coconut went on to crack against the wall behind so hard, that it burst open, showering its milk everywhere.

'Oh, bad luck!' called Cordelia.

As the others joined in lobbing as hard as they could, there came a sudden and quite unexpected hail of coconuts coming back at them from the stall.

'What on earth's happening?' screamed Persimmon as she dodged a violently slung coconut, missing her by fractions of an inch.

'Great, isn't it?' yelled Cordelia. It seemed the stall was fighting back and thank goodness everyone had taken a shield.

Getting a prize from this place was becoming decidedly unfair. Coconuts, violently shot from the stall, were swerving through the air, blasting into the witches from all directions. The nuts were not only bouncing off their shields, but walls, pathways, and other stalls close by too.

'This is absolutely ridiculous!' squealed Persimmon as she caught a rogue coconut on her right shin. 'Yeowch!'

'Yeah,' yelled Cordelia, 'you've got to watch those low one's coming in from the side... Keep your shield moving, Pers, that's what I do.'

'Use your magic too!' added Mer, feeling a bit sorry for Persimmon's cruel initiation.

Sadly, no sooner had Mer given her this invaluable advice, than she copped a particularly large coconut on her left knee.

The challenge was becoming a nightmare. Delia took control.

'Close ranks!' she cried, and they huddled to form a tight group with enough shields to protect every angle.

'Trouble is, we can't throw now,' complained Persimmon.

Though, she was grateful at least that the bombardment of nuts wasn't hitting her anymore.

Cordelia was hoping to win an eye-catching black box that contained *Johnson's Standard Collection of*

Dangerous Books, something she'd always wanted, but now it seemed more out of reach than ever. Mer had set her heart on a black charmed dress, as did Persimmon, Delia a new broom; and Meryl an amazingly large crystal ball.

'I agree with Cordelia, we're never going to win a prize at this rate,' added Meryl, 'and my cousin Dugal says it's terrible bad luck if you come away from a fair without winning anything –*your legs tie themselves together in a wicca knot!*'

Everyone laughed.

'If I can get a decent shot, and those pesky targets don't move,' said Delia, 'we might stand a chance at winning something.'

'Got it!' yelled Cordelia. 'I might have a spell that'll make our shields open one way, and closed the other!'

'What is it?' asked Persimmon, 'and, hurry, we're getting precisely nowhere here!'

'Well, from Edwardo Flynt's book How To Throw Stones in Glass Houses, there's his One-Way Spell; you could easily spend all day throwing in a greenhouse if you feel like that, and not break a single pane; everything simply passes through!'

'That means we can lob ours out, but their coconuts can't get in,' said Delia. 'Brilliant!' added Mer.

'And, would you even believe it,' said Meryl, 'don't I have cousin Dugal's *Stay Where You Are Spell* to keep those target thingies from jigging around?'

At last, a plan had been hatched, and once they'd cast the spells, Cordelia threw a coconut as hard as she could.

Like a bullet, it effortlessly shot through their shields, flew high in a wide arc; and whacked the once obstinate target straight on. Meryl's use of her cousin Dugal's spell worked a treat.

'Bull's-eye!' cried Cordelia, and the whole stall burst into life with lights and trumpet fanfares.

An angry voice crackled over the stall's speaker system. 'I'm not sure that strike was fair, number one. If you're cheating, woe betide you!'

Not knowing whether they'd cheated, which is surely what one *should* do at an *Unfair Funfair*, he at first denied their win, then reluctantly called out, 'Come on, come up and select your damn prize, and I really hope you don't get hit by any of our stray coconuts on your way here.'

Cordelia raced off to grab her so longed-for Johnson's Standard Collection of Dangerous Books, fending off a barrage of hostile coconuts with her shield in the process.

Soon, the others hit their bulls-eye too; and a now more-annoyed-than-ever voice came over the speaker, reluctantly inviting them to get their winnings. The voice went on to say that in all the history of Sergei Molotov's *Original Dangerous Coconut Shy*, never before had so many prizes been won in a single game, by so few.

The crackling voice started coughing and choking, the man finally breaking into tears as the loudspeaker was switched off.

The girls proudly walked off carrying their prizes on way to find a small lock-up, where they could leave them safely whilst enjoying the rest of the Unfair Funfair hands-free.

There were countless alleys of tents, stalls and sideshows to choose from; and it seemed impossible to believe so many things could be on offer. Eventually, the witches

343

found a lock-up; an odd-shaped iron-clad building that had light shining from a pattern of holes drilled all over it, rather like a giant lantern.

The ironwork sign at its entrance read; Cragertha's Locked, Stored & Bolted. A tall, wizen, and very sinister looking witch guarded it.

She wore a full-length black lace dress with high collar, long sleeves, and sharp, very sharp, pointed boots. The earrings she wore looked odd to Cordelia as well, so she asked the witch what they were.

Cragertha, for that was indeed her name, looked at her with sharp black eyes; and, ignoring her question completely, barked, '*WE'LL HAVE NO TROUBLE WITH YOU LOT!*'

Cordelia reeled back from this; she certainly wouldn't have trouble with any of them as far as she was concerned. Anyone would think at least three times before attempting a run-in with the likes of her.

'She's a good choice to guard this place,' quipped Cordelia to the others.

Not daring to laugh, Persimmon asked Cragertha politely if they could store their stuff at her lock-up.

The change in the witch was as dramatic as her appearance.

'Oh, my lovely ones, so, you haven't come to claim anything after all!' she cooed sheepishly.

'Well, certainly you can store your prizes here! Why', she added whilst patting Cordelia on the head, 'here's an adorable young witch, to be sure.'

At that she cackled with a very dry-sounding laugh. Kneeling down to Cordelia's height, as she was incredibly tall; the witch asked, 'So, you like my little earrings, do you?' 'They're great!' replied Cordelia with a grin.

'Not great, dear, they're just very, very little. Tiny witches in fact, ones that I shrank earlier for *TRYING TO STEAL FROM MY FLAMING LOCK-UP!*' she roared, eyes bulging with paranoid force.

This didn't intimidate Cordelia at all, and looking at Cragertha curiously, she asked, 'Don't I know you from somewhere?'

The witch smiled and gurgled loudly. 'Ever been to Pain's Wood, dearie?' she asked.

'No,' replied Cordelia, 'but I have been to a rather grand Witch Ball at Nightshade Hall,' she replied, finally remembering that Cragertha was in fact the witch who'd tried to steal Mer's Darkington Chalice.

'Oh,' she said jerking back from her, 'what a remarkable memory for one so young. Still, all's fair during battle, isn't it?'

Again she kneeled, whispering in a low, threatening sort of voice into Cordelia's ear. 'Now, off you run, sweetie, and leave all your precious cute things with your Aunt Cragertha. Be a nice, sweet child, and maybe there won't be any fights between us.'

Cordelia smiled in a way that said yes there will, and moved back with the others as Cragertha took the belongings from each of them. She smiled wickedly at what was handed to her as if she'd just been given the Crown Jewels, no less.

'Something tells me that's the last we'll see of that lot!' quipped Cordelia as they made their way to another amusement.

'Well, we did get a ticket from her,' assured Persimmon. 'Trouble is, the writing's so small, I don't think anyone could read it.'

'You might need a magnifying glass' offered Meryl.

'Or made to be very, very small,' added Cordelia; everyone quickened their pace at the thought of her remark.

'Where shall we go?' asked Delia, excitedly peering up at Pandorah Pontigue's amazingly high *Biggest Dipper* that seemed to disappear into the clouds.

Pandorah's *Biggest Dipper* is a roller coaster unlike anything else on the planet. The hand-painted sign proudly announces, *"Climb the Clouds, Dive to Hell!"*

It was unquestionably an invitation to some, like this bunch, whilst a definite repellent to other more sensible people, but, there weren't a lot of them at this fair. Meryl, watching Delia gazing at this remarkable structure, could only suggest leaving this ride to last.

'I don't think my stomach could take this at the moment, I feel as though I've just finished one of *Grandma Rhoswen's specially charmed Belly-Burster Puddings!*'

In the midst of their chatter, a ground-shaking boom from Pandorah's Biggest Dipper gained everyone's attention.

A large oddly shaped capsule containing a dozen or so screaming witches and warlocks shot into the air, seemingly guided by a thin wisp of magic energy.

It can only be supposed that this wisp of bright green power was in place of the usual rail that most roller coaster cars are attached to. It was damn effective.

The capsule followed its twists and turns, eventually shooting into the clouds, illuminating them brightly as it punched through. The girls were amazed by this fantastic display, and decided it would definitely make the ideal ride to end their visit.

Turning away, they hadn't walked far when Persimmon held her nose and groaned. 'What's that awful pong?'

'Oh, WOW!' screamed Meryl in shocked delight. 'Look, it's the *Tunnel of Vile!*'

'The what?' asked Pers.

'Oh, man, Vile is so cool –you mean you haven't heard of it?' Meryl enthused.

'No,' replied Persimmon in disgust.

'You don't know what you've been missing! OK, so the tunnel's a bit messy and stinky 'cos it's absolutely vile to get through, but if you do, the magic you gain is mind-boggling! I so love all the sludge covered arms of vile witches trying to catch you too!'

Persimmon was now totally convinced Meryl was stark staring bonkers.

Everyone stared at the tunnel's slimy green entrance and thought better of it.

'I don't know if my stomach would be up to it,' said Mer.

Persimmon agreed, and both Delia and Cordelia suggested it might be worth doing a bit later.

They'd not walked much farther, just to the corner of a set of marquees and stalls, when Cordelia froze in her tracks.

But, it wasn't as a result of any charm Cragertha had cast upon her, rather a different kind of spell, and soon they'd all be under it.

Cordelia looked straight ahead with eyes glazed, not moving a muscle. It wasn't long before the others were similarly transfixed. Ahead was perhaps the most thrilling and most dangerous ride in all of the Unfair Funfair's history.

A gust of freezing wind and a ghostly sigh chilled them further.

A dark band of faded and worn gold lettering announced, that's if you were fast enough to read it; *"Xylia Vago's Infamous Misery-Go-Round –Everyone's Dying For a Ride!"* which, probably, would be more correct in saying *"Everyone's Riding to Die"*.

The mere thought of Ms Vago's diabolical carousel sends cold shivers up the spines of most witches, warlocks, even wizards; especially those who'd rather stay indoors tinkering with magic or reading heavy volumes on other people's magical misfortunes.

Not this lot, though.

Cordelia saw the growing numbers of people scrambling to join the queue to get on and yelled *'Hurry!'* There followed a desperate rush.

Despite the barging and pushing, they'd managed remarkably well to get so close to the front; there were only about twenty people, mostly hostile witches, before them. And they were intent on standing their ground, growling and hissing at Cordelia and her party. 'Blimey!' she quipped, 'I ain't tangling with them.'

Not many could imagine the size of this *round-about* thing, even if you were to explain to them the facts and figures; like it stands a hundred and ten feet high, has a width of over three hundred feet, and can hold up to three hundred and fifty idiots, as no doubt Mrs. Merryspell would describe them. It rotates at approximately one hundred and eighty miles per hour at full speed too. However, there's a little more to it than that. Firstly, the Misery-Go-Round never stops, ever.

It can't; once the spinning charm was cast over it, the machine became unstoppable.

To join, you have to 'catch' a ride whenever a demented horse, creature, ghost, or some other inexplicably weird passing object takes your fancy. Quite simply, it would be a major folly to simply reach out and grab your ride; apart from losing half your body in the process, not even the most extreme spell could repair you afterwards.

That's why the owner of this dreadful machine, rather benevolently, offers each witch a broom so that participants can fly to their chosen mount and climb on mid-flight. Once they're mounted though, if the speed won't get them, something else a darn sight more sinister inevitably will.

Cordelia's eyes and ears were still transfixed upon this huge rotating beast. Its almost disturbing quietness, broken only by the gentle thrumming sound of forceful movement, pulled a blur of strange-looking creatures attached to poles extending from under its shadowy canopy.

The droning roundabout had them all excited. Cordelia and Mer's fascination reached a crescendo as they approached the barrier with their three friends close behind. 'One at a time!' barked a witch on admission duty, pushing her back. There were six witches overseeing altogether, and each kept a sharp eye upon the entire goings-on.

'One at a time!' she screamed afresh, pushing away several more young witches who were eagerly grabbing at brooms stood upright in a large brass cage. 'I won't tell you again,' she continued, 'otherwise it's back to the end of queue for the lot of yer!'

The young witch at the head of the queue, desperate to join the amazing ride, had successfully acquired one of the ratty brooms out of the brass cage. It barely seemed fit for sweeping a floor, let alone anything else. Nevertheless she now stood mounted and waiting to go.

With a witch's hat that had no conical top, front and back rims sweeping sharply to a point and sporting a long black feather that sailed backwards some three feet or more, the group's leader looked to her rear and the oncoming rides with deep concern.

A massive flash of green and blue sparks sent her on her way to join the rides on Xylia's fantastic Misery-Go-Round. She was gone, possibly never to return. Only a residue of hazy smoke was evidence of her ever standing there. Her friend's faces lookedsomewhat whiter. Another young witch was next in line and hesitantly mounted her broom. The attendant, seeing her nervy state, placed her hard, bony hand upon her shoulder for reassurance.

'Look back, now,' she rasped. '...Steady...steady...go!'

Another flash of sparks and hazy smoke filled the space where the young witch once stood. Before long, the group ahead of them had disappeared into the blur of rides and soon it was Cordelia's turn.

'Good luck,' reassured Mer as she walked up to the brass broom cage and took the first one to hand.

She mounted and peered back to select her target ride, which resembled a giant sabre-toothed deep-sea Viperfish jetting toward her at fantastic speed. She turned sharply to the front and in an instant was almost blinded by a flash of green and blue light.

At once the exhilarating sensation of tremendous speed set in and, for the first time, Cordelia could actually see all the bizarre rides mounted by a mass of witches, warlocks and young wizards whizzing around with her.

Now Cordelia understood a little of what was in store, and not all of it was nice. Her Viperfish ride was soon alongside, irritably snapping with those giant, glistening and well-honed sabre teeth. Grabbing the pole it was attached to, Cordelia held on for dear life as she jumped onto the Viperfish's spiny body.

The broom she once rode shot away in a puff of smoke. Attempting to stay on this ride, she dug her heels into the fish's leathery skin. It reared its sharp fins and shook its grisly-looking head as if caught by a great fishhook. It was all Cordelia could do to remain mounted as the monster writhed and bucked at her unwelcome presence.

The creature's huge curved razor-sharp teeth and fully-extended jaws looked set to devour something; hopefully, not me, she felt whilst struggling to gain control.

But, as her confidence grew, so too did her skill at managing the beast. Even though it was joined to the pole she once held onto for dear life, it was only an assumption that the pole and the ride were actually joined to anything else at all; the canopy above her was too obscured to see even basic detail.

Cordelia could swear there were clouds above her, and strained to peer into the murkiness of the canopy. There were clouds, and oddly, they moved at the same speed of the rides. They were dark ominous and billowing too, which didn't add to any feeling of confidence.

Just then though, a few yells of *'LOSER!'*, *'COME ON...GET A MOVE ON!'* and *'GET THAT UGLY THING OUT OF THE WAY!'* cheered her immensely as Mer, Delia and Meryl, mounted on equally bizarre creatures, caught up and moved in alongside her.

'A *Pterodactyl?*' she exclaimed to Delia. 'Who on earth would ride a Pterodactyl... especially being ten times bigger than you?'

'Ah, but it flies like the wind!' she bragged. With that,

Delia pulled on the prehistoric bird's reins; its long beak opened and snapped shut a few times displaying some seriously huge shark-like teeth.

'D'ya wanna swap?' called Cordelia.

'Crikey no!' answered Delia, more than happy to keep the Pterodactyl, despite its constant lunges to snap off her head.

Meryl, as usual, chose something decidedly freakish in the shape of a giant lizard with a skeletal lion's head, whilst Mer seemed content riding a traditional fairground horse.

The fairground horse fascinated her. The hand-painted, obscure designs appealed to the artist inside. The horse also had an engaging if not peculiar face. Mer found it disturbingly appealing.

Little wonder everyone else quite rightly supposed this outwardly dangerous ride to be something even more fearful than what met their eyes.

'Where's Persimmon?' cried Cordelia.

'Don't worry,' answered Meryl, 'she's OK, she just chickened out, that's all.'

'That's right,' added Mer above the incredible wind hitting them full on, 'She's going on the *Screaming Cat*.'

'Blimey!' shouted Cordelia in surprise. 'Does she know what she's in for?' '

Probably not, but what a way to learn...and on your own!' replied her sister. Their attention was soon drawn back to riding the weird creatures, and thinking about the infamous perils of the *Misery-Go-Round* that yet awaited them.

Not far off, Persimmon was walking toward an amazingly tall black tent that looked akin to a really large witch hat. Inside was the incredibly dangerous *Screaming Cat*'.

She couldn't avoid the noise of screaming either -it was so loud. But, the screams sounded human rather than feline.

The witch who inspected her ticket seemed remarkably feline; tall, graceful with an air of superiority, and Pers was sure she had cat's whiskers to match.

'Have your strongest spells ready before confronting the cat,' she mewed, 'try and stop the cat from screaming...if you don't succeed, you'll probably lose your hearing, even some of your hair, in the blast. Great fun, great prizes if you can do it... no-one has today, still, it's only early...come on now, move along quickly... cowards can exit to the left.'

She said all this in a remarkably musical voice. Persimmon was dumbfounded and immediately started searching for any spell books she may have on her.

'If only Cordelia was here!' she blurted out loudly in front of a bunch of other young witches.

They immediately looked at each other and burst into laughter, much to Persimmon's embarrassment. Climbing the rickety wooden steps up to the stage before the screaming cat was probably similar to the feelings of some poor soul climbing the gallows.

Persimmon couldn't turn back now, even if she'd wanted to, which she didn't because the group of sniggering witches she'd just encountered were staring at her every move.

Persimmon eventually got to the centre of a long stage and stood apprehensively before massive black curtains hanging in front of her.

She could easily hear the deep panting of something considerably large, breathing behind them; the curtains were swaying in rhythm with its heavy breath too.

This might have been the perfect time for her to exit

at speed, *stage left*, as offered by the attendant. It *might* have been, because the opportunity was fleeting, and the black curtains began parting almost instantly to reveal a cat that beggared description.

Before her was an astonishingly huge black cat, nearly twenty feet in height. Surprisingly and of great concern, the beast wasn't tethered either, completely free to move or even pounce wherever it wanted to.

Strangely, its shape was exactly like any cat familiar that you'd see around the house, except, alas, for its monstrous size.

Its two yellow eyes with wide black pupils stared with pure uninterruptible concentration, only moving at Persimmon's slightest twitch or fidget.

It became a lot more interested in her as she fumbled around searching for a spell book even the smallest book would do, she pleaded inside. And that's precisely what she did find.

Not much meatier than a pamphlet, it was given to her by Cordelia some weeks back for use in *"dire emergencies"* as she put it. To be honest, Persimmon hadn't taken much notice of it before this night, dismissing the booklet as a nice gesture perhaps, but more of a politely accepted nuisance.

That might explain its creased and tatty appearance. But, the title on the booklet's cover made her immediately feel she should have taken better care of it. *100 Ways of Avoiding Certain Death* it read, and the author was none other than Cordelia's favourite magician, Melchior Fizz. Persimmon's spirits lifted as she opened to find *"Deathly Screams −The Counter-spells."*

There was no doubt about it; her good friend had saved her. She took a deep breath and cried out the first line,

'*Be gone horrid, wretched screech,*' but before Pers could finish even the first sentence, her ears were filled with pain; she was pushed backwards with the force of a locomotive, or so it seemed.

A tremendous ripping sound began her brief journey, and Persimmon flew through the air thumping into a stack of well-placed hay bales.

She couldn't stand, she could hardly move and her blurry eyes just made out the hat-shaped black tent before her, now around fifty yards away and with a giant tear down its centre; evidence of her recent expulsion.

The tear quickly repaired itself, which was more than would happen for Persimmon, in the short term anyway. It was most unfair, she never stood a chance; but that's what one should expect at an *Unfair Funfair.*

Eventually, Persimmon did manage to stand again, and, rather pathetically, she staggered away from the Screaming Cat and blearily strode onto another so-called amusement. The witches that had been making fun earlier had raced outside to laugh and mimic Pers staggering off.

It wasn't fair, but she moved on regardless. She arrived at a cute-looking tent that to her seemed remarkably tame by comparison, featuring a host of gorgeous coloured lights and sounds reminiscent of a tinkling music box.

The only slightly menacing thing about it was the sign above the wide entrance, which simply read *Dead Dragon's Claw.* Though, with the letters in bright pink surrounded by drawings of sweet-looking baby dragons, it would hardly be cause for concern or acute anxiety – or maybe it would.

Right in the centre of this very inviting and well-lit tent, on a circular wooden plinth, was a tall six-sided glass paned case, measuring some eight feet in width and over twelve feet high.

It was choc-a-bloc with the most amazing gold and silver jewellery one could possibly imagine.

Its shimmering glitter and sparkle certainly caught the eye of a throng of young witches, including Pers, who couldn't wait to find out the amusement's purpose. Pers eventually managed to get a look in, standing close enough to be completely overwhelmed at all she saw.

Hanging from the top and middle of this sparkling arena, protected understandably by thick glass, was a withered-looking arm, that, as the sign had indicated, probably once belonged to a dragon; though from its dried condition it would be a little hard for anyone to be completely certain that such was the case. At last, Persimmon had figured what it was all about.

She'd remembered seeing something similar in an ordinary fairground involving a crane with a bucket that one could lower to pick up valuable items. Now, she knew what to do. Trouble was, how could she get the claw to do what she wanted? There were no handles or levers anywhere in sight, except for a *Collect Your Prize Here* button.

But, like all witches, she searched her memory for a spell that may help. The words that came flashing to the front of her brain were those of Esmeralda Potworthy, who'd many years back invented a spell to control objects by mere thought.

With a deep furrowed frown, the spell was expressed by intense concentration. At the same time, the young witch beside her screamed as the dragon's arm sprang horrifyingly to life; Potworthy's spell had worked. And, almost as if its hand and claws could actually see, the thing moved around similar to a snake's head, darting toward anyone standing too close to the glass panes.

Pers stood her ground though, not scared at all by this oddity, and concentrated even harder on commanding the dragon's arm; willing the hand to open as wide as possible and forcing it to grab a huge bundle of precious objects.

Remarkably, she achieved her aims amid the many gasps and squeals of delight from those now closely gathered around.

After Persimmon had conjured the dragon's arm into position, and with its full load, the clenched claws hovered right above a wide chute designed to convey any winnings to the lucky person waiting outside of the glass enclosure.

This was usually the time in ordinary fairground amusements that the thing would stop and return to its resting position, annoyingly taking with it all the treasure one had worked so hard to get. And, being that this was indeed an unfair funfair, the same would probably be true here.

Not so. To her disbelief, the claws released their prize, sending a shower of incredible riches down into a chute. But, despite peering into the opening in front of her, fully expecting a trove of hard-won valuables, there wasn't a thing to be seen.

It was empty, no prizes at all.

'That's totally unfair!' she yelled furiously, repeatedly pushing the prize button. Having no luck, she began kicking thumping and shaking the case, which was most unlike Persimmon.

The witches who'd been watching her moved back from

her game-rage, and without any warning, the dragon's claw once again sprang into life. With sharp claws it smashed through the glass panel in front of her, grabbing and pulling Persimmon into the huge case.

Screaming and terrified, she was left hanging above the wide chute, designed to convey winnings not witches.

Poor Pers could only struggle helplessly.

In seconds a falling sensation overwhelmed her as the dragon's claw let her go. She slid out of control down the chute at tremendous speed. Her journey was awful.

Persimmon raced through mud slime and putrid waste of unknown description, not having a clue where she was bound, only aware of the occasional rising and falling as she sped along.

'Damn, I must've entered the Tunnel of Vile!' she called aloud. She opened her mouth wide to yell more but her gob was literally stopped by a huge splat of slime.

Choking, Pers retched and spluttered on this torturous journey that seemed to take forever. She used her legs and arms to keep herself from tumbling over.

With a mighty whoosh, she exited the chute like jettisoned effluent, flew a short way in the air, and landed in an icy-cold swamp.

Covered in freezing mud and now thinking rather fondly of Xylia Vago's Infamous Misery-Go-Round, the young witch cast a quick spell to remove as much of the foul stinking ooze as possible, and climbed onto a grassy knoll where she couldn't help but notice a sporadically flashing neon sign.

With overly garish letters, the sign read "Aunty Belicia's Beloved Lucky Dip Swamp" and underneath it went on to invite those lucky, or indeed, unlucky enough, to *"Dip in and pull out a fortune!"*

Persimmon was not impressed, and after stumbling deeper into the ever-thickening swamp, she heard strange wailing moans, which broke through the swamp's eerie silence. 'Who's there?' she called. Again, there came more distressing cries.

'I'm not afraid of you!' she announced fearfully. The pitiful appeals were from nothing more horrifying than a few mud-bound witches and warlocks.

'Please help me,' came one mournful cry. *'I'm holding a golden treasure chest, and daren't let go for fear of losing it,'* the voice called quite pathetically.

Persimmon peered through the swirling mist to see if she could spot the individual calling out.

'I'll go you halves, if you help me,' continued the voice, sounding a little more anxious. Using one of her favourite lifting spells, Pers began the rescue.

'How cruel of you to cause so much distress!' she shouted out loudly; rebuking the swamp for just being a swamp.

Strangely, these words were nearly identical to the words going through Mer's mind, and no doubt everyone else with her. They were still battling the infamous Misery-Go-Round. But, worse followed. A deluge of giant hailstones the size of cricket balls rained down. The whopping orbs of ice thundered from the menacing clouds that hung ominously beneath the ride's huge canopy.

Bruised and battered and trying desperately to dodge them, Cordelia manically pointed toward the belly of her ride.

'CLIMB UNDER YOUR RIDES, YOU FOOLS!' she screamed at the others.

Her message eventually got through, and each of them

copied her, clambering below their beasts to take shelter.

'I don't know how long I can stay like this. My brain isn't used to thinking the wrong way up!' Meryl, called, holding desperately onto her giant lizard's writhing body.

The simple purpose of Xylia Vago's infamous Misery-Go-Round is this: the longer you remain on your ride, the greater your reward. In fact, it's a promise of Xylia that anyone who survives her contraption for more than an hour will qualify for a whole week at a place called *Weird Castle*; a peculiar establishment, designed and built for the amusement and education of witches, wizards and warlocks in all things magically weird.

It is a place that most only ever dream of going to. A visit alone requires the winner to have an ironclad constitution. Not only must they be able to withstand the rigours of severe and bizarre magic, but the strangest environment known in all of witchdom. Understandably, very few survive her Misery-Go-Round, even fewer Weird Castle itself.

'Can you smell burning?' yelled Mer, sniffing the air.

'It's your hat!' called Cordelia dryly, pointing toward the top of Mer's head.

'In this rain and hail?' she shouted back.

'Yeah, *she* did it!' accused Cordelia, pointing to an enflamed fire witch hovering just above seated on a roll of fiercely burning hay.

'*WHAT!*' screamed Mer, and she ripped her singed hat from her head, beating it furiously on her fairground horse to put it out.

With a groaning, splintering rip, the head of the hand-painted wooden horse turned round in surprise. It looked her straight in the eye, and screamed an objection.

'And, you can shut up too!' she yelled back, nearly at the end of her endurance. Regaining her composure, Mer muttered a short spell, which caused the fire witch to spin off in a roar of flames.

'Woo–hoo!' cheered Mer. 'So much for fire witches – they'll have to do better than that!'

But sadly, the effect of Mer's spell was temporary.

In no time about fifty of them, burning furiously, swarmed around the young witches, pulling chunks of burning hay from the small bales they were riding; throwing them like missiles. Everyone ducked and dived.

'This is more like it!' yelled Cordelia, wanting a fight. She began by catching and returning the chunks of burning hay from where they came.

She was using a spell to help quell the flames too. It was a curious charm, usually read aloud to dampen an out-of-control fire in someone's living room grate. When observing the spell at work, flames would seem to disappear into themselves.

Well it could work here, as the bales are definitely out of control...I s'pose. thought Cordelia, repeating the words by Edwardo Flynt, over and over. *'Out, out, flicker and choke, go you flames, back to smoke!'*

But, despite her efforts, the fires under the blazing witches weren't reducing which allowed them to draw nearer and nearer.

'This isn't working!' screamed Delia, who, atop her great pterodactyl, was in a good position to know as the ends of her new dress were already smouldering.

'Out, out, flicker and choke, go, you flames, back to smoke!' repeated Cordelia to help quell the menace. It was no use.

Now, the flapping sound of wild flames, whipped by the speed of air, fully occupied their senses. The ever-nearing extreme heat of the burning witches and choking black smoke took care of any remaining senses they had.

Cordelia's hat then went up in flames. Edwardo's spell had lost its potency. The fire witches were unrelenting. They swooped confidently within mere inches of the girls, attempting to cause whatever they wore to instantly combust.

And, it was no use trying to dampen any flames, as the fiery creatures returned again and again screaming and crying at the top of their burning voices. They were determined to set their victims alight, come what may.

'This has got to stop!' cried Delia.

'What we need,' suggested Meryl, 'is a few large drops of good ol' Irish rain. I might just have Ashling Ó Brolly's *Wet Spells* on me somewhere! Now, she's really good on bad weather charms!'

'Whatever!' called Delia, not really convinced her spells would help.

Yet, just when all hope had seemed to desert them, Delia noticed the fire witches departing.

'Hey, we've scared them off!' she cried.

'You're right,' answered Meryl, 'and these little fires of mine are definitely going out!'

Cordelia began cheering, and was about to say, *'Thank goodness!'* when a massiv ball of stinking ooziness slapped her straight on the face.

'Oh yuck!' she squealed.

Delia burst into fits...but not for long, as she and the others were pelted too.

'OMG!' gurgled Mer through the slimy ooze. 'This has

to be worse than a few singed clothes!'

Everyone was fending off lump after lump of this disgusting slime, holding their noses tightly.

'Who on earth is causing this?' gurgled Mer.

'It ain't from the clouds,' said Cordelia. 'Someone's throwing them for sure, but I guess that's what you get at an unfair funfair!'

The stinking mire that overwhelmed them had come so suddenly after the fire witches, no-one a chance to avoid it.

'It's them!' yelled Delia from high up on her pterodactyl mount. 'Look, it's from a bunch of Swamp Witches!'

She was right, these vile creatures are unforgivably disgusting, caring not who knows it. Their stench and stinking mud, usually caked on them, was now flying off from every part of their putrid bodies, bringing even more misery.

Swamp Witches love swamps. They can't get enough slime, ooze, or awful-smelling swamplands. They find slimy frogs, toads, snakes, worms, leeches, as well as a myriad of biting stinging insects most highly desirable too.

'Get away, you revolting creatures!' yelled Mer, waving her arms about in hopeless opposition.

'I don't know how much slime is left on them,' spluttered Delia through mud-spattered lips, 'but, I'm out of here!'

She jabbed her heals into the neck of her monstrous mount to fly higher. It was not a very wise action.

The grisly pterodactyl turned its fierce head, opened its beak revealing rows of sharp shark-like teeth, and commenced snapping at her. Well below, Mer screamed in shock, which was more than Delia did. Instead, she kicked her legs out at it.

At that unlucky moment, the pterodactyl's closing beak caught the pointed tip of her left boot and began tugging at Delia to throw her into its mouth and almost certain death.

The whole drama of her struggle was akin to watching the *death-roll* of a crocodile; every time she attempted to get free, the beast twisted and turned its head to prevent escape. Clearly, Delia stood no chance against it.

But just as she was about to be bitten clean in half between the massive beak of her ferocious pterodactyl, a sinister irony put a stop to Delia's and everyone's disastrous misery riding Vago's terrible machine.

Approaching, like a hoard of blurred shadows, came a swarm of greatly feared *Dark Witches*; ones who'd sworn allegiance to the Witches of Ice, and carried out their bidding to cause death and destruction.

Hope, it seemed, had disappeared once more. And, from out of the middle of this blur of darkness, shot forth the worst possible instrument of death these beings could unleash upon their victims.

The Witches of Ice had commanded them to use of one of the deadliest forces in dark magic: *Black Lightening*.

Only very powerful wizards can withstand this negative energy; certainly not a witch or warlock; and certainly not inexperienced ones like these four.

Cordelia's eyes were filled with horror as terrifying shafts of high energy Black Lightening darkened, roared and singed their way around her mud-caked Viperfish. The Black Lightening was amazing to watch; that's if you weren't the object of its destination.

Its violent forks crackled thunderously through the air, but were the very opposite of ordinary lightening. Their black evil energy sucked inward any form of life it encountered, making the surrounding area the absolute essence of death.

What happened next would have broken anyone's heart as a powerful strike shot through the frigid air, cracked along the surface of a nearby ride, and instantly consumed Meryl.

Without warning, she'd vanished. Instantly. Evaporated in fact before her friends' eyes. Only seconds before, she'd commenced a chant to protect herself from this terrible might. It was a waste of breath.

The shock and horror was too much for the three remaining. They jumped for their lives, despite the savage risk of being mangled by other rides crossing their path.

Again, with horror, Cordelia and Mer, both casting a spell for a broom to help in their escape, looked back to see Delia hit full force. In a black strike of lightening, she disappeared from sight too.

Having no time to get their heads around this, they simply leaped onto the abruptly materialised brooms that skidded alongside.

In a rush of fear and panic the two flew off, vanishing into the windswept haze below them. Forks of deadly power banged and exploded after them, missing only by sheer luck.

Meryl. Delia. Both gone. Gone in a black flash of evil. It was too much to bear.

From a distance, the sight of Xylia Vago's Misery-Go-Round, if not extraordinary enough, was attracting a growing number of intrigued observers. Not knowing what was actually happening, they watched with amazement as flashes of darkness from the Black Lightening circled about, replacing the usual grey blur of speeding madness. The deep hollow thunder, which accompanied these strikes, no doubt added to the curiosity.

Abruptly, Cordelia and Mer shot out of this maelstrom, circling several times until their speed decreased enough to allow them to land. *Land* though wouldn't be an adequate description –more like thump, bounce, skid, roll and crash.

As they lay in pain, gasping for air, many from the crowd of onlookers rushed to their aid. Picking them up and offering comfort, they managed to get them both safely away from the thundering Misery-Go-Round.

Mer and Cordelia, suffering grief at losing their two special friends, howled with a deep cry from the heart. Tears of inconsolable remorse poured from their stinging eyes.

Unaware of what had just transpired, the caring witches and warlocks who'd rescued them could only attempt genuine reassurance. The two girls hugged and wailed, not understanding for even a moment how it could have come to this.

After leaving their rescuers, despite being offered a safe passage out of the Unfair Funfair, and spells to heal their injuries, they hobbled off into the shadows; determined not to be found by the Dark Witches.

It took nearly an hour for the two of them to piece together all that had happened, nonetheless resolving not to be beaten by the evil around them.

'First Maxim,' wailed Mer, 'now Delia and Meryl...'

She broke down once again.

'Bloody why...why?' sobbed Cordelia.

'I don't know if I can do this anymore!' howled Mer. 'Poor Meryl...poor Delia.'

'But, we have to,' sniffled a tearful Cordelia, 'We have to do this, if only for them!'

More bitter time passed with empty moments of desolation and regret. The two hardly looked at each other, though needed each other's presence. After the tears dried away, a strong determination filled the air and the awful silence was broken by Mer.

'That's it, I'm following the Witch-Whisper,' she pronounced.

Cordelia looked up, shocked.

'Mer, I don't want to lose you as well!' she shot angrily. 'Haven't we had enough of people setting us deadly traps? Don't do it, please. Besides, first we must find Pers and tell her the untellable.'

'I don't want to lose you either,' returned Mer. 'I'm just heartbroken...and angry, angrier than you'll ever know.'

Cordelia relented and put her arm around her sister.

'Listen, we'll find Persimmon, I promise. But that *Witch-Whisper* is nagging me to follow its instructions. I hadn't explained, but the whisper told me to be at Aunty Belicia's Lucky Dip Swamp; and to meet someone who'd be in the centre at witching hour.

'What's more, I know it's *him!*' she cried aloud, with more tears of despair. 'It's Maxim, I feel this deeply, Cordelia; he's at the fair, I'm convinced.'

Although Mer felt strongly that was Maxim, Cordelia though had other ideas. Cordelia hesitated.

'I will respect your wishes, Mer, but I will follow you to Belicia's Swamp nevertheless, and I'm going to stick you like wizards' glue, and you know how strong that stuff is!' she said with a smile. 'It's true, I'll be on guard all the way –not leaving your side for one second. That's just in case someone, or something rather nasty is waiting for you instead.'

Mer appreciated her sister's concern, and they both set out for the long walk to Aunty Belicia's swamp.

Their journey took them past a fantastic array of stalls and amusements. On better days, there wouldn't be one they'd pass by. Harriet Mistletoe's *Exploding Dodgem Cars*, Vidsava Obnoxia's *Tower of Disappearance*, Cuthbert Hang's *Extreme Ghost Train*, Helen Blackberry's *Strange Cabinet of Peculiar Events*, or even Thinius Murk's *Diabolical Wheel of Chance* – that's if anyone ever gets to stay on his diabolical wheel long enough to win anything.

They also managed to get past Penny Ditherington's *Penny Arcade*. Penny nearly caught them a few times, although they certainly weren't in the mood for any of her menacing antics. The two even avoided William Bullstrode's *Got You!* shooting range –not getting shot at even once with one of his disgusting dung balls.

There wasn't yet the slightest temptation to stop either as they passed *Witch-Glitz Galore* –the fair's finest stall of hand-made witch jewellery; or even divert their progress via *The Crumbling Magic Bridge*, where no doubt they would have trodden upon one of countless unsafe stones; inevitably to end up in the teeth of several rather vicious creatures.

Alas, with them being so understandably distraught, they traipsed forward in a daze; intent on getting to the lucky-dip swamp; Mer more than Cordelia it seemed.

At last they'd passed the furthermost collection of amusement tents and game arcades; and were finally upon the unlit swampy road that led to Aunty Belicia's dangerous attraction. It was set back from the main arena of Horace Brill's Unfair Funfair simply because of its perilous nature; and, revoltingly, its foul stomach-churning reek.

The rain that had plagued the fair had abated for now, allowing a growing mist to rise up from the swamp, covering the only pathway to its main gate. It blanketed so thickly, they could hardly see where they stepped.

'We need a glowing spell,' called Cordelia. 'especially when we reach the swamp itself.'

'More like a *see-where-we-should-be-going-spell* you mean,' added Mer, still caught up by the horror of all they'd been through.

'Yes, that's it,' replied Cordelia, 'a spell that not only glows, but glows the way forward!'

'Daft question,' said Mer. 'but, have you got one?'

Before she'd finished asking, Cordelia had removed a small scrunched-up piece of paper, set fire to it with one of Pontigue Popp's trusty *Everlasting Non-Strike Matches*, and threw it into the mist.

The spell written on the paper was rather clever, as it caused any plant or creature nearby to glow and shed a pathway of light. It was Mott's *Light-Mapping Charm*, developed one foggy night after Mr. Mott lost his way home from *The Steaming Imp*, his local pub.

Walking quite quickly now, the illumination from the tall iridescent gates of Belicia's unfair masterpiece soon glimmered through the mist; and, after holding up their damp though still-charmed tickets, the gates momentarily disappeared to allow them through.

'I've been thinking,' said Mer, 'what if it isn't Maxim waiting for us, but someone else, like say ...an Ice Witch for instance?'

'Now you get it!' sparked Cordelia. 'Why do you think I'm so nervous? You must have wondered?'

'Obviously I did,' replied Mer emotionally, 'but after all that we've suffered, losing our best friends and all...'

Her voice choked. She didn't continue with the sentence.

'Yeah, I know,' comforted Cordelia, who, it seemed had grown in wisdom by about five years in as many months.

Mer then stopped and yelled, 'Persimmon! ...We mustn't forget about Pers!'

'I know,' answered Cordelia, 'And we won't either. At least we know she went away from danger and off to the Screaming Cat...mind you, supposing she's...'

'No, no! Don't even think it,' interrupted Mer, 'Goodness knows what I'd do if...' She stumbled for words once more, trying desperately to keep from breaking up. Cruelly, very cruelly, the Witches of Ice had added yet another dimension to their unending barbarity.

As Mer commenced walking once more, she missed her footing, almost falling headlong into the swamp that was present both sides of the narrow path.

She was saved though by a fortuitously placed rock; landing on it with both feet. It moved unsteadily beneath her, sinking deeper into the slime with her added weight.

Fearing it ultimately submerging, Mer quickly regained her balance, leaping back onto the path. Had she'd given the rock a closer look, which happily she didn't, the both of them would have been in even deeper despair. Sadly, it was no rock, but a huge lump of ice containing the frozen body of Persimmon.

She'd encountered a Dark Witch too, and its evil had put paid to any escape. As they walked off completely ignorant of this dire circumstance, Persimmon's frozen body slowly sank deeper and deeper.

Not far from this sad spot, their glowing spell unexpectedly stopped working, leaving them in near total darkness before a large grassy knoll. Only the dim light from the far-off fairground arena helped them see anything at all.

'How did that happen?' complained Cordelia, who immediately fumbled for another scrunched glowing spell. She didn't find one.

'Look over there,' whispered Mer abruptly, her voice quivering with fear and anticipation. 'Someone's standing in the centre.'

She was right, the figure was tall, much taller than she remembered Maxim to be.

'Perhaps he's a ghost,' mumbled Cordelia. 'Ghosts can appear larger than what they were in life. Well, that's what our Aunt Eunice believes anyway'.

'Oh, shut up, please!' snapped Mer, too frightened to move. They simply stared at the tall figure; who seemed to be wearing a full-length robe. Its arms lifted and a deep hard voice roared out.

'Stop! You have come far enough.' Instantly, they knew it wasn't Maxim, ghost or not. He spoke again, though not with a roar this time, more kindly, with a hint of underlying wisdom.

'We live in troubled times,' he said. 'There are things concerning a terrible evil within witchdom that I must relate to you.'

'Who are you?' called Cordelia boldly.

The man pushed back the hood that shrouded his head

to reveal a friendly and wise face. A face aged with frowns and smiles from years and years of life. 'I am your humble servant, Melchior... Melchior Fizz, that is.'

The two of them were stunned for words; and the only expression they could manage wouldn't be hard to guess.

Without thought, the witches leapt onto the knoll, not for one moment thinking that the being who claimed to be this great magician was anyone else.

They stood before him; and at once Melchior developed one of the broadest smiles they'd seen. It warmed their hearts as much as anything could on this cold and grievous day.

'I understand your troubles,' he broke in a concerned voice, 'I really do. But I must tell you to continue having enormous courage. The greatest fight of your lives is about to happen.'

Mer became tearful, and Cordelia managed to say the words Mer couldn't.

'But, you don't understand, we've lost two more of our friends. Gone in an instant... they're dead, *both of them*!' pleaded Cordelia in anguish, trying desperately to fend off hundreds of tears waiting to appear on a face so unaccustomed to them. 'How could you know what we're going through?'

'Ah, alas, but I do, many times over. I'm so sorry, but I cannot unwind the terrible events that have been visited upon you, no-one can,' he said, trying to understand how they felt. 'But I can say this; trust in yourselves first, then trust in others that trust you. You must know that deep inside everyone exists a core harder than diamond. OK, we may be sensitive, kind and forgiving on the outside, but in here,' he said pointing to his heart, 'it's rock-solid all the same; allowing us us to withstand the horrors that life sometimes throws in our path.'

Melchior's words were wise, but not enough to take away their pain. He knelt beside them and added softly, 'Yet, even so, I have to tell you something.'

Melchior looked down searching for the right words. 'There is a certain thing which you both possess that has the power to defeat the Witches of Ice!'

'What does it look like?' urged Cordelia.

'Who has it... me or Cordelia?' asked Mer.

'No, it's not that simple,' he chuckled; if it were, the Ice Witches would have it by now. This is something you need to think on. All I can say is that this possession cannot be broken or stolen. It is sought after by many, and once revealed can never be destroyed. I can tell you no more.'

He stood back. 'I must leave now; it's becoming dangerous for me to remain. Remember what I have told you, hold firm; all is not lost.'

'Can't we at least have a clue to what this thing is?' demanded Cordelia.

'Search your souls!' he cried, and his body immediately began disappearing.

'Your destiny lies in the Forest of Gloom. I shall send you a Witch-Whisper at the right time. Think well upon all I've told you. The lives of many depend on this.'

Cordelia was in the process of firing another question when the magician was gone. Just the mist replaced him, and once again they were alone, but somehow not. The two trudged back toward the Unfair Funfair.

Strangely, Cordelia found another scrunched piece of paper where she was certain she'd already searched, and recommended the glowing spell to shine their way through the treacherous swamp.

Above them, high above, cruel eyes watched their everymove. They did not interfere though –no, not yet. Their time was surely coming; and despite Melchior's guidance; this pair were, after all, only two young witches possessing limited knowledge, and an even smaller amount of hope.

The moon shone through a break in the heavy clouds, but soon hid again once their cruel eyes scowled at it.

Chapter Eleven

Chapter 11: *Forest of Gloom.*

Except for a swirling grey whiteness, nothing at all could be seen in the fogbound Forest of Gloom.

No matter how high one looked; to the left, right or behind, not a single object could be made out with any definite shape. In fact, however one looked at it, visibility itself seemed almost invisible. In addition, the whole forest was deathly quiet.

Even the birds refused to sing. It was as though a black death had covered the place; leaving no-one alive to warn any who may happen to stray there. Evil was unmistakably in the air.

The stench of damp undergrowth and rotting leaves pervaded the atmosphere too. Any surviving leaves of winter that were on the trees, if you could see them, hung limply from each twig or limb.

Unseen Cobwebs draped from countless sprigs and tall weeds, loitering with intent to trap their next victim. But, all of them remained empty except for a covering of tiny beads of moisture, and these clung desperately to the webs for fear of dropping like discarded jewels to the wretched soil below.

There wasn't even so much as a breeze to take away this heavy fog. It seemed as though the entire forest was waiting, waiting in quiet anticipation for something dramatic to occur.

At last, something did happen, the crack of a breaking branch snapping through the air. It was a remarkable event amid all this stillness as it meant someone or something was definitely there, but whom?

Part of the answer came in an alarming and surprising way. The disturbing roar of two dark objects, rushing along at enormous speed, screamed through the fogbound Forest of Gloom.

After they'd gone, the forest became still once more and the grey-white fog remained just as thick, just as sound absorbing. For some time this morbid peace continued undisturbed.

Arrogantly, another windswept whoosh shot through the mist, followed by another just as fast. How anything could be travelling so quickly in such a dense fog like the one today, especially without causing itself some kind of fatal collision hardly made any sense at all.

But there *was* sense to it, and it came in the form of Cordelia and Mer.

They were on a deadly mission, flying especially charmed brooms loaned to them by Gran and Uncle Wistar. Fortunately for everyone concerned and mostly the entire world of witchcraft, their mother hadn't a clue what they were up to.

Both were desperately searching for their archenemies, Kaldre and her coven; *the Five Witches of Gloom*, and time was running out.

Despite Kaldre and her despicable sorcerers trying everything in their power to prevent these two from hearing Melchior's vital *Witch-Whisper*, the girls eventually did, and what a shock they got. Melchior's whisper revealed that Delia, Pers and Meryl were very much alive. Cordelia and Mer were totally stunned and overjoyed to say the least.

However, their friends wouldn't be alive for much longer, as the message went on to reveal the girls were now in the clutches of the Witches of Ice; and they had some very not-so-nice plans for them.

So, it was imperative they find the Witches of Gloom,

as they were the only ones who knew where their friends were being kept. Yet, they knew from previous encounters, that capturing these old crones would be deathly difficult, even more so getting the truth out of them.

Their task though was just about impossible. Worse still, if these two couldn't capture the Gloom witches, there would be few others that could. Failure would mean time's-up for their friends, and conceivably everyone else living in the present world of witchcraft.

'I'm scared to bits of Kaldre, and I'm not even sure if we're ever going to find her at this rate' sighed Mer as the two came to rest hovering above the trees.

They were exhausted from spending most of the day rushing from one end of the forest to the other upon brooms that although deeply charmed, were beginning to feel the strain as well.

'I could go back to Gloom castle, if you like?' suggested Cordelia 'have another look?'

'Maybe after dark' answered Mer.

'Yeah, Kaldre and her bunch of weirdo's have got to eat sometime...or, even someone!' added Cordelia meaning every word.

The sun still couldn't be seen, but its reddish orange light of late day already coloured everything with a copper tinge.

'The river!' yelled Mer 'we haven't flown along that yet.'

'That's right!' realised Cordelia 'I know, you take the North, and I'll search from the South.'

In a flash, she'd gone not even allowing Mer's plea for her to 'wait!' reach her ears. She'd wanted to warn her sister that Mrs. Spry, the *river witch collector* had been seen recently, and already six witches had gone missing.

'Just typical of Cordelia' she muttered turning her broom

northward 'never lingers for a second once her impulsive mind's made up!'

Far from the mutterings of her sister, Cordelia raced southward to where the River Gloom commenced its journey through this foreboding forest.

It was named *Gloom* forest some nine hundred years ago, perhaps because of the effect it had on people who came close to it. Cordelia certainly hadn't experienced any gloominess though, just the opposite in fact.

Suddenly, she spotted them, Kaldre and her four ancient cohorts all riding five equally old pushbikes. With enormous effort, she managed to slow and turn Gran's charmed broom. Yet the forces of this dramatic turn, made the handle split and splinter. She held it with all her strength. Fortunately, the splitting hadn't caused it to break, so she was able to fly down for a closer look.

I bet it is them! she thought *But, why would they be riding bikes and not flying; and where are they heading in such a hurry?*

It was ponderous, and as she got closer, being careful not to be spotted, her suspicions were confirmed.

'Kaldre!' she nearly yelled, stifling her delighted cry at the last moment. 'I knew it!' she whispered under her breath

'If only Mer was here to see them, she'd be so impressed. *There again...*" considered Cordelia *"perhaps she wouldn't. Once more, no doubt, it'd have to be me coming up with a plan, as she'd be too busy criticising and worrying to get the job done! -No, this is something I have to do myself.*

Cordelia was battling hard to justify her intended actions, as deep down she actually respected Mer's opinions; that's probably why they worked so well together on such problems. But her sheer determination to finish the task on this occasion won through.

Cordelia continued following the old witches from high above, rather than racing back to Mer for help. As she spied upon the five careering down the narrow pathway, an idea suddenly struck.

Divert the path, that's it! she mused. *Cause them to crash, and whilst they're in confusion, cast a sleeping spell. When they're knocked out, I'll bind them and go and get Mer. Crikey, job done! She'll be overawed!*

Cordelia smiled, smugly it must be admitted. She began reading from one of her favourite very old and extremely potent spell books, Edwardo Flynt's *Powerful Charms & Moving Enchantments*, whilst keeping a wary eye upon the five's progress.

Although she'd used it before, it was a book Cordelia was totally banned from possessing. If discovered by her strict mother, it would land her in more trouble than it was worth.

Nevertheless, she found the very chapter: *"Flummoxing Roads & Puzzling Pathways"*.

'Excellent!' she stifled. Cordelia went on to read Edwardo Flynt's guide to Changing Directions.

After skimming through all the usual warnings and dire cautions, which, to be honest, Cordelia wouldn't have taken much notice of anyway, she found the spell that would do the job perfectly as she thought.

But, where shall I do it? she wondered. *I mean, if I'm seen, I'm dead! ...I know, I'll fly ahead and find a place where the path twists and turns; that's it, I'll hide amongst some thick ferns and bushes – they won't spot me in that lot!*

Feeling rather proud of herself, she sped off in pursuit of the ideal place.

In the rapidly fading twilight, meanwhile, Mer had begun worrying about her sister. *I'm halfway along this silly river, and no sight of them. I bet Cordelia's met up with the coven and tried to capture the lot of them, all by herself too – typical!*

Mer knew this was a distinct possibility, but couldn't afford to dwell upon negative thoughts; so she pressed on, keeping to the river, now hoping she'd see the Witches of Gloom before Cordelia did.

At the other end of the river meanwhile, Cordelia had just found the perfect spot to set a trap. It was where the path twisted between a stand of ancient oaks.

Hidden deep in a clump of ferns using the dodgy light of her torch she read out Edwardo Flynt's remarkable incantation. Hopefully it would make the pathway change course, sending the Witches of Gloom scattering.

Waving her left arm in the air and moving her hand about in pure drama, as if trying to point at some confused butterfly, Cordelia read the following:

> *"Road, path and crooked track,*
> *Give up your route and turn your back,*
> *Take a journey in squiggles and twists,*
> *Lead astray those in the mists!"*

She stared unflinchingly at the mist-damp pathway for some time looking for even the minutest change in the path's direction. Nothing, not even the smallest piece of gravel budged an inch.

'So much for Edwardo's charm!' she thought aloud *I'm going to need a spell that's a damn lot more perilous than this. I need a deep hex.*

She sighed *And a really powerful one –one to shake the very earth!*

Reaching inside her cloak again, she fumbled around for the ultimate solution. As if her fingers had eyes themselves, they found a hexagonally shaped book and immediately grabbed it. Pulling it out Cordelia read the title and promptly remembered the book and how hard it had been to acquire.

It bore the title; *"Deadly Dangerous Hex's –Surviving the Worst Spells Ever Conjured"*, and naturally, the book was by her all-time favourite magician-wizard, Melchior Fizz. Cordelia recalled there was some kind of caution attached to this particular volume, but couldn't quite put her finger on it.

Breaking the bright red glowing seal, warning of impending danger, she gingerly prized the covers apart.

'BANG!' went a massive blast followed by an intolerably bright flash from the book. Her face was smoking and blackened with soot. Her eyes and face stung, ears singing.

And before she overcame that shock there followed another, a terrific ripping and tearing noise. It seemed like a miniature earthquake; and was strong enough to send her tumbling to the ground.

The young witch dropped her broom and precious volume. Hazily scrambling to pick them up, Cordelia looked back to see an amazing sight: the old pathway, which had probably been undisturbed for hundreds of years, had snapped away from itself tearing the ground apart.

The new end of it snaked its way to rest slap bang in front of a massive elm. Her bright eyes shone through her sooty face.

'Get out of that one, Kaldre!' she cried 'I didn't need Melchior's help after all...good old Edwardo Flynt!'

Cordelia immediately ran back to her hideout in the ferns with smoke still rising from both herself and Melchior's charred volume. The young witch sat there for quite a while waiting, waiting in the gloom for the fun to start.

Cordelia was as patient as could be, and eventually it paid off. The Five Witches of Gloom, headed by a determined-looking Kaldre, raced toward her, hunched over their rickety pushbikes with fierce expressions and spindly legs peddling like mad.

Down the narrow pathway wove the five at great speed, seemingly unaware that the course of their path had been changed. They rounded a bend and passed between the large oaks as they usually did. Cordelia watched, rubbing her hands together in great amusement.

Too busy gossiping and cackling, none of them had noticed the sudden change in the path's direction; why should they? The old witches would've been along the same route for years. Their bikes no doubt could have steered them on this journey all by themselves, which to be honest, they probably did. Free-wheeling some of the way, brake-skidding the rest, it was all too easy for the coven, all too *done before*.

That's probably why the witches rode so happily along the altered pathway, and why the following occurred.

With a bone-snapping, metal-twisting, ground-thumping clatter, the five women bounced off the giant immoveable elm tree and landed in a pile, one atop another. The groans and curses emanating from this heap of nasty women were awful. Suffice to say their language was totally disgusting.

Their curses; even though not aimed at anyone in particular –simply because they didn't know who or where the culprit was–would have instantly disintegrated the recipient into a small heap of something not very pleasant at all.

At once, Cordelia chanted the necessary sleeping spell. Immediately, the witches fell silent. Regrettably, this peace lasted for a mere four and a half seconds as one piercing black eye after the other opened to focus upon her.

With a reconstituted roar, they each screamed her name. *'CORDELIA MERRYSPELL!'* Their war cry echoed off every tree; rattling loudly throughout the surrounding forest.

It's time to go, thought Cordelia wisely and she hurriedly disappeared into the thick fog.

Flying at enormous speed between the trees, sometimes missing them by the mere thickness of a leaf, Cordelia raced along, zigzagging away from the pathway and Gloom River.

After travelling for goodness knows how far; and to goodness knows where, she felt safe and faraway enough to slow down. It was a foolhardy feeling.

Twilight had set in and Cordelia knew full well the oddity of it being neither day nor night. Twilight is when weirdness takes hold, transforming ordinary things into peculiar shapes and situations. A time best spent indoors if you have no powers to hand.

Creatures become shadows, shadows become horrifying creatures, and, as Cordelia was about to discover, this twilight was to become a great deal more tormenting.

Coming to rest, Cordelia landed between some trees, and peered through the gloominess of Gloom Forest hoping to find her bearings. Even finding her occasionally nagging sister seemed a little more desirable than before.

'For goodness sake, where on earth am I?' she said aloud, her voice bringing some relief to the disquieting stillness. No-one was listening; well, to her knowledge anyway.

'Of course, my trusty compass!' she cried, fumbling to find it, but strangely, it was missing.

There was no moon that night either, so she could only rely upon the remaining half-light and her fast-fading torchlight.

'Better make for home, wherever that is,' she said grabbing her broom.

But, just as she was about to fly off, a fallen branch, withered and gnarled, sprang to life and moved along the ground, roughly grabbing her ankle. Cordelia jolted away but couldn't escape as the branch twisted and bound her ankle tighter and tighter. Then, from out of nowhere, came a long snaking tongue, which at first she thought was a creeping vine. It coiled mercilessly about her waste.

'HELP!' she screamed but there was no-one to hear. With her hands free, she desperately rummaged through her pockets for a spell.

Alas, this was put paid to when a raven landed on her left shoulder and began viciously pecking. And, as if that wasn't enough, a sizeable rat scurried up her body and sank its long sharp teeth into her right arm.

The pain of the bite caused her to scream even louder. Almost immediately her cries were muffled by an obnoxious slimy toad, which jumped right into her wide-open mouth. The revolting creature commenced swelling, making it impossible for her to cry again for help.

Five different attacks from five different entities, and there was nothing Cordelia could do about it, except to think back to the Five Witches of Gloom she'd left piled amid a tangle of broken bikes and broken tempers.

As she wrestled helplessly, now realising who was responsible, she felt all hope of survival disappear from her mind.

At the same time, Cordelia began slipping away from consciousness; which at least was a welcome relief from the pain and panic.

Heaven must be like this, Cordelia thought as she awoke in a warm, cosy bed, peering out to greet the golden light of a new day. The smell of exotic scents, tea, and freshly baked cake filled her nostrils; and the sweet winter chorus of Song Thrush, Blackbird, Greenfinch, Nuthatch, and Robin caressed her ears.

Yet, Cordelia's memory flickered and occasionally dire images of what had happened previously disturbed her blissful thoughts.

As she sat up, it occurred that maybe these flashbacks belonged to some kind of nightmare; and that she'd fallen asleep in Gloom Forest.

'Yes, that's it!' she cried, feeling a lot happier, 'some kindly lady has rescued me and this is her pretty little cottage.'

Gently, the door to her delightful room opened and in walked the very lady she'd just imagined. Her smile was as broad and welcoming as her generosity. She was carrying what seemed like a tray of breakfast. Cordelia smiled back and said, 'Good morning, dear lady. Thank you for rescuing me. Where am I?'

The woman's face changed from a delightful smile into a snarling crinkle and she barked, 'Shut your face you vile little witch, and mind your own damn business!'

'That reply was totally uncalled for,' rebuked Cordelia sharply. As she tried to climb from her bed, she felt and saw the cuts and bruises from last night's ordeal.

'So, it wasn't a nightmare,' she gasped. 'This is for real!'

The young witch jumped from her once soft and comfortable bed and stood firmly before the woman.

Once comfortable, because the bed where she'd been sleeping could now be seen for what it really was; hard splintery wooden boards, covered with nothing more than a moth-eaten blanket; and a sack of dried cockroaches for a pillow.

Obviously Cordelia had been charmed into believing it was totally luxurious. For that matter, the pleasingly curtained windows and cheerfully painted walls had fooled her too. At once she saw the windows were barred and draped with old cobwebs, the walls dingy and made from coarse stone.

Her obstinate eyes fixed on the witch. 'You have no power over me, you old crow!'

With that, she fumbled through her many secret pockets for a spell to deal with her. Nothing, not as much as a pamphlet could be found; all her spell books were gone.

'Have you lost something, dearie?' asked the strange

person in an extremely sarcastic tone, 'like maybe a hundred or so foolish books on sorcery perhaps?'

With that she snickered, snorted, coughed and spat with laughter. It was a good job that Cordelia had moved a few feet back to search for her spell books.

Cordelia's face reddened. She opened her mouth to insult, but couldn't say a thing.

'What's the matter, little one, has a toad got your tongue?' asked the crone. Again she spat in fits, but Cordelia was determined not to let it have any affect.

'Don't worry, I have loads of spells,' she added defiantly.

'Oh, really?' asked the witch.

'Yes... up here!' Whereupon Cordelia pointed to her head.

'How clever you are,' replied the woman. 'Well, why not amuse me?'

Unfortunately, as much as she tried, Cordelia just couldn't remember the endings to any of her spells. Her memory seemed blocked. After several attempts, with the witch bursting into splutters whenever she couldn't complete the charms, Cordelia had no choice but to give up.

'Oh, what a tragedy,' mocked the woman. 'Shall I have a go? Ummm, how about this one:

> *"Old hags wrinkled with age,*
> *Turn into mice trapped in a cage,*
> *Feast on apples poisoned and red,*
> *Cough and splutt..."*

'Oh dash... what were those last words now? Have you any clues? I just soooo can't remember,' she hissed, 'those last... precious... words!'

This taunt greatly amused the witch, especially seeing Cordelia's despising look. 'Perhaps you could help me with the ending?' she scorned.

'Very funny... not!' replied Cordelia, and in a flash ran for the door. Halfway to it, though, her running slowed dramatically, as if she were dashing through an enormous bowl of extremely thick slime. Eventually she came to a complete stop frozen in space and just inches from the door.

Fully conscious, she tried like hell to keep herself moving forward, but to no avail.

'That's right, dearie, you're stuck... stuck just like a fly in a web, and what a web we've woven for you!' Her hideous laughter and disgusting spluttering recommenced, showering poor Cordelia with copious amounts of putrid witch's spit.

After her revolting laughter abated, the hag pushed her wrinkled face uncomfortably close to her young victim and whispered, 'I find it so moving that you can't move. And shortly, you'll have lost your will to move altogether... even your will to live! Not yet, but soon though, very soon, my pretty.'

Cordelia couldn't even grunt an objection, as her stiffened face was totally paralysed, like the rest of her. The iron latch on the heavy, gnarled door snapped upwards allowing it to open with a rusted groan. Four other witches of the coven, equally as nasty, entered into what now appeared a dungeon.

'How's she doing?' questioned the tallest in a tall voice that grated like a knife blade on a grindstone.

'Nearly done,' replied the first witch as if reporting the progress of a cake merrily baking away in an oven.

'Good, that's what we like to hear,' she continued. The

witch smiled deeply, which really did her looks no favours at all. The woman began introducing herself and the other four witches whilst tickling Cordelia's chin with fastidiously sharpened nails, rather like how an adoring grandmother tickles a baby, hopefully without the dagger sharp claws like hers.

'You don't remember us, do you?' she asked 'No, of course you don't with your poor little mind being all *fuzzy-wuzzy, woozy and wavy.*'

The witch said this whilst moving and weaving about, ridiculing Cordelia's light-headedness. She was enjoying making fun of her.

'We are the Five Witches of Gloom,' she announced. 'My name is Kaldre, and the adorable lady you've been chatting with is Ulla. And, perhaps I can introduce you to the rest of my coven. Now, here we have Rioghnach, Wyn, and Meag... aren't they all rather lovely?'

Cordelia's response at their evil, gloating faces was immediate, though somewhat stifled. All she could utter was a frustrated growl that came out as an annoyed moan.

'What was that, dearie?' questioned Rioghnach.

'I think she's trying to tell us something... what is it, my love?' Meag asked, whilst engaged in knitting a rather awful-looking baby's bonnet.

Cordelia strained once more to get the words out. 'I... know... who... you... rotten... creeps... are... now!'

Her memory was beginning to return, but the stubborn reply met with no surprise from the five.

'Plainly you do, now that I've released my spell a little,' affirmed Kaldre. 'My memory's fine, you know. I mean, how could I ever forget the nasty trick you and your wicked friends played on us at Nightshade Hall?'

'And again, at the markets!' snapped Wyn harshly.

'As well as last night in the forest!' compounded Ulla. 'Our bicycles are completely wrecked... you ought to be ashamed of yourself.'

Cordelia, although immobilized, noticed everyone's changing expression and it wasn't nice.

'You may well have cheated us at the Crystal Palace of Death,' snarled Kaldre.

'And out of the Darkington Chalice!' interrupted Wyn once more.

Kaldre flashed her colleague a look of displeasure. Wyn bit her lip and Kaldre continued. 'But now, you will pay the price of these misdeeds with your life; and no-one will be able to stop us this time!'

Kaldre's remark sent a wave of spitting cackles throughout the five of them, and a cold shiver up Cordelia's spine.

'By the way,' continued Kaldre, 'I expect you're missing your wonderful sister Mer, aren't you?'

A slow, drawn out 'yes' drawled from Cordelia's mouth and both Kaldre and the rest of her cronies smiled in anticipation.

'Well,' burst out Wyn, 'you won't be missing her for long; at this very moment we're setting a trap for her!'

'...Oh, is it OK for me to tell her that?' she asked Kaldre, looking a tad stupid.

'Well it's a bit late to ask now, isn't it?' spluttered Kaldre angrily. 'But she's right, we've been waiting a long time to capture you two, that's why we've left a trail of clues for Mer to follow... like a trail of breadcrumbs. What a diligent little thing she is!'

Cordelia strained to say something more, but no-one could understand what she was straining to say, so Kaldre asked her gathering, 'Shall we let her speak?'

They nodded and she relaxed the spell a little more so as to hear what Cordelia had to say.

'My sister's no dimwit!' she cried clearly and loudly, 'and she won't fall for your ridiculous trap!'

Kaldre frowned. 'Do you know, you're probably right. Why, a clever little witch like Mer would see your precious books and belongings, all scattered, ripped and mangled, and think *"Gosh, my sister's either very stupid or extremely careless!"*'

'That's true,' sided Wyn, 'she may think; *"How untidy is that Cordelia, leaving her things strewn about? Just because everything looks like its been through the wars, doesn't mean she's in any trouble. I think I'll just pop back home!"*'

'No, no, no, you and I both know she'd be most alarmed!' oozed Kaldre. 'Mer would definitely follow our little trail of breadcrumbs back here, foolishly planning to rescue you all by herself.'

Kaldre stared hard at Cordelia whilst nodding as if to say *you know I'm right*. Everyone burst into more spluttering and spitting, leaving Cordelia without even the option to wipe her face.

'Laugh as much as you like,' she retaliated, 'but only whilst you can. My sister will have a cunning scheme to take care of you lot.'

Kaldre looked daggers at her but soon smiled again as a raven flew into the dungeon, landed on her shoulder, and began whispering something.

Her face immediately lit up.

'So Mer's not easily fooled, eh? Well, accept your fate, dearie... at this very moment I'm reliably informed that your dear clever little sister is flying toward Gloom

Castle in great haste, weeping and holding what appears as your ratty broom snapped in half. But, as you said, she simply wouldn't just enter the castle to see if you're trapped and injured... no indeed, she'll have worked out a plan to snare your evil captors, wouldn't she?'

Tears welled in Cordelia's eyes and trickled slowly down her cheek. She knew deep inside that Mer wouldn't have any cunning plans at all; she'd only want to rescue her.

Kaldre drew near to her once more. 'Stupid Mer... stupid Cordelia, now we have both your souls.'

She raised her crinkly eyebrows as she said this.

Cordelia simply couldn't respond to Kaldre's alarming remark. A wave of cold awareness took hold as she realised with Delia and Meryl dead and Persimmon possibly held prisoner by the Witches of Ice, the remaining three of them could all die together.

As awful as this thought was, she refused to show any sign of submission to Kaldre.

Not far off, in the rapidly fading daylight of late afternoon, Mer stood outside before the steep, age-weary and battle-scarred edifice of Gloom Castle. As she walked across the keep, holding her broom tightly in case an urgent escape was needed, Mer observed with horror several Dark Witches circling above the main tower.

They were keeping their black heartless eyes on everything that moved, including her if she wasn't careful. Scared, she darted through the giant opening and speedily made for the entrance of the main tower.

The stone steps spiralling upward were wet from rain pouring through the broken wall. They seemed to go on forever. Mer was about to use her broom for a quicker ascent when something awful stopped her in her tracks.

Her heart was pounding, mind racing. Yet, there was this something obstinately standing in her way. It was grey, or was it black? Transparent, or was it solid? She couldn't make up her mind because it was all of these.

The one thing she felt for sure though, was her fear of it. With a thunderous voice, the thing that stood in her way roared a loud '*NO!*'

In shock, she let go of her broom; looking back only to watch it bounce down the stairs, far from her reach.

That was a valuable means of escape she could ill do without. But Mer's determination to find Cordelia remained resolute. Despite the spirit, or whatever it was doing its best to stop her, she strode forward.

The grey-black being spoke once more. '*Go no further, witch; doom and death await you!*'

Mer said nothing, partly from fear, partly because she was trying to work out a way past.

'Who are you?' she asked.

There was no answer and the air became like ice with mist forming from her breath. What followed was a pained cry from the being sending her backwards, almost tumbling down the stone steps to follow her broom. All at once, this grey-black thing became formed; and she felt it could well be a ghost, though she had to make sure.

Its face, now clearly seen, was drawn and scared-looking, its body, smoke-blue where there was any substance to speak of; and where not, emptiness. Mer could easily see the stone wall and stairs behind it. Her unease began to grow, but still she wasn't fully convinced that this 'thing' was a ghost.

Some charms can totally fool the senses, she reminded

herself.

It *was* a spirit however, shimmering and changing shape as if made of liquid or gas. All the time, its completely black eyes kept staring into the young witch's, searching for her innermost thoughts and anxieties; and there were plenty of those.

A shivering coldness surrounded it too, making Mer feel incredibly uncomfortable. At last, it spoke to her again.

'Turn back,' it cried, holding up a thin sliver of a hand, as if that's all it would take to prevent a witch in full-flight from passing. *'A trap awaits you; your sister is lost, I have seen it with my own eyes, such as they are.'*

Mer looked aghast. 'You're lying! My sister is laying hurt somewhere in the castle; and for some strange reason you're preventing me from saving her!'

Using all its might, the ghost screamed with such a shrieking moan it caused the very stones to shake. Mer stumbled backwards in shock once more. Regaining her balance and some courage, she challenged the spectre.

'Let me by!' she demanded, but her plea was met with silence. Stubbornly, she attempted to pass but stopped abruptly. To her surprise, the spirit now opened its arms beckoning her to pass through if she dared.

'Very well... survive this ordeal,' wailed the being in a disdainful tone, *'and notwithstanding, you'll pass through me to your sister, but I warn you again, death is waiting beyond me.'*

Mer took up the challenge.

If this isn't a ghost, she thought, *it'll soon run scared the moment I walk up and cast a vastly powerful spell.*

She searched her mind for the deepest spell possible. Then, denying what would have seemed obvious as a *ghost* to many who might stand before such a creature (that's if anyone else would have been crazy enough to be there in the first place), Mer approached the spirit, reading the *Vanquishing Charm*, learnt incidentally, off Maxim.

If only he was here now, she thought sadly.

But instead of the thing running off, like she thought it would, the being stood firm even as she charged forward.

In the blink of an eye, she passed into the very body of the ghost itself.

The first feeling she had was of immense coldness. Her breathing as she entered the spirit's misty translucent body was almost impossible; it pained her to even allow the tiniest amount of frigid air to enter her lungs.

Her eyes instantly froze open too and stung like hell; her hearing became muffled and filled with different voices speaking all at once.

She felt as if her body had been invaded by some kind of freezing, invisible gel-like substance pumping through her veins; and for a while she was taken over by the ghostly being. So much so, Mer could feel all its pain and suffering and wanted so badly to cry for it.

What made things more woeful, she was unable to continue moving forward. Her limbs were in limbo, her mind awry with emotions both good and bad; and throughout this whole ordeal, she was utterly, utterly freezing cold.

Even the view before her began shaking just like the ghost had when she'd first caught sight of it. Mer was terrified to say the least, and for a split second doubted her very reason. Though, her determination to save Cordelia soon returned.

Yet, just as she began feeling forever bound to the ghost,

she passed through it. The sensation of her own body heat rushing back was as painful as the immense coldness she'd first experienced.

All the same, it was welcoming; and tears of joy and relief streamed down her face as her eyes could see properly again. Normal sounds clattered into her eardrums once more. Mer had done it, actually passed through a ghost, and lived to tell the tale.

Now to rescue her sister; her resolve over this had not decreased one bit. At the top of the tower's stairs, she stood on the open battlement; curiously, there arose another much thinner tall tower to one side; it too was made of stone and thrust into the ever-darkening sky.

She desperately scurried over to the nearest wall in a vain attempt to hide from what she immediately recognised above as circling Witches of Ice. Too late, they'd already seen her, so too had others much closer.

'Ah! The final piece in our puzzle!' came a voice starkly familiar. It was Kaldre, expectedly; head of the Five Witches of Gloom, and she was most delighted to see her. 'Welcome, Mer Merryspell. Come forward, dear. There's *everything* to be scared of here!'

Mer immediately felt the same paralysing sensation that Cordelia had experienced earlier that day. No longer could she move, talk or even change her expression. Worse still, as Kaldre spoke to her, she was abruptly lifted into the air and floated over to somewhere on the battlement.

'We failed the last time with the Darkington Chalice,' cried Kaldre. 'Our mistake, I must admit. But, not this time.'

She pointed upwards, smiling sickly. 'See them above? As you've realised, they're our wonderful Witches of Ice, and like me, they thought they'd got you too, once. But, you lot have proved unreasonably good at your craft...not your own doing, more by getting your friend Melchior's help; it has to be said.'

Mer, although hearing Kaldre's every word, couldn't respond, even if she'd wanted to, which she did. She'd love to give her a piece of her mind...*and a few choice spells, come to think of it.*

By now, Mer had ceased her involuntary floating, arriving where Kaldre had intended, directly above a pile of firewood and kindling.

She looked down helplessly at the unlit bonfire in despair.

'Oh, you've noticed it then?' asked Kaldre. 'A little scorched bird told me you like fires, and this pile of kindling will become just one of the *Five Fires of Unending Darkness.* Yes, indeed it will!'

Kaldre smiled. 'Would you like to see my four other captives?'

Mer didn't, but knew she had no choice in the matter. As her almost-paralysed eyes were moved to see across from one side of the battlement to the other, she noticed a further four unlit bonfires. These were illuminated in a blue light by simple a wave of Kaldre's arm. If Mer could have screamed, it would have at least allowed her to vent an expression of horror.

Immediately, she saw that above each of these tall fire stacks, evenly placed around the battlement perimeter, floated Cordelia, Meryl, Delia and Persimmon. They were paralysed by the same enchantment. But, more importantly, and to Mer's joy, they were still *ALIVE*... well, for now at least.

'Yes, my dear,' broke in Kaldre, 'they *are alive*! And, it's wickedly ironic, don't you think, that all you ever wanted was to help each other live, but actually only ended up helping each other to *die*!'

She choked with laughter at her cold observation.

Unseen up 'til now, Kaldre's four other Witches of Gloom revealed themselves lurking in the shadows and added to her conceited laughter; they were clearly integral to the whole dire scheme, and couldn't wait to take part in the deaths of all five young witches.

'We have a covenant, you see,' confided Kaldre as she blew onto a firebrand, setting it instantly ablaze with purple flames that shot from her wizen mouth. 'A deal, if you like. It's with the Witches of Ice. Look at them, go on; iciness has never been more deadly!'

They had no choice but to look as their eyes were forced upwards to observe. The deathly beings swooped in and out of the billowing clouds with ease.

'This covenant,' continued Kaldre, 'is simple. We destroy you and your friends for them, and as payment, we get to keep your life-giving souls. Two problems taken care of with one action!'

'You see how brilliant it is?' asked Kaldre, rhetorically and smugly. 'It's all part of this new order of witchcraft; eagerly led by those delightful Witches of Ice, and naturally, by powerful allies like us. Believe me, witchcraft is about to change for the better, well, for us at least!'

Both Mer and Cordelia, who, like their three friends, were very much awake, thought back to the dire warnings of Melchior and Maxim.

The suspended young witches watched Kaldre walk to the centre of the battlement to join the other four of her coven. '*Do we still need your souls?* Well, yes actually, we do! How could we pass up on acquiring youth and beauty; how else could we gain such a rare commodity in such a stingy old world, I ask you?'

Kaldre smiled and swiftly reached over with her firebrand to set alight the firebrands held high by the other four.

'Yes' she added, 'whether people like it or not, witches and warlocks everywhere will soon be under the control of the Witches of Ice.

Even we've accepted that. No-one should fight it. Get rid of all your *wishy-washy* nice spells to help everyone, I say. Use magic for what it really stands for; power and control!'

'As well as endless riches and pleasure!' added Wyn.

Kaldre growled at her to '*Shut... up!*' This had been quite a speech from Kaldre.

Thank goodness she's finished at last, thought Cordelia in her dazed state. Still able to muster a little humour, she mused, *I thought we'd die from boredom!*

But, things weren't done with quite yet. Outside the stern stone walls of Gloom Castle, amid the gathering wind and pitiless cold, arrived two strange souls.

They'd journeyed far to assist Cordelia and Mer, although none of the witches knew of their intentions. They'd come to see if these two brave young witches could turn the tide of misfortune that had swept over witchdom.

Melchior Fizz and *a very much alive* Maxim Dashkov had battled painfully through some of the darkest magic, ready to join a fight they likely couldn't win; but were willing to try if the girls failed.

Maxim, it must be declared, had been in hiding from the Witches of Ice and their many corrupted followers who'd supported their evil. It was as Cordelia and Mer had previously suspected.

Melchior's intervention had saved Maxim from dying in the molten chambers of the Earth's centre after being dragged away by Kaldre whilst on the Deathwych underground train. It was Melchior and some extraordinary magic that had drawn him back from that burning fate, and hidden him. How Kaldre and her coven survived certain death must be down to the Witches of Ice for sure.

Yet, now there was work to be done. And, as they raced over the keep, sped up the stairs of the castle's steep central tower, they knew time had probably ran out.

Upon the battlement, the coven of Gloom witches, each holding firebrands licking with purple and green flame, made their way over to a waiting fire stacks.

'The bonfire stacks beneath you,' proclaimed Kaldre triumphantly, 'are woven with gnarled and twisted sticks and branches, as gnarled and twisted as the curses and enchantments we've cast onto them!'

With that, Kaldre and her cohorts leant forward, setting the stacks ablaze beneath the paralysed witches.

Maxim and Melchior climbed up onto the battlement and were immediately confronted by this awful sight. Yet, before they could let out so much as a gasp of horror, terrifying strikes of Black Lightening exploded beside them.

Conjured by the Witches of Ice, who'd seen their arrival, the strikes sparked about relentlessly. In anger, Maxim attempted a counter-charm.

Seeing him defiantly chanting out in the open, and importantly that Maxim's charm had actually begun working, Melchior roughly grabbed his sleeve, dragging the inexperienced young wizard away. He forcefully led him through the strikes to take shelter in the small tower on the far side of the battlement.

'NOT NOW!' he screamed at him. 'THIS HAS GONE BEYOND SPELLS!'

They fled up the tower's narrow stone steps, their hearts pounding fit to burst. The tall, tiny structure was probably only built to support some kind of flag or banner once proudly announcing the family crest of a lord or prince.

It may also have been the last place to flee in the event of a siege, confirmed by the regular placements of arrow slits all the way up. But, this mattered not to these two, who were just grateful for its meagre protection from the Witches of Ice.

There were serious gaping holes in the stone wall too, caused hundreds of years ago by canon and slingshot; and this concerned Melchior. Every time they passed one, the Ice Witches, who could see them very clearly from where they hovered, shot more bolts of Black Lightening to fizz through the frigid air. This constant bombardment held the magicians back even further.

And anxiously, through each gap they managed to jump past, the wizards could see the mysterious fires burning under their friends growing greater by the second.

'JUMP, MAN!' yelled Melchior, encouraging Maxim to leap up five steps in one go. It was the only way he could pass the large gaping holes fast enough. He promptly took a few steps back, rushed forward, and sprang upwards with every ounce of his strength.

He landed safely and Melchior grabbed his arm to stop him falling down again. Quickly, they made it past each opening, Black Lightening thumping and fizzing past their legs as he and Melchior disappeared behind the safety of stonework.

'WELL DONE!' cried Melchior upon reaching the

summit. 'Now Maxim, watch and learn.'

The two had a clear view of the awful drama from the top of the narrow tower, though had to keep ducking to avoid being struck by the powerful dark energy unleashed upon them.

Cordelia, Mer, and their three friends were still suspended above the roaring purple and green flames. Already the fires had begun to work their evil; the young witches' souls had become much weaker.

Above each of them hovered one of the five Witches of Gloom mounted upon a broom, and mercilessly chanting the darkest incantations known. They bathed arrogantly and blissfully in the weird flames that arose, cheerfully consuming the girls' souls that were evaporating into Kaldre's *Fires of Darkness*.

'I CAN'T WATCH THIS!' screamed Maxim at last; angry at being made to feel so helpless by Melchior, who still insisted that he hold back from casting any counter-spells at all. 'We must rescue them, Melchior, before it's too late.'

'I hear you, lad, but there's naught I can do,' he replied, but it only served to make Maxim more restless.

'They're all going to die if we stand here doing nothing!' he yelled.

Melchior understood his anxiety; and once again tried to impress upon him that the answer wouldn't come from spells and counter-spells; it could only come from their friends, who tragically, were being killed before their very eyes.

'I can't explain why this has to happen, Maxim. I can't tell you lest my very words dilute all that I trust will eventuate. It breaks my heart to add this, but unless that certain something isn't forthcoming from at least one of those poor young witches, the whole world of witchcraft, as we know it, will disappear forever.'

Maxim remained frustrated and perplexed by this. Yet, although Melchior seemed to be speaking in riddles, deep down Maxim remained convinced of the man's sincerity, though he still desperately wanted to take action.

By this time, Cordelia felt overwhelmingly faint; her soul was ready to leave her to replenish the cruel soul of Kaldre waiting above. Although the magic flames could not burn as ordinary flames do, they nevertheless were causing the girls to die.

Cordelia, for the last time perhaps, surveyed the cruel scene around her, settling her tearful eyes upon her sister and each of her friends one by one. Again she looked at Mer, precious Mer, not only her sister, but also her dearest friend. Hardly able to prise her burning lips apart, she managed a grieving farewell.

'Mer,' she called, 'I love you.'

Those three words: *I love you*, are the most powerful words in the whole world. Stronger than hate, more lasting than gold, more effective even than the worst spell, charm, bomb or weapon known. So powerful, they actually undid the hostile spell now at work. They were, in fact, precisely the words Melchior wanted to hear.

The flames beneath her stopped at once. And, as her sister turned and said the very same, her flames died too, the fire beneath spluttering out.

Tears of joy and relief poured from their eyes as Cordelia screamed, 'I love you Delia... I love you Meryl!'

Mer joined in too. 'I love you Pers!'

With that, their friends commenced calling back the

same sentiment over and over again. The fires beneath them had all but gone out, and the witches of Gloom were faltering on their brooms.

Maxim screamed for joy, dragging Melchior from their hiding place to commence a ridiculous dance of joy and celebration.

'THEY DID IT, *THEY DID IT!*' he yelled with tears mixed with laughter. Melchior joined in as the two of them continued to jump and reel.

Kaldre immediately and painfully tried halt their rebellion.

'*STOP IT! CEASE THIS GARBAGE INSTANTLY,*' she cried. But already she and her nasty, warped little coven were beginning to shrivel. Their faces and bodies became like toasted prunes.

Holding up her withered hand she at last screamed, '*WHAT ARE YOU DOING TO ME? STOP THIS, STOP THIS AT ONCE... STOP... STOP... STO... OP...*'

Her voice soon faded to nothing and the witch was quickly naught but dried skin stretched over crumbling bone, her shrivelled lungs unable to gasp the tiniest breath. Her cohorts similarly writhed and spat and spitted as they too began diminishing.

With the fires and the coven vanquished, the young witches were freed, falling onto the twisted stacks now extinguished by their own love.

Immediately the girls could hear the yells and screams of joy from Maxim high in the flag tower; they could hear the pained cries too from the Five Witches of Gloom as they continued to shrivel and buckle with instant age; eventually all dispersing into clouds of *un-empowered dust*.

The monstrous spell they'd cast upon their prey had

reversed on them. One great act of love had caused their demise. In no time Cordelia and the others raced to greet Melchior and once-lost friend, Maxim.

'I knew you weren't dead!' yelled Cordelia. 'You wouldn't make a very convincing ghost anyway!'

Mer and everyone laughed.

'But, it's thanks to Melchior I'm here at all!' added a still-jubilant Maxim. Mer chuckled and just couldn't take her eyes off him, almost if she expected him to evaporate any second.

They were so busy cheering and screaming, no-one had even noticed the quiet departure of the Witches of Ice circling above. Until Meryl realised that is.

'Now isn't that a little peculiar?'

'What?' asked Pers.

'Yeah, go on, I know... you saw this *all in a dream!*' Delia said in a spooky wailing voice.

'No, the Witches of Ice... they've gone!'

'Blimey!' cried Cordelia, looking up, 'you're right Meryl, it's over, the Witches of Ice have scurried off... *cowards!*'

Melchior's wise face creased with a frown none of them had seen before. 'Yes, we've won the fight here, it seems, but I still have my doubts.'

'You see,' he said, whilst slowly shaking his head, 'I fear there's a much longer road ahead in the battle for witchdom.'

Despite Cordelia's optimism, she knew deep down he was right, especially after what she and Maxim had read on his dire warnings, bitter though the thought was.

Melchior was a careful wizard; rightfully concerned about the possible return of the Witches of Ice.

'I fear their hearts – cold as Neptune, merciless,' he added, staring into the dark foreboding clouds, the

A time for celebration...or maybe not.

moon still shy.

The gathering became sombre, and Melchior, seeing their gloom, picked his thoughts from the blackness to offer a smile. 'Forgive me. We must still celebrate; after all a great victory has occurred today!'

Melchior turned to go. 'Sadly, it's time I left. I expect you've many things to do as well. Though I do need to tell you something important before I go...'

He paused to wipe a little moisture or maybe tears from his eyes.

'Magic, you know,' he began, 'is simply fantastic with all its whizz bang wizardry; but, as you've each so painfully discovered, without love, understanding, and respect, it really isn't magic at all.'

They smiled in agreement and the wizard vanished into a cloud of mist, leaving Cordelia, Mer and all their friends staring at where he'd disappeared.

'Mmm,' pondered Cordelia, 'don't get me wrong, cool wizard, great books, but he really needs to lighten up!'

Everyone stared at her. Then they broke into laughter.

Eventually, they turned, and Delia added; 'All I can say is that we massively need another adventure!'

'I couldn't agree more,' added Maxim, 'and interestingly, I read this book recently. Someone, about six hundred years ago, had lost all of his magical belongings in the Forest of Evil; it's not that far from here, actually... anyone care to check it out with me tomorrow?'

They all looked stunned. Then, the place erupted once more, especially after Cordelia conjured a few of *Bumble Bee's Best Quality Spoilers.*

As the group wandered away from the grim fortress, a ghostly sigh and cold wind echoed across its high battlements. Nobody heard it though; perhaps they were too busy chattering about all they'd experienced. And, the fact they still remained alive.

THE END.

...now, take a sneek-peek at the prologue & first two chapters of **'Cordelia & Mer and the Witches of Ice' Book Two: Doom.**

W. F. Gadd

Cordelia & Mer
and the

WITCHES
OF ICE

Book Two: Doom

Illustrations by Maxine & William Gadd

Cordelia & Mer and the Witches of Ice.
Book Two: *Doom*

Prologue.

On Friday the thirteenth, at exactly three pm and seven minutes, a merciless flash of dark magic, in the form of Black Lightening, violently struck an unremarkable little house.

It was aimed to strike a group of witches who had just rushed into this supposedly 'safe' house.

The Black Lightening missed. They'd escaped by the skin of their teeth.

This powerful blast struck their front door as it closed behind them with a flash of blackness, searing red flames, and deafening roar.

Black Lightening could be compared to ordinary lightening, but that would be folly, as it possessed something far worse; deathly magical energy that not only burns the body, but the soul as well.

The devastating explosion not only destroyed the front door, which duly burst into flames and smoke, but shook the whole house and the houses next to it.

The witches' eyes bulged, hearts pounded, legs weakened as they scrambled for the most protected part of the abode, the living room. It was the home of Mrs. Valerie Pitheringae, Nineteen Lovehoc Lane; a usually respectable looking terrace-house, on an equally respectable-looking lane.

During the strike, red and green sparks flew here and there. Smoke of various colours billowed up and the foundations of the whole house shook from this spell-driven blast. So much so that the living room they now skulked in still shimmered with a dull blue glow.

Such a shocking event in the normally sedate little village of Lower Wyshing had never ever occurred before.

All four had been chased there by a few of what are best described as Dark Witches, at the command of the Witches of Ice. And no adequate description of these evil creatures could ever relate the sheer horror of their power and presence.

Approximately an hour after this terrible event, all seemed clear, no further attacks taking place. They felt, maybe at last, a tiny bit safer, hoping against hope they'd survived.

The small room they huddled in, still slightly glowing and smoking from the attack, remained winter-dark and tense. These four acutely scared sorcerers well knew the dread of impending doom.

Next door, Mr. Baffle, a tall elderly gent, who collects pet snails and has a dog called Whine, never felt or heard the blast of magic when it happened. To him, all was normal and peaceful at the time.

During the drama, he remained engrossed reading a strange little book he'd discovered at the local library. The book, entitled *How to Travel to Unusual Places by Broomstick Without Being a Witch or Wizard* was a real gem. In fact, he'd already purchased his broom from the local hardware store on Sunny Street, owned by the dubious Mr. Sneeze.

Mrs. Bayeux, on the other side however, had jumped so much when the blast occurred, she'd bashed her head on the inside of the kitchen cupboard she was meticulously cleaning. Immediately, the woman had grabbed a saucepan to bang on Mrs. Pitheringae's wall.

She was getting more than a little upset lately with this rather odd neighbour; peculiar noises in the dead of night, weird chanting, offensive smells from whatever was being cooked. She didn't know Mrs. Pitheringae, nor cared to either.

The four of them inside number nineteen, though, ignored Mrs. Bayeux and her pot-banging, simply remaining seated whilst worriedly staring into space.

A whiff of strange potions and coal smoke filled their nostrils, as Mrs. Pitheringae had hurriedly conjured alight a fire in the grate near to where they sat.

The smoke and heavy perfume from a cauldron of various potions made the stale air almost choking to breathe.

Each witch gathered in the room, including Hepsibah Merryspell, Olivia Jute and Hilda Huggitt, was quite terrified. So terrified in fact, that even with all their powers they were afraid to be caught outside.

Mrs. Pitheringae's home was their last remaining refuge. This was the safest place any of them could be, and the almost unbreathable air helped keep it that way.

Finally, the world of witchcraft had become poisoned by these Witches of Ice. Stark evil was taking over *witch-by-witch, death-by-death*.

The four sat huddled for goodness knows how long around a small table in Mrs. Pitheringae's living room, and close enough to the slow-burning coal fire to warm their chilled and exhausted bodies.

They were vainly attempting to pretend everything was OK. It was foolish, and each knew it, really. But, maybe being in denial was a whole lot more comfortable than the desperate truth that they were going to die by the evil from the Witches of Ice.

That's why, in those moments at least, they had chosen to distract themselves by playing tarot cards, or should that be reading them? No, they were definitely playing them, as one of the witches had flippantly yelled, 'SNAP!'

During their game, eyes darted from one person to another, from one thing to another.

A small piece of still-glowing coal had dropped through the fire's grate; rolled onto a tiled surface, and lay there to die a slow death. Its fading demise wasn't unnoticed by any of the witches.

A moth too, who'd persisted in killing itself amid the flame of a nearby oil lamp, didn't go unseen; and glints of gold leaf print upon the spines of spell books, collected in much better times, winked at each witch in turn every time a flare jetted from the homely fire.

Heavy, suffocating curtains played their part in the depressive environment as well; excluding whatever dingy light was meanly given by the miserable sky outside. Only the greeny-blue glimmer from the once-shaken walls, a cautiously lit oil lamp, and the fire of course, she'd enough light for any of the four witches to see well enough.

Mrs. Pitheringae decided to break the tension by reaching and bringing over a plate of instantly conjured food resting upon a smallish side-table behind her.

'Care for a slice of Tilly's inside-out-upside-down cake, anyone?' she asked.

Apart from them already suffering so much, she really wanted to discuss with her gathering of friends how they were going to escape from this terrible trap, and whether their magical world could survive. Maybe a piece of this peculiar cake would ease them into it.

So, with a kindly smile, Valerie simply offered around the plate of Tilly's treat, sliced and arranged as best as possible into a five-pointed star.

To many an outsider, the cake would seem utterly revolting; pieces like a creature's innards jutting out here and there; red-mauve coloured orbs hanging on tendrils, similar to strawberry-sized clots of blood.

And woven throughout the dark cake was a seam of thick greenish

414

cream, appearing to all intents and purposes as some unfortunate person's phlegm. Yet, despite these failings, Tilly's cake was amazingly delicious to eat.

'Olivia!' suddenly screamed Hilda whilst avoiding the presented plate of cake, 'that's a Le Mort card you've placed! Maybe we are going to see the death of witchcraft as predicted after all!'

Hilda's shocking remark nearly caused Valerie to let her plate crash to the floor.

'OH! You're right, dear,' replied Olivia in alarm. Hesitantly she'd slid the offending card out of harm's way, nervously replacing it with the next one from her other hand. It wasn't much better either; The Hanged Man could be interpreted as meaning a scapegoat or victim was to be found. .

Valerie eventually recovered from this minor drama, pushing the plate towards Hepsibah. Mrs. Merryspell duly picked up a wobbly slice between her thumb and two fingers. But, before the poor lady could get the delicious morsel near to her waiting mouth, it had frozen, splintered and evaporated into a wisp of blue mist.

She shook her stinging frozen thumb and fingers in alarm, wishing she'd used the solid silver tongs instead. One by one, the other slices on the plate froze and evaporated before anyone else had a chance to get near them; not that they would want to.

Every beady eye in the room had focused onto the empty plate held by their host who'd suddenly let it go with a pained cry as it too instantly froze. The plate vanished in front of them amid another wisp of blue mist. Valerie gasped and choked.

'They're here!' she spluttered in a terrified scream. Everyone stood up and looked about for the vile creatures she was referring to.

'No, not in person, ladies, in spirit! The Witches of Ice have sent their magic here into my living room, probably down the chimney,' she added, 'it is amongst us now, casting and weaving evil!'

Valerie shook her hurting hand once more. With the other, she comforted her throbbing brow in distress.

'Who'd have thought it, Dark Magic, here in this very room, cast by those evil Witches of Ice!' stressed Hilda Huggitt.

"Yes,' grated Valerie in a voice quite withered, 'I feel their ethereal presence all about me.'

'No, not now, surely not,' cried Hepsibah. '...there's nowhere left to hide!'

'But even supposing you're right, Val,' suggested Olivia, 'haven't we enough power between us to deal with them?'

She looked about for agreement, feverishly, searching too for odd shadows or things that didn't quite look right.

Though, Valerie knew they hadn't enough power, and shook her head solemnly.

'No, not even witches as strong as us would stand a chance against them,' she groaned, 'and what happened to Tilly's cake is just the beginning... we've run out of time.'

One by one, they looked toward Valerie for some kind of solution, though they knew there wouldn't be one. So, they deserted their pointless game, and muttered various hexes whilst continuing to scour the room for any peculiar signs.

'You won't find any!' blurted Valerie. 'They're too clever for that. And as I said, we have no time anyway. We'll have to plan on how to get away from here as soon as possible!'

Everyone appeared a shade whiter, which was hard to imagine for witches as experienced and capable as these four.

Mrs. Pitheringae's clock, resting on the neat and orderly mantlepiece, slowly and regularly ticked away each second.

A teapot set on a fine silver tray in the middle of the table where they'd sat began steaming and Valerie Pitheringae shakily poured its brew into each waiting finest bone-china cup. There was probably no time for this idle ritual either, though perhaps it was some way to restore a kind of balance to the room.

'Sugar... milk?' she'd asked, already knowing in fact who took what.

Her friends easily felt the strange disturbance in the air. Olivia seemed the most worried, fidgeting with her cup and saucer stirring the tea with a swish of her left index finger held above it.

'But, if we make a plan now,' whispered Hepsibah, 'surely they'll hear our every word, and be waiting for us, won't they? My daughters, Cordelia and Mer, have come to me with harrowing stories of their supernatural cunning and how close the two of them have come to death. The Witches of Ice seem to know our thoughts before we do ourselves!'

The worry-lines on her already worried face creased more and more.

'For a little while, we're safe,' breathed Mrs. Huggitt, who'd just finished muttering the *Word-Twister Spell*. Hopefully it would twist everyone's words enough so as to confuse. even the Witches of Ice.

Though that was doubtful.

'These evil creatures,' she continued, 'they're even having an effect on my Curiosity Shoppe!'

'No! How awful for you, Hilda,' sided Mrs. Merryspell.

'Yes, my magic fountain pen Spell-Writers aren't working; they just lay there on the parchment, won't even stand up to write by themselves!'

'Goodness me,' gasped Olivia. 'Have you tried changing their ink?'

'The first thing I did! Even Wizard Scribe's Deepest Formulation, you know, the ink Emily Starch-Stiffington uses for her punishment book, doesn't work; not even a scribble!'

It was true; Mrs. Hilda Huggitt's Celebrated *Fountain Pen Spell-Writers*, used by countless witches and wizards everywhere, would, in normal circumstances, automatically write down the spells requested; or, users would even be able to let these remarkable fountain pens come up with entirely new ideas. But for now, the pens just refused to work.

Olivia frowned deeper, appearing paler than the rest. She at once tied another knot in her charmed lavender wreath. That was six more knots she'd tied in those last few minutes alone, and each knot was supposed to offer the owner of the wreath at least a day of protection from evil spells or supernatural intervention.

'Our predicament is very numbing,' she uttered lowly.

'Where shall we go? I mean, not even the woods are safe anymore!' said Mrs. Merryspell. 'I don't even know how we can get out of this room without being got at.'

The others mumbled a nodded agreement. Clearly, things were looking grim for all the witches of Lower Wyshing, indeed, witches right across the whole country.

Valerie's mantle clock chime then struck six times in a strictly accurate beat, once again breaking the nervous expectant silence. Mrs. Huggitt looked up. The six chimes were actually rather odd, as the time just then was in fact was only five-thirty, not six pm; and Valerie kept everything she possessed in a state of absolute precision.

'Splintering hickory-sticks... your clock, dear,' burst Mrs. Huggitt, 'it's wrong!' She held up her solid silver pocket watch for all to see. Everyone looked aghast.

This had never, ever happened before. One thing about Valerie was she didn't allow standards to slip, clocks and timekeeping especially. Her timepiece was governed not by one charm, but several, all interconnected too. Thus, if one charm was out by a mere microsecond, the other charms would set it right, indeed they would. That was, up 'til then, of course.

Olivia confirmed the terrible truth with her charmed Shadow Pendant. Naturally, it wasn't strictly accurate. But, of the twelve shadows it cast, the strongest one nevertheless did mark the hour of the day. And with both the fifth and sixth shadows being equally as dark, it certainly indicated around half-past five.

So, for this small gathering of witches, desperately attempting to survive the remains of a particularly dangerous afternoon, life looked like it was about to get decidedly worse.

Chapter One: Ms. Emily Starch-Stiffington's ordeal

No more than a twisted crow's flight away from the woodlands surrounding Lower Wyshing, past some decidedly treacherous iron gates, up a meandering and equally dangerous pathway; and through an obnoxious wooden front door, clearly possessed by something that felt its sole purpose was to keep strangers out, things were getting out of hand for the headmistress of a particularly strict and disciplined school for supposedly well-behaved young witches.

In a certain room of this weird school, a bothered and irritable Ms. Starch-Stiffington sniffed then barked into a grey well-used hanky, wiped her flu-ridden eyes with it and took a deep inhalation of Smith's Magical Industrial Grade Anti-flu Potion, guaranteed to clear away the worst infections; providing, of course, the correct spells had been read correctly.

Ms. Emily Starch-Stiffington was grumpy and foul, more so than usual, which wouldn't be nice if you happened to be with her in the stuffy dark room she called her office.

The walls were lined with shelves of report books, written years and years ago but now cobwebbed, dusty and dispensed with. Kept more likely as a comforting reminder of countless punishments enjoyably given to even the most trivial offender.

Strangely, sat upon various creaking small tables, placed in a particularly dark corner, rested child-size large domed bottles of glass. Reminiscent of storage jars in fact. Close scrutiny wouldn't be advisable though, as even in this gloominess they appeared occupied. Errant young witches knew well to avoid conflict with this ruthless woman.

Emily's black fountain pen (the blackest she owned) was in a right old mood too, almost pushing out her words of vitriol quicker than she could write them.

'Merryspell... Mer, Merryspell...Cordelia,' she croaked angrily, 'Severe and Cruel Detention for one week.'

Her fountain pen eagerly scribbled her instructions onto an abjectly bleak punishment form. The miniature storm, whirring around the top of her pen, let loose a bolt of tiny lightening which managed to burn a pin sized hole in the paper it wrote upon, much to Emily's satisfaction.

Just as she'd finished writing her report, though, the dark grimy windows of her depressing office shook violently. Before she knew it, the heavy hand-carved wooden desk, where she'd determined so many damming and unfair judgments of pupil behaviour, suddenly levitated.

To the woman's great astonishment, it took her and the creaking chair she sat upon soaring upward, swaying her violently from side to side.

She screamed, calling out her most powerful protection spell, which was useless, and tried grab as many beloved report papers as possible.

Her tall pointed hat scrunched into the ceiling and poor Emily's cranium followed not long after, thumping loudly against its hard surface. The blow sent her odd-shaped glasses flying onto the desk. She reached to put them on again, but the desk instantly and surprisingly sped back down to the floor with a rush and massive crash.

Emily tried to compose herself, and looked about to see who'd caused the attack. *Surely not any of my pupils, they wouldn't dare*, she thought, though a couple of likely names entered her mind. Yet, this was more than a prank; someone actually wanted to harm her. The desk was broken by the fall; legs and hard oak panels twisted and splintered.

Before another thought could circle through her cerebellum, Emily's beloved black fountain pen was wrenched from her hand, moved around in front of her, and then committed to writing by some invisible hand. The black ink inside haemorrhaged out of the pen onto her desk in gushes as if there was no limit to its supply.

The message spelt and spilled onto Emily's desk instantly froze and was instantly read. It made no sense; "Beware the early hours!" proclaimed the written message in iced black ink before her.

The thin pointy headmistress was angry, livid in fact.

'HOW DARE ANYONE INTERRUPT THE PLEASURE OF MY PUNISHMENT-HOUR!' she vented with incredible loudness. Her annoyed shouting was so violent it shook her office windows once more.

'Early hours, indeed... I'll give them early hours!' she blasted. With that, Emily rescued her frozen pen, snapping it off the frozen ink, grabbed her broom and flew off down the corridor to find the audacious perpetrator of this alarming crime.

Chapter Two: The Terrified Wizard

Several miles due North, amid the now-blustery night, the wind was whipping a small stone house beside a turgid angry river. The smoke from its tall chimneystack whipped around and about.

Amid the wailing wind came another kind of wailing, although this from what appeared to be a demented man dressed in flowing dark robes that billowed in the storm. His left arm was stretched out, pointing toward the walls of his house, calling something in a strange tongue.

Even more astonishing, as he moved his arm, words of burning light appeared on the stonework itself. So intensely hot were the words, they caused the very granite to become molten.

The man was the wizard Melchior Fizz; and he was in great earnest to complete the urgent task of protecting his home from deadly attack. Melchior knew the Witches of Ice were after him, and by writing these powerful words around the circumference of his house; there was every chance they couldn't get at him.

Yet, he had very little time. Fortunately, there was less than a yard between the first word he'd written and the one he was currently burning into the stone – a gap betwixt survival and total annihilation. His index finger now glowed with energy too as he commanded more and more magic energy to complete his task.

With the seconds ticking away, only twenty inches remained to finish. Once complete he would be free to rush into his house, there to stand within the extra safety of a double-witch's circle, suitably hexed.

In this moment though, the unthinkable happened. The section of stone wall where hewrote crumbled and collapsed inward on.his beloved home.

Soon after, because his etching of strange words was incomplete, all the walls of his ancient house cracked and fell to the power of this strange magic, causing the once-grand pointed roof to crash down with a roar.

There followed a wanton destruction of countless magical instruments and priceless parchments inside with fire and wind. Above in the clouds came a cry of pitiless laughter followed by a swirl-fall of ice crystals. The Witches of Ice had found Melchior.

In the dark confusion of this storm-wracked night, the wizard ran away, ducking and diving between trees and thick undergrowth to escape capture. Without any magical devices, or his vast collection of spells and powerful hexes to rely upon, his flight was all but in vain.

He hid momentarily beneath a tightly woven thicket of briar to gather his breath.

Shortly, a rushing crackling sound filled the air accompanied by flaming red light. Melchior looked up to see a stream of fiery words similar to those he'd written on his once stout walls. He watched them circle through the air like a serpent.

They were seeking something, someone, Melchior in fact. The wizard positioned himself lower, if that were possible, chanting under his breath a charm of invisibility. It seemed the charm had worked, giving him a chance to read those fiery floating words. .

But, Melchior really wished he hadn't. They evilly read, *"Kill the wizard... kill Fizz"*.

Cautiously, Melchior crept away from his hiding place, constantly looking back at the circling words urgently seeking their prey.

Disaster struck again. He tripped on an unseen fallen branch whilst keeping an eye on the pursuing fiery words. Had he been looking ahead, he wouldn't have stumbled and caused such a noise.

Immediately, the serpent of words saw him laying crumpled and in pain, and shot toward Melchior for the kill. The wizard scrambled in agony to escape, and became momentarily hidden from view by thick undergrowth.

Crawling slowly, he made it to the embankment of a nearby river. It was swollen and violent. But, the flaming burning stream of words caught sight of him once more. They rose up like a giant fiery serpent, ready to strike.

His choice was simple: the river or the words. Neither was desirable, but the burning words were a great deal more dangerous and final.

Fizz couldn't swim; he doubted whether he could float. Yet, the only course open to Melchior was the awful dark surging river.

He slipped in as easily as an escaping fish loosed from a broken line. All went dark for the man; cold, and water drenched; dragged down to drown. If this was the fate for a powerful wizard such as Melchior Fizz, then surely no-one could stand against the Witches of Ice.

Cordelia &Mer and the
WITCHES OF ICE
Book Two: Doom

*...Coming soon as an eBook on various
digital platforms, and in paperback.*

W. F. Gadd

Cordelia & Mer

and the

WITCHES
OF ICE

Book Two: Doom

Illustrations by Maxine & William Gadd

Made in the USA
Las Vegas, NV
12 June 2023